DEADLY DECEIT

This Large Print Book carries the
Seal of Approval of N.A.V.H.

HARBORED SECRETS, BOOK 2

DEADLY DECEIT

NATALIE WALTERS

THORNDIKE PRESS
A part of Gale, a Cengage Company

GALE
A Cengage Company

LIBRARY OF CONGRESS CIP DATA ON FILE.
CATALOGUING IN PUBLICATION FOR THIS BOOK
IS AVAILABLE FROM THE LIBRARY OF CONGRESS

ISBN-13: 978-1-4328-7297-7 (hardcover alk. paper)

Published in 2020 by arrangement with Revell Books, a division of Baker Publishing Group.

Printed in the United States of America
1 2 3 4 5 6 7 24 23 22 21 20

G.I. JOE, your unconditional love gives me the freedom to dream big with the security of knowing you're right there beside me.
Without you, this dream never would've happened —
thank you, my love.

ONE

In the face of small-town news, all creativity left Vivian DeMarco.

"And Walton Elementary will raise enough money to support Home for Heroes and end the war, bringing peace to the whole country. And everyone will find true love. Have two adorable children. A cute puppy." Vivian stamped out the words on her keyboard with more force than necessary. "And everyone will be happy and live happily ever after. Forever. And ev—"

Yuck. Vivian stopped typing, leaned back in her chair, and exhaled. *It's only temporary.* Sitting forward, she tapped the delete key. *Tap. Tap. Tap.* And then held it down until she erased the last paragraph of her story on Walton Elementary's 5K race to raise money for Home for Heroes.

It's only temporary.

Those three words had become her mantra every day for the last 180 days, though lately she'd recited them to herself less frequently than she had when she first drove into town. A fact that frightened her a little bit. Those three words were her daily reminder that *this* was not where she belonged. It was a means to an end.

Clackity clack clack. Clack clackity clack clack. Clackity clack. Ding.

Vivian frowned. The vintage typewriter ringtone belonged to only one person and a quick glance at the time on her phone said it was past his bedtime.

"Harold?"

"Oh, good. I was hoping you were still up." Harold's twangy voice was barely above a whisper. "Where are you, dear?"

"At the office."

"So late?"

"Doing the final copy editing on a few of my pieces and finishing up some stories." Vivian could hear some noise in the background. "Where are you?"

"I just left the g—" Harold coughed. "Excuse me. I'm leaving the basketball game."

That explained why her boss was still awake at such a late hour. Harold was an avid sports fan, and the Anderson College men's team had made it to state . . . or was it the division finals? That was the other reason why Harold was at the Friday night basketball game. Vivian didn't do sports. She had always been the last one picked in PE and the first one targeted in dodgeball when that heinous sport was allowed in schools. Covering sports was the one thing she wouldn't budge on when it came to her job at the *Gazette*. She'd cover the insane number of festivals, fundraisers, dedications, cook-offs, and 5K races filling the Walton community calendar, but if Harold wanted a sports story, he'd have to cover it himself. Besides, no one was going to respect a writer who didn't know the difference between an ump and a ref.

"Did they win?"

"They did, but that's not why I'm calling. Can you meet me at the house?"

"Your house?" Vivian looked at the time. It was half past eleven. "Now?"

Harold coughed again. "Yes, dear. I know it's late, but I need your help."

A tingle of worry spread through Vivian's chest at his ominous tone. "Are you okay?"

"Oh, yes, dear." He cleared his throat. "They used quite a lot of pyrotechnics at the game. Some of the smoke must be bothering my throat. I'll be at the house in ten minutes."

"Harold, are you sure this can't wait until

tomorrow? I'll even stop by the Way Station Café and pick up some cinnamon rolls. Plus, since Carol's out of town, you won't get into trouble."

Harold laughed, but it came out choked. "I've got a marmalade dropper, and I think . . . I think it's the story you've been waiting on."

Vivian sat forward. "Marmalade dropper" was Harold's unique way to tell her he had a story. A big one. But even if he hadn't used his familiar phrase, the fact that he suggested this was *her* story captured her curiosity instantly.

"Why? What's the story?"

"Vivi, I'll tell you at the house. Please."

Her heart pulled at the sound of the nickname Harold had dubbed her with almost as soon as she began working for him — ignoring her insistence that her name was "just Vivian." Nicknames were familiar. Familiarity meant affection. And affection was harmful. Still, she couldn't ignore the strain in his voice.

"Fine." She closed her laptop and grabbed her keys. "I'll be there in fifteen minutes."

Ford Avenue was congested with game-night traffic. Vehicles covered in cheers for the Cougars written in shoe polish on their windows honked playfully at residents young and old as they waved their red and silver banners in the air. Kids with faces painted like the school mascot rode on their dads' shoulders or tugged their moms in the direction of Sandy's Ice Cream Shop, which apparently had extended its hours in honor of the win. The town was alive with celebration.

It was all a pitiful reminder of just how lame Vivian was.

Several blocks farther down, Vivian turned into The Landing, a subdivision of stately homes with wraparound porches and wide lawns manicured to HOA standards. She parked behind Harold's white Volvo on Marshford Avenue, the light from his living room illuminating the path up to his porch.

Vivian knocked on the door. What kind of story was important enough for her to be standing here this late at night? She didn't have a clue. This was Walton, Georgia, where people lived happily ever after. The words she had typed earlier came back to her. She'd been in the news industry long enough to know there was no such thing.

Vivian knocked again, then moved to the front window and peeked in. Her heart stopped at the sight of his body crumpled on the floor.

"Harold!" She grabbed for the doorknob and it turned. Shoving the front door open, she ran to Harold's side. "Harold!"

His face was red, lips blue and swollen. His chest heaved, but only shallow wheezing escaped his throat. "Harold! What's wrong? Are you having a heart attack?"

A subtle shake of his head and Vivian remembered. Harold had a peanut allergy. "Allergic reaction? Are you having an allergic reaction?" More wheezing, but his eyes widened a bit before closing. *No, no, no.* He couldn't . . . "Stay with me, Harold."

She pulled out her cell phone and dialed 911. After Vivian gave the emergency operator Harold's address, the woman directed her to find his EpiPen. Harold had made sure Vivian knew where he kept it at the office, but this was his house. She looked around, not knowing the first place to look. Her eyes swept across the living room until they landed on the familiar briefcase. It was Harold's and she knew he'd have one in there. Vivian squeezed Harold's hand. *Please don't die, Harold. I can't lose you.* "Hang on, Harold."

Vivian popped open the satchel and dug through it until her hands landed on the pen. She grabbed it and then rushed back to Harold's side, where she removed the cap and pressed the pen to his leg and injected the medicine. The 911 operator stayed on the line to explain what should happen next — only nothing was happening. "It's not working. He's still struggling to breathe. Please help me!"

"Ma'am, help is on the way."

"Vivi —" The strangled whisper from Harold's lips hurt Vivian. "Help . . . her."

"Harold, don't try to speak." Her fingers trembled as they clutched his hand. "Help is coming."

He moved his head to the side, closing his eyes.

"No, Harold." Emotion ripped at her throat. "You stay with me. You made me drive all the way over here in the middle of the night because you have a story that you just *had* to tell me." Vivian's attempt at humor felt puny, until Harold's brown eyes met hers. "That's right. A real marmalade dropper, remember?"

His lips parted. "Lau-ren."

What was he saying? Vivian leaned closer. "What?"

"Help . . . Lau—" He gasped. "Marma . . . Lauren."

Vivian blinked. She leaned in closer. "What? Lauren who?" She felt guilty for making him talk, but the urgency in his eyes pulled at her.

Whatever Harold was trying to tell her fell silent in the desperate gasp. She squeezed his hand, but it fell open. *No!* Panic slid cold fingers around her heart and squeezed. He was dying. Harold was leaving her, and she'd be all alone again.

"Please!" Vivian pressed the phone to her ear. "Tell me what else I can do! Can I give him another shot?"

The blare of sirens outside interrupted the operator's words. Vivian dropped her phone and yelled. "Hurry! He's in here!"

Two EMTs ran into the house and started working on Harold. A man wearing a blue shirt with the fire unit's number on the pocket moved her to the side. "Ma'am, are you his daughter?"

"No." Vivian's eyes were fixed on Harold's body. The paramedics opened his shirt, revealing a chest that wasn't moving. The wheezing had grown too soft — almost silent. She watched them try to stick a tube down his throat, but it wasn't working and her heart was shattering. Steeling her emotions, she looked into the firefighter's concerned eyes. "No, I'm just a reporter."

Deputy Ryan Frost had no expectations for his first day back on duty. Okay, maybe one

— easy. It was Walton, after all, and Friday nights remained relatively quiet, aside from an occasional noise complaint or juvenile shenanigans happening on the outskirts of town. Possibly a drunk driver passing through from Savannah. But not even the excitement from tonight's basketball championship garnered much more than a few reminders to college students against disorderly conduct.

He was beginning to wonder whether the agency recruiters were right about his skills being wasted in Walton. Then the call came in. He'd been in town less than twenty-four hours, on patrol less than eight, and he was already investigating a death. Ryan spotted the brunette sitting stiffly on a leather chair talking to Deputy Ben Wilson. According to the first responders, she was the one who found Harold Kennedy and called in the emergency.

"Deputy Frost, we're about done here." Troy Bennett walked up, removing his latex gloves. He was the first EMT on the scene and a classmate from high school. "Medical examiner is on the way." He tipped his chin in the direction of the home office. "You might want to let her know that there was nothing more she could do. Allergic re-

15

actions are unpredictable. It was just too late."

Ryan looked over his shoulder, his gaze meeting her blue-gray one. A sense of familiarity raced through him. Did he know her? He searched his memory, but nothing came up. "How is she?"

"Seems fine." Troy looked toward the ambulance where his partner was finishing up. "Pretty composed, actually."

"It's not shock?"

"She said she was shaken but okay to go home."

Ryan thanked him and the rest of the first responders after he verified their names for his report. He was taking some pictures of the scene when the medical examiner entered the house.

"Hi, I'm Josie Carlisle, assistant ME for Chatham County." The blonde was half a foot shorter than he was and looked way too young to be a medical examiner. She must have read his thoughts, because she smiled widely and gave him a wink. "Graduated high school last week."

Ryan flinched.

"Just kidding." She pulled a pair of latex gloves out of her bag. "I really wish I had a camera every time I said that."

"Deputy Ryan Frost."

16

"I'm told you're the man in charge." Her blue eyes swept up over Ryan's shoulder. "Or would that be you?"

Ryan turned to find Deputy Wilson's hulking frame standing behind him, his smile bright against his dark skin.

"You're looking at me like I'm gonna have a problem going home tonight when my shift's over while you stay and fill out paperwork for the chief." The man was roughly the size of a refrigerator and took great pleasure in intimidating Ryan. "First man on the scene is the rule, right?"

"Guess that answers that. I'll do the paperwork." Ryan returned his attention to the ME. "Anything you need from me?"

"Only to stay out of my way unless I have a question." She pulled the blanket from Harold's face. "Told this was an allergy-related death."

"Peanut allergy."

The medical examiner let out a whistle. "Ain't it a shame." She snapped her gloves on. "Okay, boys. I'll take it from here."

Ryan and Wilson stepped back, giving her space to work. "What's our caller's connection to Mr. Kennedy?" Ryan asked.

Wilson smirked. "You don't know?"

"Should I?"

"I figured you would've recognized her."

Wilson pivoted, giving Ryan a full view of the woman still sitting in Harold Kennedy's office. She was twisting a piece of dark, wavy hair around her finger. "She practically camped outside our office last year."

Last year?

"And my wife thinks I'm oblivious." Wilson handed Ryan his notes. "Check out her name."

Ryan did and his pulse jumped with recognition. "She's not blonde anymore."

"And you ain't scrawny anymore." Wilson chuckled. "Change happens — even the miraculous kind."

"What's she doing here?" Ryan asked, ignoring Wilson's jab.

"Works for Harold."

"Doing what?"

Wilson held up a meaty finger. "I'll give you one guess."

Right. Reporter. Really?

"Look, I don't know what them boys taught you up in Quantico, but gawking at the witness isn't really professional."

Heat raced up his face. Ryan quickly looked down at Wilson's notes again. He wasn't gawking . . . he was looking. Trying to reconcile the tenacious reporter he remembered from a year ago with the one sitting twenty feet away from him.

18

"I told her you might ask her some follow-up questions."

"Right." He didn't dare look at Wilson. Ryan could tell from the tone of his voice what his coworker was implying and he wasn't going to give Wilson the satisfaction. Ryan hadn't spent the last nine months training with the Advanced Tactical Response Task Force to get tripped up by Vivian DeMarco. "I'll be back."

"Famous last words," Wilson mumbled under his breath.

Ignoring him, Ryan stepped into the office and cleared his throat. Vivian turned and looked up at him.

"Did I do something wrong? Is that why the medicine didn't work?"

"It's not your fault." Ryan felt drawn to reassure her of this fact. He sat in the leather chair across from her. "The EMTs said you administered the EpiPen correctly, but it's possible the medicine couldn't react to the allergy fast enough. You did everything you could."

An empty stare met his.

"How long have you been back in town?"

"Long enough to know you haven't been, Deputy Frost."

It took him a second to realize he hadn't introduced himself and her using his name

19

meant she recognized him. "Right. I was up in Virginia. Training." He looked down at his notes, praying Wilson was not hearing this. "Deputy Wilson said you stopped by here because —" Ryan read the note again. "Marmalade dropper?"

"Yes, it's something Harold liked to say when he had a story idea. Means the headline will be so big it'll make you drop the marmalade."

"What was the story?"

"He never got a chance to tell me."

Ryan saw it. The way her eyes shifted quickly to the side. She was holding something back. "You're sure about that?"

A flicker of the obstinate reporter he remembered from a year ago lit her eyes. "Yes, I'm sure."

He studied her features, the set of her jaw daring him to press her further. He wouldn't. Not because he was intimidated — no. She did unnerve him though. A year ago it was the scrappy way she went after each deputy in the station, hungry for information on Walton's first murder. Tonight *that* reporter wasn't sitting here. The woman in front of him now was . . . vulnerable.

"Look, I think we have everything we need for the report." Ryan stood. "I have your

20

contact information if I need anything else."

"Yes." Vivian rose slowly. She glanced over at the ME examining Harold's body.

"I'm sorry for your loss."

Her eyes met his, and for the first time all night he saw a shimmer of emotion, but it lasted only a second. She offered a sad smile. "Leave it to Harold to die with a story on his lips."

"Maybe some stories are best left untold."

There was a sad tilt to Vivian's lips. "I don't believe that."

An uneasy feeling settled in his gut as he led her to the front door and watched her get into her car and drive away. What story was so important that Harold would call Vivian to his home? Ryan turned on his heel and walked to the place where Harold had died. He began picking up the discarded trash left by the EMTs and noticed a piece of paper. He was about to add it to the trash when he saw a name on it.

Lauren.

Who was Lauren? Did this name have something to do with Harold's big story? Something told him Vivian had the answers. And if she was still a tenacious reporter, anxious and willing to dig up dark secrets to fuel her need for a headline . . . then she was already a step ahead of him.

Two

Ryan drummed his thumb against the steering wheel, trying to keep his mind occupied. Listening to Pastor Price's sermon this morning on the Song of Solomon had left him uncomfortable and unable to stop thinking about Vivian DeMarco.

It had been two days and the shock of seeing her back in Walton still hadn't worn off. Why hadn't Charlie mentioned anything? *Because he was too busy getting married to Lane.* While Ryan was eating dirt up in Quantico, his best friend had been consumed with wedding plans and his new bride.

Vivian's presence demanded attention, and it was hard not to give it to her. She was beautiful. Was still beautiful . . . maybe even more so with the darker hair. He also noticed she wore less makeup than before, and he liked that too. Ryan shook the errant thought from his mind. Yes, she was beautiful. And *way* out of his league.

Why was she in Walton? He'd imagined she'd be up in New York City reporting for the *Times*. Vivian certainly seemed destined for bigger and better things. Ryan flexed his fingers. Those were the same words Agent Hannigan from the FBI had told him a few weeks ago in his bid to get Ryan to accept their offer.

Ryan wheeled his Jeep into the driveway behind his mom's Camry, forcing his thoughts back to the task at hand — mulching his mom's flower beds. He climbed out of the car and caught sight of the bright pink blooms in a sea of dark, shredded wood bark lining the front porch. *What?* He glanced at the dogwoods . . . someone else had taken care of the yard.

Surveying his mom's yard, Ryan scratched the back of his neck, confusion rising. He'd hired a handyman named Ralph before he left for Virginia. Ralph had come highly recommended by Sheriff Huggins and promised to take care of anything his mom needed. So, when Ryan called yesterday evening to find out what he owed the man, he was shocked to hear that his mom hadn't called Ralph in two months.

The yard had been mowed, the flower beds cleared and ready for the mulch Ryan had brought over. He even noticed the rain gutters had been cleaned. Had she hired someone else? It bugged him. It was his job to make sure his mom was taken care of, and the last thing he needed was for her to hire some dude he hadn't run a background check on.

He went up the porch two steps at a time, then entered the house, annoyed she had left the front door unlocked. He'd talk to her about that after he found out who she had hired to take care of the yard.

"Mom." Ryan walked through the front living area and into the kitchen. Empty. "Mom!"

"Ryan?" The back door opened and his mom stepped inside, carrying an empty coffee mug. "What's wrong?"

He appraised her. Face pink from the sun, blonde hair poking out beneath a straw hat, dirt smudged at the knees of her pants. Gardening. "You left the front door unlocked."

Linda Frost's cheeks pinched into a warm smile. "You sound like a parent."

"Or a deputy who knows the first line in home defense is a locked door."

She set down her mug and walked toward him, putting both palms on the edge of his jaw. "The kindest, handsomest deputy who needs to find someone other than his mom to worry about. Besides, this is Walton."

Ryan's mind skipped to Vivian DeMarco. Those fiery eyes claimed more of his thoughts than he cared to admit.

"Ry-annnn!" A shrill voice echoed through the house. "Your stupid Jeep is taking up half the driveway." Ryan's sister stepped into the kitchen, dropping her backpack at the door and tossing her keys onto the counter. "Didn't anyone teach you how to park?"

"Good morning to you too, Frankie." Ryan eyed his sister's attire. Fringed jean shorts and a cropped T-shirt that revealed more skin than he was comfortable with. "Didn't anyone teach you how to dress?"

Frankie blew out an exasperated breath that lifted her strawberry-blonde bangs off her forehead for a second before they fell back over her blue eyes. The same eyes she rolled in an exaggerated way before turning them on their mom. "Can you tell Mister Law Enforcement that it's Frannie now?"

"What's Frannie now?"

"Her name." His mom's eyebrows lifted in amusement. "She doesn't like being called Frankie. Prefers Frannie or Francis now."

Ryan grinned. "Oh, Frankie's a big girl

now that she's about to graduate high school."

Frankie stuck out her tongue before her eyes grew wide. "Did you tell him?"

Their mom shook her head. Frankie disappeared down the hall.

"Bring your brother's mail too," their mom called after her. She turned to Ryan. "Want some sweet tea?"

"Tell me what?"

Without answering, his mom opened the fridge and pulled out a pitcher. When she let the door swing closed, his eyes caught on the magnetic notepad. Blank.

Every Sunday that pad of paper held a list of tasks and chores his mom needed done: replace batteries in smoke detectors, fix torn screen, clean gutters, change oil in the car. Jobs the man of the house should've taken care of but became invisible to his father as he reached for his next beer. Pulling double shifts at the truck stop restaurant six days a week left his mom with little energy, and she didn't have the money to hire a handyman.

So Ryan became one. Using the school computer, he watched how-to videos and started crossing off items on the list. It didn't take long for his mom to figure it out, and he never forgot the tear-stained expression on her face. He'd become the man of the house in his father's inexcusable absence. But today something wasn't right. His mother's slanted script was missing.

He reached for two glasses from the drying rack next to the sink. "I talked to Ralph yesterday. Said it's been a couple of months since you've called him to do anything. I picked up mulch, but it seems that's already been taken care of."

"Oh," his mom said as she busied herself pouring the tea. "I forgot to tell you about that. It was expensive and —"

"So, where are you moving?" Frankie interrupted, resuming her position on the counter as she thrust a handful of envelopes into Ryan's hand before taking his glass of tea. "DC? New York? Ooh, LA." Frankie rolled her eyes up in delight. "I would love to go to California. Hollywood. Famous actors."

Ryan frowned at his sister. "What are you talking about?"

Frankie pinned him with a wide-eyed stare. "You're moving, aren't you?" She poked a finger at the stack of envelopes in his hand. "Taking a job with the FBI, CIA, or FDA, right?"

"Food and Drug Administration?"

27

She made a face. "You know what I mean."

He looked down and saw the familiar letterhead of the agencies that had approached him in Virginia. Ryan swallowed. The recruiters wanted him to commit, but he hadn't made a decision yet and had been avoiding their attempts to contact him since returning home.

"Besides, I need to know where you'll be so I know where *not* to be."

Ryan lifted his eyes to meet his sister's excited expression. "What?"

"For college!" Frankie squealed, revealing two envelopes she'd been holding behind her back. "I made Mom wait so I could tell you when you got home, but I got accepted to Georgia State and the University of South Florida!"

"Wow." But the word didn't match his tone, and Frankie picked up on it immediately.

Her smile drooped. "That was real enthusiastic, Ryan."

"I'm sorry," he said. "I'm in shock, I guess."

Frankie's smile returned. "Me too." She waved the envelopes at him. "My guidance counselor suggested I apply to more colleges than just Anderson and —"

"What's wrong with Anderson College?"

She narrowed her eyes at him. "It's *here.*"

"Which makes it perfect for —"

"Linda?"

Ryan started, when a man's face peeked through the back door. He crossed in front of his mom and sister, forgetting that he wasn't in uniform, and reached for his weapon that wasn't there. "Who are you?"

"It's okay, Ryan. This is my friend." His mom moved around him and opened the back door, allowing the man to step inside. "And the main reason why my chore list is blank."

"He's a handyman?"

Frankie snorted.

"He's a dentist," his mom said. "Dr. Evan Murphy."

Dr. Murphy held out his hand, but Ryan ignored it as he assessed the man: mid- to late fifties, soft around the middle, brown hair graying throughout, and a lined face that seemed to see a lot of sun. Nothing struck him about the stranger's profile except the man's ease in walking through his mom's kitchen.

"It's nice to meet you, Ryan. Your mom and Frannie have told me so much about you."

Frannie? Ryan slid a glance to his sister,

29

who tucked her chin to avoid eye contact.

"I was hoping to introduce you two at dinner next week," his mom said.

"Why? My teeth are fine. Not looking for a new dentist."

His mom's expression tightened. Over her shoulder she gave Dr. Murphy a smile. "Give me a minute. I'll be right out." As soon as the man stepped out of the house, her focus pinned on Ryan. "This wasn't how I planned to do this, but . . ." She smiled. "Evan is more than just a friend."

Oh, he could see that without a single word being uttered. They had stood too close, their gazes lingering. "How long has he been more than just a friend?"

"A few months."

"*Months.*" The word came out in a low grumble. "You've been dating for months? Here I was worried about Frankie bringing home some guy —"

"Hey," Frankie whined.

"I never even considered worrying about my mom bringing home a stranger."

"He's not a stranger." His mom pressed her lips together, giving him a look that said he was close to crossing a line. "I met him before you left, but it didn't start getting serious until recently." Her tone softened. "He's a good man. Helps out around the

house. Cares about me. And Frankie and I
—"

"I need to go." Ryan pulled out his keys
and started for the front door. "I've got
some work to do."

"Ryan, please stay."

His mom called after him, but he didn't
stop. He couldn't. Hurt seared his chest.
How could his mom not tell him about this?
Or Frankie? Single parenthood hadn't given
his mom the luxury to look after herself. It
had become his job to look after her and his
sister. To make sure they were alright. He
had been gone for only nine months and
they'd . . . replaced him.

"Ryan, wait!"

Opening his Jeep door, he paused. Frankie
ran up to him.

"You forgot your mail."

He took the envelopes from her and tossed
them onto the passenger seat before climbing in.

Frankie stepped to the driver's-side window. "Mom's happy. If I go to college in
Florida, I'll be happy." She punched him
playfully on the arm. "One of these days
you're going to see that we're alright. You
did your job looking after us." She lifted her
chin at the envelopes. "Maybe it's time to
find a new one."

Vivian's eyes burned, and it wasn't from the bright rays of light cutting through her curtains, telling her it was well past morning. Rolling over, she picked up her phone and checked the time.

"Well done, Viv, you've officially slept through half of Sunday."

She dropped her head back to the pillow and let her wrist fall across her eyes. There had been no sleeping. Between the nightmares, Vivian had managed to doze off only to startle herself awake at the same point in her dream each time.

The scene played out just as it had on Friday night. Harold called and asked her to come over. She drove there, but something always slowed her down. First, she couldn't find her keys. Then it was her car not working properly or getting lost on her way to Harold's house. The worst was seeing Harold through the window and not being able to get into the house. But the part that tortured her were those final moments at Harold's side. The way his eyes looked into hers, desperate for her to help him. In the end she was always too late.

Vivian groaned and shoved herself out of

bed. Her feet smacked across the wood floor toward the kitchen of the small two-bedroom cottage she rented. She needed coffee. And something for the ache in her head. Deputy Frost's words rolled around in her mind. *"You did everything you could."*

Once the deputy got over his initial shock of recognizing her, she could see the sincerity in his attempt to console her, but it didn't lessen the pain pulsating in her heart. Or the guilt that maybe, just maybe, she could've gotten there earlier and given Harold the shot in time to save him. Vivian placed both hands on the counter and dropped her chin to her chest, her breathing constricted.

Get a grip. He was my boss. I worked for him for a short while — not enough time to get attached. This is only a temporary gig to get me where I want to be.

Man, she wanted to believe that.

Regaining her composure, Vivian started a pot of coffee and searched the fridge for something to feed the gnawing in her stomach. She wasn't really hungry, but at this point she was looking for anything that would keep her busy and her mind off Harold. And Deputy Frost. He'd invaded her bad dreams a few times, only it felt less like an invasion and more like . . . well, whatever it was, she wasn't going to allow her mind to explore it — even if she'd been just as surprised at his Samson-like transformation as he'd been about finding her in Walton.

A faint ringing echoed from the bedroom. She walked back in there and picked up her phone. "Well, you wanted something to keep you busy," she muttered before answering. "Hi, Mom."

"Did you just wake up? You sound like you just woke up. What time is it there?"

"It's a little past two. And no, I've been up pretty much all night." Vivian had no intention of revealing the reason behind her raw throat. "Might be a cold."

"Oh. Make sure you take some zinc. That's what the girls and I do to stay healthy on the planes."

Genevieve DeMarco had worked as a flight attendant before Vivian was born and returned to the job she loved right after Vivian left for college.

"Did you just get home?"

"Yes. The red-eye from Paris." A rustling noise. "Oh, I got you some perfume."

Vivian walked back to the kitchen and chose her largest mug and filled it to the brim with coffee. "Thanks."

"Anyway, I'm calling because a piece of

mail came for you. I think it's a card. Or maybe an invitation?"

"An invitation?" Vivian frowned. It had been at least ten years since she'd lived at her mom's address. Anyone wanting to invite her to something would know that. "It's probably junk."

"It doesn't look like junk."

"Mom, the whole point is not to make it look like junk so people will open it."

"I'm going to open it."

Before Vivian could tell her no, she heard ripping. Something in her gut told her there might be a reason a piece of mail with her name on it would arrive at her mother's address, and it turned her delicious coffee into sludge.

"It's a birthday card . . ." Vivian's mom's voice faltered. "Oh, uh, it's from —"

"I know who it's from."

"I guess he wanted you to know he remembered your birthday."

"If Russell wanted me to know, why did he send the card to your house?" But it wasn't really a question. The card going to her mother's house was only further proof that her father, the famous Russell Bradley, wanted it to look like he cared. But really, he didn't care enough to know where she lived in the first place.

"You won't let me give him your address."

"He asked?"

"He's called a few times. To check on you. Said you don't respond to his emails."

"And that surprises him?" Vivian dumped her coffee into the sink.

"Vivian."

"Nope. Not going there." But it was too late. Vivian's thoughts were already transporting her back fifteen years to when the man betrayed her. The man who pretended to be something he wasn't and now he was pretending he cared enough about her to remember —

Wait. "What's the postmark on the envelope?"

"March 22. Hmm, that's weird. I wonder why I just got it — oh, here it is. The address is wrong. It must've gone to the neighbor's by mistake and they put it in my mailbox. At least he tried."

"Mom. My birthday's March 12." Vivian groaned. The pressure was building steadily in the back of her head. "He sent the card ten days *after* my birthday."

"It was probably a simple mistake."

That was typical of her mom. Sweep the real issue under the rug. Or hide it altogether like she'd done for fifteen years. Vivian's anger throbbed. "Sums up my life about now."

"Vivian Renee Bradley."

"DeMarco." Vivian ground her molars. She walked into the bathroom, phone clutched between her cheek and shoulder, and searched the medicine cabinet for pain pills.

"You know I hate when you say things like that."

Resignation and exhaustion filled her mom's voice, but it did little to ease the hurt Vivian had pent up inside her.

"I think your dad wants a relationship with you. We made mistakes, you know that. He's trying." Vivian fought hard not to say something that would embarrass her mother. She wasn't prone to cursing, but sometimes thinking those horrible, awful words made her feel better, at least temporarily.

"All I'm saying is that maybe it's time to forgive. I'm reading this new devotional, and it talks about how forgiveness can release us from bitterness. It's what God wants —"

"Fine." Vivian swallowed two pills without water. The last thing she needed right now was a lecture on God. "Not like it matters anyway since my birthday has passed, but I'll respond the same way he did the day I graduated high school."

"Vivian —"

"Look, I've had a really bad weekend and this isn't making it better. I'm going to go back to bed." And pretend all this is a nightmare.

"Alright, I hope you feel better. Get some zinc. And Vivian" — her mom's voice grew soft — "I'm sorry. For my part. His part. For all of it. I want you to be happy . . . and I know he does too."

This wasn't the first time her mom had apologized, and Vivian wanted to offer forgiveness but couldn't. It felt like doing so would somehow make what happened okay. And it was not okay. "I'll talk to you later, Mom."

Vivian hung up the phone and flopped down on the couch. She had no energy to argue with her mom. Nor did she want to. *God.* He seemed to have disappeared from her life about the same time her dad did. She reached for the chenille blanket and curled up into a ball, trying to ignore the return of an ache for something she hadn't realized had been missing deep in her soul. And she knew why.

Vivian had allowed Harold Kennedy to fill a void she didn't dare admit she was experiencing. He might've started out as just her boss, but at some point he had become more. He extended her grace when she had called him about a job. Offered wisdom and encouragement when she had questioned and doubted herself. And filled the vacancy left by a man who should've been there for her.

With practiced movements, her fingers glided over her phone's screen until the email popped up. The one she had looked at so many times while she was packing up her apartment in DC. And by the end of the eight-hour drive to Walton, she knew the message verbatim.

Heard you're no longer working for the *Herald.* If you need anything . . . I'm here.

R. Bradley

Ha! Her sadness roiled into burning resentment. If she needed anything? There were many things Vivian needed — had needed — but they weren't going to come from Russell Bradley. The man had made his choice.

Vivian wiped angrily at the stray tear falling down her cheek. She wouldn't cry. Crying didn't do anything but make her look weak. And she wasn't weak. She never should have allowed herself to get attached to Harold. She hated herself for it. It was a mistake she wouldn't make again. She came to Walton to do a job, and she would do it, because there was no way she would ever ask her father for a single thing. Ever.

THREE

What in the world had made her think coming here would be a good idea? Vivian went to the large picture window of the *Gazette*'s second-story office and swung it open. She breathed in deep, willing her lungs to exchange the sweet tobacco scent of Harold's chicory coffee for the honeysuckle that clung to the brick exterior of the former bank building.

The afternoon sky had darkened, bringing with it the promise of a thunderstorm. Perfect. The weather was exactly what this day called for.

A gust of wind blew in and toppled the stacks of paper from Harold's walnut desk. The old wood had been polished smooth by thousands of hours of stories typed right there. And Vivian couldn't shake the phantom vision she kept seeing of her boss sitting in the leather chair, smiling at her.

Vivian swallowed the lump of emotion in

41

her throat. She had come into the office because it was Monday. And there was a paper to print . . . except the eternally optimistic editor with a penchant for spinning stories into something people enjoyed reading was gone. Leaving just her, the other half of this small press, to figure out what to do next.

She turned to scoop up the scattered papers. This was just supposed to be a job — a stopping point on her way back to the career she unintentionally threw away a year ago. If that were true, then why did she have an aching, hollowed spot in her chest?

Because she'd gotten too close to the quirky man who dressed like Mark Twain and had the manners of someone who still believed it was proper to tip his hat to a lady no matter her age, and he . . . recognized her.

Blinking back tears, she started to return the toppled pages to Harold's desk when footsteps sounded behind her.

She turned and found herself staring into a pair of familiar eyes on a man she did not recognize. Wiping her face, she straightened and took in the stranger's khaki shorts, polo shirt, and dock shoes sans socks — he must be lost.

"Can I help you?"

"You must be the infamous reporter."

There was an unnerving look in his brown eyes. "The reporter part is accurate."

The man stepped farther into the office. His gaze roamed around the open space until finally landing on the desk behind Vivian. He walked around her and spun Harold's leather chair.

A sad smile spread across his face. "When I was a kid, my uncle used to spin me on this until I couldn't walk."

"Your uncle?" Her voice was barely audible over the alarm sounding inside her brain. Standing in front of her was the heir of the *Atlanta Tribune* and editor of the *Savannah Daily.* He was also much younger than she had expected, maybe a few years older than herself, and with a wave of brown hair falling across his brow, he looked more the part of surfer than newspaper man.

He stopped the motion of the chair and glanced up. "Shep," he said as he held out his hand. "Harold was my uncle."

Vivian shook his hand. "Shep?"

"Well, my given name is George Shepherd Kennedy, but I was never a fan of being called junior and George is my father." He sat in Harold's chair and ran his hands along the armrest like he was getting a feel for it. "Shep's easier."

Trying not to be bothered by Shep's comfortable clothing, she quickly glanced at her own outfit. Floral skirt, white sleeveless blouse, and flats. Nothing memorable, but at least her look was professional.

"I'm sorry for your family's loss."

"Me too."

"How's Carol?" Vivian heard Carol had flown in from Florida on Saturday, but she hadn't had the nerve to call Harold's widow yet.

"Still in shock. I think we all are."

Vivian nodded.

Thunder bellowed. Ominous timing. She moved to the window and pulled it closed just as the pitter-patter of drops began to fall. When she turned, Shep was watching her.

She licked her lips. "Harold had the layouts prepared for the next two papers. I've finished the community events column as well, and I —"

"Ms. DeMarco, that's why I'm here."

Vivian's breathing slowed, preparing for what she was afraid was coming next.

"The *Gazette*'s final publication is scheduled for the last week of September. My father and I intend to keep the *Gazette* running until then. My writers at the *Daily* will handle the news content." Shep rose from

44

the chair. "My father informed me Uncle Harold had made you a deal."

"Harold knew moving here wasn't going to be easy for me —"

"My uncle always had a soft spot for those in need."

Vivian's cheeks flushed. "I wasn't in need."

"So you had other job options?"

"No, but —"

Shep held up his hands, palms facing her. "Ms. DeMarco, I'm not here to question my uncle's decision to hire you. He was a smart man and my father and I trusted his intuition —"

"And yet, here you are, questioning my position." Vivian took some pleasure in the shock on Shep's well-bred face. Apparently, he was not accustomed to being inter-rupted.

"I'm not questioning your position. Your editorials on Walton's social events are well received, as are your blog posts." He quirked an eyebrow at her. "But I have yet to see what you can contribute as an investigative reporter to the *Tribune*."

Vivian's defenses surged. "I can print you out a résumé, if you'd like, but I don't think it's your place to question my ability. My position at the *Tribune* is up to your father now."

Shep smiled. "And one day my father's legacy will pass to me, and I want to make sure I can trust my reporters to report the story without hesitation."

Ah, so that was what this was about. A year ago, she was in this very town reporting on its first murder when she overheard Lane Kent — the daughter of Senate hopeful Judge Raymond Sullivan — confess her role in the death of her husband and chose not to write the story. The decision was not well received by her editor back at the *Herald* in DC, who didn't care to know the rest of the story behind Lane's admission because those details didn't sell papers, and he let her go.

That one decision had tainted her reputation with other news corporations. So after months of job searching, she had no other option but to accept Harold's job offer and move to Walton in the hopes she could prove herself. And now she was being called out on her decision.

"Mr. Kennedy, I don't know what reservations you have about my ability, but your uncle didn't share them. And from what he told me about your father, I believe them both to be men of their word. At the end of the summer, my expectation is to move into a position at the *Tribune,* where I can prove exactly how good of an investigative journalist I am."

Shep's eyebrows rose at her speech. "We'll see, Ms. DeMarco. I'll be in touch."

And with that, Shep gave the leather desk chair a final spin as he left the office. Vivian's chest heaved with indignation. Was that how he was going to leave it? Question her as a journalist and leave her wondering if, after she fulfilled her commitment to the *Gazette,* there might not be a job waiting for her? A frightening thought took over. Did George Shepherd Kennedy really have a say over whether his father hired her? Or would his assumption of her ability to be an investigative journalist keep her from the job?

The idea sickened her. She looked around the office. When had she grown to love the place? She reached for Harold's chair, then sank into the soft leather and breathed in the chicory scent that would forever remind her of the man who knew the rest of the story. Story . . .

Vivian sat up. Marmalade dropper. Friday night Harold said he had the story they were looking for. What did he mean? Shep was right. Vivian wasn't currently writing investigative pieces worthy of the *Tribune,* but this was Walton. Big-city scandals didn't happen here like they did in DC, New York, or Atlanta. Maybe that was it.

She stared at the mess of papers, ads, invoices, and story notes piled on Harold's desk. If he had a story, it might be somewhere in this mess. All she had to do was dig for it and prove she had the gumption Harold had seen in her.

Vivian flipped on the desk lamp and rubbed her eyes. She turned to the window and realized the sky had grown dark, except for the flashes of lightning still streaking across the glass. What time was it? She stood and stretched. *Ooh.* She needed to use the restroom. She walked to her desk and grabbed the key, then went down the hall to the restroom.

Washing her hands, she looked up in the mirror and could see the weight of what the last few days had done to her. She untwisted her hair from the messy bun and ran her fingers through it, when everything went black.

"What?"

A loud crack of thunder rumbled and Vivian flinched. Feeling her way to the door, she opened it and let her eyes adjust to the darkness. The glow of the red exit sign led her back to the office and she stopped.

Her breathing hitched. The feeling that she was no longer alone sent chills coursing down her skin. She held her breath, listening, but whatever she'd heard was gone. Maybe it was her imagination.

Creak.

Nope. Definitely not. "Hello?"

A shadow emerged from the darkness and Vivian screamed.

Ryan paused. *What was that?* He moved his flashlight from side to side as he walked down the alley behind the old bank building. Mrs. Bernard's skittish cat didn't care for bad weather and had managed to escape out of the house. Again. He looked between a dumpster, calling for the calico, before rounding the corner and searching along the side of the redbrick building. A deputy's job in Walton wasn't complete if he didn't get called out to at least one domestic animal disturbance a day.

Scratching his head, he stepped back onto Ford Avenue. Where else —

"Aghhhh!"

A scream jolted Ryan. He jerked around and stared up at the old bank building. Reaching for the glass doors, his eyes caught on the gold lettering of the *Gazette* sign.

He pounded up the stairs two at a time, sweeping the beam of his flashlight over the space. Why was it so dark? He radioed his location and trained his weapon forward.

"Walton County Sheriff's Department! Is anyone here?" A mumbled cry echoed from down the hall. His light caught on the brunette sitting on the floor. "Ms. De-Marco?"

She turned, and the sight of blood dripping from her chin sent a surge of adrenaline coursing through him. He went to her side.

"Are you okay?"

"Yes, I think so. He came out of nowhere."

Ryan swung the beam around. "Which way did he go?"

She lifted a hand and pointed toward the emergency exit at the back of the building. Ryan radioed in the information before turning his attention back to Vivian. He could see fear swirling in eyes that were more gray than blue tonight. His fingers moved the hair from across her face and the touch of her skin sent a zing through him. "I need to secure the building. Are you okay to walk downstairs with me?"

She nodded.

Ryan helped her up and escorted her down the stairs, where another unit was already walking in. He left her with Deputy Benningfield, and he and Deputy Hodges secured the real estate office on the first floor, the bathrooms on both floors, and the small insurance office on the second floor across from the *Gazette.* Just as they finished searching, the power returned. He headed outside and walked over to the ambulance, where an EMT was bandaging Vivian's chin. The tech said something that made Vivian laugh and Ryan found he didn't like the way that made him feel. Not that it mattered — it didn't. This was a crime scene. It was serious. And Vivian had been injured.

"Doesn't look like you found him."

Vivian's words brought Ryan's thoughts back. "Uh, no. But we've got a BOLO out based on the description you gave Deputy Benningfield."

"Big guy in black seems like the standard costume of thugs."

Ryan smiled. "How are you?"

Vivian's fingertips touched the bandage. "Feels like I got sucker punched."

"You've been sucker punched before?"

"No. But I imagine this is what it feels like." The EMT finished and gave her some extra bandages. "I didn't even see him before he rushed at me."

"Doesn't seem like he was expecting you."

Vivian shook her head. "He had to have been waiting." She shuddered. "Waiting until I went to the restroom."

"Deputy Hodges said a breaker had been tripped, but the lights are back on now. If you're up for it, I'd like you to walk me through the office so I can take account of anything missing or damaged."

Ryan followed her back up the stairs and into the *Gazette*'s office. The only things occupying the open space were some filing cabinets, a copier, a table with a coffee-maker and supplies, and two desks. A large one in front of the window and a smaller one that faced the large desk but was next to a wall with photos taped up on it. He guessed that one belonged to Vivian. "Do you see anything missing?"

Vivian looked around. "It's hard to tell, really." She walked to her desk and lifted a bunch of papers. Then her gaze shot to the large desk. "Harold's laptop."

"It's missing?" Ryan noticed the empty spot where a laptop would most likely sit. He pulled out his notepad. "Do you have the serial information?"

"Probably, but I wouldn't know where to even look for it. Maybe Carol would —" Vivian stopped abruptly and bit her lip.

"Sorry. I was just thinking that this is the last thing Carol needs to deal with."

Her compassion surprised him. The woman had just been assaulted by a burglar and her concern was what this would do to Carol. He felt an urge to wrap Vivian in his arms and comfort her, which freaked him out. He rocked on his heels and tapped his pen against the desk. "Uh, is there anything else?"

Vivian swallowed. "No, but it's weird."

"What?"

"Well, they stole Harold's dinosaur of a computer but left mine here."

"It was dark. He probably grabbed the first thing he saw."

"Yeah . . ."

A small wrinkle formed between Vivian's eyebrows, indicating something was churning in her mind. "What?"

"Nothing," she said a little too quickly.

Remembering the note he found in Harold's house, Ryan took purposeful steps toward the desk. "So what brought a big-city girl like you back to this small town, Ms. DeMarco?"

"Vivian." She eyed him, suspicion clouding her eyes. "Short story is that I lost my job in DC at the *Herald* because I didn't give them the story about your friend's wife.

53

Papers aren't really fond of journalists with morals. Harold told me to call him if I ever found myself needing a job. So I did. And here I am."

He wasn't sure if what he heard in her voice was disappointment or sadness. "I have to say it was quite a shock to see you here."

"I'm surprised your buddy didn't let you know I was in town so you could keep your distance." Vivian pulled her hair back into a ponytail, revealing her slender neck. "Shouldn't surprise me though. I'm probably not his favorite person, considering everything that happened with Lane."

"Charlie and Lane aren't like that." Ryan slipped his pen and notepad into his pocket. He took several pictures of where Harold's laptop had once been. "They've been through a lot. Makes a person more forgiving than most. I'm surprised you've been here as long as you have and managed to avoid them."

"I wouldn't say I avoid them. I just have really good timing to make sure I'm not in the same place at the same time as them."

"Or the right place at the right time." A shadow crossed Vivian's features, making them tight. He circled his finger in the air. "You know, because you're a reporter. Have to be in the right place at the right time . . . Never mind."

Ryan's cheeks warmed. Talking to girls had never been his specialty. Wearing the uniform had at least given him an authoritative confidence to do his job. But not even a badge and a gun could diminish the effect Vivian DeMarco had on him.

"Deputy Frost, we've run the fingerprint kit on the doors out here." Deputy Benningfield popped her head into the office. "Where would you like us to start in here?"

"The desk." Ryan pointed and Deputies Hodges and Benningfield began their work. "We'll just stand out here to let them work. When they're done, you can get your things and leave."

Vivian followed him out. She rubbed her elbows and Ryan noticed a bruise beginning to form on her left forearm.

"Are you sure you're okay?"

"What? Oh, yeah. Sore, I think."

"It'll probably get worse tomorrow morning. Maybe you could take the day off."

"Oh no, I'm fine." She shook her head. "The paper never sleeps, ya know."

Ryan took in the frantic reassurance that she was okay. Curious. "Working a big story are you?"

That stopped her. She eyed him. "I'm a

journalist, Deputy Frost. I'm always working a story."

"I meant to ask, do you know someone named Lauren?"

Vivian frowned. "You'll have to be more specific."

Ryan leaned against the stair railing. "I think she might be a friend of Harold's."

Ah, there it was. A flicker of recognition lit her eyes, then just as swiftly disappeared. "You know her?"

"I know a few Laurens, but unless you have a last name, I can't say that I know who you're talking about."

Ryan rocked back on his boots. That was not what her expression told him. He'd spent nine months training to read body language and Vivian's was telling him she knew exactly who he was asking about.

"Deputy Frost, we're finished in here."

"Thanks, Hodges." Ryan looked to Vivian. "If you can get me the serial number on Harold's computer, I'll put it in the system in case we find the guy."

"What are the chances?"

"I imagine the computer will show up in a pawn shop. With the serial number out there, we'll get a call and maybe catch him." He glanced over his shoulder at Harold's desk. "You don't think there was something on that computer worth stealing it, do you?"

Vivian looked at the desk and then back at him. "I don't have a clue."

He studied her. If there was a clue, it would be buried among the clutter on that desk, and Ryan guessed Vivian would be in search of it the second he left.

"Ms. DeMarco, if there's something more . . . it's my job to find it."

"Don't worry, Deputy." She squinted. "I won't get in your way."

"If you're trying to reassure me, you're doing a horrible job."

Her face softened. "Have a nice night, Deputy."

He brought his hat to his head and tipped the brim to her. "You too, ma'am."

Vivian rolled her eyes, but he caught a hint of a smile playing at her lips before she slipped back into the office and closed the door behind her. Ryan made his way down the stairs and exited the building onto Ford Avenue, knowing two things after tonight. First, Vivian DeMarco would most definitely be getting in his way, and two, he wasn't entirely sure he was upset about it.

FOUR

Preston Northcott III
CEO, Owner of Northcottpharm
Dublin, Ohio

"Turn it off." Preston couldn't take any more. His stomach balled into a tight knot of anguish and utter rage. Sophia's quiet sobs weren't helping. He looked away from the computer screen, wishing he could erase what he had seen from his mind.

"What would you like me to do, boss?"

Preston took in a deep, deliberate breath, trying to collect his emotions and thoughts. "You weren't able to trace the email? Where it came from? Or who this *Watcher* is?"

"No, sir." Kayson Gray shook his bald head. "There are too many firewalls. The Watcher — whoever he is — made sure there was no way it could be traced back."

"And the link to the bank account?" Preston snapped. "Don't tell me your men couldn't figure out who's going to get paid for this . . . this . . ." He swiped his hand at the frozen picture of his daughter's face on the computer screen. "Who did this?"

Sophia, frightened, lifted her tear-stained face from her mother Erica's shoulder. A tear slipped down his wife's cheek as she clutched their daughter to her chest.

"I'm sorry, Daddy."

Preston's chest squeezed. "I know, honey." He gave Erica a look and she stood. "Take her home. I'll take care of this."

When Erica and Sophia had left the office, Kayson moved to the door and stood in a wide-leg stance, folding his arms over a barrel of a chest that proved whatever free time he had outside his job as Preston's head of security was spent in the gym.

Preston turned his attention to the other man in the room, his lawyer. "Flynn, tell me we have recourse."

Flynn's pasty, arthritic hands tugged at his silk tie. "Like Mr. Gray said, we haven't been able to verify who sent the video. And when we checked the account, my sources confirmed that the name on it is most likely an alias."

Preston balled his fingers into a fist. "How did this happen?"

"I believe Sophia wasn't aware she was being set up."

Preston glared at Kayson. "You think I don't know that? I want to know by who. How did they know who she was? Where she was?"

"Sophia said they met the boys at a night-club in Panama City. The boys suggested they go to a private party in the penthouse of Hotel Del Mar." Flynn opened a leather portfolio. "The name on the room was an alias, paid online with a credit card under the same name. Sophia and her friends went up to the room. She was too drunk to realize the pills had been slipped into her purse. Or that a camera had been set up."

Preston rubbed the bridge of his nose. "Have you found the boys?"

"Not yet, sir," Kayson spoke up. "I have a friend at the Miami-Dade County Sheriff's Office who's looking into it, but given the fact that thousands of college kids converge on the area during Spring Break, it's not going to be easy to find them."

"It could be they just got lucky," Flynn said. "Had the drugs there and then realized who Sophia was and decided to cash in."

"No." Preston shook his head. He pointed at the computer. "This was a setup. They knew to use drugs from my company and set up those cameras to make it look like Sophia was distributing them."

"We can go to the police," Flynn suggested quietly.

Preston stood and paced toward the window overlooking the Ohio River Valley. "And you think they'll find the dirtbags behind this?"

Silence met his question. He spun around. Flynn shook his head. Preston looked to Kayson, who gave an imperceptible shake.

"So I just pay $250,000 and this will go away?"

"Considering the alternative, Preston, it's a small price to pay."

"A small price to pay?" Spit flew from his mouth. "There's a video of my daughter snorting a medication my company is currently trying to get the FDA to approve."

Flynn remained calm. "That's why I think you should pay and let this disappear."

"How do we know it'll disappear?" Kayson voiced.

"Exactly. Who's to say that once I pay, the video still won't go viral?"

"We don't." Flynn lifted his shoulders. He removed a sheet of paper from his folder and set it on the desk. "The Watcher's email states that when payment is received the video will be destroyed."

"Hrmph." Preston crumpled the piece of paper in his fist. "I'm supposed to trust his word?" He threw the balled paper at his lawyer.

"What would you like me to do?"

Preston stared at Flynn. The man was supposed to protect him. *And Preston was supposed to protect his daughter.* The image of his drugged-up daughter infuriated him, but more than that, it scared him. Facing the FDA, Preston had been questioned extensively on the role prescription drugs were playing in the opioid epidemic. He'd seen the photos and was heartbroken for the families affected, but his company was also on the cutting edge of developing medicine to treat diseases like Alzheimer's and Parkinson's. This video being released would set not only his company back but also the progress his scientists had made.

"Fine."

"Fine?"

"Make the payment."

Flynn made a note and stood. "I'll get confirmation as soon as the transfer's complete."

Preston grumbled his consent and waited until his lawyer was gone before fixing his gaze on Kayson.

"Reach out to your contacts and find him. I don't care what it costs or how you do it.

I want this Watcher in a grave before one cent of my money is spent."

FIVE

Ryan clicked through the arrest reports from last week. No one matched the description Vivian had given him of the man who broke into the *Gazette* Monday night. He ran a hand through his hair and stared at the screen. He had zero belief Vivian was going to just let him do his job. There was a spark in those unwavering blue-gray eyes when he mentioned the name *Lauren,* and though he didn't know who Lauren was, he did recognize trouble when he saw it. And Vivian was going to be trouble.

Maybe he could print off a few of the mug shots and run them by the *Gazette* to see if she recognized anyone. It wouldn't hurt, right?

His desk phone rang. "Deputy Frost."

"Good morning, this is Josie Carlisle. I'm the medical examiner working the Harold Kennedy case."

"Yes, ma'am." He remembered the spunky

blonde. "How can I help you?"

"I'm about to email you the initial report, but I wanted to call you about some of our findings."

Ryan leaned forward, grabbing a pen and pad of paper. "Go ahead."

"During the routine processing of the body, we emptied the victim's stomach contents, and despite the information from the EMTs on the scene, I found no evidence to suggest this man died from ingesting any form of peanuts."

"He didn't die from his allergy?"

"He did. Our labs just didn't pick up anything containing peanuts, or any nuts for that matter, in the contents of his stomach. After receiving those results, I went back and reexamined the body. There was some discoloration near the victim's mouth. I swabbed the area and ran more tests that came back positive for peanuts."

"But you just said he didn't eat peanuts."

"Correct. It was peanut oil," she continued. "Trace amounts were found on and around his lips, chin, and nose."

"He ingested peanut oil?"

"Most people don't drink oil — especially an oil that can kill them. I checked the rest of his body and found peanut oil on both of his hands, but a higher amount appeared on his right hand. Was Mr. Kennedy right-handed?"

"I don't know."

"My guess is he was. And his right hand was most likely the first point of contact with the oil."

"And simply touching the oil was enough to kill him?"

"I studied a case a few years back where a little girl with a severe peanut allergy ended up in the hospital after walking through a grocery store barefoot over the exact spot where a gallon of peanut oil had spilled earlier that day."

"Did she die?"

"Fortunately, no. Her mother recognized her symptoms and administered the EpiPen on the way to the hospital."

Ryan's mind went to the scene. An EpiPen had been used, but the medics said it was too late. "Why didn't the EpiPen work on Harold?"

"His blood work showed the medicine was in his system. EpiPens are a critical first step treatment, but depending on the severity of the allergy and how much time passes after exposure . . . for your victim, it was just too late."

Ryan started to run his hand over his mouth and chin but stopped. "So he accidentally poisoned himself."

"Maybe."

"Maybe?"

The medical examiner let out a breath before she spoke again. "My daddy and both my brothers work in law enforcement, Deputy Frost. You sit around the dinner table long enough and you learn a thing or two. The amount of peanut oil residue found on your victim's mouth might indicate a simple accident, but we found a substantial amount of peanut oil on Harold Kennedy's right hand. More than enough to kill him."

"You think someone used peanut oil to kill him?"

"You're the deputy."

A throat cleared behind him and Ryan swiveled in his chair to find Sheriff Huggins standing there. "Thanks for calling, Ms. Carlisle. I'll investigate further and keep you posted."

Ryan hung up the phone and started to stand, but the sheriff waved his hand and sat in the empty chair next to Ryan's desk.

"Everything okay?"

"That was the assistant ME, Josie Carlisle. She said Harold didn't die from ingesting peanuts but from peanut oil she found on his right hand."

"Hmm." The sheriff was approaching eighty and had the stamina of men half his age. Beneath a shock of white hair, his blue eyes had the gentle spirit of a man who had seen and heard it all but didn't allow life's curve balls to interrupt his game. "Interesting. What's your plan?"

Ryan hadn't had even a second to think about it. "Harold died at home. There's no reason to believe he'd have anything inside his home that contained peanuts or peanut oil." He rubbed his hand down his face and cringed. Then looked up. "But maybe he touched something with the oil on it." His gaze met the sheriff's. "Either at the game or on his way home."

The deep lines of the sheriff's face pulled into a knowing smile. "That's why those agency boys keep calling me." He rapped his knuckles on the desk. "Know a good thing when they see it."

"Agency boys?"

Sheriff Huggins stood, then he removed an envelope from his pocket and set it in front of Ryan. The letterhead said it was from Breckenstone Security. He wasn't familiar with the company, but he guessed it was another private firm interested in hiring him.

"You know they're both proud of you."

Ryan looked at the framed family photo sitting on the corner of his desk.

"We all are. And that's not going to change if you decide to pursue bigger things."

Bigger things. That's what his father had done. Chased after dreams because his life — his family — in Walton wasn't enough.

"My mom's dating."

"Dr. Murphy. Good man."

Ryan's eyes flashed to the sheriff. "Am I the only one who didn't know?" He pushed the Breckenstone envelope across his desk. "What happens if I leave again? Frankie gets married and has kids?"

"Lord willing, yes." Thick white hair fell over Sheriff Huggins's forehead, crowning a face lined with wisdom and experience. "Isn't that what you want for her? For your mom? A life filled with blessings and opportunity?"

"Yes, of course, sir."

"Then what makes you think they don't want the same thing for you?"

He hadn't thought about that, but it didn't matter what he wanted. He needed to make sure they were taken care of. "What if I'm gone and they need me or something happens?"

"You're fooling yourself, son, if you think

you ever had control over that. Besides, your momma and sister did pretty good on their own while you were up at Quantico."

"If you call Mom dating and Frankie looking at colleges out of town good," Ryan mumbled.

"They're a lot stronger than you give them credit for," Sheriff Huggins said. "Maybe it's time they stop being your excuse to avoid" — he tapped a finger on the envelope — "what the Lord has in store for you. Trust him to do his job and care for them so you can do your job."

The sheriff was never one to mince words. He delivered truth with gentle humility, but it was always direct. Ryan had learned so much from him — could still learn so much from him. That was enough, wasn't it? To stay in Walton, content to keep his community safe? Or was the sheriff right? His mom and Frankie were doing pretty good. Had been for a while, if he was honest with himself. Then why couldn't he just accept a job and leave?

Two hours later, Ryan put Deputy Hodges in charge of running forensic tests on Harold Kennedy's Volvo. His talk with Carol Kennedy concerned him. A thorough search of the home confirmed there was no peanut oil or anything else containing peanuts on the property. Harold had been managing his allergy since childhood and Carol assured Ryan he was diligent about it. He rarely ate out, and when he did it was only at places he trusted not to cross-contaminate their food products.

Ryan had seen the concern in Carol's eyes when he questioned her. "Why are you really here, Ryan?"

"I'm just making sure we're covering all our bases." Carol peered down at the wedding ring she was spinning on her finger. "Is there anything you want to tell me?"

Her hazel eyes met his. "It's probably nothing, but there was something in his voice that day. An energy I hadn't heard in a long time."

"You said he was going to the Anderson College basketball game that night."

"Yes, he loves basketball, but that's not the kind of excitement I'm talking about. When I asked Harold how his day was going, he told me it was good . . . but he hesitated. When I pressed him further, the excitement I heard in his voice began to sound more like anxiousness. I knew he was working on a story and he wanted to talk to Viv about it, but I just can't help wondering if he got so worked up on something he

71

overlooked his own health somehow."

That bit of information grabbed Ryan's attention. "Vivian knew the story Harold was working on?"

"I'm not sure, but I know he trusted her."

Ryan glanced at the plastic evidence bag sitting in the passenger seat next to him. Harold's phone was inside and with it, Ryan hoped, was the information he'd need to lead him through Harold's final moments before he died. An upsetting revelation was gnawing at him, given what the medical examiner had told him and Carol's concern over the story that had made Harold anxious and prompted him to seek Vivian's opinion. Did it play a role in Harold's death? And if so, was Vivian's life also in danger?

An invisible battle was permeating the air inside the cafeteria of Walton Elementary. Between the red-faced, sweaty kids filing in and that afternoon's spaghetti lunch, the aroma was enough to make Vivian pity the custodians.

Lifting her camera, she snapped a few more pictures of the students still energized despite the run they just completed to raise money for Home for Heroes. Today's event would require more pictures than words in the next issue of the *Gazette*. Vivian knew the kids would love seeing their photos in the paper, leading their parents to dutifully cut them out and tack them up in a prominent location for all to admire.

And this event was something to admire. Following behind the children came a group of men and women of various ages, some with prosthetic legs or arms, some scarred, some carrying invisible evidence of their injuries, but all of them with one thing in common. They were part of the Home for Heroes rehab facility and had paid heavily for their service to their country. Vivian snapped a few more pictures as emotion rolled through her chest. Harold would've loved seeing these photos. Her vision blurred, obscuring her next shot.

It had been a week and she still hadn't found anything in Harold's notes about someone named Lauren. And yet, the name was important. The night Harold died he had tried to say something to her, but in the chaos of the moment she hadn't really understood what he was saying. When Ryan asked about it the night Harold's computer was stolen, it came back to her in a rush. Harold was trying to tell her something about Lauren. But Vivian still didn't know who she was.

The cacophony of excited chatter hit a

high when teachers wheeled in platters of fresh fruit and cookies and coolers with bottled water. Vivian moved her camera around the room until it landed on Deputy Ryan Frost. What was he doing here?

"Hey, girl!"

Vivian brought the camera from her face to find the beaming smile of a petite woman wearing scrubs standing next to her. "Hi, Pecca."

She knew only one neighbor by name — Pecca Gallegos. A vivacious woman who'd made it impossible for Vivian to keep quietly to herself. Of course, Pecca's homemade empanadas were impossible to resist, and she was pretty sure the lady wielded her culinary skills like Wonder Woman wielded her lasso of truth.

"This was a great turnout. Our heroes were so excited to cheer on the kids."

"It's awesome you were able to bring them to the event."

"Are you kidding? When they found out the kids wanted to do this, they wouldn't take no for an answer." Pecca leaned over. "I actually used it as an incentive to get some of my stubborn patients to do their exercises."

"Whatever works, right?" Like a magnet, Vivian found Ryan again. He was holding two cookies over his eyes like eyeglasses to the delight of the children around him. She seized the opportunity to take him in. Lifting kids into the air exposed the ripple of muscles in his forearms and Vivian found it hard to look away. It was like Ryan left as Steve Rogers and returned as Captain America.

"The kids love him."

Vivian swung her gaze back to Pecca. "Who?"

Pecca laughed, her eyes lighting up. "Ryan."

"Oh, yeah." Vivian watched a blonde teacher wearing a cardigan and capris move around the students until she was next to Ryan. Hands on her hips, she said something that made Ryan and the kids laugh and gave her the opportunity to flash a perfect smile. An ugly feeling flared inside of Vivian. *Not only the kids love him.*

Vivian, feeling her cheeks grow hot, busied herself packing up her camera equipment.

"If you two move a little to your right, I'll be able to snag a whole tray of snickerdoodles and meet you out front." The whispered voice speaking behind them sent a zing up her spine. "No one will even notice they're missing."

The blonde teacher looked over her shoulder in their direction and Vivian caught a flash of hurt in her eyes. "I think you might be missed."

Ryan moved to her side, stuck his thumbs in his gun belt, and puffed out his chest. "Yeah, I've been known in these here parts to be unforgettable."

"And here I thought you were the shy, humble deputy."

"Pssht." Pecca rolled her eyes. "Traded that in for muscles and contact lenses in Quantico."

His cheeks pinked and Vivian felt hers warm too. There was something endearing about catching glimpses of the man she remembered from a year ago. Underneath the hunk, he was still the same witty guy.

"So, are you two like best friends now? Going to trade secrets about me? Fight each other for me?"

"What?" Vivian dropped her notepad.

"Be serious." Pecca playfully punched Ryan in the arm. "I was just going to ask Viv if she wanted to come to game night this weekend. Now she probably won't because you're being a total dork."

"Viv?" Ryan lifted an eyebrow in Vivian's direction.

"Oh." Pecca's eyes rounded. "Sorry. Is that okay? I shorten everybody's name, right, Ry?"

He shook his head. "Like my name is so long it needs to be cut in half."

Pecca laughed and Vivian liked it. There was something very genuine about her. Ryan winked at Pecca and Vivian wondered if there was a thing between them. She wasn't catching a romantic vibe, but it didn't mean they didn't have feelings for each other. And why in the world that bothered her she did not know and would not explore.

"So, are you game? Ha! Pun totally intended!"

Ryan snorted before joining Pecca's infectious laugh.

Vivian bit the inside of her cheek, a smile warring to be released. "Um, this weekend . . . I don't know."

"Always working a story, right?" Ryan crossed his forearms over his chest, his gaze holding hers. "Not getting in the way, are you?"

Those azure-colored eyes captured her. There was something playful but also serious in the question.

"Wait!" Pecca put both hands on Vivian's shoulders, turning her so they were face-to-face. "Please say you'll come. I've invited one of my patients, but I'm still not sure she's coming, and that means I'll be stuck as the lone girl with three boys." Pecca's expression grew serious. "Please. I can't handle one more night of burping, lame knock-knock jokes, and never-ending fart noises."

"That sounds super appealing," Vivian deadpanned.

"She didn't mention our epic dance wars." Ryan's arms jerked in a robotic motion, his boots sliding across the linoleum tile. The dance grabbed the attention of the children closest to them and they started laughing and clapping enthusiastically. "You see? My moves make the crowd go crazy."

Pecca shook her head. "So, it'll be two boys and" — she hitched her thumb toward Ryan — "him."

Half a dozen excuses came to her mind, but Vivian couldn't make herself say a single one of them for fear of disappointing the vibrant woman in front of her. She shrugged. "Okay. Maybe. Possibly."

"Yay!" Pecca clapped. "Ryan can pick you up at six."

Before Vivian could remind her that she only lived a few houses down and didn't need a ride, Pecca was off gathering her patients. "Can anyone say no to her?"

"No." Ryan reached into his pocket and

held out a card. "Here, in case you need a ride . . . or anything else."

Vivian took the card, their fingers touching for just a second, but that was all it took to jolt her pulse.

"I hope you can make it though."

She swallowed. "I'll, um, try."

He smiled — the kind that made her really, *really* want to try.

Vivian tried to make sense of what was happening. What was the harm in going to Pecca's house and playing a game or two? And it wasn't because of Ryan. No, definitely not. Pecca was funny and sweet and the kind of friend Vivian could see herself becoming attached to — and therein lay the problem. Attachments never ended well. Not in her life, anyway. And she needed to stay focused on Harold's story.

Her phone chirped.

Vivian sighed as she climbed into her car and then opened her email. When she'd first started working for Harold, she set up his email to forward all unopened messages to her a week after they were received to make sure she caught anything he might've missed. She scrolled through a few, taking note of the ones she'd need to respond to, but then stopped on one. Clicking it open, her heart dropped to her gut.

A grainy video began playing. Vivian recognized Harold's signature attire — linen slacks, button-up shirt rolled at the sleeves, tie, and straw fedora. Vivian brought the phone closer. *What in the world?* Harold was talking to a woman she didn't recognize. From the woman's pained expression, Vivian could tell she was upset about something. Harold's hand reached for her shoulder before they embraced.

An ugly feeling settled in Vivian's stomach. She stared at the familiar way they looked at each other. Vivian shook her head. "No, not Harold. Not him. Why?" But her question died on her lips when the video ended and a message popped up.

The Watcher respectfully requests a deposit to be made in the amount of $100,000 in exchange for fiduciary discretion. A link has been attached with payment information. Hesitation to pay will result in the release of this email's contents within forty-eight hours.

Regards,
The Watcher

Six

Harold was being blackmailed. Or extorted. Or something. As alarming as that was, Vivian couldn't shake the looming despair over what the video implied. Nor could she stop watching it. She hadn't called the sheriff, and maybe she should have, but the idea of showing it to someone and having them believe what they were seeing about Harold — she just couldn't.

It can't be true. There has to be an explanation.

Vivian pressed back from her desk. She'd adopted Harold's chair and let the soft leather comfort her. Who would do this to him? And why? Harold was an upstanding citizen. Loved his wife and family. Worked hard on the *Gazette.* The idea had crossed her mind that maybe Harold had angered someone, wrote a story they felt was unfair, but she easily crossed that off her mental list. Across the world, journalists were often insulted, assaulted, and sometimes killed for pursuing a story. But the *Gazette* was different. Harold had wanted it that way. He had wanted stories full of hope. Not that he obscured the truth, but rather his focus was on finding the light in the darkness of humanity. He'd told her, *"There is always light in the truth."*

Vivian wasn't exactly sure she agreed. When she found out the truth about her father, it smothered the light right out of her life. She'd been trying to make her way through the darkness ever since. And now this? Could she really have been fooled twice?

Her cell phone rang and Vivian answered it, hoping the caller was about to shine some light on this ugly mess.

"Sorry, Vivian. I've never seen an email so well protected in my life." Smasher exhaled into the phone. "Whoever set this up did not want to be found and took extensive measures to that end."

Smasher had dated her roommate during her freshman year at VCU. He was a genius at coding and received a coveted internship at a tech software company in San Francisco after he graduated. Though his relationship with her roommate had ended long ago, Vivian and Smasher remained friends and often traded skill sets. Smasher provided her with informal computer help. She offered him advice on women he met on the internet. It probably wasn't a fair trade, but Smasher didn't seem to mind and was still seeing the woman Vivian picked out for him five weeks ago.

"You're telling me not even your nerd squad could trace it?"

"I'm telling you that I've got a $4,000 laptop that is close to being fried because some Trojan virus infected it when we tried hacking one of the firewalls. Nerd squad? That's the best your writerly brain could do? Disappointing."

Vivian ignored his playful retort. "What about the link to pay?"

"Same thing. It's a maze of firewalls and dead ends," Smasher said. "But here's the curious thing. Something caused the Watcher to retreat from his threat."

"What do you mean?"

"You received the email a week after it was sent, which means at least the deadline to pay him off had passed and yet there's no video floating around of your boss with the chick."

She frowned. "You're right. What would make him do that?"

"My guess, whoever it is didn't know their

target was dead until after he sent the email. Realized demanding money from a dead man might look suspicious."

Vivian straightened. "But Harold died because of his peanut allergy, Smasher."

"You do read what you report, right? Killers are creative."

Vivian's eyes went to the empty spot where Harold's laptop once sat. Had someone used peanuts to kill Harold? And did the theft of his laptop have something to do with it? And what did the video — she shot up. The story. The one Harold was trying to tell her about before he died.

"I gotta go." Vivian grabbed her keys, ending the call as she raced down the stairs to her car. She'd been avoiding this errand long enough and now she couldn't wait to get there.

Eyeing the front porch of the craftsman-style bungalow, Vivian wondered if this was a good idea. Maybe there was a way she could do this over the phone and avoid seeing the place —

"Vivian?"

She blinked, not expecting to see Shepherd Kennedy standing in front of her. Vivian climbed the steps. "Oh, hi. I'm looking for Carol —"

"Vivian, is that you?" Carol Kennedy, a beautiful woman with cropped brown hair and just enough age lines to show she smiled more than she worried — or used to — stepped forward. "Oh, honey, it's so good to see you. Shep, let this sweet girl in."

Shep moved aside, holding the screen door open for Vivian. Curiosity colored his brown eyes as she passed.

"You've met Shep."

"Yes," Vivian said, glancing at the man standing protectively next to his aunt. What did he think she was here to do? Tattle on him?

"He couldn't stop telling me how pretty you are —"

"Aunt Carol," Shep said. "I only agreed with you that Ms. DeMarco was pretty feisty."

"He's a sweet boy." Carol rubbed her nephew's arm. "Works too hard in my opinion."

Shep's face pinched and Vivian passed him an amused expression. She swore that if Carol hadn't been standing there, he would've stuck out his tongue at her like a petulant child.

"But we still love you, don't we, Shep?"

He pressed a kiss to Carol's temple. "I'm headed to the airport to pick up Dad. Do you need anything while I'm out?"

"I don't think so, hon."

"Ms. DeMarco." Shep winked — actually winked at her — and then left.

"I'm so glad you're here." Carol embraced Vivian. "It's been so busy. And since the funeral I haven't had an opportunity to call you and tell you how much it meant to know Harold wasn't alone that night."

Vivian pressed her lips together in an attempt to stay the emotion welling up inside of her. Her eyes fell to the spot in front of the couch . . . she didn't want to be there. Should turn around and leave. Find the answers to her questions another way.

Carol released her. "Come into the kitchen. I just made a pitcher of sweet tea."

If Vivian had learned one thing living in the South, it was that when someone invited you in for tea, you weren't going anywhere at all. She followed Carol into the kitchen, where several dishes lined the counters and table.

"Wow."

"I know. Everyone has been so generous, but there's no way I can eat all this." Carol pulled a pitcher of tea from the refrigerator. "Would you like something? Cookies, cobbler, pie? I'm afraid sugar and butter is the way of comfort here in the South."

"I'm fine, thank you."

After she poured the tea, Carol sat and reached for Vivian's hand. "It really is so nice to see you."

"Ms. Carol . . . I just want to say how sorry I am. If I had known Harold was in trouble, I would've gotten here faster. Given him the injection quicker. Done something else." The words spilled out in one breath. "I'm so, so sorry. I keep thinking about what else I could've done."

"Oh, my dear child." Carol scooted her chair closer. She wrapped her arm around Vivian's shoulder. "I know you did everything you could. Lord knows I miss him, but my Harold is in a better place. Can you imagine the stories my newspaper boy is hearing right now?"

Vivian searched Carol's face, and though she saw immense sadness in her hazel eyes, there was also peace. And love. Even in Carol's grief, Vivian recognized the immeasurable love she still had for Harold. Vivian had witnessed in Harold the same kind of love for Carol. There was no way he would have been capable of dishonoring her.

"Now, tell me why you're here."

Vivian looked down. Was her face that readable? Her intentions obvious? "I, well, I wanted to tell you how sorry I am for your loss."

Carol smiled. "I appreciate that dear, but there's something else." A knowing expression filled her face. "You have that look. The one Harold" — her voice caught and a sheen of moisture filled her eyes — "used to get when he was working a story."

Vivian blushed, feeling bad. Was this appropriate? Harold's funeral was only two weeks ago. *"Find the story, my dear."* Harold's words echoed in her ear. But what if the story led to breaking Carol's heart? Vivian had already convinced herself she would not tell Carol about the video until she had no other choice. Until she knew the truth — no matter how ugly it might be.

"Does this have something to do with Ryan stopping by?"

"Ry— I mean, Deputy Frost was here? Why?"

"He came by and asked about Harold's allergy. I told him Harold would've never accidentally eaten anything with peanuts. You know how he was." Vivian nodded. "Anyway, one of his deputies took the Volvo to run some tests on it. Did some here too. On the door." Carol looked at the kitchen door leading to the detached garage. "Ryan didn't tell me what they were looking for, but he did ask me if I use peanut oil when I cook."

Vivian blinked. "Peanut oil?"

Carol shook her head. "Anyone with a peanut allergy knows the oil is just as dangerous."

Smasher's words came rushing back to her. "Carol, did you or Harold know anyone named Lauren? Someone maybe Harold was —" Vivian hesitated, not wanting to suggest anything. "Like maybe a past student or employee?"

Recognition lit Carol's eyes. "Oh, you know, there was a Lauren" — she tapped her finger to her lip — "Lauren . . . Holt. Yes, Lauren Holt. She was a teacher at Anderson, if I remember correctly. Invited Harold to speak to her class every semester."

"Does she still teach at Anderson?"

"I'm not sure, dear."

The doorbell rang.

Carol rose. "Will you excuse me?"

This was as good a time as any for Vivian to make her exit. "I should probably go." Vivian stood. "Thank you for the tea. And if you need anything, please let me know."

"Just promise me you'll stop by for sweet tea every once in a while. Talk newspaper with me."

Vivian started to leave and then paused.

In a move that didn't feel entirely of her own doing, she took a step toward Carol and wrapped her in a hug. The woman stiffened — probably from shock — but a second later she leaned into Vivian's arms and whispered in her ear.

"Harold said you were the best part about his job these last six months." She pulled back. "Your presence brought back a joy I hadn't seen in him for a long time. I'm forever grateful for that."

The ugly ball of emotion Vivian was struggling to keep at bay returned, leaving her only able to nod. She walked with Carol to the front door and slipped by the neighbor bringing in another casserole dish. Outside of the house, she hurried to her car, allowing herself only one thought: find Lauren Holt.

Friday afternoon at the Way Station Café was just as Ryan had expected it to be. Packed. He maneuvered around the busy tables toward the counter and the employee with the bright purple streak running through her strawberry-blonde hair. *Now, when did you do that?*

It would've been his first question for Frankie — or Francis or Frannie or whatever she wanted to be called — if his attention hadn't tripped on the woman she was talking to. Vivian. When had he learned to recognize her from behind?

Ryan stepped to the side and saw that Frankie and her friend Bethany were leaning in, silly smiles plastered over their faces.

"But are there cute guys in journalism?" Bethany rubbed her fingers together. "My teacher made us watch *Dead Poet's Society.* The guys in that movie were pretty cute."

"Ew." Frankie wrinkled her nose. "You realize those guys are as old as our dads."

Ryan took another step closer, not liking the theme of this conversation.

"I like guys with sexy abs —"

"Frankie." Three heads turned in his direction. Frankie rolled her eyes.

"There's a line." Frankie pointed to the one man standing at the counter staring up at the menu. "Your badge does not give you special privileges."

The amount of sarcasm dripping from his sister's lips could drown a person. Vivian looked between them like she was trying to figure out the connection.

"I'll help you, your majesty." Bethany gave him a curtsy, batting her eyes.

Vivian hitched an eyebrow in confusion before realization rounded her eyes so much that Ryan could see they were a little bluer today. "Frannie's your sister?" She pivoted back to Frankie. "Wait, this is your brother, the one you said" — she made air quotes — "is a super genius computer hacker?"

Ryan frowned at his sister. How many times had he told her to stop saying that about him? Frankie lifted her shoulders in mock apology. Every time she brought a friend home, it was the first thing they would want to talk to him about. They would ask questions, like how did he hack into the DEFCON in Las Vegas, and could he teach them how to do it?

"We talked about that." Ryan lowered his voice.

"So it's true?" Vivian's voice wavered between disbelief and awe.

"Yes, it's true." Frankie answered before Ryan could be offended by Vivian's shock. "And if my brother would stop being Deputy Do-Good, he could totally cash in on his skills and make bank."

Heat flamed Ryan's cheeks, but he wasn't sure if it was annoyance or embarrassment.

"Deputy Do-Good, huh?" Vivian smirked, eyeing him. "Sounds about right."

"No way." Bethany shook her head. "It's Prince Harry."

Ryan closed his eyes, wishing he had packed his lunch.

"That's it!"

His eyes popped open and he found Vivian closer than she was before. Close enough that he picked up on the delicate fragrance of her perfume as she . . . was she checking him out?

"I knew you reminded me of someone."

He didn't know if it was the way she was looking at him or what, but his nerves were sending signals to his heart that had him shifting beneath her gaze. "Uh, I'm just here to talk to Frankie."

Frankie pushed back from the counter. "And that's my cue to get back to work."

"Is that what you were doing a second ago?" Ryan teased.

"It's called customer service. I was helping a customer" — she lifted a hand to Vivian — "and she was helping me."

That grabbed his attention. Ryan looked from Vivian to Frankie. "Help with what?"

"She said Georgia State has a good journalism program. They also have internships at the *Tribune* — which did you know Mr. Kennedy's brother owns? — and Vivian is going to be moving there at the end of the summer. Maybe she can help me get a job."

"I told her that I'd help her create her portfolio when she interviewed."

Vivian was moving to Atlanta? Definitely

a good reason to ignore his overreacting nerves and focus on Frankie's desire to leave Walton. "I thought you were looking into accounting? Here at Anderson?"

Frankie rolled her eyes, pulling out her phone. "Oh, look at that, my break is over." She stuck her phone back in her pocket. "Thanks for the help, Vivian. I'll talk to my adviser tomorrow."

"We still need to talk, Frankie."

Frankie groaned. "I already know what you want to talk about, and honestly, Ryan, the person you *need* to talk to is Mom."

With that, his sister spun on her heel, grabbed a rag, and moved around the counter to start clearing tables.

"She'd probably make a great journalist, ya know." Vivian sipped on her drink. "She's very curious. And likes to talk."

He watched Frankie clear plates away while joking with some customers at another table. She was nothing like him. Outgoing, friendly. Unafraid to try anything, even if she knew the odds of succeeding were beyond her reach. His sister had this ability to imagine anything was possible and to chase after it without any fear of what could happen.

Unlike him.

Ryan analyzed the risks, then made a plan

for how to proceed. He'd seen firsthand what chasing after the wind could do to a family. Those failures fell on his shoulders and he wasn't about to let Frankie set out on a path that would leave her disappointed, or worse.

"There's a bit more stability in accounting."

"What's wrong with journalism?"

"There's journalism at Anderson."

"But Georgia State's program is better."

Man, she is incorrigible. "Harold taught at Anderson."

Vivian pressed her lips closed, emotion dimming the soft blue in her eyes. Ryan felt bad. Clearly, there had been a connection between her and Harold. "Late lunch?"

"Working lunch/dinner."

"What are you working on?"

Vivian's nose wrinkled. "Wouldn't you like to know."

Ryan leaned against the counter. "Actually, I would."

"You first." Vivian's eyes narrowed in a challenge. "Carol told me you're testing Harold's car for something. Took his phone too. What are you looking for?"

He studied her for a second. Vivian was definitely not to be underestimated. "I thought you weren't digging for a story."

Vivian's lips twisted playfully. "Frannie says you're a computer hacker. Explain, Deputy Do-Good."

"Not a hacker," Ryan said, aware of her tactic to shift the conversation. He pulled out a stool and gestured for Vivian to sit. She did and he sat on the one next to her. "One time." He held up his index finger. "One time I did this thing where I hacked into a gaming convention and won."

"That doesn't sound genius to me."

Was she challenging him? Ryan pulled out his cell phone and began typing a text. After a minute, he held his phone out to Vivian. "Yes."

Vivian scrunched her forehead. "What?"

"Your text to me."

She took the phone from him and looked down at the screen. He watched her expression transform from confusion to shock.

"How?" She stared up at him. "I didn't send this to you!"

Ryan pushed his elbows over the counter. "I don't know, Ms. DeMarco. Looks like you sent me a text asking me out."

"I did not." She looked at the text again. "How did you do that?"

"I'm a genius." She narrowed her eyes at him and he shrugged, liking the way she was trying to read into him. "It's simple. All

96

I did was send myself a text message and then go in and switch my contact info with your name."

Vivian looked impressed and confused. "I'm going to pretend like I understood what you just said. So what did you win?"

Ryan frowned. "Win?"

"You said you won."

"Ha. I won the attention of every federal agency in the nation and a meeting with the FBI. And let's just say they weren't at my door to congratulate me."

"Really?"

"Sheriff Huggins convinced them not to charge me since I was only fifteen —"

"Fifteen?"

"Anyway, Sheriff H. convinced them not to charge me in exchange for my promising to never do it again and to contact them after I graduated high school when I could begin my prestigious career posthaste."

"But you're still here."

"My boy-crazy sister is enough reason to stick around here," Ryan said, unsure if his discomfort was from the memory reminding him of a dream he once had or the way Vivian's statement challenged him the way Sheriff Huggins had. He gave a quick wave to the woman approaching him with a to-go bag in her hand. "Afternoon, Ms. Byrdie."

"Hello, Ryan, Vivian." Ms. Byrdie was Sheriff Huggins's wife and the unofficial First Lady of Walton. She practically raised several generations of residents and was happily spending retirement baking delicious meals at the Way Station Café with Lane Lynch. "I stuck an extra cookie in there for you." Ms. Byrdie's gaze moved between him and Vivian and a smile he'd seen before lifted her lips. "Should I pack another sandwich? Today's a beautiful day for a picnic lunch at the memorial garden."

"Oh, no." Vivian stood too fast and her leg got caught on the stool, pitching her backward into Ryan's arms. Her body pressed against his for just a moment, but it was long enough for an energy to pass between them. He helped her back to standing position.

"Thanks." Her cheeks were pink.

An eruption of clapping, cheering, and whistles bellowed around them. Apparently, their little move had been entertaining. Vivian unwound herself from his hold.

"You okay, honey?"

"Yes, Ms. Byrdie." Vivian tucked a strand of hair behind her ear. "I need to go."

Bethany thrust a bag across the counter. "Here's your lunch."

Vivian handed over a $10 bill. "Keep the

change."

Something was up and Ryan didn't think it had anything to do with the number of people still watching them. "Vivian."

"I've gotta run. Work."

Ryan watched her hurry out of the café. "Wonder where she's rushing off to."

"Anderson College, if I had to guess."

"Anderson?" He looked over his shoulder at Ms. Byrdie. "What for?"

"She was asking about a teacher. Lauren Holt."

Ryan spun around to the doorway through which Vivian had disappeared. *This is not staying out of the way, Ms. DeMarco.*

SEVEN

The clapping and hollering still echoed in Vivian's memory as she tapped her fingers on the steering wheel. It felt like every eye had followed her out of the Way Station. Her graceful exit out of Ryan's arms had left her cheeks hot and her heart thumping. This was becoming a problem. Something about being around him triggered emotions she'd denied herself. A relationship, any kind, promised pain. It wasn't worth it. She made a mental note to call Pecca and cancel. Going to game night this weekend would only make leaving Walton harder. And she was leaving Walton.

It would be in her best interest to stop letting Ryan's roguish smile set a kaleidoscope of butterflies loose in her stomach. She smiled, replaying the banter that had taken place between Frankie and Ryan. It became obvious they were brother and sister when she saw the similarities between the two of them. They shared the same blue eyes that shined with flecks of amber, strawberry-blonde hair — though Frannie's now sported a bright purple streak — and their smiles. Wide and full of life and love for each other. Vivian had noted one small difference — Ryan's lower lip was slightly fuller. *Kissably fuller.*

Vivian flinched. Where had that come from? *Left field,* she thought. *Definitely left field.* Shaking her head, she forced her attention back to what it needed to be on — Harold. Or, more curiously, Lauren Holt.

If the woman was a teacher at Anderson College, she wasn't one any longer. Vivian had run a search through the list of faculty on the school's website and come up empty. So she called Carol to see if someone at the school might know what happened to Lauren, and Carol gave her the name of a journalism professor, Christine Mercer, who'd been at the school for almost twenty-five years.

Unfortunately, Mrs. Mercer was currently in class, so Vivian had to wait until class got out.

She found a parking spot off-campus on a nearby street lined with dilapidated homes. Vivian wasn't sure any of them were occupied anymore based on their rotting porches, overgrown yards, and boarded-up windows. Though a group of men lounged on the cracked cement steps of one, so maybe people lived there. At least other cars were parked along the road.

Vivian cranked up the air conditioning in her car and unbuckled her seatbelt. She typed Lauren Holt's name into the internet browser on her phone, then pulled a photo from her purse. Smasher had enhanced a still shot from the video of Harold and the woman and sent it to her. She compared the image of the woman with light-brown hair and a pretty smile with those on her browser. *Hmm.* This was interesting.

Everyone had a social media presence these days, even grandparents, yet Lauren Holt — the one Vivian was trying to locate — did not. Unable to make a match, Vivian clicked on the images tab and began scrolling through pictures of women named Lauren Holt until she found what she was looking for.

She recognized the background immediately — the gold dome atop Savannah City Hall, the river behind it. The woman in the picture had shorter hair, but her eyes, her smile . . . it was Lauren Holt. Vivian found another photo of Lauren smiling with a group of friends on a boat. Farther down was a photo of Lauren standing in the middle of students all wearing Anderson Cougars shirts. It was blurry, but there was a banner with the name *Atkins* on it. Why did that sound familiar?

Vivian opened another tab and searched for Atkins and figured out why. This year the Savannah Yacht Club gala was honoring Congressman Atkins, a longtime resident of the coastal area. Vivian clicked back to the images of Lauren and studied her. *Who are you, Lauren, and what were you doing with Harold that night?*

Tweet-tweet.

The sound of someone unlocking their vehicle pulled Vivian's attention away from her phone. A few students were walking back toward their cars, which meant class was out. Vivian tucked her phone into her purse, then stepped out of her car, locking it while she crossed the street.

She worked her way through the current of students who were anxious to begin their weekend, filing from their classes in Bailey Hall. Streamers and banners of red and silver boasting the basketball team's championship win still hung on the walls.

Room 117 was an amphitheater-style lecture hall. Vivian waited for a female student to finish talking to the woman standing at a lectern before approaching.

"Mrs. Mercer?"

"You must be Vivian." Christine Mercer looked to be in her late fifties, with brown hair that was twisted into a bun. She crossed the room. "Carol sent me a message that you were on your way." The professor had a surprisingly firm handshake.

"I appreciate you speaking with me and promise not to take up too much of your time." Vivian pulled out the photo of Lauren Holt. "I wanted to ask you some questions about Lauren Holt. I believe she was a teacher here."

"She was. Taught political science. Left about two years ago." Mrs. Mercer's expression shifted from friendly to one Vivian knew well. It was the look someone gave when they *wanted* to help but couldn't — or wouldn't. "Carol mentioned you'd be asking about Lauren, but I'm afraid I didn't know her very well."

"What about her relationship with Harold?" The question slipped through Vivian's lips before she could stop it, but there was a flicker of something in Mrs. Mercer's expression that said she'd asked the right question. "I know Harold came in to speak to Ms. Holt's classes each semester. Can you tell me what kind of relationship they had?"

"Professional." Her tone was terse, factual, and resolute — as was the look in her eyes. "Harold loved speaking to the students about journalism and storytelling. And he adored Carol."

Vivian felt chastised, but she had to get to the truth. "I wasn't implying —"

"Maybe you weren't, but all it takes is a whisper to ignite a flame capable of destroying." Mrs. Mercer eyed her. "As a reporter, you know this better than most."

"I do." Vivian straightened. "I also know that a lie can lead to death, but the truth can be freeing."

"Quoting him, huh?" Mrs. Mercer said, looking impressed. "Harold said you were ambitious. Saw great potential in you."

The compliment sent a burn to Vivian's cheeks. "He was one of the greatest men I've ever known, and all I'm trying to do is get to the truth behind the story he tried telling me before he died."

The lines of her face softened before she glanced over Vivian's shoulder toward the door. "Harold was a kind soul. It was his calling to help others, and he did it often without thinking of the consequences."

Vivian's pulse surged.

"No one here really knows why Lauren

left Anderson, and truthfully, it's not anyone's business." Mrs. Mercer began gathering her belongings. "I think Harold saw a bit of his daughter in Lauren, but it was never more than that."

A small weight of relief lifted from Vivian's shoulders. "When was the last time you saw Lauren?"

"Maybe a week or so before she quit. I could tell she was upset, but I figured it was none of my business."

Vivian frowned. Mrs. Mercer was a journalist. Sure, she'd been teaching for almost a quarter of a century, but why wouldn't she be curious about a colleague's distress?

"Did Harold ever mention Lauren to you after she left?"

"I'm sorry, but I really should be going."

Frustration mounted. "What about now? Is Lauren teaching somewhere else? Are there any other teachers here who knew her that I could speak to?"

Mrs. Mercer skirted around Vivian, aiming for the exit. "I wish I could be more help."

Vivian started to open her mouth, when the woman turned and faced her. "Harold was an asset to Anderson and a dear friend. He'll be missed." She sniffled. "If I knew anything that could help you, believe me when I say I'd tell you."

It didn't look like the woman was lying and why would she? Vivian retrieved a card from her purse and walked forward. "If you think of anything."

Mrs. Mercer took the card and nodded. "He was a good man."

Vivian tucked her chin. "A really good man."

And it was the truth. Vivian didn't need anyone else to corroborate that. When she called him out of the blue asking about a job, Harold didn't ask a single question. He welcomed her to Walton with not only a job but also his family's cottage home to use until she moved to Atlanta and took the job he had prearranged with his brother on her behalf. *"He said you were ambitious."* Harold Kennedy's belief in her was Vivian's driving motivation to prove he wasn't wrong about her. She would not let the story he was trying to tell her disappear with his last breath.

Vivian left Bailey Hall and decided to walk around campus. A slight breeze left the normally muggy air feeling light and cool. Passing groups of students, Vivian wondered if any of them knew Lauren Holt.

A bump from behind jarred her forward.

"Oh, I'm sorry." A tall, lanky black kid smiled down at her. "I didn't see you."

Two more boys jogged up behind him.

"Dude, you ran into a teacher," the boy with hair so blond it was almost white said. "That's a point deduction."

"At least ten points." The other one piped in. His dark, curly hair was pulled into a bun. *A bun.*

Vivian noticed she was staring up at all three boys. They were giant. At least eight inches taller, maybe more, than her own five-four.

"Ross, Fellows, Alonso." A male voice spoke up from behind her. "What are you doing?"

A man wearing a red polo shirt with a cougar stitched on the pocket walked up. His dark brown eyes glanced in the direction of the trio of giants. He too had to look up.

"Just messing around, Coach. Didn't see her," the black boy said. He dipped his head sheepishly. "Sorry, Miss —"

"DeMarco. But I'm not a teacher."

That bit of information transformed all three of the boys' faces. Suddenly, they were looking at her with interest.

"Aren't you boys supposed to be in the gym?" Their coach shooed the boys forward before giving Vivian an apologetic look. "Sorry. Apparently, I've kept them in a dungeon so long they've forgotten how to interact in civilization."

"A dungeon?"

He smiled. "They seem to think so." He held out his hand. "Coach Robbins."

Vivian knew the name. Harold had mentioned it more times than she could count in the last couple of months. Pete Robbins was the men's assistant basketball coach and a key reason Anderson now had a title.

"Vivian DeMarco."

"You're not a teacher?"

"A reporter."

Coach Robbins's eyes lit up. "Oh yeah? Here to do interviews on our amazing team?"

Vivian cringed. "Afraid not. Don't know much about the sport, but my boss loved it."

"Well, if you ever want to learn . . . I make a pretty good teacher."

"I'll keep that in mind." Vivian refused to look into his eyes. He wasn't bad looking but a bit too old — and *nothing at all like Ryan.* "I should go."

"Have a nice day, Ms. DeMarco."

A shiver skittered over her skin. At one time she used to appreciate — even strive for — approving glances from men. She'd spend hours a day picking an outfit, applying her makeup, paying excessive amounts of money at hair and tanning salons, and working out to make sure she looked good. Looking good gave her the upper hand. It was a lot easier to get someone to do what you wanted them to when they liked what they saw.

When she lost her job at the *Herald,* Vivian struggled with emptiness. It didn't matter how much she dressed up on the outside — it wasn't enough. She wasn't enough. Now the idea of using her looks to . . . manipulate . . . It made her feel cold.

Vivian crossed the street and was leaving Anderson's lush campus when a shrilling wolf whistle slowed her steps. A quick glance over her shoulder revealed three men converging behind her. She couldn't tell if they were the same ones she'd seen earlier, but she wasn't going to stick around to find out. Keeping her eyes on her car, she picked up her pace.

"Hey, you!"

Vivian's heart catapulted into her throat. She dug into her purse for her keys. Her heel hit a hole in the asphalt, causing her to stumble forward. Why hadn't she pulled her keys out earlier? Or at least her Mace? *Because this isn't DC.*

The biting stench of body odor hit her

before she felt fingers digging into her arm. "I was talking to you, girl."

Vivian's eyes flashed up to the man holding her, fear throttling her throat. "Let me go."

A wicked smile exposed stained teeth and breath that made her gag. "Nah, Juliet. You and me are going to have some fun."

She tried yanking her arm free, but the man held tight. "I said, let me go!"

"Hey, fellas, what'd you say we have some fun with Juliet, here?" He looked over his shoulder at his two friends. They hung back, shifting on their feet with uncertainty and confusion etched into their dirty faces.

He turned his gaze back to her and Vivian gasped. "It's you. You stole Harold's laptop." She didn't know how she recognized him, because the last time she saw him it was pitch dark except for the flashes of lightning, but she had no doubt that this was the same man.

Confusion clouded his eyes before it cleared. He jerked his hand back like touching her suddenly burned and started backward, shaking his head.

Vivian took a step toward him. "Stop!"

"Hey!"

Vivian turned and saw Ryan jogging toward her. Where had he come from? She didn't care. He was here and she needed him. "That's him, Ryan. The one who broke into the *Gazette.*"

"Stop!" Ryan ran past her, hand on his holster. "Walton County Sheriff's Department."

The man turned and started to run, aiming for a grassy knoll, but before his foot hit the dirt beyond the pavement, Ryan's body barreled into his side and sent him face-first into the ground. Vivian rushed over.

"Your timing is impeccable."

Ryan grunted, turning the man over on his stomach and cuffing him. "And you have an impeccable ability to get into trouble."

EIGHT

Ryan made his way to Vivian. She was leaning against her car, slender legs crossed at the ankle in heels that were probably meant to pound the streets outside of the DC Capitol or New York City searching for a story. *Or Atlanta.* Frankie's comment about Vivian's intent to move for a job with the *Tribune* came back to him.

He glanced over his shoulder at the man handcuffed and sitting in the back of Deputy Wilson's squad car. Was that what this was all about? Ryan's gaze returned to Vivian. Black skirt, silk camisole, shiny hair that seconds ago had been coiled around her shoulder but was now pinned up, revealing an elegant neck that . . . Ryan shook his head.

Vivian's conspicuous beauty was like the signal at a train track crossing — warning him that she was here, passing through town, with a better destination in sight.

"How is it that trouble seems to follow you around, Ms. DeMarco?"

Vivian's forehead creased. "You realize *he* attacked me, right?"

Ryan wouldn't admit it had felt good to lay into the man who had his filthy hand clamped around Vivian's arm or that it had taken him far too long to regain control over the anger that still had his pulse ramped up. "He doesn't have any identification. Are you sure it's him?"

Vivian followed his gaze. "Pretty sure. I didn't get a great look at him that night, but I remember his eyes."

"How did you know he would be here?"

"I didn't." She narrowed her eyes, seeing the disbelief he wasn't hiding well. "You really think I'd confront the guy who attacked me at my office?"

"I'm thinking it's a little too convenient that you came to Anderson looking for Lauren Holt and ran into the guy who attacked you."

Indignation lit her eyes. "I'm doing my job."

"And I'm doing mine." Ryan, interested in why Vivian was searching for Lauren Holt, hadn't known what to expect when he came to Anderson, but it was becoming obvious she wasn't going to just let him do his job.

Deputies Wilson and Hodges had gathered the two other men and begun searching through their bags and backpacks, as well as a shopping cart they had with them. They were looking for the one thing that would confirm the man who grabbed Vivian was the same one who had broken into the *Gazette* and roughed her up.

Harold's laptop.

It was unaccounted for. Not that Ryan believed they would find it among the man's stuff. His bag held a lot of things — empty bottles, a single sock, half a computer science textbook, and a handful of used cigarette butts. Nothing struck him as odd, except for the wad of cash the man had stuffed in the bottom of his shoe. They wouldn't have even found that if the shoe hadn't come flying off when Ryan tackled the two-hundred-pound man to the ground. A move that had left his shoulder slightly sore.

"You believe me, right?" She looked up at him beneath dark lashes. "I had no idea he was here."

Ryan cringed internally. There were only two women in his life who had the power to cripple his resolve, but now . . . with Vivian standing in front of him, those eyes . . . he began to wonder if she might be the third. His kryptonite.

"I believe you."

And he did, but he also didn't have any evidence other than the money, which could've come from dealing drugs. Or been stolen. He could've sold the laptop, but even pawn shops hesitated to purchase items these days without some kind of proof of ownership if they believed an item might be stolen. So if he hadn't stolen it to sell for money, where was it?

There were enough unanswered questions to give him sufficient cause to bring the man in for further questioning, but first he had to rein in the growing concern he held for the woman standing in front of him. She'd been chasing a story and it led her to trouble. Again. Though to be fair, the break-in at the *Gazette* wasn't her fault. Still, his eyes slid to Vivian, who wasn't one to let something go.

"Who is Lauren Holt?" Ryan tried again.

Vivian's lips parted and then pressed into a firm line.

"You do realize you've been attacked twice," he said, using her own logic against her. "It's not a wild assumption to believe it might be connected."

"Maybe."

She wasn't giving him anything. "Vivian, if it is connected, then you're stepping into a big pile of trouble."

"Have you considered that maybe my trouble began *because* you've arrived?" She looked up at him suspiciously. "Why were you even here? Are you following me?"

Ryan swallowed, heat warming his cheeks. "I, uh —" He cleared his throat. "When you left, I was concerned. Ms. Byrdie said you were coming here to look for Lauren Holt." He straightened his shoulders, unsure why he was explaining himself. "Doesn't matter why I was here, only that if I hadn't been, who knows what could've happened to you. And all this after I asked you not to get involved."

"You said you were concerned for me." Her eyebrows winged up. "Why?"

Her question sent his heart thumping in an erratic rhythm. He studied her, letting his gaze drift to her full lips. He blinked, bringing his focus back to her question. What was she asking? "It's my job to be concerned for everyone in Walton."

"And I appreciate that. But it's also my job to follow the leads on a story, no matter the risks."

"Vivian —" Deputy Wilson shot Ryan a

questionable look and Ryan moved so he couldn't see Wilson's penetrating gaze. "It seems like you cared a lot for Harold, which leads me to believe he cared a great deal for you too." Her gaze grew glossy and he unconsciously reached for her hand. The second her skin met his, an electrical current radiated through him, forcing him to withdraw his touch.

Ryan took a step back, putting an appropriate amount of space between them so he could stay focused. "I don't think Harold would've ever asked you to put yourself in danger, no matter the story."

He thought he caught a shift in her expression — hope — making him believe he'd gotten through to her. His eyes slipped to the scrape on her chin from the altercation at the *Gazette.* There would be a scar, but it didn't mar her beauty. In fact, it only added to her spunky nature.

"Deputy Frost, we're ready to roll."

Ryan looked past Vivian's shoulder to Deputy Wilson and gave him a nod. "I can have a deputy follow you home."

Vivian shook her head. "I'm fine, thanks. Heading into the office first, but I'll be fine."

"Vivian, maybe you should call it a day."

A smile tipped the corners of her lips. "Do you know your accent adds an extra syllable to my name when you say it? *Viviannn.*"

Deflection. Incorrigible. Or maybe flirting? It wasn't like he had a whole lot of experience in that department. *Probably wise to just stick to the job then, Ryan.* "Just try to stay out of trouble."

By the time Ryan led Otis Jackson into his holding cell, the sun had set and a fingerprint match to ones taken from the *Gazette* had confirmed he'd been there the night of the break-in, even if Otis had zero recollection of the crime or hurting Vivian.

It quickly became clear the man was on drugs and probably had been the night of the crime. It was also likely that the drugs were the reason nothing coherent came out of the guy's mouth and wouldn't until he detoxed. Ryan yawned. He was tired and ready to go home, but his thoughts remained on Vivian. Had she gone home like he'd suggested? Or was she still at the *Gazette*?

Forty minutes later, he had his answer. When he drove by the old bank building, the *Gazette* office was dark, which meant Vivian was home. He came to a stoplight and, against his better judgment, pulled up her address on his computer. It wouldn't take more than ten minutes to run by her place and make sure all was well.

Ryan took a left and headed toward Bristol Circle. A blanket of stars covered the sky. This kind of cosmic beauty was absent beneath the glaring city lights of DC. Sure, the Metro had its own kind of historic richness, but he would miss this if he left. The quietness of Walton was what the rest of the world was missing, right? He didn't have to chase any dreams because he was happy here. Content.

If that were true, then why was he still holding on to a handful of offers? Ryan had officially turned down a few, including the one from Breckenstone Security, but he hadn't been able to reject the ones from the FBI, CIA, and another private security firm outside of Bethesda. Why?

His thoughts kept rounding back to Sheriff Huggins's counsel. Was he using his family as an excuse not to leave Walton? The sheriff had been right about his mom and Frankie. They were both doing fine — better than fine, otherwise Ryan never would've left for Quantico when the opportunity to attend ATRT training came up. That meant his hesitancy could be the result of only one thing . . . or person. *His father.*

Ryan never understood what it was his father craved, only that it had taken him away. How many years had passed with Ryan sitting at the front window of their house waiting for him to return? Except he never did. Ryan figured his father had found whatever he had been chasing after, and it was better than his life there in Walton with his family.

Even if part of Ryan still hungered to fulfill his dream of protecting the nation, his father's actions overshadowed it. His father had chased after a dream to the detriment of his family. Ryan sighed as he turned onto Bristol Circle. Was Vivian doing the same thing? Only her chase was to the detriment of her safety?

Porch lights illuminated homes settled in for the night. A child's bike left out, a dog barking to be let inside, trash cans pushed to the curb — everything looked normal. As it should. He passed Pecca's home and slowed when he arrived at the end of the cul-de-sac, where 1996 Bristol Circle was dark. A BMW parked in the driveway assured Ryan that Vivian was home. And probably asleep.

He was about to head home when a flash of light caught his attention. Ryan put his car in park, rolled down his window, and flipped on his spotlight, directing the bright beam onto the cottage home.

The sound of chirping crickets filled the night air. Whatever he thought he'd seen was gone. He pressed the button for his window when a muffled scream pierced the air. *Vivian!*

Ryan jumped out of his car and raced up her driveway. "Dispatch, 10-67 at 1996 Bristol Circle."

The sound of crashing glass lured him onto the front porch. He drew his weapon and held it up, then pulled out a flashlight. "Hello, Vivian? It's Deputy Frost. What's going on?"

"Help, please!"

Ryan's pulse jumped. He tried the front door, but it was locked. "Vivian?"

Her scream echoed, and he kicked his foot into the door. The wood splintered beneath his boot, sending the door flying open and crashing against the wall.

"What did you do?" Vivian asked.

Ryan's gun and flashlight trained on Vivian, who was holding a frying pan in one hand and a can of spray in the other. He quickly lowered his gun but kept his flashlight on the shocked expression staring back at him. "Are you okay?"

"Yes." Her eyes flashed to the door barely hanging on to the hinges. "What did you do to my door?"

"I heard you scream for help." His heart was pounding. "Are you sure you're okay?"

"Yes, I'm fine."

Ryan's brow furrowed in frustration. He radioed back to dispatch an all clear and then studied Vivian. "Why are you screaming? Why is it dark in here? And what are you doing with those? Are they your weapons or something?"

"Weapons?" She looked at the items in her hands. "Oh. Yeah. I need them to protect me from the monster hiding in the bedroom."

Monster? Ryan passed the beam of his flashlight over Vivian's eyes. "Have you been drinking?"

"No, I haven't been drinking." She mocked him. "There really is a monster in the bedroom."

Ryan holstered his weapon, the tension he felt seconds ago lingering. "What are you talking about?"

Yeowwwl.

Ryan aimed his flashlight in the direction of the hair-raising yelp. "What was that?"

Vivian lifted up the pan and spray defensively while stepping closer to Ryan. "I don't know," she half whispered, half hissed. "When I came home, the lights wouldn't turn on and I heard a noise. I screamed. It ran."

"Where?"

"Down there." She used the frying pan to point in the direction of the hallway. "In one of the bedrooms."

"The first thing we need to do is get the lights back on. I'm going to check the circuit breaker."

"And leave me by myself with that . . . that thing?"

Vivian pressed closer into him and he wanted nothing more than to stay right there in the dark with her. But he stopped his thoughts before he latched on to an improbable possibility.

"If we both leave, whatever's in the bedroom might take off or find a new place to hide. Do you want to play hide-and-seek with it tonight by yourself?"

"No. Definitely not."

"Okay, so you stay here with this." He handed her his flashlight. "And I'll go flip the switch so we can see what we're dealing with."

"What if he tries to escape?"

He looked at her and was instantly reminded of his sister's favorite Disney movie, *Tangled*. "Nail him with the frying pan, Rapunzel."

Vivian told him where to find the electrical box, so Ryan stepped out of the house and through the side door into the garage. With a simple flip of the main switch, the lights in the house lit up. Now to figure out what kind of monster Vivian had trapped inside the house.

"Hurry, I think I heard it move."

Vivian stood in front of him in a tank top and running shorts, her long hair swept into a messy ponytail and her hand wielding a weapon of . . . "Is that hair spray?"

She lowered her arm. "Yes. It's all I had."

"You were going to knock it out and then do its hair?"

"No." She stuck out her lip defiantly. "Spray it in the eyes so I could run away."

Scratching and another hideously loud screech made Vivian cover her ears. Ryan started down the hallway, listening to the hissing coming from the first bedroom. He reached in and let his fingers play against the wall until he found the light switch. Flipping it on, he caught movement at the edge of the mattress. He dropped to his knees and looked under the bed. The baleful eyes of a cat glared at him.

Vivian had discarded her weapons and leaned forward, but not close enough that she couldn't bolt if the monster charged.

"What is it?"

"A cat. Feral by the sounds of it." Ryan squatted back on his haunches. "How did it get in here?"

"I don't know."

Ryan reached for his baton and extended it.

"You're not going to hit it with that, are you?"

He swung his gaze over his shoulder. "This coming from the woman ready to crack its skull with a cast iron skillet?"

"That was before I knew it was a cat. Poor thing is just scared."

"I'm not going to hit it," Ryan said as he stood up. "I'm going to make some noise and hopefully scare it out of the room. Go open the front door and then stand in the hall so it doesn't dart into another part of the house."

Vivian frowned. "Maybe I should be the one chasing it out of the room."

"No, I don't want you to get bit."

"Good call." Vivian looked down the hall. "Just give me a second and I'll tell you when I'm ready."

Ryan kept his eye on the cantankerous cat and waited until he heard Vivian call out to him.

"Ready."

Ryan tapped his baton on the floor. For every step he took around the room, the cat moved farther under the bed in the direction of the door and freedom.

"Hey, kitty-kitty. Time for you to leave."

The cat hissed, ears back and teeth exposed.

Tap-tap-tap.

The cat inched out from under the bed.

"Get ready," Ryan said before he tapped his baton quickly against the floor and took a quick step toward the cat, sending it scurrying out of the bedroom and down the hall.

"Aghhh!"

Ryan hurried out of the room to see Vivian high-stepping onto a chair with a seat cushion from the couch positioned in front of her like a shield.

"What? Where did it go? Did it leave?"

"Yes! Yes! Out the door!"

"Then why didn't you shut the door?"

"I didn't want to get bit."

Ryan closed the front door and returned to Vivian. He held his hand up to her. "Aw, poor thing is just scared."

Vivian arched her eyebrows. "You better be referring to that cat, Deputy," she said, taking his hand. She stepped down from the chair and tossed the seat cushion onto the couch. "You're sure that thing isn't coming back?"

"One second." Ryan slipped his baton back into his belt and faked a call into dispatch. "10-91a. Resident safe. Animal chased into hiding by frying pan and can of" — he found the can of hairspray — *"Aqua Net."*

Vivian's mouth gaped. "You're awful, you know that?"

Ryan smirked. "It's fine. We get RFI calls all the time."

"RFIs?"

"Rabid Feline Intrusion."

"You think it was rabid?"

It was impossible not to laugh. Vivian tried to look mad, but her scowl slipped into a smile and Ryan liked it. A lot. He needed to go. "So, if you're fine, I'll be going."

"Um, before you leave, would you be willing to check out the rest of the house with me? Make sure there aren't any more unwanted pets lurking beneath beds or hiding in closets?"

"Sure."

Vivian followed him through the small two-bedroom, one-bath home, finding nothing else save for dust bunnies and a hole in the master bedroom's window screen.

"That's most likely how the cat got into the house. I've got some extra screen at my

place. I'd be happy to fix it, make sure
don't get any late-night visitors."

She shuddered. "That would be gre
Thank you."

"Tomorrow? Before the games?"

"Games?"

Ryan swallowed. He'd seen the hesitatio
in Vivian's expression when Pecca ha
invited her, but he really thought she'd go
Hoped. "Game night?"

"Oh, yeah." Hesitation clouded her eyes
again.

"You don't have to go, ya know. Pecca will
understand. I mean, she'll probably be
angry for a couple of weeks. Avoid you.
Spread rumors and such, but —"

"She will not."

Ryan smiled. "No, she won't. But she'll
definitely corner you and demand to know
why you turned down a night with the likes
of me. *And . . .* I did save you from a rabid
monster."

Vivian's lips slipped into that smile that
made his pulse sprint. She leaned against
the doorframe. "I'll be ready tomorrow and
if you show up to fix my screen, I won't turn
you away."

"Yes, ma'am." He tipped his hat. "I won't
be late." He turned on his heel and forced
himself to *be cool.* But coolness went out

the window the second he got into the safety of his dark squad car. Grinning like a fool, he tapped his fists triumphantly against the steering wheel, completely ignoring the teeny-tiny warning in the back of his head telling him that chasing a woman like Vivian DeMarco might be detrimental to his heart.

NINE

Blaise Taylor
Cougar Point Guard
Carter Hall

The Porsche 911 series was hot. Blaise Taylor imagined himself driving down Montgomery Boulevard in it, turning every head. He clicked through the many model options. These bad boys were *sweet*.

"Completely impractical," he could hear his momma saying. Blaise didn't care. He'd worked hard for this opportunity and deserved something for his efforts. And he'd paid plenty of times. Blaise ran his fingers over the scars on his knuckles. By fifth grade he already towered over his peers but lacked the muscle to defend himself against the bullies. His only saving grace was the fact that his legs were longer than everyone else's, giving him the head start he needed when the bell rang. He ran until his legs tired and discovered it took him one county

over. To the Boys and Girls Club, where Coach Mike took pity on the sniffling kid and told him to work out his frustration on the court.

So Blaise did.

From fifth grade until his senior year of high school, Blaise worked the court from the time school let out until the sky grew so dark he had to use a flashlight to find his way back home. He glanced at the lineup of luxury cars on his computer screen. *Carmine Red.* He clicked the color so the model reflected his choice. A red so bright no one could ignore it. Not even the kids who had made his life hell — like Jamal Thurgood.

Jamal had made it his life mission to prove the only king on the court was him. And up until their senior year it had been hard to tell who was the better player. What Blaise lacked in aggression, he made up for in skill. And what Jamal lacked in skill, he made up for in illegal jabs, picks, and the violent personal foul that broke Blaise's nose and ended Jamal's chances to play college ball.

A *ping* alerted him to an email. Blaise swiveled around in his desk chair and grabbed his phone from the bed. His excitement over the car died the second he opened the email.

Your presence is required at the following address:

173 Lewis Road

Tybee Island, Georgia

Accommodations will be provided.

Information regarding your date is attached.

Acceptance of this invitation within one hour is demanded before further action is taken.

The Watcher

Blaise ran both hands through his hair, his fingers gripping it tight. *Before further action is taken.* He knew what that action would be. This wasn't the first email the Watcher had sent him, and they haunted him almost as much as his own stupidity did. He should've reported the email the first time, but that would have meant telling on himself.

The screen on his phone changed to an incoming call from his mom. Tears burned his eyes. He was a twenty-one-year-old white kid from a hickville town in Georgia still aching for his momma to comfort him.

"Hey, Mom," he said, clearing the emotion from his throat.

"What's wrong?"

He wiped his eyes. "Nothing."

"Are you sure?" Hearing her concern gutted him. His dad always teased him about being a momma's boy, but not in a demeaning way. It was more playful. His dad knew if anything ever happened to him, Blaise would take care of himself and his mom.

"I'm fine." He reread the Watcher's note. "Just ready for this to be over."

"Soon, honey. All your hard work is going to pay off soon, and then you'll be living your dream." Her excitement trickled through the phone. "That's why I'm calling. Mr. Morris helped me arrange our tickets. We're flying into New York the morning before the draft." Blaise heard his father in the background yelling about finding the best pizza place. "All your daddy can think about is food." She giggled. "I bought a new dress. Do you want me to send you a picture?"

"Sure." Blaise stretched out his legs. "Are you sure Dad should be flying?"

"Honey" — his mom's voice dropped in volume — "this is all your daddy is looking forward to. His nurses say it's helping him fight the cancer."

The colon cancer had ravaged his father's body, taking with it the strength of the man Blaise admired more than anyone else in his life. The diagnosis had stolen not only his father's health but also his job at the plant. The small company couldn't afford to keep him, and his parents' insurance lapsed. Blaise had been using part of his scholarship money to help pay the bills, but it wasn't enough. When his agent called and said he was being considered for a second-round draft pick, Blaise knew it would answer his family's problems.

His eyes found the email and he balled his fists. There was one thing keeping him from helping his parents. One thing capable of sending his dream crashing down around him. His phone vibrated against his cheek. He pulled it away and saw the photo his mom had sent him of her dress. It was blue and matched her eyes.

"It's beautiful, Mom."

"You think so?"

"I do." He didn't know how she had paid for it, but he would put another deposit in their bank account to cover the cost.

"Oh, honey, we're just so proud of you."

He squeezed his eyes shut. "Thanks, Mom."

If only she knew the truth. Devastation would replace her pride. It would break her heart. And it would kill his father.

What if it didn't? Part of him was so tired of the threats. So tired of hiding the secret, he thought maybe if he just told the truth, everything would be okay. Wasn't there a saying about the truth setting you free? That's what he wanted. Freedom. But he was chained to his past, just as he was chained to this email inviting him to a party he didn't want to go to — and Blaise knew the consequences of rejecting it.

"Mom."

"Yes?"

Just tell her. The confession was at the tip of his tongue. *Momma, it's all a lie. I lied to you. To Dad. I'm nothing but a fraud.* All those teachers had been right. Blaise would never amount to anything. He wasn't as smart as the other kids, so he did what he had to do to pass.

"Blaise, what's going on, honey?"

He blinked, the memory of his sins slipping back into the recesses of his mind, along with his courage. "Nothing, Momma."

"How are your classes? Did you pass that math test?"

"Got a B plus."

"So Coach Robbins was right?"

Blaise scratched behind his ear. "Yeah. He doesn't want the draft to distract me from what's important." The invitation glowed — a not-so-subtle reminder that the Watcher didn't seem to mind distracting him.

"That's right. He's a smart man."

A red flag popped up on his inbox. New message. Blaise's fingers shook as he moved the cursor and clicked.

A timer ticked, along with a link.

"Mom, I need to go."

"Okay, honey. Take care of yourself and try to get some rest. You sound tired."

"I will." Ending the call, he dropped the phone onto his desk with a clunk. He was tired. Tired of this.

He clicked the link and a familiar video filled the screen. There he was in all his black-and-white glory, walking into Professor Bludworth's office. When Blaise had first gotten the email to meet with his teacher, he was sure it was to discuss his failing math grade that would put him on academic probation, preventing him from playing in the season's opener.

Blaise watched himself sit in the empty chair across from Bludworth's vacant desk, looking around the office and then at his watch. He had been worried about being late for a date with Valerie. Blaise grunted. The nursing major had been too smart for him and had figured it out after their second date, which also ended up being their last.

Several minutes passed before Blaise rose from the chair and walked around the desk. His focus was on the photos of Professor Bludworth's travels across the globe. Pyramids, some ancient structure Blaise thought he'd seen in a *Transformers* movie, and a few taken in front of landmarks he recognized from his World History class.

The second his eyes landed on the file of answer sheets, guilt knotted Blaise's gut. Watching himself pick through the folder, he knew exactly what he had been thinking. It was the answer he needed. The quick fix to bring up his grades so he could play, because not passing meant he'd fail and failing meant he'd lose his scholarship and losing his scholarship meant he couldn't take care of his family.

"I just needed to pass." Blaise's words came out a harsh whisper.

He'd been telling himself that for years now. In fact, he'd forgotten how many times he'd broken into his teachers' offices in high school to steal test answers. Enough times to help him graduate high school so he could play basketball in college.

"You better hope you can make something of yourself on the court, because you've got a pile of rocks in that head of yours."

Blaise had wanted to prove Mrs. Van Buren wrong, but no matter how hard he tried, the failing grades on his tests only proved her right. So he did what he had to do. If basketball was all he had, then he wouldn't let anyone get in the way — even himself.

Without having to study, Blaise was able to hit the courts harder and longer than anyone else, upping his game. Securing a scholarship to play ball in college was all that mattered . . . and then his father got diagnosed with cancer.

Basketball seemed like the only thing that brought life back to his father's dim eyes and lifted his mother's weariness. When Coach Robbins offered him the scholarship to play for the Anderson Cougars, it felt like things were going to be okay no matter how he had gotten there.

Blaise was able to send money to his parents. And the harder he worked on the court, the better he became. Eventually, talk about him getting drafted made him believe that somehow God had forgiven him for cheating and was blessing his efforts by giving him a way to take care of his parents.

According to the ticking digital clock on the screen, he had thirty-seven minutes left to decide what to do, but that wasn't necessary. Blaise opened up the original email and clicked the link, accepting the job. He might not have known a security camera was filming him stealing the test answers from Professor Bludworth's office, but somehow the Watcher did, and now he had the power to make Blaise do whatever he asked.

This time the Watcher was directing him to attend a party with a girl. The last time he had to show up with a camera at a hotel. Blaise didn't ask questions. He did what he was asked and prayed the Watcher would keep his word and not release the video exposing Blaise for the cheat he was. So far, he had.

Blaise's agent informed him that several security directors had been looking into his family. Visiting his hometown to talk to his old friends and teachers. Even kept tabs on his social media pages. NBA owners weren't willing to risk the reputations of their teams over a player with questionable integrity — especially in regard to cheating.

The face of a girl popped up on his screen. She was young. Beautiful, but definitely young. He read through the details provided to him by the Watcher and nausea crept up his throat. He didn't know what the Watcher had planned or why it involved this girl, but if he thought too much on it, he was afraid his conscience would win out. Blaise looked over at the family photo tacked to his corkboard — a painful reminder that his conscience no longer mattered.

He grabbed his phone and pressed the number of his friend. "Dude, I want to get drunk."

"Aw, man, we've gotta be on the court tomorrow before the sun comes up."

"I don't care."

"Dude, we're gonna be hurting."

Blaise shut down his computer. "Are you coming or not?"

"Yeah, man. Give me a minute to get my shoes on."

Ending the call, Blaise grabbed his wallet and shoved it and his phone deep into his pocket. He didn't care how much it would hurt in the morning. Tonight he would drink until the guilt over what he had done and what he was going to do didn't bother him anymore.

TEN

Vivian was finding it very hard to convince herself that staring at Ryan was a bad idea. *It is a bad idea.* Very bad, considering the erratic beating in her chest. He was just there helping her out. Doing a favor. Being neighborly. Only Ryan technically wasn't her neighbor, and she could've easily taken the screen into the hardware store to be fixed. *But then I would have missed the way Ryan's broad shoulders pull taut the Captain America T-shirt that so appropriately fits in more ways than one.*

Ugh. She needed to get a grip. Now was no time to start entertaining whatever it was stirring her heart. Vivian watched Ryan lift the repaired screen back into the window. It might be easy to ignore his hunky transformation, but it was difficult for her to dismiss the tender way he teased his sister or how he hadn't thought twice when he offered to fix her screen. He was kind, protective, genuine — and who was she kidding? Those ridiculous blue eyes and the tilt of his lips when he smiled . . . impossible to ignore.

"Done." Ryan stepped back, appraising his work. "That should keep your house free of any more feral intruders."

"Thank you." Vivian shook her head, bringing clarity back to her thoughts. "I really appreciate it."

Ryan looked at his watch. "And just in time. You ready?"

"I think so."

Vivian grabbed her purse, then they walked to the front door and out onto the porch. Ryan waited for her as she locked the door behind them.

"Have I mentioned that you look really nice tonight?" His cheek pinched into a smile. "Living in the South becomes you."

"Thank you." Vivian assessed her outfit. A silk tank, linen shorts, and flip flops were nothing to write home about, yet her heart hungrily took hold of the compliment. From the corner of her eye, she looked him over. Out of his uniform, he was more relaxed. His thick reddish-blond hair fell over his forehead, giving him a charming look, and the dusting of afternoon stubble lining his jaw — she needed to stop.

Ryan's compliment distracted her. *He*

distracted her. They started down her driveway in the direction of Pecca's house. She had taken great efforts to minimize her interaction with the town of Walton. She kept it professional because she knew full well the consequences of letting things get personal. And if she wanted to get her career back on track, she needed to keep her distance.

"So, Captain America?"

"My sister got it for me." Ryan smiled. "She's in love with, like, every Marvel super-hero."

"She could be in love with worse."

"I'd prefer her not to be in love with anyone right now. She's too young."

"You sound like her father." Ryan blanched at her comment and regret curled over her shoulders. She didn't know what the story was with Ryan and Frannie's dad — only that there was one. "Sorry. I'm sure Frannie hasn't made it easy to keep an eye on her."

That brought a smile to his lips. "She's not the only one."

"Are we back on that?" Vivian teased. "It's not my fault trouble finds me."

Ryan gave her a look that said he didn't believe that for a single second, and it filled her with a delicious, warm feeling that set off an internal alarm. She was getting a little close to the line she'd drawn in the sand long before coming to Walton. This attraction — or whatever it was — buzzing inside of her had to stop. Now. Thankfully, they were standing in front of Pecca's door.

"It's about time you two showed up." Pecca's infectious smile greeted them. She pushed open the screen door and stood to the side. "Come inside."

Vivian followed Ryan and Pecca inside. She heard the playful squeals of kids drifting from the front family room. Unlike Vivian's small cottage, Pecca's expertly updated house had three bedrooms with an open floor plan.

"Maceo, Noah, come get your plates."

"Noah?" Vivian's pulse skipped. Noah was Lane's little boy. And right now his mom and her new husband, Charlie Lynch, should be on their honeymoon.

"He and Maceo are in the same Sunday school class, so he's here for a sleepover." Pecca's hips had a way of sashaying when she walked, like her heart beat a happy tempo within her, as she led them into the kitchen. "I hope you guys like tacos."

"Tacos are my favorite." Ryan high-fived Pecca.

"Ryan!" Two voices echoed in unison from

a pair of boys scrambling around the couch.

Vivian recognized the sweet blue eyes of Noah. He was looking more and more like his mom, and Vivian's heart tugged at the loss he'd already experienced in his young life. The second little boy maneuvered around a chair, not letting his prosthetic slow him down, and Vivian couldn't help but smile. Maceo had the same black hair as his mom, as well as her dark, thick lashes and an ear-to-ear smile that never seemed to waver.

"Ryan, Vivian, this is Sergeant Elizabeth Reynolds." Pecca introduced them to a woman sitting at the kitchen island. "She's a —"

"Army sniper," Maceo yelled before he and Noah began making shooting noises, using their arms and hands to mimic guns.

"Really?" Vivian took in the woman she shook hands with. The sergeant wore black yoga pants and a T-shirt, along with running shoes. Her short, curly black hair was pulled back with a headband, showing off dark, clear skin. She looked far too youthful to be a sniper.

"Yes, ma'am."

Ryan flashed a grin. He leaned in and whispered, "Are you going to tell her not to call you ma'am?"

146

"Are you kidding?" she whispered back. "She kills people for a living."

Ryan snorted.

"Okay, you two, let's eat." Pecca handed the little boys their plates before stepping back. "We eat casual here, because who has time to get fancy? Plates are there" — she pointed to the stack near the tortillas — "cups are in the cabinet next to the sink. Drinks are in the fridge. There's plenty of food, so don't hesitate to get up for seconds. Or thirds." She shot Ryan a glance.

Once everyone was seated at the table and enjoying the delicious meal Pecca had prepared, Vivian began to feel herself relax. She liked the jovial conversation and the way the little boys hung on every one of Ryan's words. The whole atmosphere was warm and inviting and reminiscent of the one time in college when Vivian last experienced such a familial setting. She hadn't realized she missed it so much.

"The tacos were delicious," Vivian said, helping Pecca clear the table. She could hear the boys, Ryan included, trying to pick a game from the closet. "Maceo seems to be doing well."

"Just like my patients, he has good days and not-so-good days." A sadness always seemed to dip Pecca's mood a little bit lower when she talked about her son. "He's going to have to get a new prosthetic soon, and those always lead to harder days."

Pecca was amazing. She didn't speak much about her past, so Vivian only knew that the single mom moved here from Texas with Maceo and not only provided all the care her son needed but also devoted countless hours to her patients at Home for Heroes. And she did it all with a smile on her face.

"We've got it," Ryan announced, sliding a game across the table. "Trivial Pursuit Superhero Edition."

Pecca groaned. "Not fair."

"You said we could pick, Mom." Maceo pulled out a chair and hopped in it, his prosthetic leg clinking against the metal.

"Yes, but you picked a game you know you're going to win."

"How about we make this interesting?" All heads swiveled toward Vivian. "Guys against girls. Whoever loses has to do whatever the winner chooses — no questions, no grumbling, no matter what."

Pecca frowned and Elizabeth, unconcerned, lifted her shoulders.

Ryan arched his brow. "Are you sure?"

"I'm not worried," she said, taking her

seat between Pecca and Elizabeth.

"You should be." He winked and she knew he was right — but not because of the game.

Two hours later, the game hinged on a single question. Ryan held the card in his hand with the boys already giggling excitedly about their win.

"I'm going to make my mom eat a mud pie."

"With worms," Noah added.

"Yeah, with worms." Maceo smiled.

"Please tell me you know the answer to this." Pecca looked worried and a little sick at the prospect that she might have to follow through with Vivian's bet.

"I've had worms," Elizabeth said. "They're not that bad."

The boys went wild.

"Should we start a countdown?" Ryan tapped his watch. "For the win, ladies. Or you could just declare us menfolk the champions."

"We are the winners!" Noah lifted up his arms, flexing.

"Not so quick, little man." Vivian looked at Ryan. "Read the question again."

"Name the two goats that pull Thor's chariot."

"Is that even in the movie?" Pecca asked.

Elizabeth shook her head. "No."

"I'm going to be eating a mud pie with worms, aren't I?" Pecca sat back, resigned.

Vivian reached for the final colored wedge. "The names of Thor's magic goats — dear, sweet *menfolk* — are Toothgnasher and Toothgrinder."

Ryan's eyes about bugged out of his head and Vivian laughed.

"Wait? Did we just win?" Pecca grabbed the card from Ryan's hand and whooped. "We just won! We beat the boys." She danced around the table, squishing each boy's little cheeks. "Who's going to eat mud pies with worms? Not this girl!"

"As much as I'm enjoying this, I should probably get back home." Elizabeth pushed back from the table. "If you want me to teach you how to cook the worms before you put them into the mud, let me know."

"Ew." The boys wrinkled their noses and ran away from the table.

"I should probably head home too," Vivian added, though a part of her didn't want to leave. She hated herself for all the times she had come up with an excuse to turn down Pecca's invitations. What had been so wrong with coming tonight? It was fun. A lot of fun. She hadn't laughed so much in a long time. She looked around the room until her eyes finally landed on Ryan's face and realization settled in. That line she'd set up all those months ago about keeping her distance . . . somehow, between a feral cat invading her home, tacos, and Ryan's insanely attractive knowledge about all things superhero, the line had blurred. Was it really so bad to stick her toe across the line? Test the waters? What was the worst that could happen?

"I'll walk you home." Ryan found his voice. He still wasn't sure how Vivian knew the answer, but it only reminded him how little he knew about her and how the burning desire to know more was growing with every minute he spent with her.

"That's not necessary."

"Actually, it is. My Jeep's there."

"Oh, yeah."

Ryan and Vivian said goodbye to Elizabeth and Pecca and the boys before he led her back down the street toward her house. "That was a lot of fun. I'm glad you decided to come."

"It was." Her voice sounded wistful. "Reminded me of when I was in college."

"Oh yeah?"

She nodded, her eyes reflecting in the moonlight. "I'm not a fan of holidays and usually stuck around campus. There was a lady from a local church who invited students unable to get home over to her house, and one Thanksgiving she convinced me to go." Vivian chewed on her lower lip. "I wasn't sure what to expect, and I didn't want to be the only stranger there, so I planned on stopping in and then coming up with an excuse to leave early."

"But you stayed."

"I did," she said. "When I got to her house, I realized there were other students, church members of all ages, and neighbors. It was like this hodgepodge collection of people all gathered together, and after dinner we played games. It was fun and reminded me of what I thought families should be like."

Ryan's eyes drifted to Vivian. It sounded like there was something painful tucked in her words and she'd let him in. He didn't want to push her for more, but that tiny glimpse only drove his desire to know more about her.

"So beneath that beautiful exterior, you're just a geek like the rest of us."

Vivian glanced up at him. "You think I'm beautiful."

Her tone said she was being playful and not at all fishing for a compliment. "I also said you're a geek."

She laughed. "More than meets the eye."

"Seriously?"

"How could you not love a toy that transformed from a tank to a robot?"

Ryan squinted at her. "I think you're a bit young for that generation."

"Yeah, but you gotta admit Mark Wahlberg makes it easy to be a fan!"

He rolled his eyes at her laughter but memorized the sound. She was nothing like he had imagined her to be. The woman walking next to him was down-to-earth, playful, and yes, if he had to admit it again he would — she was beautiful.

"What made you decide to become a journalist?"

Vivian pressed her lips together and gave a firm shake of her head. "Nope. My turn. From one geek to another" — she winked — "what's keeping you from taking one of the many jobs being offered to you by the federal agencies?"

The muscles in Ryan's shoulders grew tight. "My sister talks too much."

"She's proud of you and doesn't understand why you're settling."

His pulse ticked up a notch. "I'm not settling." The words came out harsh. He took a breath. "I don't see anything wrong with staying here." He held out his arms. "It's past ten at night and it's quiet. You lived in DC. Tell me how many nights I'd be able to experience that there."

"You have a point."

Vivian's house came into view and Ryan hated the disappointment filling his chest. "Do you think I'm settling?" He wasn't sure why he was asking, but part of him wanted to know her opinion.

They made it to her front steps before she answered. "Truthfully? I kinda think you are. Part of what makes a journalist good at their job is the ability to listen and observe." She sat on the steps, surprising him, and waited for him to join her. He did, their shoulders brushing, but Vivian didn't move.

"Last year, thanks to your stubborn friend, Charlie, I was forced to observe. A lot. But I wasn't just watching him. I was watching you." She gave him a bashful look. "You're smart. Sydney Donovan's murder was solved because of your skills." She held up her hand as if to stop him from protesting. "Sheriff Huggins said as much. What I'm saying" — Vivian turned so she was angled toward him — "is that there's a lot of junk happening in this world, and in my job I feel like I've kinda seen it all. Wouldn't you want to use your . . . your, I don't know, superpowers to, like, stop evil?"

154

"I'm not a superhero."

She poked his chest, sending a burst of heat racing through him. "That's not what your shirt indicates, Cap."

"I could do that here. Stop evil."

Vivian pulled her hand back, leaving the spot cold. "You said it" — she swiveled so they were side by side again — "this place is quiet. Hardly in need of a hero."

Ryan forced himself to look around and not at the woman whose compliment was making his pulse surge. When he was up in Quantico, he took trips into the city and there wasn't more than a few minutes between the sound of sirens penetrating the air.

"Think of how bad our world would be if Cap, Thor, Hawkeye, Iron Man, and Hulk kept their powers to themselves?"

"Hulk?"

"Bad example, but you know what I mean." She pressed her shoulder against his. "Don't hold yourself back."

Was that what he was doing? Or was he afraid? After that fateful day with the FBI, Ryan started to dream about what it would be like to work for them — or the CIA or NSA. Sheriff Huggins said God gave him a gift, but it needed to be used wisely. Was it wise to chase after the dream? Ryan wasn't sure. His dad had a dream and it chased him away from Walton — and away from his family.

"Ryan, if I tell you something, do you promise not to get angry with me?"

He took her in. The porch lights haloed her silhouette, softening her features. Even in the shadows she was beautiful, but he could see tension pulling at the corners of her eyes and it made him nervous. "I'm not sure there's anything you could tell me that would make me angry with you."

"Hold that thought." She rubbed her hands over her knees. "I have need of your superpowers."

"What?"

"Your genius computer-hacking skills."

"For what?" he asked, unsure he really wanted an answer.

"Okay, first, remember that just like you, I have a job to do." Yeah, he did not like where this was going. "And I'm not trying to get in your way, but that sorta comes with the territory —"

"Does it?"

She gave him a look. "Yes, it does. Anyway, you know how you were asking if maybe whoever stole Harold's laptop might've wanted it for a specific reason?"

"Yes." Ryan thought about Otis Jackson

sitting in the holding cell. "I'm not sure that's the case anymore."

"Oh?"

She waited for him to tell her more, but he couldn't. Wouldn't. It was an open investigation. "Go on."

"Right. The other day I got an email with a video link in it. I think whoever sent it didn't know Harold was dead and might've come back to steal his laptop."

Ryan frowned. "Say that again."

Vivian took a breath. "Harold's emails get forwarded to me if he doesn't answer them within a week. Sometimes he got a little distracted and it helped me make sure we didn't miss anything. I forgot about that until I got several of them forwarded to me. Most were general newspaper stuff, but there was one that wasn't."

"What was it?"

"Well, first you have to promise me that you won't jump to conclusions."

"Vivian, just tell me what's in the email."

"Let me show you." Vivian pulled her phone from her back pocket and tapped the screen a few times before handing it to him. "Just watch."

The email was unnerving. Someone named the Watcher was asking for money, but it was the attached video that chilled him. Harold was talking to a woman who appeared to be upset. Harold reached for her . . . was he consoling her? Or —

"You don't think he —"

"I don't," Vivian said. "And I'm glad that was your first instinct as well."

"Let me guess, that's Lauren Holt."

Vivian nodded.

"When was this?"

"The afternoon before Harold died."

Ryan set his elbow on his knee, still staring at the video. Just like in the Donovan case, pieces of information were beginning to form a picture . . . a very frightening picture.

"There's more. See the link at the bottom. A payment was supposed to be made to the Watcher so that he wouldn't release the video, but by the time I got the email, the link was no longer active. And as far as I know, no one else has seen the video but you, me, whoever sent it, and a friend of mine."

"A friend?"

"A source, really. He's pretty computer savvy, but he said whoever set up that link made sure he couldn't be found. Even set up a virus in case anyone tried. I was hoping maybe you could try."

Ryan handed her phone back. "I don't

want you working this story."

"What? Why?"

"Vivian, there's more to Harold's case. I need you to let it go."

She stood, her posture stiff. "Let it go? Harold was trying to tell me something the night he died and I think this" — she held up her phone — "has something to do with it, and you know I can't let that go."

"It's an open investigation." Ryan stood. "If you interfere, there could be legal issues —"

"Legal issues?" Betrayal lined Vivian's forehead. "I shouldn't have mentioned anything to you." She started up the steps. "I'll take care of it myself."

"Vivian." Ryan reached for her hand, her foot stopping on the final step, putting her eye to eye with him. They were impossibly close — close enough she could probably hear his heart beating in his chest. But the increase in his heart rate was due to fear. For her. For what she might get herself into if she kept pursuing the case. "If I promise to check out the link, will you promise to stop digging into my case?"

Her eyes searched his face, and before the words left her lips, he knew the answer.

"I'm sorry, Ryan." She withdrew her hand. "It's my job."

ELEVEN

Ryan thrummed his fingers against his desk,
agitation churning the delicious cinnamon
roll he had for breakfast into a ball of
sludge. It had been just over two weeks
since he watched the questionable video of
Harold and someone who might be Lauren
Holt. Ryan tried to confirm the identity of
the girl from the video, but if it was Lauren,
she was no longer living in Walton. Her
move was sudden according to her neighbors and left him very interested in finding
her.

But he was equally, if not more, interested
in whoever was behind the video and link.
Harold was being blackmailed by someone
who had enough computer skills to leave
Ryan stuck. He'd tried every trick he knew,
even reached out to a few of his friends, but
they were right back to what Vivian's friend
had said. Whoever the Watcher was, he
didn't want to be found and had gone to

extreme lengths to protect himself.

There was only one other option. Ryan *could* use some of his not-so-legal methods to track down the origin of the email, but . . . He picked up the phone and dialed someone who could help keep him out of prison if he decided to try it.

"Tell me you've finally decided to join the team."

Ryan rubbed his forehead. "Sorry, sir. I've been neck deep in a case, which is why I'm calling, actually. Need a favor."

"If you're calling me, then you're either stroking my ego or breaking a law."

"Justifiably doing the former to earn favor to do the latter."

"Tell me what you got, kid."

Agent Robert Hannigan was the director of the FBI's Cyber Crimes Division and one of his instructors at ATRT in Quantico. He was also brilliant and the only person Ryan believed could break through the Watcher's digital fortification.

After Ryan finished explaining the situation, he was met with several seconds of silence before Agent Hannigan let out a long, low whistle.

"It sounds like you've exhausted every avenue we'd pursue."

"Legally," Ryan added.

"Correct." Agent Hannigan chuckled. "You have an idea?"

"I do, sir, but it's not exactly going to make your agency happy." Ryan pulled open his top drawer, eyeing the stack of envelopes still awaiting his response. "Or anyone else for that matter."

"You're not hearing this from me, and I'll deny these words ever left my mouth the second I hang up. I'll also destroy the recording of this conversation."

Ryan laughed. "Go on."

"If, say, you decide to go through with whatever your idea is — and it's better I don't know at this point — then all I ask is that if you hit something that looks *official,* you back off. I'll run a check on the Watcher character, but I don't need you interfering in an ongoing operation."

"Yes, sir." A familiar face filled Ryan's vision. "I'll keep you posted if I make any progress."

"You better. And this favor better give the FBI the advantage in your decision."

"Yes, sir." Ryan ended the call with Agent Hannigan and stood to greet his friend. "Marriage looks good on you, man."

Charlie Lynch shook Ryan's hand before pulling him into a brotherly hug. "Marriage is fantastic. I highly recommend it."

Ryan's cheeks warmed. "How's Lane?"

"Amazing." Charlie's eyes shone.

The man was definitely smitten, and a tinge of envy fluttered within Ryan's chest. Would he know that kind of adoration? Vivian's smiling face appeared in his mind and he shook away the image. It was coming far more frequently and only added to his stress. The woman wasn't staying in Walton — he needed to remember that. And to remember that his job was to keep her safe until she left.

"Sheriff says a certain reporter is keeping you on your toes."

Ryan cleared his throat and his thoughts, again. "That's the truth."

Charlie sat in the chair across from Ryan's desk, setting a piece of paper on it. "This probably isn't going to help."

It was the forensic report with the findings from Harold Kennedy's car. Trace amounts of peanut oil were found on the steering wheel, seat belt, and radio panel, most likely transferred by Harold's hand from the origin, which was determined to be on the outside handle of the driver's-side door.

"Someone put peanut oil on Harold's car." Ryan met Charlie's grim gaze. "It's official. Someone wanted Harold dead."

"Appears so."

"If Vivian finds out about this . . ." He didn't want to think about it. This information in her hands would only spur her forward in her search for the story Harold had wanted to tell her — or had died while trying to tell her.

"Then keep her close."

Ryan blinked. "What?"

"You and I both know Vivian goes after what she wants . . . aggressively" — he raised an eyebrow — "if necessary. My opinion, if you want it, is to keep her close. Work with her. Share a little information with her. Get her to trust you so she shares what she has with you."

"I'm not sure it's a good idea — she was injured in the break-in at the *Gazette.*" Ryan couldn't believe his friend was suggesting this. Maybe Vivian did have information that could help him solve this case, but at what cost? Would Charlie offer the same advice if Lane were the one being put in danger? "Isn't our job to keep her safe — away from danger?"

Charlie's jaw flexed, understanding filling his eyes. "What better way to keep her safe than to keep her close?"

Ryan wasn't sure that was the best idea. He was already toeing the line when it came to remaining professional with Vivian. "What about Sheriff Huggins? I don't think he'll agree."

"Ask him."

"That easy?"

"It's only as complicated as you make it. If there's one thing I learned last year, it's that things often line up exactly the way they're supposed to. It may not seem like it in the moment, but you'll see looking back that had it happened any other way, you'd be less than blessed."

Ryan wasn't certain if Charlie was talking faith or what, but it only took a brief glimpse into his past to see that blessed wasn't exactly what Ryan would call his life. He smarted. Was that really true?

He was here in Walton, working as a deputy. Frankie was getting ready to graduate and go to college. His mom . . . well, his mom was doing good. He kept trying to check into the dentist, *Dr. Murphy,* but Harold's case and Vivian's involvement had him preoccupied. At least his mom seemed to be happy. Was Ryan looking at the complications in his life and missing the blessing? He rubbed the back of his neck, thinking of Vivian. Where did that put her? Complication or blessing?

"I'll talk to Sheriff Huggins."

The Georgia sky had melted from a bright blue into a delicious peachy-pink color, reminding Vivian that dusk had arrived. The grumbling in her stomach was another reminder that she'd missed lunch. Again.

Lunch was the last thing on her mind, however. Ever since her conversation with Ryan, she'd spent every free second, in between her work for the *Gazette,* trying to figure out what he'd meant when he said *there's more to the case.* She'd seen the worry in his eyes when he asked her not to keep digging. Genuine concern. She so wanted to do what he asked, but in the end, she couldn't. Harold had a story and her gut told her it was important.

Her cell phone rang. A quick glance and her mood buckled into irritation. *Why was he calling?* She declined the call with an enthusiasm most therapists would say was unhealthy. A minute later, her phone pinged with a message.

Just erase it. Vivian's finger hovered over the delete button . . . but she couldn't. A glutton for punishment, she hit the play button.

"Hello, Vivian." He cleared his voice.

"Um, I wanted to call because I heard about your boss and wanted to say . . . well, to see how you are." She rolled her eyes. This was rich. Her father calling to see how she was handling the death of the man who'd acted more fatherly to her than he ever did was ironic. "And, uh, if you need anything . . . you know I can help you find another job . . ."

A fiery heat burned inside her chest. Did Russell Bradley think he was playing some role? A hero coming to her rescue? She deleted the message, not caring what else he had to say. She did not need rescuing. And even if she did and he was the only one left in the world, she'd rather die.

Whatever reservations Vivian had about pursuing this case her father effectively erased the second he offered his help. She did not need it. She did not need him. An ache ricocheted inside her chest, sending angry tears to her eyes.

"Vivian?" She jerked her teary gaze up and found Ryan standing in the doorway. "Is everything okay?"

Talk about timing. Vivian hadn't seen Ryan since their talk on her porch, and here he was showing up during an unexpected bout of emotion. She quickly wiped her eyes, sniffling. "Yeah, yes. Allergies." She tilted her head toward the open window. "Honeysuckle outside."

His frown said he wasn't buying it, so she redirected her attention and unfortunately — or maybe fortunately — it landed on his muscular legs. Ryan was wearing a pair of khaki shorts and a T-shirt that invited her to take in the noticeable expanse of his defined chest.

Avert! Avert! She turned and picked a piece of paper from her desk to focus on. *First Family Church Potluck Social.* Yes, definitely a safer choice for her attention — though not nearly as appealing. She bit her lip. "So, uh, is there something I can help you with?"

"Dinner."

Her eyes swung up to his. "Dinner?"

"I want to take you to dinner."

Vivian licked her lips and looked around. "I've got a lot to do —"

"I promise it'll be worth it. A real marmalade dropper." He winked, holding his hand out to her. "Besides, it looks like you could use a break."

Even if he hadn't piqued her curiosity using Harold's saying, the hunger pangs in her stomach were making it impossible to resist. And she *did* need to eat. Yeah, she was going with that. "Fine."

Four blocks later, Vivian and Ryan were sitting at one of a handful of picnic tables outside a tiny screened-in restaurant called Smokin' Hog, licking barbecue sauce from their fingers and breathing in the woodsy scent wafting from the smokers.

"This is really good." Vivian dropped a rib bone she'd stripped clean.

"I can't believe you've lived in Walton for months and haven't eaten here before."

"I like to cook." She didn't sound convincing at all. "And who would've guessed the best barbecue in Walton was a joint connected to a gas station?"

"So you like to cook and get into trouble." Ryan wiped his face with a napkin and balled it up. "What else should I know about you? Names and numbers of your parents in case they need to bail you out of jail?"

Vivian threw her napkin at him and he ducked. "My record is clean, thank you very much."

"I know — I ran your prints."

Her mouth popped open. "No you did not."

"Maybe, maybe not." He sipped his sweet tea, a smile playing on his lips, making him look . . . irresistible. "Well?"

This was not Vivian's favorite topic. Talking about her parents had a souring effect, which maybe wasn't a bad thing given the rapid speed of her pulse since Ryan asked her to dinner.

"Hey, Frost." A guy with wavy brown hair walked over. His navy blue shirt matched the tactical pants he was wearing. Vivian recognized him as one of the EMTs who took care of her after the break-in. "How are you doing, Ms. DeMarco?"

"I'm good, thanks."

"Hey, Troy." A flicker of something passed through Ryan's face. Was it jealousy? "Picking up food to take back to the station?"

Troy smiled, picking up on the not-so-subtle hint. "Yep, but I'm glad I ran into you. Peach Bowl is coming up and the guys back at the station are wondering if you're going to play this year."

Ryan shifted on the bench. "I'm not sure."

"What?" Vivian squeaked. According to Harold, the Peach Bowl was Walton's summertime claim to fame. The event put on by the First Responders' League brought out the crowds to root and cheer for firefighters, paramedics, and law enforcement officers who signed up to play kickball on a tarp-covered field laden with water and soap, making it dangerously slippery. She would be there to take pictures for her column. Watching Ryan play would be icing on the cake. "You have to."

"Why?" Ryan's eyes slid to Troy and back to her. "It's a broken leg waiting to happen."

"Aw, come on," Troy said. "It's fun. And frankly, we're ready for some real competition."

"Doesn't the fire department beat you every year?"

Troy cringed. "Yeah, but some of them backed out this year because they got hurt."

"See?" Ryan gave her a pointed look. "Not interested."

The man at the counter called out a number and Troy waved. "That's me." He clapped Ryan on the shoulder. "Think about it, man. Show your beautiful date what a stud you are."

When Troy had collected the station's order and left, Vivian fixed her attention on Ryan — who was doing his best to avoid eye contact with her.

"So?"

"So what?" he said, sipping the last of his sweet tea.

"Are you going to show me what a stud you are?"

He raised his eyebrows. "Do I need to?"

Vivian's cheeks flushed. She waved the waitress over and was handing her cup over for a refill when an idea — a brilliantly evil one — came to her. "I'm cashing in."

"Excuse me?"

"The bet from game night. Remember? You have to play in the Peach Bowl this year."

"You're kidding."

"Nope." She accepted her drink back from the waitress. "The deal was you had to do anything I asked."

"Are you trying to kill me?" He eyed her suspiciously. "Or are you trying to take me out so you can chase after your story?"

"Ooh, I hadn't thought about that." She winked at him. Why was flirting with Ryan so easy?

"Fine." Ryan forced a pout to his lips and Vivian had to look away. "But only under one condition."

"Nope." She shook her head. "A bet's a bet."

"You might want to hear this one out, De-Marco."

Hearing him say her last name like that tickled her nerves. It had been a long time since she had actively flirted with anyone while not trying to get information for a story. Was this a good idea? No — she was leaving town. She bit her lip. Yes. Maybe? She liked the way Ryan made her feel . . . it was okay to indulge in a little harmless flirtation, right?

"I've got a proposition for you."

Her unsweetened tea sprayed everywhere — including Ryan's shocked face. "Oh. My. Goodness. Ryan, I'm so sorry." She grabbed a handful of napkins and started wiping at his face, her face, the table.

Ryan's sudden laughter captured her attention. "That was awesome, DeMarco."

Vivian's mortification melted. "That was so embarrassing."

He shrugged. "No big deal, but let me rephrase that. I wanted to see if you'd be open to helping me with Harold Kennedy's case."

Thank goodness she hadn't taken another sip of her tea. "What? Really?"

"Before you get too excited, there are some ground rules —"

"I don't do well with rules."

"I know." Ryan smiled. "Which is why I made them."

She narrowed her eyes playfully — *flirtatiously* — at him. A warning voice echoed in her head that she was treading very close to the line she'd set out to protect herself, but at the moment the line was fuzzy at best. "I'm listening."

"Next to Harold's wife, you were the closest to him. You knew his schedule, what stories he was working on, the details of his life outside of the home." His blue eyes grew somber. "Harold's death is being ruled suspicious."

Vivian's heart twisted. "Why?"

"You can't repeat any of what I'm about to tell you. Sheriff Huggins has given me permission to bring you in on the case because he thinks you can help us."

"I'm a journalist, Ryan."

"I know, and we're not asking you not to do your job . . . just to hold off while we investigate."

She thought this over for a few minutes. Working with Ryan would give her access to details she wouldn't have otherwise . . . and she'd be working with him. What would that be like? Would he distract her? Prevent her from digging deep when her instinct said to? Would she be better off going forward on her own — with no one to answer to or rely on? "Okay," Vivian agreed.

"You promise?"

"Yes." No matter what questions were swirling in her head, she needed to follow her heart on this, and if that meant working with Ryan . . . well, she'd have to remember she had a job to do and a story to find.

"The ME's report came back. Harold

didn't accidentally ingest something with peanuts — he was poisoned with peanut oil."

Vivian listened in utter shock as Ryan gave her the details of the medical examiner's report. Her heart ached. *Someone had killed Harold.* The video replayed in her head. Was it the Watcher? Lauren? Her eyes met Ryan's. "What do you need from me?"

Ryan licked his lips. "I don't think the break-in at the *Gazette* or Harold's stolen laptop or the email are coincidental. The night Harold died, there was a paper next to his body with a name on it — Lauren. I know you're looking for her, but I don't want you to do it alone. If she had something to do with Harold's death, then she's dangerous. Moving forward, we work together — and that means sharing information."

She hesitated a second. "Okay."

"I'm serious."

His skepticism bothered her. "You don't think I will?"

"I've seen you at work, DeMarco." His fingers played dangerously close to hers again. "I wasn't kidding when I said your safety is my priority."

Vivian set her cup of tea aside. There must be something in the water in Walton. Something that turned her resolve to absolute mush. Moving here had been a calculated step. A step back into the industry that so quickly dismissed her when she had allowed her personal feelings to interfere with a story. Writing about Walton's social events wasn't as adrenaline-pumping or attention-grabbing as, say, uncovering a politician's ties to the mafia, but the former had unsuspectingly been just as fulfilling. Maybe more so, if she were honest with herself — and that felt personal.

Harold's death was personal. The story silenced by a killer was personal. And the sentiment lingering in Ryan's eyes said it was personal.

"I won't pursue any leads without letting you know first."

"And you won't do anything to put your life in more danger —"

"Than necessary," Vivian added before he could finish.

"DeMarco," he warned.

"I'm still a reporter, Ryan, sheesh." She smiled. "Yes, I'll do my best not to put myself in any danger, but" — she held up her finger — "I cannot be held accountable if trouble finds me."

His blue eyes locked with hers and her breathing slowed. What was he thinking?

Did he know what she was thinking? What *was* she thinking? That working with him was going to put her heart in danger and maybe she should back out.

"Good." Ryan called for the check. "We start tomorrow."

TWELVE

"Has anyone ever told you how much you look like Prince Harry?"

Ryan had barely stepped into the Way Station Café. Lane had one hand on her hip and the other threw a towel she was holding over her left shoulder. "But like the bulkier, post-military-training one — with the muscles."

"Aah. He looks like a Boy Scout to me," a scratchy voice called out from the barstool at the counter.

"Hush, Ducky." Lane pulled her towel down and playfully swatted at the old fisherman who frequented the café more than anyone else. "It's good to see you, Ryan."

"Hello, Mrs. Lynch." Ryan hugged Lane. "It's a good thing you're back to keep your customers in check." He flashed a pointed look at Ducky. "That one was especially disagreeable while you were away."

Ducky's weathered face pinched into a

scowl. "Still don't see what that young deputy has that I don't."

"Yeah, Lane." Ryan put his hand on his gun belt and rocked back on his heels. "What does Charlie have that Ducky doesn't?"

"Teeth," she hissed with a smile.

Ryan's mouth opened at the same time Ducky's thin shoulders pulled back in a fit of laughter that had him hacking loudly.

"Hold on, Ducky." Lane flashed Ryan a see-what-you-made-me-do look before slipping around the counter and grabbing a cup. "I'll get you a cup of lemonade on the house."

When it came to Ducky and several other special customers, everything was on the house. Lane gave back to the community in a huge way by feeding not only empty stomachs but also empty souls. Charlie was extremely lucky.

"Don't you have a job?" The snarky question came from his sister. She rounded the corner, tying her apron around her waist. "This isn't a donut shop, you know."

"Donuts?"

"Yeah, doesn't your kind, like, hang out at donut shops or something?"

Ryan narrowed his eyes. "Why would I go

to a donut shop when I can annoy you here?"

"Har. Har." Frankie gave him a fake smile to go with her fake laugh. "You're so funny you're killing me — literally killing me."

He could've schooled her on her improper use of the word *literally,* but he was actually more concerned about why she wasn't in school. "Aren't you supposed to be in class right now?"

"Half day, and I'm working a double tonight for Bethany."

"On a school night?"

"Relax, *Deputy.* Mom already said I could, and besides, Bethany has a hot date. Hot dates are priority." She wiped the counters. "Speaking of Mom, why are you acting like a teenage girl and ignoring her calls?"

"I'm not ignoring her calls —"

"I hope you're not ignoring calls, Deputy." A smooth, feminine voice drifted over his shoulder. "That's not becoming of an officer or a gentleman."

Ryan smiled. "Hi, Holly." He greeted the blonde beauty with a side hug. "Are you playing hooky from school?"

"No." She batted her eyelashes up at him and Ryan caught Frankie rolling her eyes. "I'm picking up food for our teacher luncheon."

"Ms. Byrdie will have your order right out," Frankie said. "Now, if you'll excuse us, my brother and I were having a conversation. I think they teach something about interrupting in kindergarten, don't they?"

Ryan gasped, heat rushing to his cheeks. "Frankie." He looked at Holly, who was smiling. "I'm sorry, my sister was dropped on her head as a child."

Holly laughed, pressing into Ryan's side in a way that was both uncomfortable and improper of the Southern belle, who'd had no idea he'd existed in middle school or high school. "I think she's cute."

Frankie's eyes bulged and Ryan was relieved when Ms. Byrdie came around the corner with the elementary school's order. He did not feel like arresting his sister for assault.

"Have a nice day, Holly," Ryan said, as Holly followed Ms. Byrdie to the register. He turned his focus on his sister. "You didn't have to be so rude."

"Didn't you hear her? I was being *cute.*" Frankie cast an unfriendly glance in Holly's direction. "Besides, you think I'm going to be nice to some girl who suddenly becomes interested in my brother because he's gone all Five-O?"

Ryan smirked. "You think I look like Steve

McGarrett?"

Frankie rolled her eyes. "Can we get back to why you're avoiding having dinner with Mom?"

"I've been busy."

"So you said." Frankie leaned her elbows on the counter and stared at him until he couldn't help but stare back. "Did you really think Mom was going to spend the rest of her life single? I'm going to college, you've moved out and are living your life. Doesn't she deserve to live hers?"

"I never said she couldn't." Ryan moved the salt and pepper shakers around. "I just don't know why y'all didn't say anything about Dr. Murray."

"Dr. *Murphy,* and because Mom didn't want to say anything until she knew for sure he was the guy."

Ryan swallowed. "She thinks he's *the guy*?"

Frankie nodded. "She does, and I agree. He's a good guy, and you would know that if you actually talked to him."

"Here's your lunch. Two turkey clubs, extra bacon, hold the onions." Lane handed him a paper bag. "And two blondies."

"Two?" Frankie's eyes grew round. "Now who's holding stuff back?"

"Stay out of trouble, Frankie." Ryan slid

his money across the counter and turned for the door.

"Call Mom, Ryan," she said. "Or I'll tell her *you're* hiding a girlfriend."

Part of him wanted to turn around and convince Frankie he did not have a girlfriend, but the larger part of him knew doing so would only fuel her. And she had this weasely way of twisting his words until she got exactly what she wanted from him. Maybe he should convince her to get a job in law enforcement as an interrogator.

Ryan headed out the door and crossed the street, where he caught a glimpse of Vivian waiting for him on a park bench near two huge Magnolia trees.

"Lunch is served." Ryan held up the bag. "I hope you weren't waiting long."

"Nope." She smiled, clearly unaware of what that simple gesture did to his pulse. "I brought Harold's calendar. Do you want to eat or work first?"

"Wanna do both?"

Her smile grew. "I was hoping you'd say that." She took the bag from his hand and spread it out between them, then her expression shifted. "Uh, I think someone wants your attention."

Ryan looked over his shoulder to find Holly waving at him. He waved back.

"That's Holly. She teaches kindergarten at Walton Elementary."

"I think I remember her." Vivian's tone was low. "She's pretty."

He gave a quick glance behind him and shrugged. "I guess. Nothing special about her though."

Vivian's cheek lifted subtly and the beginning of a smile played at her lips. Was she jealous of Holly? She had no reason to be. Girls like Holly were a dime a dozen here in the South and brought nothing exciting to life — unlike Vivian.

Ryan sat. "Would you mind if I said grace over our meal?"

"Uh, yeah, sure." Her expression was uncertain. "You're not going to ask me to say anything, right?"

"No." He smiled. Then he took her hand in his, giving it a squeeze before closing his eyes and saying a quick word of thanks for their meal and asking for protection and guidance to find the answers they needed. When he was done, Vivian withdrew her hand and gave a bashful smile. "See, not so painful."

Between bites, Ryan caught Vivian up. "I think the best way to approach this is with a timeline charting Harold's moments leading up to Friday night." He paused, taking in the soft features of Vivian's face. "Is this going to bother you? Talking about Harold's death?"

Vivian shook her head but let her gaze fall to her pink toenails. "It's not personal — it's a story."

The platitude sounded rehearsed and unconvincing, and her body language the last couple of weeks reflected the exact opposite of it being just a story. "Okay, but if you need a break or anything —"

"I'm fine, Ryan." Her fingers grazed his as their eyes met. "Really."

He straightened, turning his attention back to business. "Working backward, we can assume that by the time Harold called you, the oil was already in his system."

"Right." Vivian swiped at a crumb on her face. "His voice was scratchy and he was coughing. He thought it was smoke or something from the game."

"I spoke with Daphne Ross, the arena's facility manager, and she confirmed their food services do not use peanut oil because of allergies."

Vivian finished chewing a bite, then wiped her mouth with a napkin. "Was the oil put on his car before or after the basketball game?"

"After." Ryan finished the last of his

sandwich. "The ME talked with a couple of physicians, and based on how severe Harold's allergy was, if he had come in contact with it earlier . . ."

"He would've died earlier," Vivian said. "Okay, so it's safe to assume someone poisoned Harold at the basketball game. What's next?"

It was disconcerting to hear the detached tone in her voice. Was that how she handled the hard news she reported? Charlie had mentioned soldiers doing that when they were at war, but pushing down the emotional impact of what they witnessed always found a way to the surface. It didn't usually end well. He'd keep an eye on Vivian, and if he noticed any signs she was losing herself to the story, he'd pull her off the case.

"Hello? Ryan?" Vivian waved her hands in front of his face. "Did I lose you?"

"Sorry." He redirected his thoughts back to the present. "Ms. Ross mentioned video cameras over the parking lots, but the video from that night has already been erased."

"Darn."

"I do have" — Ryan pulled out a folded piece of paper from his pocket — "a list of all the addresses from Harold's GPS for that week."

Vivian picked up the calendar. "Let's start

cross-checking them."

She reached for them, but Ryan moved the paper. "Just a minute, Ace. This is a sharing program, remember? I gave you my info, now you give me yours."

"Fine." She adjusted the strap of her top and Ryan noticed a dozen freckles sprinkled over her shoulder. She pointed at a line on the calendar in her lap. "This is the address for the *Daily* in Savannah. Harold went there once or twice a week. This one here" — she pointed to another — "and here are related to a story he did on the school board adjusting the calendar for next year." She tapped her finger on the page, studying the rest. "There's only one that seems out of place. Here."

Vivian lifted the calendar and showed it to him. The street name was the only thing familiar to him. "That's a residential neighborhood not too far from Anderson."

"It's not Lauren's address — she lived in Savannah." She slid a sideways glance up at him. "Don't give me that look. I checked her place before we made our deal. What's interesting is that, according to his GPS, Harold was at this address when he was supposed to be meeting Lauren on Monday. He went there again on Friday, a few hours before he died."

Ryan leaned in, taking in her findings, and immediately picked up on the soft floral scent of her skin. He moved back.

"What do you think?" She looked up at him. "Is this important enough to check out?"

He wasn't sure, but he was certain that he wasn't ready for her to leave. And the scary part was, he knew it was coming. Not just this afternoon when they were done working on the case or when the case was finished, but on that day when Vivian packed up and left Walton for good . . . potentially taking his heart with her.

"Ryan?"

He stood quickly. "You up for a field trip?"

Vivian fiddled with the strap of her purse. She was sitting in the passenger side of Ryan's squad car, trying not to sneak peeks at him. Her eyes hadn't deceived her. Moments ago, she'd caught him looking at her in the way every girl understood, a way that spoke of feelings. And instead of scaring her — like it should have — it delighted her.

Of course, there was *Holly* — the perfectly pretty Southern belle whose feelings for Ryan were visible all the way across the street, as was her atrociously blinding floral Lilly Pulitzer dress. The kindergarten teacher might've been smiling like a composed debutant, but Vivian recognized the stiffness in her posture. The flames of her feelings for Ryan were unmistakable, as was the warning look she gave Vivian.

Did Holly have anything to worry about? Did Vivian?

"That's it."

"What?" Vivian looked to where Ryan was pointing. "Oh, yeah." The house on 803 Shoreline was impressive. It was a modern two-story home with bold black trim that contrasted nicely with the white siding and lavish landscaping that spoke of a yard service. A Cadillac Escalade was parked in the driveway next to an open house sign. "It's for sale."

"Dead end?"

"Not at all. Park." Vivian pointed to a spot in front of another house. "We're going in."

When Ryan parked, she opened the door. "We know Harold came to this house twice the week he died. What better opportunity to snoop than when the owners aren't even inside? Legally, anyway," she added with a wink. "Hurry, it ends in five minutes."

She was halfway up the walkway when Ryan caught up to her. He leaned in close. "We can't just snoop in someone's house."

"What are you talking about?" She rang

the doorbell and knocked. "That's the point of open houses."

Vivian could see he was about to argue, but a woman wearing an insane amount of makeup opened the door.

"Hey, y'all! Are you here for the open house?"

"We sure are. Is it too late?" Vivian pleaded at the woman with her eyes. "I had to drag my fiancé away from work — ya know, protecting the innocent and all that." Vivian threaded her arm through Ryan's and leaned into his side, which was a bit difficult with the bulky vest and gun belt. "We promise not to take long."

"Sure, honey." She let them in. "I've never been able to resist a man in uniform. Take your time. And if you need anything, just holler. My name's Ramona."

"Thanks, Ramona." Vivian pulled Ryan into the front room. "Look, honey, it's got the crown molding you like."

"The what?" Ryan hissed in her ear.

Vivian cast a glance over her shoulder and saw Ramona lingering. "Just keep looking around like you want to buy this house," she said through gritted teeth. "What's the square footage?"

"Just over three thousand."

"That's a good size." Vivian took in the

large family room that opened up to an expansive chef's kitchen. The furniture, art, plants, even the cake stand holding freshly baked cookies made the home feel comfortable, inviting, and *staged*. There was nothing personal to indicate who was living here, and Vivian was certain Harold wasn't in the market for a new home.

"Can we check out the bedrooms?"

"Sure. There are three upstairs, including the master, and one downstairs."

"Let's go, honey." Liking this ruse very, very much, she laced her fingers through his and escorted him upstairs. "In case we want kids."

Ryan's eyes bulged, and Vivian stifled a laugh as she stepped into the first bedroom.

"What are you doing?"

"I'm digging." Reluctantly, she let go of his hand.

"Here?" He looked around the room. It too was staged. Bed, dresser, mirror, vase of flowers. "For what?"

"For who lives here." She went into the next room and found it just like the first. So, no kids. Vivian peeked downstairs to make sure Ramona wasn't eavesdropping. But just in case she was . . . "Honey, I think this would make a perfect nursery, don't you?"

Her words echoed, and she shot Ryan a look.

"Uh, yeah, sweetie pie."

Vivian scrunched her nose and mouthed "sweetie pie?" He made a face and shrugged. Shaking her head, she waved him into the master bedroom.

"My entire apartment in DC could fit in this room."

"It's a bit much." Ryan stood in the room, his arms crossed over his chest. "I prefer something more cozy."

"Cozy means small in real estate lingo."

"Small is easier to clean."

"Good point." Vivian peeked into the closet, which was *actually* the size of her bedroom. Rows of shirts, dresses, and slacks hung neatly on both sides. At the end were floor-to-ceiling shelves filled with every designer shoe Vivian once drooled over. "Wow."

"Is this a closet or a clothing store?"

"Whoever lives here has very expensive taste." Vivian lifted up the sleeve of a hoodie. "Do you know how much this Victoria Rose sweatshirt costs?"

"Do I want to know?"

She shook her head, eyeing the rose-gold sequins that lined the seam. "No. Definitely not."

"I don't see anything in this room except evidence these people have more money than they know what to do with."

Vivian reached for the closet light when her eye caught on something that stopped her. She moved quickly to the built-in dresser and picked up the framed photo of a man and woman standing on a beach. Vivian moved the picture closer. There was something familiar about the man — had she seen him in Walton before?

"Ryan," she whispered loudly. "Come here."

"I have to say my fiancée is a bit bossy."

She quirked her head to the side before thrusting the frame at him. "Do you know them?"

He took the picture and looked at it. "The guy looks familiar . . . and maybe I've seen the wife around town?"

"That's not helpful."

"Yoo-hoo," Ramona's voice called up the stairs. "I'm sorry to rush you, but I do have to get back to the office."

Vivian replaced the photo and shut off the light. "We're coming."

Ryan's footsteps followed behind her.

"If y'all are interested, you could come by the office and talk numbers," Ramona said, her expression hopeful.

"It's such a beautiful home. I can't imagine why the owners want to sell. Are they downsizing?"

"I'm sorry, I can't give you any information on the sellers, but" — she leaned forward — "I will tell you they are motivated."

"Motivated?" Ryan walked to the banister and gave it a shake. "Is something wrong with the house?"

Ramona moved swiftly to Ryan's side, taking his hand off the banister. "Not at all, Officer."

"There must be something wrong if the sellers want to dump the place." He stepped out of Ramona's line of sight and wiggled his eyebrows at Vivian. "Maybe we should keep looking, sugar pie."

"Okay, okay" — Ramona pressed her palms on Ryan's bulletproof vest — "what if I can assure you there's nothing wrong with the house?" Ryan looked down at Ramona's hands and then lifted his brows at her. She giggled and dropped her hands. "Sorry," she said, looking at Vivian.

Oh. Fiancé, right. Vivian moved to Ryan's side. "We're listening."

"I can promise you that Daniel and Trisha Atkins have taken very good care of this home."

Atkins? That name sounded familiar. Vivian looked down. Where did she know — "Congressman Daniel Atkins lives in this house?"

"Yes," Ramona said, looking around in case someone overheard. "But I can assure you they're being very reasonable about the price, considering."

"You've given us a lot to think about." Vivian urged Ryan toward the door. "We'll get back to you."

"My card," Ramona called after them.

Vivian kept moving toward the squad car, a dozen thoughts tumbling through her head. Harold was here to talk with Congressman Atkins a few hours before he met with Lauren. There was a photo of Lauren at Atkins's campaign. Vivian was trying to make sense of it all when a horn blast snapped her attention back.

"Whoa there." Ryan pulled her away from the curb. "Good thing they were paying attention."

"Sorry." Vivian gave an apologetic wave to the woman driving the Lexus. Her gaze followed the redheaded driver as she steered her car into a driveway one house over. She probably wouldn't have given it a second thought, except under the current circumstances, Vivian's Spidey senses were on high alert. "Go, hurry. Get in the car."

"What?" Ryan asked, following her quick pace. "What's going on?"

Vivian pulled on her sunglasses and slipped into the car as soon as Ryan unlocked the door. When he got in, she told him to drive.

"Tell me what's happening, Vivian."

"That lady in the car, the one who almost hit me, that's Trisha Atkins, the congressman's wife."

Ryan looked in his rearview mirror. "So?"

"*So,* Lauren Holt worked Atkins's campaign with her students. Harold's GPS puts him at the Atkins home twice that week. The last time only a couple of hours after he met with Lauren." Ryan looked like he was trying to follow along, but even she could hear the disconnect in her thoughts. "Look, I don't know how it all fits together, but something brought Harold, Congressman Atkins, and Lauren together."

"What about the video? Do you think Congressman Atkins is the Watcher?"

Vivian settled into her seat. "Maybe?"

"You think it was Lauren?"

"Taping herself? No." Vivian shook her head. "She was upset about something."

"So what do you want to do next?" Her

eyes met his and he smirked. "Find Lauren Holt."

"The quicker, the better."

THIRTEEN

Bethany Price
Walton, Georgia
Sunday Morning

The lock on her bedroom door rattled, sending Bethany scurrying to the corner of her room where her dresser was. She reached for a tissue and wiped her eyes, her skin raw.

"Bethany, are you ready?"

"Um, I'm not feeling well. Can I stay home?"

"Sweetheart, open the door."

Locking the bedroom door in the Price household was acceptable only if someone was changing. Her parents believed in an open-door policy, meaning that if the door was open, trouble was less likely to happen. Tears stung her eyes. *If only I had listened to them.*

"Bethany." Her mother's tone was no longer concerned — it was now stern.

"Open the door."

Nausea rose in her gut, but Bethany did as she was told.

"Jeremy is already in the car — Bethany, what in the world?" Her mother moved into her bedroom, crowding Bethany backward until the back of her knees hit the edge of her bed. "Honey, what's wrong?" She pressed her hands to Bethany's cheeks. "Are you sick?"

"Yeah." It was only a half-lie. She was sick, but it wasn't the kind of sickness any medicine could fix.

"Get back in bed this instant." Her mother pulled back her bedspread, revealing the soft rose-colored sheets that Bethany had twisted and turned in all night. "I'm going to call Daddy and tell him we won't be at church this morning."

"No." Bethany shook her head and sat. "I'm not that sick. I think it's just a bug. Maybe something I ate." *Dear God, please don't let her see I'm lying.* "Go to church with Jeremy. I probably just need some rest."

Her mother sat at her side, stroking Bethany's blonde hair from her face. The motion, which her mom had meant to be comforting, now churned Bethany's stomach, forcing a sob into her throat.

"Oh, honey, are you sure? You look on the

verge of tears."

"Momma, please." She took her mom's hand from her face. "I'll be okay."

Her mother tucked a strand of her own blonde hair — curly, unlike Bethany's stick-straight locks — behind her ear, revealing the gold hoop earrings Bethany and Jeremy had saved up to buy her for Christmas. They were gold-plated, but from the joy on their mother's face that morning, you'd have thought they'd have given her jewelry from Tiffany's or Cartier.

"I think I should stay —"

Bethany wiggled under her covers, reaching for her stuffed bear. "I'm just going to sleep. I shouldn't have gone out last night." *I should've stayed home.*

"I've heard there's a summer flu going around. Maybe that's what it is?"

"Maybe."

"Okay." Her mother stood, straightening a white cardigan over her floral dress. "But I'm only going to stay until Daddy begins his sermon. I'll sit in the back and sneak out to check on you."

All Bethany could muster was a weak nod. She was afraid that if she tried any harder to convince her mother to leave, she'd become suspicious.

"See ya later, Bethany-gator."

When her mom left the room, Bethany counted off the seconds, listening for the front door to close and the sound of her mother's car driving away before she buried her face into the blankets and released a painful, silent sob. Her cries had grown inaudible over the last two weeks, like there was nothing left in her soul to release. *Her soul.*

Bethany wasn't sure what made her most sick. Going to her father's church knowing what she did and having to pretend she was still the same virtuous pastor's daughter everyone believed her to be, or sitting there and listening to her father preach about the destruction of sin when he couldn't even keep his own daughter from it.

Suddenly, being tucked into her bed felt strangling. Suffocating. Bethany kicked and tore at the covers until her body was free, and she slid to the floor, pressing her face against the cool wood of her nightstand as she closed her eyes. She took in deep breaths and forced them out until she could feel the vise around her chest loosen.

Opening her eyes, she took in her room and it felt like she was a stranger. Photos of her and her friends pinned on the wall showed the face of a girl who had it all even when she hadn't realized it. Why had she thought she needed more — needed him?

She caught sight of the white romper with pink flowers still crumpled on the floor near her desk. She'd aimed for the trash basket and missed. Now it sat there on the floor like an ugly reminder of what she did that night. Only she didn't need a reminder. Bethany had the Watcher to do that.

She reached under her bed and dragged out her backpack. Inside were the clothes from last night. She wanted to throw them away — burn them — but her mother might notice, and then what would she say? "Sorry, Mom, but these clothes remind me of my dark, ugly sin, and I'm no longer the girl you thought I was."

Bethany's words echoed in her room. She went to the laundry room and dumped the items into the washer, wishing her mother hadn't taught her how to do her own laundry when she was little. Maybe then she could *accidentally* pour a bottle of bleach into the load and ruin them. That's what she needed. An entire bottle of bleach to cleanse her. Plain old soap wasn't doing the trick — the raw skin beneath her clothes could testify.

Back in her room, Bethany slid to the floor and curled into a ball, closing her eyes. Why couldn't she remember what happened?

Of course, she didn't need to remember to know what took place. It was all there on video. Someone had taped her. Someone had captured her mistake and was now forcing her to . . . she swallowed the bile that seemed settled to remain in her throat.

She sat up, grabbed her cell phone, and pulled up the message, but not because she wanted to see it again or watch the video of her seducing the boys at the party — that was burned in her memory forever. She needed to figure out a way to get the money and make this all go away.

Dear Bethany

Bethany's stomach roiled at the condescending tone of kindness.

It is unfortunate when our sins find us out. Even more so when hypocrisy paints a vivid picture that can condemn an entire family. You will begin receiving texts from an untraceable number with instructions on how to keep the attached video from finding its way into the spotlight. After all, "Consider what a great forest is set on fire by a small spark."

Anger bubbled at the Watcher's use of a

Bible verse, but the point was clear. If the video of her sleeping with those boys got out, it would destroy her father's career. Who'd want to listen to a pastor preach about sin when his own daughter hadn't merely sinned but was now being forced to engage in moral depravity at the beck and call of some monster unless she paid.

She should've gone to the police that night, but what would she have said? How many school assemblies had she attended that talked about the consequences and risks of underage drinking? Maybe she should've paid attention. When she woke up the next morning, the memory of what had happened was grainy — and she was grateful for it. She hoped God was sparing her the reminder of her sin, but then the email came . . .

As your Lord says, I would be thoughtless if I didn't give you a way out from under your sin — a payment of $50,000 can be transferred to a link that will be provided when you respond. Any hesitation to respond to either option within four hours will result in the video going public.

The Watcher

Bethany had watched the video in horror. It showed her walking into a room with a guy, who then offered her a drink. Shame forced her eyes closed the second she saw him taking off her romper. The act lasted only a few minutes from what she could tell before the next guy came in. The first time she watched, she couldn't hold back the vomit. She rushed to the bathroom and heaved until every muscle in her body ached and nothing else came out.

Bethany clicked on the link just to shut off the video, not thinking what agreeing to the Watcher would mean. She just wanted it to stop. Except it didn't.

Three days later, she received her first message with an address only. It was to a hotel room. And before she could back out, another text message arrived warning her what would happen if she did.

$50,000

It was just under the amount Gigi had promised her to help pay for college. Bethany lifted her eyes to the University of Georgia poster she'd received when the school had accepted her as an incoming freshman. Not only had Bethany worked her tail off to get accepted, but her GPA and test scores had awarded her enough scholarship money to pay most of her tuition and fees. Her mom and dad had promised to cover room and board, but Bethany wanted them to keep the money they'd saved.

If she used the money from Gigi for room and board, then her parents could take the dream vacation they always talked about but neglected because it was more important to give to the church or a charity or some poor, desperate soul who showed up at their doorstep from time to time.

Bethany admired her parents for their generosity and hoped she could give something back to them for all they'd done for her. If she used her money from Gigi to pay off the Watcher, then she'd have no other choice but to accept the money from her parents and hope she could find a job to cover everything else.

Or maybe she wouldn't go to UGA at all. Staying in Walton wasn't the worst thing. And she could pick up extra shifts at the Way Station Café. Anderson College was a good school, and if Frannie went there, it could be fun —

The buzzer on the washer went off and Bethany forced herself off the floor. She went to the laundry room and moved her clothes to the dryer, disappointed they hadn't been miraculously destroyed. Her cell phone chimed from her pocket, the sound sending her heart plummeting into her stomach.

Surely, he isn't sending me out again. Bethany's fingers fumbled as she tried to get her iPhone screen to open up to the messages. When she did, she wanted to cry. Tears of relief came this time, because instead of being from the Watcher, the message was from Frannie.

Beth, where you been, girl? Guess who came in last night?????

Did you guess Henry? YASSSSS!!!

He asked about you.

Is everything okay?

Maybe we can go see a movie this week. I'm in a Hemsworth mood.

Come on, girl. It's senior year!!!! YOLO and all that right???

Bethany shoved her phone back into her pocket. "You only live once" was a stupid saying. All it had taken was one night to ruin her entire life, and now she was paying for it with her body and soul.

FOURTEEN

It was here. Walton's main event had finally arrived, and Vivian was more excited than if she had exclusive access to interview a newly elected president. This wasn't an election, but she did have exclusive access as the only reporter on-site at the Walton Peach Bowl.

Unlike the annual and legit college football Peach Bowl game, this sporting event took challengers of all shapes and sizes and put them onto a giant tarp covered in water and soapsuds for a friendly, hilarious, and injury-waiting-to-happen game of kickball.

"I don't know how you talked me into this, DeMarco."

Vivian turned to find Ryan standing next to her. She snapped a picture. "Is that your war face?"

Ryan tapped his cheeks, which had been blackened with face paint. "Maceo and Noah said it makes me look cool. No?"

She wrinkled her nose, shaking her head. "Is cool the look you were going for?"

A group of teenage boys walked past, their clothes soaked and smeared with mud. One was holding a bag of ice on a swollen and purpling brow.

Ryan adjusted his sunglasses on his head. "Are you really going to make me do this?"

"A bet's a bet, buddy."

A bullhorn blew and Ryan gave her a look. The kind that said "Please don't make me do this."

"Good luck." She smiled. "I'd watch out for that guy." She tilted her head toward a hulk of a man wearing a Walton FD shirt. "I saw him lifting an ambulance to warm up."

"Good grief." Ryan shook his head. He turned and stepped close to her. "You'll tell them won't you?"

She swallowed, her eyes shifting to see if anyone was watching. "What? Who?" Her voice came out breathless.

"Frankie and my mom. You'll tell them of my heroics on the field today?" Serious blue eyes stared into hers before humor crept into them. "Even after I'm gone?"

She pushed him back. "Get out there."

He turned and jogged over to his team members, who were only identifiable by their green shirts. Already the players' legs were slipping and sliding from beneath them. For some reason little kids and even lanky teenagers had the agility to keep upright, but within a few minutes the grown men of the Walton fire department, rescue, and sheriff's department were struggling to stay upright — Ryan included. He tossed her a playful scowl.

"This is going to be fun."

Vivian recognized the voice of the woman who had just walked up.

"You know this is the first sport he's ever played? Spent all night asking Charlie for tips." Vivian turned to Lane, whose long auburn hair was swept up into a ponytail. She wore a green tank top with white shorts.

"Ryan's going to die out there, isn't he?"

Lane smiled and it filled her whole face. "Nah, he's got some meat on those bones now."

This was weird. Vivian was standing next to the very woman whose reputation she could've destroyed a year ago and they were chatting like . . . friends?

"Noah can't stop talking about the girl who's going to make him and Maceo eat worm pie."

"You know I'd never make them do that, right?"

"I know." Lane laughed. "But he doesn't know that and Charlie's having fun with it."

"Congratulations on your wedding." Vivian fiddled with her camera strap. "I heard it was beautiful."

"Thank you."

Loud cheering erupted and Vivian lifted her camera in time to catch Charlie kicking a red rubber ball over the heads of the fire department's team. His run toward first started out well, but as he rounded the base, his legs slid in the opposite direction of his body, sending him sprawling on the wet tarp to the delight of the crowd.

"Ooh, that's gonna leave a mark." Lane giggled.

Vivian tapped her camera. "I'll make you a copy."

Ryan was next. There was a strut to his step as he made his way to home plate that was more mocking of his courage than evidence of his actual ego. Vivian heard a woman call out his name from the stands and sighed when she saw Holly waving enthusiastically. Apparently, she had gotten the team green memo too based on her still outrageously bright outfit. He smiled up at her, and Holly's face beamed like she'd won the Miss America crown.

A tinge of jealousy slithered inside Vivian's

chest. She positioned her camera in front of her face, hiding any revealing emotions. Ryan wasn't hers. Sure, they'd grown a lot closer over the last couple of weeks while working on the case, but their relationship was professional. A professional relationship with an expiration date. Because, like it or not, Vivian's job at the *Gazette* was coming to an end and she needed to figure out where that left her.

As many hours as she and Ryan had put into the case, they weren't any closer to finding Lauren or the identity of the person who blackmailed and possibly killed Harold, which meant she didn't have the story she needed to prove to Shep or his father she was the journalist Harold had believed her to be. Truthfully, her aspiration for that position was waning with every extra second she spent with Ryan, and that scared her.

"Run, Ryan!"

Lane's scream shook Vivian out of her introspection. Through the lens of her camera she watched Ryan run to first base and almost eat it like Charlie did, but he was able to regain his balance enough to make it to second base.

"I think you should consider dating him."

"What?" Vivian's expression must've matched the shock in her voice because

Lane laughed.

"I'm not asking you to marry him, though I could see the two of you together."

What is happening? "Uh, I don't think we're a good match." Vivian's eyes landed on Holly. "I'm sure there's a better choice."

Lane turned to the stands. "Who? Holly Newman?" Lane laughed. "She'd have to get through Frannie first."

"They're perfect for each other. She lives here and he wants to stay here. She's the epitome of all things Southern and he's a gentleman."

"You left out boring and the fact that he won't shut up about you."

That should've thrilled Vivian, but it only worried her. "I'm leaving," she blurted out.

"So?" Lane waved Vivian closer to the action and into the shade of a big oak tree. "Ryan's getting close to making a decision about whether he's going to leave Walton. Maybe you two end up in the same city." She shrugged. "You never know."

A tickle of excitement blossomed in Vivian's chest at Lane's suggestion, but then she shut it down. "I don't think Ryan's going to leave Walton."

"Don't get me wrong, I love Ryan and don't want him to leave, but I think he's scared of chasing after a dream he doesn't feel worthy of."

"Agencies are literally fighting for him. I'd say the dream is just waiting for him to accept."

Lane took hold of Vivian's hand and pulled the camera away from her face. "You're not hearing me. The chase isn't after the job — it's you."

If it were possible, Vivian could have sworn she felt the earth beneath her feet shift. Ryan felt unworthy to chase after her? She turned her gaze back on the game until her eyes found him. Funny, kind, humble, and he considered *her* the dream? How could Lane be so sure?

"Oh, Charlie made it back home. I'd better get over there and make sure he's okay." Lane picked her bag up from the grass. "I hope to see you at the next trivia night."

Vivian searched Lane's soft features. The shy woman who'd experienced deep trenches of pain and sadness didn't joke, which meant her invitation was genuine.

"I know what it cost you not to print my story." Empathy emanated from her green eyes. "Truthfully, you still intimidate me a little, but I know we've all got our stories — no pun intended." She winked. "And I would really like the opportunity to become your friend."

There were no words. Vivian was still feeling unsteady from Lane's earlier comment about Ryan — and now this? It was more than she could handle. The many emotions flooding her system made her afraid speaking might pop this bubble of a dream.

"Look out!"

Vivian's attention whirled around in time to see a human wall of muscle, fear in his blue eyes, hurtling toward her. Lane jumped back, but Vivian wasn't quick enough. Ryan's body slammed into her, sending them both somersaulting into the air. She felt his arms wrap protectively around her a second before they hit the ground.

"Vivi, you dead?"

She wiped the soapy water from her face. "Did you just call me Vivi?"

Ryan rolled so he was facing her. "You took that hit like a champ."

Beneath the war paint and suds, there was a blush coloring his cheeks. He was avoiding her question, but she didn't really need an answer — it was there in his eyes. Her hands moved to his face, gently wiping away the stray pieces of grass, her finger lingering on his lower lip.

Kissable.

Their eyes met, and before she could give herself a million reasons why this was a bad idea, she pulled him toward her, closer and closer until finally, *finally* their lips met.

Thank goodness he was already knocked flat on the ground. Ryan's arms wound around Vivian's back, pulling her closer as their kiss deepened and they shut out the rest of the world — until someone cleared their throat loudly.

Ryan groaned as Vivian pulled back. No regret in her eyes. She'd meant to kiss him. His lips pulled into a smile. "That was awesome."

Vivian couldn't help smiling. She wriggled her arm out from underneath him. "How long before the whole town finds out about this?"

"I'd say they're already planning the wedding." Charlie reached for Vivian's hand to help her up. "I'd complain that Frost lost us the game, but I'm not sure he cares."

"Not even a little bit." Ryan grinned as his buddy helped him up. His gaze slipped to Vivian, their eyes locking. Neither of them were able to keep the smile from their lips. Her lips . . . man, he wanted them back on his. And soon. "Are you okay?"

"I'm good."

He was grinning like a fool and he knew it, but he didn't care.

"I think you owe her dinner or something, Ryan," Lane suggested, eyeing Charlie.

"Oh yeah. It's the least you can do since you almost killed her."

The smile melted from his face. A concussion. Maybe he'd hit her so hard she didn't know what she was doing when she kissed him.

Vivian smirked. "My house, six o'clock. Bring dessert, and it better not be a cobbler."

"I really think you're going to like him, Ryan." His mom had called to ask how the games went and to once again invite him over to officially meet Dr. Murphy. Ryan had finally caved, and it was most likely due to the woman he was getting ready to meet for dinner. That kiss, *that kiss* — his mom could ask him anything right now and he'd do it without a second thought.

"Would it be okay if I bring someone?"

Seconds of silence passed. "You want to bring someone? Is it a girl? Frannie said something about a girl —"

"Yes, Mom." Ryan cut in, pausing in front of his bathroom mirror to run a hand through his hair, which was still wet from the shower. His body was sore and a few bruises were beginning to rise to the surface of his skin. He checked his watch. He was going to be late if he didn't leave soon. "Mom, I gotta run, but I'll call you later to find out what I can bring."

"Okay. Don't worry about the food, I'll have plenty. Just bring yourself and your friend."

Ryan couldn't end the call fast enough. His drive to Vivian's was interrupted by a quick stop at the Way Station Café where Lane had a warm batch of chocolate chip cookies waiting. He would've kissed her if Charlie hadn't given him the stare of death. It was fine. Ryan really wanted to kiss just one person tonight and she was standing at her door watching him walk up now.

He held out the box. "Not a cobbler. Chocolate chip cookies from Lane."

"Excellent choice." A smile filled her face as she took the box from him. "Do you like pizza?"

"Doesn't everyone?"

"You'd be surprised." She stepped back and let him in, setting the cookies on a small table. Her long hair was pulled up in a bun, with a few loose strands framing her face. "I was going to order Greek food, but I wasn't sure if you'd like that and there's only one place in Savannah, but they don't deliver, so I made cheese with sausage and spinach pizza. Is that okay?"

She sounded nervous, and Ryan couldn't explain why seeing her off her game made her even more attractive. He didn't care what they ate or where they ate as long as he was with her. "Pizza sounds great, but if you really want Greek, we can go get it."

"No, it's fine." She tucked a piece of hair behind her ear. "Look, about today, if that was awkward —"

"Was it awkward for you?" Ryan paused. Had he misread her intentions? Or maybe she had changed her mind.

"No. Unexpected but definitely not awkward."

"I thought it was nice. Really nice."

She smiled and took a small step toward him. He brushed his knuckles along her jaw and saw expectation fill her eyes. He reached for her hands and moved them around his waist and she obliged, pressing closer to him.

"I'm going to kiss you, Vivi."

She nodded, her lips parting.

He leaned down and breathed in the scent of her shampoo, floral and feminine. It drew his lips to her temple and then her cheeks. She inhaled sharply, her fingers clutching his shirt. He kissed a trail along her jaw until he could no longer take it and had to have her lips on his.

The kiss was deep and filling and just as ground-shaking as the one in the park. They moved against the wall, his body coupling with hers as though they were made for each other. She kissed him deeper and he was certain he'd never be the same again.

When she pulled back, she gave him a shy smile. "We should eat."

He didn't want to stop kissing her, but he also didn't want to rush whatever this was. "So, Greek, huh?"

Vivian grabbed the cookies and carried them into the kitchen. "Have you ever had it?"

Ryan shook his head. "Can't say that I have."

"There's a really great place in northern Virginia called Angie's. It's a hole-in-the-wall type owned by a couple who moved from Greece. It's the next best thing to actually eating there."

Ryan remembered the photos taped to the wall behind Vivian's desk. "Have you been to Greece?"

Vivian picked up a stack of paper plates and napkins. "No. One day, maybe." She pointed at the fridge. "I've got water, some cans of Diet Coke Pecca left behind, and before you even ask, no sweet tea."

"What's with you and sweet tea?"

Vivian speared him with a look. "It's liquid calories."

"And cookies are?"

"Worthy of the calories."

Ryan laughed. "I'll take water and don't let Ms. Byrdie hear you speak that way about the official beverage of Georgia."

"Oh, she has. Won't let me leave —" Her eyes met his, the unspoken reality of her words crashing into their night like an unwanted guest. "Without her recipe."

"Should we talk about that?"

Vivian grabbed two bottles of water from the fridge before moving to the couch. A pizza was already waiting on the coffee table. Ryan followed. "Actually, I'd prefer to talk about why you're still here in Walton."

"What do you mean?" he asked as he grabbed a slice of pizza.

"Come on, Ryan. What's really keeping you from accepting a position with the FBI or CIA or whoever else is trying to hire your genius brain?" She passed him a plate. "Is it because of Frannie and your mom? Are you afraid of leaving them?"

Leave it to a reporter to get right to the hard questions. Ryan finished chewing his bite of pizza and wiped his lips. "My dad walked out on us when I was twelve. He was chasing a dream because his life here didn't satisfy him enough to stick around. If I'm afraid of anything, it's following in his footsteps."

"But you'd have your family's support, right?"

"I do, but would God really call me away from them?"

Vivian frowned. "I don't know about God, but you can't let what your father did stop you from doing what you're good at." Her voice grew tender. "You're a protector. I see it in the way you look after Frannie and the way you've —" She tipped her chin. "I would hate to see you hold yourself back."

"What if it doesn't work out?" He hadn't voiced his fear out loud before and he worried that Vivian would think it was silly. "What if that dream isn't what I thought it was?"

"What if it's everything you wanted and more?"

Ryan tilted his head, taking in the amazing woman in front of him. "There's a position in DC with the FBI Cyber Crimes Division . . . maybe you could show me that Greek restaurant."

Vivian set her plate aside and snuggled into Ryan's side. She traced her fingers over his until finally lacing them together. Her charcoal-blue gaze found his. "I think I could do that."

Ryan kissed the top of Vivian's head, his mind playing a dozen scenarios of what his future might look like if he did as she suggested. A stack of envelopes with job offers that could take him all over the country and world was just sitting in his desk waiting for him to make a decision. It should be easy, but it wasn't. Because now the one hesitation Ryan couldn't ignore was whether any of those choices included Vivian at his side.

FIFTEEN

He did it. After several weeks, Ryan finally struck gold. Using brute force, he decoded the hashed password and unlocked a link that was now flashing brightly from his laptop screen. Running his fingers through his hair, he took a breath and started to press the enter button but stopped. If the Watcher had gone to all this trouble, Ryan wasn't going to go another step without recording what he found. Satisfied the online recording software was running, he moved the cursor back to the link and clicked enter.

His stomach hitched in disappointment when a black-and-white video began playing. He leaned forward. There were two beds, a nightstand, and matching pieces of art on the wall — nondescript, so he guessed it to be a hotel room. A second later, the room was crowded with a group of college students. Though there was no sound, he could tell from their facial expressions and exaggerated movements that they were all drunk or well on their way.

Ryan searched for a time stamp and found the video was a few months old. Weird. He continued to watch the screen. It appeared the vantage point of the camera was positioned on the television. Since none of the kids seemed to be paying attention to it, Ryan guessed they didn't know it was filming them. But why?

His question was answered when several minutes had passed and about half of the kids left the room. Only five remained. A girl with light hair swayed her way to the bed, helped by a young man. Ryan held his breath, afraid of what was going to happen next. But the young man went to a bag and pulled out a pill bottle. A conversation happened between the two of them. A minute or two later, someone brought a tray to the bed, emptied the pills onto it, and crushed them up. Ryan watched as each of the kids took their turn snorting the medicine.

He squinted, trying to read the label on the bottle when the screen went black. "What happened?"

A link popped up similar to the one Harold had received on his video. When Ryan clicked it, an error occurred. What did that mean? Had the Watcher been paid? And which of these individuals had been the target?

Before he could try to figure it out, his laptop *pinged* again. What? Ryan clicked on the link and froze. Another video. An older man and a younger lady were getting very close — Ryan averted his eyes. He felt like a peeping tom but worse because his computer was still recording.

Another *ping.*

Twenty minutes later, Ryan had opened up a Pandora's box of blackmail videos and wanted to scrub his eyeballs. How many more were there?

"Frost." Sheriff Huggins walked up to his desk. He tilted his head in the direction of his office. "We need to talk."

"Yes, sir." Ryan hesitated to turn off his computer but wasn't willing to risk anyone walking by and thinking he was watching these . . . nope. He set up his computer to keep tracking the videos as they came in and caught up to Sheriff Huggins just as he entered his office. "Sir, I'd like to give you an update on the Watcher case."

"Were you able to trace him?"

"Not exactly." Ryan slid into the chair across from Sheriff Huggins. "The password to the Watcher's link was hashed and salted —"

"Frost, like you're talking to Frannie."

"Right. Sorry, sir. You've heard of the cloud, right? Virtual storage saved on the internet rather than on a computer's hard drive?" The sheriff nodded. "All clouds are connected to an IP, which is basically your computer's network address so the internet knows where to send your emails, files, photos, et cetera."

"I know what an IP address is, Frost."

There was a low grumble to Sheriff Huggins's voice that said Ryan needed to be quick and succinct. "The Watcher used a password that was hashed, meaning the numbers are scrambled with a key, and salted, meaning a random string of characters were added to the beginning of the password. When I was able to break into that, I tried tracing the IP address, but it was spoofed and led me to a dead end. Most likely intentional. But it also led me to a cloud where more videos had been saved."

"With Harold?"

"No." Ryan shook his head. "College students doing drugs. And there are more. Men, women . . . they make Harold's video look like *Pollyanna.*"

A deep chuckle filled the office. "You've seen *Pollyanna*?"

"My sister went through a phase," Ryan grumbled, feeling an embarrassing heat curl over his shoulders and up his neck.

"You'd better not let Deputy Wilson or Lynch find out." Sheriff Huggins wiped at his eyes and cleared his throat, bringing seriousness back to the conversation. "Recognize anyone in the videos?"

"No, sir, but I'm considering reaching out to Agent Hannigan again. Maybe have him run facial recognition through the FBI's system."

"You don't think we'll get any hits on our system?"

Ryan hoped he wasn't offending the sheriff. "Sir, the Watcher — whoever he or she is — is setting people up. Those kids had no idea they were being taped. It didn't appear Harold and Lauren knew either. Vivian never heard Harold mention anything about Lauren, and it's been two years since she quit teaching at Anderson." He took a breath. "If I send these videos to the FBI, they might be able to figure out who the victims are. Maybe find a connection between them that'll lead to the Watcher."

"Good plan." Sheriff Huggins shifted in his seat, tugged open the top drawer in his desk, and pulled out an envelope. "Speaking of the FBI." The sheriff slid it across the desk. "That came in today."

Ryan lifted the paper and recognized the letterhead. Strategic Neutralization and Protection Agency or S.N.A.P. was a private contract security company that operated all over the country.

"I'm not sure they're the right fit for me."

Sheriff Huggins lifted his brows. "Any closer to a decision?"

"There's a position with the FBI Atlanta office that I'm considering." Ryan thought about his dinner date with Vivian and the tease of imagining a future with her. "And one in DC with Cyber Crimes."

"But?"

"It's gotten a bit more complicated."

"Because of a certain reporter?"

Ryan searched the sheriff's face, feeling heat crawling up his own. "If I take the job in Atlanta, she'd be there and we could —" Ryan looked at his hands, unsure what he was expecting would happen if he and Vivian lived closer or what to even call what they were doing . . . dating? Flirting?

"The job in Atlanta isn't what you want to be doing?"

"No, sir." Ryan tucked his chin. "Agent Hannigan is anxious for me to be part of the FBI, but he doesn't think I'll be satisfied anywhere else but in DC."

"What do you think?"

"I'm satisfied here, sir." Ryan raked his fingers through his hair. "At least I thought I was. I don't know anymore." He blew out a breath. "I don't want to be like him."

The lines across Sheriff Huggins's forehead deepened. "If you're referring to your father, you have nothing to worry about there, son. You are nothing like him."

"Am I though? I've got everything I need right here and I'm going to walk away from it all to chase after a dream I had as a naïve kid?"

"First, I would never call you naïve. Second, your daddy was selfish. He chased after a dream he didn't share with you or your mom and sister." Sheriff Huggins picked up the envelope. "You have their support. Mine. Those in this office. We all believe God is calling you to fulfill a purpose he created you for — you just have to believe it yourself."

Sheriff Huggins's words followed him out of his office and back to his desk, where Ryan found a message waiting for him from Agent Hannigan. Was he ready to make a decision? Deep down he knew his family supported him. Sheriff Huggins and Charlie did too. Ryan picked up the phone and prayed, because no matter how confident everyone else was that it was the right thing to do, Ryan was still nervous. It felt like a big chance, but Sheriff Huggins had reminded him that unlike his father, he had the support of everyone who mattered — including Vivian. Especially Vivian.

Vivian chewed on her pen, looking at her notes. When she was working on a big story, it helped to lay out all the pieces on index cards so she could move them around and make connections. So far nothing was connecting and it was giving her a headache. "Where are you, Lauren Holt?"

Her question echoed off the oak floors in the *Gazette*'s office. Lately, it had begun to feel lonely. The heartache came unexpectedly these days — whenever she caught a rerun of *It Happened One Night* or when she walked into the *Gazette* on an especially warm day and the scent of stale chicory coffee welcomed her.

Or maybe it was because she was getting used to Ryan dropping in with lunch or coffee or a persuasive dinner invitation that often included kissing.

This is getting out of hand. Ryan was consuming too much of her head space, silencing any underlying warnings that whatever the two of them had together wouldn't last. Their conversation about him taking a position in DC had led her to dreams of evening strolls along the National Mall or eating Greek at Angie's with him. But what did that mean for her? Even if Vivian could solve Harold's case or figure out who the Watcher was . . . it was unlikely she'd find a job in DC.

Vivian's eyes landed on the latest *Savannah Daily* — what if? She picked it up and studied the headlines. What if it were possible to get a job there? Walton was sort of growing on her and —

"Excuse me."

A man with cropped black hair pushed open the door to the *Gazette* office. His eyes darted around the open space, looking for anyone else, until they landed on Vivian.

"Can I help you?"

"Are you the reporter?"

She frowned. "I'm *a* reporter. Who are you?"

He stepped into the office but hugged the wall next to the door. Weariness clung to the lines on his face. "Are you the one looking for Lauren Holt?"

Vivian sat up, taking in the lean man. His faded jeans were worn and bore oil stains that matched the ones darkening the skin around his nails. "Who are you?"

The man's jaw flexed as he eyed the door. "Why are you looking for Lauren?"

Whoever he was, he was nervous and she didn't want to say anything to send him running if that was his plan. "I'm worried."

"Why?"

Vivian took the emotion filling his eyes as a good sign. The man cared for Lauren, but she'd need to show a bit of her hand if she wanted to gain his trust. "Harold didn't just die — he was killed."

The color drained from the man's face. "Mr. Kennedy was killed?"

"Yes." Vivian ignored the twinge of guilt for sharing classified information. This was the closest she or Ryan had gotten to finding Lauren, and she'd risk Ryan's annoyance if it got them answers. "Lauren met with Harold a few hours before he died. She was one of the last people to see him alive."

He started for the door. "I need to go."

"Wait." Vivian shot up from her chair. "Lauren could be in danger."

"She's fine. Now leave her alone."

Vivian wasn't quick enough. The man was already out the door and halfway down the stairs before she could stop him. Without thinking, she ran after him. Outside, the lampposts were flickering to life, providing just enough light so that she was able to catch a flash of his blue T-shirt rounding the corner.

She chased after him and found herself in the alley behind the *Gazette* just as he was climbing into the passenger side of a Ford pickup. "Please, wait!"

His eyes froze on her for only a second before he jumped in. The truck's engine roared to life, the lights blinding Vivian. There was not enough room for the vehicle to turn around, which meant the only thing preventing it from driving off — was her.

Vivian held up her hands. This wasn't going to end well. With the lights blinding her, she couldn't see who was behind the wheel but prayed they weren't willing to run her over.

"Please, just one minute."

The engine roared again and Vivian took a determined step toward the truck.

The man leaned out of the window. "Just leave us alone."

Us? Was Lauren inside the truck too? "Just one question and I'll let you leave. I won't bother you or Lauren again."

There was no reply, but at least the revving had stopped. Vivian walked up to the truck, but a jarring blast of the horn stopped her instantly.

He leaned farther out the window, holding up his hand. "Don't come any closer."

"Fine." Short of running her over, there wasn't really anything they could do to stop her from approaching the truck. But if Lauren was in there, Vivian hoped obeying their commands would get them to trust her. "Was there something going on between —" Vivian checked her surroundings. This wasn't a conversation she wanted to have out in the open where anyone could listen, but what choice did she have? In her loudest whisper, she continued. "Harold and Lauren?"

"You don't know what you're talking about."

The engine revved.

"What about the video?" Vivian asked.

"What video?"

Vivian bit the inside of her cheek. If they didn't know about the video, then she was crossing a line that would more than annoy Ryan, but her options were limited at the moment. "The one with her and Harold a few hours before he died."

The passing seconds felt like an eternity before the engine went silent. Vivian blocked her eyes against the headlight beams, then the passenger door opened and she took a step back, wondering if she should have an escape plan herself.

The alley instantly went dark. The lights from the truck had shut off. It took Vivian a few seconds to let her eyes adjust, and when they did she saw that not only was the man walking toward her, but he was carrying a baby in his arms. The driver's-side door opened and Lauren Holt stepped out.

The guy looked at Vivian. "Do you have a back entrance into the building?"

"Uh, yeah." Vivian's gaze moved between him, the baby, and Lauren. "But it's locked and the key is upstairs."

"Go get it." Lauren took the baby from his arms and smoothed her dark, wispy hair. "We'll wait."

Vivian hesitated. Were they lying? Would they run the second she turned her back?

"It's late," he said. "Go back inside and get your keys and your purse." He exchanged a look with Lauren before returning his attention to Vivian. "Leave the building just like you would if you were going home for the night. Lock the door and come around back. We'll go in through the back exit."

What in the world is happening? The guy gave directions like he was some kind of operative — or had watched too many Jason Bourne movies. Either way, she had no other choice but to do what he asked and believe they would be here when she came back. Vivian hurried around the side of the old bank building and ran up the stairs, praying — again — that they would keep their word.

After fumbling through her desk for the key to the exit door, she grabbed her purse and forced herself to walk down the stairs. A skitter of goose bumps covered her skin. What would make them suggest such an act? Were they afraid someone was watching? Vivian's eyes searched the shadows — was someone watching her right now?

Call Ryan. Vivian knew that was exactly what she needed to do, but what if it scared Lauren away? She'd wait, listen to what Lauren had to say, and then call Ryan.

When she saw Lauren's silhouette still waiting for her, she let out a breath of relief. Without a single word passing between them, Vivian unlocked the door and escorted them in and up the stairs into the office. She'd purposely left the light on inside the office — if someone had been watching, they wouldn't be any wiser to their presence.

As soon as Vivian closed the door, she locked eyes with the guy. "Who are you and why the theatrics?"

The man glowered at her, but Lauren placed a hand on his arm. "This is Cody White, a friend of mine." Lauren sat in a chair, settling the baby on her lap with a bottle before pinning Vivian with a look. "You said there's a video of Mr. Kennedy and me?"

Vivian didn't like the exchange of control, but if she had to answer one of Lauren's questions before asking hers, she would. "Yes."

"Can I see it?"

There wasn't a reason to deny her, so Vivian grabbed her laptop, found the video, and hit play.

Lauren's face transformed from sadness to anger. "Who sent this to you?"

"Why were you there?"

"You think someone killed Harold?"

Lauren whispered the question as though she was trying to shield her child. The baby's dark brown eyes looked up at Vivian before a milky smile pulled her bow-shaped lips from the bottle's nipple.

"What's her name?"

Lauren shifted the baby so her head turned back toward the bottle. "Olivia."

"She's beautiful." Vivian smiled. "You're both very lucky."

A flicker crossed Cody's face. What was it? Anger . . . no, pain. The dip at the corners of his mouth, the crease between his brows, and the sadness in his blue eyes. Blue eyes. Vivian's gaze bounced between all three of them. "She's not your daughter."

"Let's go." Lauren shot up, clutching Olivia to her chest.

"Wait, what about the video?"

"I don't know who took that video, but it's not what it looks like."

Cody opened the door and put his hand on the small of Lauren's back, pushing her through.

"Then tell me what it looks like, because this video shows you talking to Harold hours before he was killed. Why did he meet with you?"

Lauren looked over her shoulder, pulling Olivia up to her cheek. "Please leave us alone or I'm afraid we could be next."

Vivian started for them, but Cody twisted around, his sharp gaze drilling into her. "Do not follow us."

There was a protective, almost carnal, growl in his voice that scared Vivian. Cody, Lauren, and Olivia exited the same way they came in. She did not follow them, but she did call Ryan.

"Don't tell me you're still at work?"

Ryan's voice soothed her frayed nerves.

"Are you working tonight?"

"Yeah. Deputy Wilson's little girl has colic."

Vivian's thoughts went to Olivia. "Ryan, Lauren was here."

"What? When?"

"Just now, but she left and Ry—"

Loud pounding echoed from outside . . . or was it inside? Vivian rose, tucking her cell phone between her chin and shoulder.

"Vivi?"

Was someone screaming? She opened the *Gazette* door, and a thick cloud of black smoke washed over her just as an ear-piercing alarm blared through the hallway.

"Ryan —" She coughed. "I think ther—" Vivian dropped to her knees, choking on the poisonous air.

"Vivian, what's happening?"

The rancid smoke burned her eyes. Using her hands, she felt her way toward the stairwell — toward the screaming. Was someone else inside the building?

"VIVIAN!"

Ryan's scream redirected her focus. She fought for a breath of air that wasn't contaminated by the smoke. "Th-there's a fire."

"Get out of the building right now." She heard him yelling at someone. "I've got

Benningfield calling the fire department. I'm on my way."

Vivian gripped the railing so she wouldn't lose her footing and fall down the stairs, but the smoke was making it hard to breathe and even harder to see. Her foot missed a step and she stumbled, dropping her phone. *Just get down and get out.*

Sliding on her bottom, Vivian used the sound of the pounding to draw her toward the door like a beacon. A crackling noise drew her attention up and Vivian gasped. Through black smoke, red-and-orange flames licked the ceiling. A loud pop exploded overhead and soon a cascading shower of water rained down on her from the sprinklers.

Thank God. The sentiment tasted bitter on her tongue. Leave it to her to only speak to God when it suited her needs. It wasn't her fault. God was the one who had turned his back on *her.* After her dad left, every heartbroken prayer she cried into her pillow went unanswered. Whatever she had done to push her dad away must've pushed God away too. Right now was probably not the best time to contemplate that though.

Well, if being chased by a fire wasn't a time to consider God, when was? She made it to the front door and saw Cody's panicked face through the glass door. Vivian tried the door, but it wouldn't open. She cringed. She'd forgotten she locked it earlier. Her fingers fumbled for the lock. Finding it, she twisted, but it was stuck. She shook the door and tried again. Her lungs burned, desperate for a breath of fresh air.

"Break the glass!" Her voice came out hoarse.

Cody looked around, but there was nothing he could use to break the double-paned door. He kicked at it, but that did nothing. Vivian looked behind her. The faint glow of the exit door at the end of the hall was barely visible. Should she risk it? There was a sputtering noise and then the sprinklers stopped.

"Get out!" Cody's fists pounded on the door.

Vivian's eyes burned. She laid her cheek against the wood floor, hot tears slipping from her eyes. *I'm sorry I failed you, Harold.*

Sixteen

Vivian's eyes felt like they had been rubbed raw with sandpaper. She tried opening them, but they were heavy, as were her arms . . . her legs . . . her whole body. Voices spoke around her, but it was hard to make out what they were saying through the stuffiness in her ears.

She tried to move and a hollow pain burned in her chest, forcing her to cough — the pain! Vivian cried out, her voice scratchy.

"Vivi, hang on, a nurse is coming."

That was Ryan's voice. She used more energy than it should've required to open her eyes. Opening them just a slit at first, the sting of air made them water. She squeezed them closed. Another voice broke through the congestion filling her ears.

"Ms. DeMarco, can you hear me? I'm Dr. Pickering. Do you know where you are?"

Vivian shook her head, or at least she thought she did, but it felt as though her head barely moved. "N—" She winced. It was as if someone had taken a razor and sliced the inside of her throat.

"Don't try to talk just yet." Vivian heard the doctor tell someone — a nurse, she supposed — to get a cup of ice chips. "I'm going to press a wet cloth to your eyes, which should help with the burning."

Burning. And just like that, her memory came back. The smoke, Cody pounding on the door but unable to get it opened. The flames. The *Gazette* — had it burned down? How badly was she hurt? Where were Cody and Lauren?

A beeping noise grew in speed next to her.

"Vivi, relax, you're in the hospital. You're okay." The gentle tenor of Ryan's voice was soothing. "You breathed in a lot of smoke."

"The ice chips and water will help." The doctor's voice came close and Vivian jumped when a cold compress was placed over her eyes. "This should help as well."

He was right. As the coolness took away some of the sting, Vivian replayed what she remembered last before everything went dark. Cody and Lauren showing up at the office. Them leaving. And then a fire.

"Now, let's see if you can try opening your eyes again."

The wet cloth was removed from Vivian's

eyes, and she carefully opened them. The room was blurry at first, but soon the images around her solidified. Ryan, in his uniform, worry etched into his face. He looked older. Next to him was an older man in a white coat with salt-and-pepper hair. A nurse walked over with a cup of ice in her hand.

Vivian moved her hand and felt a tube in her nose.

"That's oxygen. Are you a smoker, Ms. DeMarco?"

She shook her head.

"Well, tonight you smoked about a pack and a half in a three-minute window." Dr. Pickering checked her lungs with his stethoscope. "But the lungs are a miraculous organ. Besides an achy chest and some coughing, you shouldn't have any lingering effects."

Ryan's face relaxed. She hadn't noticed it before, but he was holding her left hand.

"Now, let's try some talking." Dr. Pickering had her open her mouth so he could look at her throat with a penlight from his pocket. "What's your favorite ice cream flavor?"

"Vanilla." The word came out sounding like she'd been a carton-a-day smoker her whole life.

The snort from Ryan turned her attention to him. He rolled his eyes at her and she frowned, unable to swallow over the pain in order to ask what he found funny.

"Vanilla isn't a flavor, DeMarco." The edge of his lips lifted into a smile that didn't quite diminish the angst still lurking in his blue eyes.

She'd normally argue, but right now she was tired. And a debate about ice cream would require more than she could give, so she let her eyes drift closed and squeezed Ryan's hand, hoping he understood she wasn't letting go.

A soft glow filled the hospital room when Vivian opened her eyes. She was grateful they didn't sting like before, but her throat still felt like the worst case of strep she'd ever had. Her gaze moved around the room, pausing on the large bouquet of white roses. Next to them was an arrangement of hydrangeas and pink roses and a vase with a collection of colorful wildflowers — who?

Vivian looked to her left and found Ryan asleep in the chair next to her bed. He'd released her hand at some point but was still wearing his uniform. From the disheveled way his hair was lying, she guessed he'd stayed with her the whole night. Or was it morning? How long had she been asleep?

His eyes opened. "Good morning, Rapunzel."

"How many —" She coughed to try to clear the scratchiness, but that was a mistake. She cringed.

Ryan pushed off the chair. "Let me get you some water. Or do you want ice chips? The nurse said ice cream would be good too. I can get that, if you like."

Oh man, if he wasn't cute before . . . "Vanilla's a . . . flavor, you know."

He handed her a cup with a bendable straw. The water was tepid, but it felt good. "We can have that argument when you don't sound like you swallowed that feral cat from your house." Vivian almost spit out her water and shot Ryan a look. "Sorry." But his eyes said not really.

"Where did these come from?" She pointed to the floral shop filling her room.

"The pink roses came from Sheriff Huggins and Ms. Byrdie. Lane and Charlie brought you a dozen snickerdoodles." He pointed at a vase of white roses. "Those" — he made a face — "came from *Shep.* And these are from me." He tapped the vase containing the wildflowers.

"They sent them —" Vivian's throat constricted with emotion.

Ryan poured her some more water and held the cup up for her. "No one sent them. They were all hand-delivered. Everyone has been worried about you."

Vivian let her hand linger on his. "Everyone?"

"Yes."

"Even Shep?"

"What?" The edges of Ryan's eyes crinkled in annoyance.

"I'm just kidding." Vivian grabbed Ryan's hand and pulled him close. The palm of her hand traced the edge of his jaw, the shadow of hair tickling her skin. "You're the only one who matters."

His blue eyes seemed to drink her in, and she drew his lips toward hers in a kiss that made her sure a dozen or more of them would cure her instantly.

"Well, it's good to see you feeling better, Ms. DeMarco."

Vivian released Ryan reluctantly. Her nurse scooted around the bed. "Don't mind me, I'm just taking vitals but probably don't need to considering your heart looks very happy."

"It is." Vivian smiled at the man making it so. "When will I be able to leave?"

"Today, most likely. Dr. Pickering starts rounds at nine."

"It's not too soon, right?" Ryan asked, taking his seat back at her bedside. "There's no rush."

"As long as there are no complications, she'll be discharged and ready to return to normal activity." The nurse winked at Vivian. "A breakfast tray will be delivered in an hour."

When the nurse left, Vivian turned her attention back to Ryan. "What happened to the *Gazette*?"

Ryan adjusted the covers on her bed. "Surprisingly, the damage from the actual fire is minimal. The fire chief said the sprinkler system shorted out, but the burst of water was enough to slow the fire down and they were able to stop it from spreading. Shep has already hired a cleaning team that will start when the scene is cleared, but I think it'll be a couple of weeks before you can return to work there."

Vivian's brow pinched. "What about Lauren and Cody?"

"They're at the station," Ryan said, his thumb circling around her knuckles. "Deputy Wilson took them in last night."

"He did?" Vivian coughed. "Are you going to talk to them?"

"As soon as I'm done here."

There was something in his tone . . .

disappointment maybe, and it stretched into the lines near his eyes. "What's wrong?"

"You promised not to put yourself in danger. Last night. The fire. That was danger, Vivian."

Hearing him say her full name was jarring after all the nicknames he'd given her. "I didn't put myself in danger last night. Lauren and Cody came to the *Gazette* to find me. Was I just supposed to let them go? We needed to talk to Lauren."

"*We* needed to talk to Lauren. The both of us."

His gaze shifted to the window. The sun was beginning to peek through the buildings, filling her room with enough light to make the dark shadows beneath his eyes visible.

"I'm sorry." She looked down at her hands. "I didn't know Lauren was going to be there. I should've called you right away." Vivian lifted her eyes to find him staring at her. "Do you know who started the fire?"

"It's still being investigated." The muscle in Ryan's jaw ticked, his expression turning serious. "Vivian, I think it's time to take you off the case —"

"No," she barked.

Ryan stood. "Vivi, look where you're sitting. In a hospital." He ran a hand through

251

his hair. "I didn't even know how to get ahold of your parents . . . or what I would say."

Vivian's heart twisted inside her chest. Ryan stalked in front of the window, his anxiety palpable. He was a provider — a guardian. When his father walked out, Ryan took on the responsibility of making sure his mom and sister had everything they needed, were taken care of, never giving a second thought to the things he was denying himself in the process.

Ryan suspected Sheriff Huggins thought he was holding himself back out of fear, and she might've believed that if she wasn't watching a man who was winning a piece of her heart every day rub worry lines from his forehead that hadn't been there the day before. It wasn't fear keeping Ryan from taking a position with an agency — it was his desire to protect them. All of them. It was as natural to him as breathing, and now she was included.

"Come here."

He shook his head.

"You're adorable, but you're not a five-year-old. Come here." She patted the space next to her. "Please."

Ryan's expression said he was annoyed, but the second he was next to her, he wrapped his arm around her and kissed the side of her head.

"You could've called my mom, but she's probably flying over Europe. She's a flight attendant for Air United and loves her job, so she works a lot." Vivian took in a slow breath. She could count on one hand how many people knew who her father was, and now Ryan would be one of them. "She met my father on a flight and, according to her, it was a whirlwind romance. They fell in love and she got pregnant."

"But he didn't stick around?" Ryan said, understanding in his voice.

"No, he did, but only when he wasn't off working." *Or so she thought.* "Ever heard of Russell Bradley?"

Ryan frowned before recognition lit his eyes. "The actor?"

"That's the one."

"Your father is Russell —"

"Yes."

Ryan's features shifted from awe to apprehension.

Vivian rolled the edge of the sheet back and forth between her fingers, imagining the questions rolling through Ryan's head. "I didn't know he was an actor. My mom didn't believe in having a television in our house, and I thought my dad traveled for his job. He would come home with all these amazing pictures of the places he'd been. The people. Animals. Landscapes. I fell in love with the adventure surrounding his stories. It never occurred to me either of them were lying."

"How did you find out?"

Vivian released a long sigh. "At a sleep-over when I was thirteen. The girls put in a DVD and there he was." Vivian looked up at Ryan. "I was staring at *my* dad playing the lead role as the father of some family."

Ryan's hand squeezed her shoulder. "What'd you do?"

Even after all these years, the memories of what happened next still felt like she'd been punched in the stomach. "I ran home, and through my sobs my mom managed to figure out what I was saying. Instead of be-ing shocked or outraged, as I had thought she would be, she just looked . . . sad. I had no idea what to expect, but it wasn't what she said next. She told me Russell was an actor who lived in Los Angeles with his wife and two children."

Disbelief colored Ryan's face. "Your da— Russell had another family and your mom knew?"

"It didn't start that way. From what I can remember of her explanation, she and

Russell fell in love, but as his career began to grow, his publicist felt his personal life needed to portray the image of the roles he was playing on-screen. So he began dating some actress, and shortly after he married her and they started raising the perfect Hollywood family."

"What about you and your mom?"

Vivian shrugged. "Like I said, he'd come to our house in between gigs, play father, and leave. Somehow they thought it was better to keep things the way they were until I was old enough to understand." She scoffed. "Like there's a right age for that."

"That's horrible. I'm so sorry." Ryan pulled her closer into him. The touch was gentle and reassuring . . . reliable. A connection that spoke to the vacancy her father had left in her soul. "Our dads are the worst."

She smiled. "They really are." Vivian wasn't sure why she had chosen to tell Ryan about this part of her life, but now that she had, it felt like a chasm inside of her chest had shifted, freeing her of a burden she'd been carrying for almost eighteen years.

"You can't pull me from the case, Ryan." She turned to face him. "I became an investigative journalist because after what Russell and my mom did to me . . . I have to find the truth and put it out there. No one should ever be blindsided like I was."

He drew back slightly, his gaze locking with hers. "Not if it puts your life in danger, Vivi. I can't have that."

"Would it be fair of me to ask you that?"

"What?"

"To stop being the deputy" — her finger traced the gold badge on his chest — "because it puts your life in danger?"

"It's different. I'm trained. I can defend myself."

"I'm trained too." She saw the skepticism in his eyes. "I know how to find the truth behind a story. You wouldn't have half the information you have now if I hadn't helped you, right?" His shoulders fell an inch and she knew she was winning him over. "And who can you thank that right now Lauren Holt is sitting in your station being questioned?"

"Well, she's not being questioned right now because I'm here with you —"

Vivian grabbed the edges of Ryan's bulletproof vest and tugged, bringing them nose to nose. "Who do you have to thank, Deputy Frost?"

His blue eyes slipped to her lips before making their way back to her eyes. "I suppose I have you to thank."

"That's right." She kissed his lips and then shoved him back playfully. "Don't forget it."

"I don't think you'd let me." Ryan adjusted his vest before pulling his phone out of his pocket. "Speaking of Lauren. I need to get to work."

"You promise to give me all the details?"

"I'll be back to take you home, Rapunzel." Ryan started for the door and then turned on his heel. He leaned in and gave her a kiss so deep it curled her toes. When he released her lips, Ryan picked up the bouquet of white roses from Shep. "I think the nurses will like these."

She shook her head. "Oh, wait, Ryan." He stopped. "Ask about the baby's father."

Seventeen

Ryan passed another package of orange fish crackers across the table. The baby squealed in delight as her mom opened them and handed her one.

"I already told you I don't know who set the fire." Lauren wiped a strand of loose hair from her face. "Cody and I were already in the truck when he saw the flames."

"Why were you at the *Gazette* last night?"

"To find out why that reporter was looking for me."

"Did Ms. DeMarco give you a reason?" Ryan was interested in hearing not only Lauren's side of the story but also just how much Vivian had told them.

"She said Harold was killed. That whoever killed him might be looking to come after me." There was a tremor in her voice, and when she handed the baby another fish cracker, he saw her fingers shake. "You don't think I had anything to do with his death, do you?"

"I'm not sure what to think, Ms. Holt." Ryan looked at his notes. "A video of you and Harold hours before he dies is emailed to him with a demand for payment. You disappear and then suddenly reappear at the *Gazette* minutes before the place is torched. There's something going on here that you're a part of, and I want to know what it is."

"I don't know anything about the tape. I saw it for the first time last night."

"Why were you and Harold meeting that day?"

Lauren's eyes shifted downward. "He sent me an email asking to meet him. Said it was urgent."

Ryan frowned. "What was urgent?"

"I don't know. When I got there, Harold asked me why I had sent an urgent email asking him to meet. But I didn't send him an email."

"Harold said you sent him an email?"

Lauren nodded.

"Is there any reason why someone would want to tape you and Harold together?" Ryan hated himself for what he was about to ask next. "Did you and Harold ever —"

"What?" Lauren gasped. "No."

"According to Harold's calendar, you'd met with him before."

"He was trying to help me."

"Help you how?"

She smoothed a piece of the baby's downy hair. "It was personal."

Ryan studied the woman in front of him. Nothing stood out about her. T-shirt, jeans, sandals. Her hand stroked Olivia's chubby cheek and Ryan noticed her ring finger was bare. No ring. Then Vivian's words echoed in his head. *Ask about the baby's father.*

"Is Cody Olivia's father?"

The question caught Lauren off-guard and she narrowed her eyes. "No."

"Harold?"

Disgust filled Lauren's face. "You're joking?"

Ryan's eyes slid to Olivia, who was contently gnawing on her fist. Lauren's gaze followed and she drew the little girl back.

"No, Deputy. If you knew anything about Harold, you'd already know the answer to that question."

He did, but he still had to ask. Lauren was hiding something. "You're right. Harold loved his wife and she loved him." Ryan hoped he could lean into her compassion. "Which is why we're trying to understand why someone would videotape you and him together hours before he was killed."

"I don't know." Lauren looked up, a tear

dripping down her cheek. "The last time I spoke with him I told him that I didn't need his help anymore."

"Help for what?" The frustration in Ryan's tone drew Olivia's doe-eyed gaze and something clicked. "Is it possible Olivia's dad might be involved in this?"

"Olivia's dad is not involved in her life." Lauren stiffened, moving the baby to her other leg. "And I would like to keep it that way."

Not a direct answer. If Lauren was finished teaching about politics, she'd probably make a great politician. A thought occurred to him. "Do you know Congressman Atkins?"

Something passed through Lauren's eyes that caused her to hesitate before answering. "I took my students to a few of his campaign events."

"Did Harold attend those events?"

Her eyebrows creased. "A few times."

"Was there any interaction between the two men?"

"I don't know."

Ryan heard the waver in her voice, and his gut told him he was getting close to something. "Do you know why Harold went to Congressman Atkins's home after meeting you the day he died?"

Lauren's face paled. She swallowed before answering, "No."

A knock at the door startled Olivia and she burst into tears. Ryan barely had to reach to open the door of the small office he was using to question Lauren. Deputy Benningfield looked apologetic. "I'm sorry, but Agent Hannigan is on the phone and said it was important."

Ryan looked over his shoulder at Lauren, who was desperately trying to console her baby. He felt bad. Just like Vivian, Lauren had obviously thought of Harold as a father figure. But was she holding something back?

Olivia's exhausted cries told him his interview was done for now. He turned back to Benningfield. "Make sure she tells you where we can find her and three ways to reach her." Glancing back, he repeated. "Three ways."

Ryan left Lauren with Deputy Benningfield and went to his desk. When he reached for his phone, the light to indicate a call was on hold wasn't flashing. *Hmm.* He picked up the receiver. "Hello, Agent Hannigan?"

Only a dial tone greeted him.

"Deputy Frost." Charlie waved to him from the doorway of the large conference room. "We got some footage of the fire last night."

Ryan dropped the phone into its cradle and moved into the conference room. Finally, maybe they'd catch a break. "When did it come in?"

"Just now." Charlie stepped around the table and powered up a television screen mounted to the wall. "A dry cleaner backs up to the same alley as the *Gazette*. The owners had some problems with someone graffitiing and installed a video camera. When he went in to work this morning, he pulled his video to see if he caught anything."

"Did he?"

"We'll see." Charlie shrugged, hitting a button on the remote.

The blue screen lit up and Ryan groaned. They were staring at a dumpster. The position of the camera faced the back of the dry cleaner, the angle giving them only a foot or two of the actual alleyway. He kept watching. He saw the edge of a truck, presumably Cody's. A blur of clothing moved by and then there was nothing for several minutes until the truck moved.

"That wasn't helpful," Charlie said.

"Can you rewind it?"

Charlie did and Ryan watched it again,

trying to piece it together with what Cody had told them. Cody and Lauren had entered the *Gazette* through the emergency exit door. From the angle of the camera, it was impossible to see them entering or leaving. Yet the camera caught a flash of fabric moving by the dumpster.

"Do you see something?"

"This came to you electronically?" Ryan asked.

"Yeah, the owner said he splurged on the camera system."

Ryan quickly accessed the video and pulled up the enhancement software. After a few key strokes, he managed to figure out that whoever ran by the dumpster was wearing a large jacket or sweatshirt.

"What's that?" Charlie said.

"What?"

"Go back."

Ryan replayed the video.

"Stop. Right there." Charlie tapped the screen. "It's like a flash or something."

"Maybe some kind of reflective material?"

"If that was a runner, it'd make sense," Charlie said, leaning back. "The military started incorporating reflective material in their PT uniforms."

"So our arsonist might be a runner." Ryan rubbed the knot in the back of his neck.

The chair at the hospital was not comfortable, but he'd have spent as many nights on it as necessary until Vivian was released. "That eliminates half the county."

"Running is good for the soul." Charlie tapped him on the shoulder. "Gets the blood pumping."

"I've got enough of that in my life, thank you very much. And does anyone actually consider that if God had wanted humans to run long distances, he would've given us four legs?"

"You sound like Lane."

"She's smart." Ryan tossed a glance at his friend. "Course, that doesn't explain why she's with you."

Charlie grabbed at Ryan's head and rubbed his knuckles over it. "Take it back."

"Are you seriously giving me a noogie?" Ryan laughed, pulling himself free. He ran his fingers through his hair. "Aren't you a little old?"

"Probably, but Noah loves it. I taught him what a sternum rub was and now I have to wear my bulletproof vest at home."

"I bet Lane loves that."

The phone in the conference room rang and Charlie answered. A second later, he held it out to Ryan. "Agent Hannigan."

Ryan spun around in his chair and took

the phone. Charlie gave him a little salute and slipped out the door, closing it behind him.

"Agent Hannigan, I'm sorry I missed your call earlier."

"Don't worry about it. My fault. Had to answer another call."

"Yes, sir." Ryan hit the play button on the video again. "Did you find out anything on the Watcher?"

"We did, and that's why I'm calling."

Ryan hit pause. "I'm listening."

"We were able to identify several of the subjects in the videos you sent us — which, by the way, our IT guys are extremely anxious for you to join the team and teach them some of your programming tricks. They're wondering how you were able to breach a Bcrypt algorithm so quickly."

"It wasn't too hard." At least not for him, but he knew the significance of what he did even if it didn't lead him directly to the Watcher at first. "Sir, you were saying about the victims in the videos?"

"Right, we contacted several of the victims, and after assuring many of them that we were more interested in finding out who the Watcher was than some of their illicit and illegal behavior, they were more than willing to help us. The first video you sent us involved Mr. Northcott from NorthcottPharm. His company has a medication that is supposed to help with Parkinson's and Alzheimer's and is currently being reviewed by the Food and Drug Administration. His security team did an extensive investigation into how a bottle of that drug made it outside their facility. I didn't ask for details, but I got the impression that Mr. Northcott's security team is military grade and didn't have a problem finding out how their medication got into his daughter's hands."

Ryan thought back on that first video. The group of college students living it up in a hotel room. How careless they were about trying a drug — never mind one that hadn't even been approved safe for the market. Would Frankie be so reckless? A tug of guilt tore at his gut. How would he protect her when she left for college? Especially if she actually did decide to go out of state?

"It seems that the drug never made it out of the plant."

"What?" Ryan blinked, bringing his attention back to the conversation. "You saw the pill bottle in the video."

"I did, but it wasn't until Mr. Northcott brought the crackdown on his labs that it occurred to him that the labels hadn't even been printed for the medication yet."

"There was a label with a lab's name on it."

"Exactly," Agent Hannigan said. "Our technicians enhanced the image enough to compare it to another label from Northcott's facility. They're not the same. Someone printed a label and stuck it on a bottle containing who knows what to —"

"Set him up."

"How'd you know?"

Ryan filled in Agent Hannigan on his and Vivian's search for Lauren Holt, the events that led up to the fire the night before, and his interview with Lauren that made him suspect she and Harold had been set up as well.

"Unfortunately, that confirms my next point." There was a weight in Agent Hannigan's tone that made Ryan suspect the worst. "Once Mr. Northcott became aware of the setup, he assumed it was a competing pharmaceutical company trying to interfere with the FDA's investigation. All the money in that man's bank account couldn't get him any closer to the Watcher's identity than you could . . . initially. However, our financial crimes division began tracking Mr. Northcott's payment to the Watcher. It wasn't easy, but we finally managed to trace a secured IPN to a computer belonging to someone in your area."

Ryan's blood ran cold as the pieces of his case began to fall into place. Harold was targeted — no, set up — because he had a story. Had he figured out someone in Walton was running an extortion ring and was killed to keep him quiet? The Watcher would have had to have known about Harold's allergy to peanuts . . .

What about the break-in at the *Gazette*? There was no way Otis Jackson was the Watcher, yet Ryan couldn't rule him out because someone wanted access to Harold's laptop and used Otis.

He looked over to the now-empty office where he'd questioned Lauren Holt. She had been just as confused about meeting Harold as he had been about meeting her. Another pawn in the Watcher's game that led to the fire that almost killed Vivian.

"Sir, I need to go, but I appreciate your call and all the information. I'll talk with the sheriff and get back to you on what we can do on our end."

"Let us know how we can help, Frost."

"Yes, sir."

Ryan hung up the phone, grabbed his car keys from his desk, and headed to his squad car. His mind was moving as fast as his body. He had to get back to the hospital — back to Vivian. The Watcher was somewhere out there trying to destroy the evidence of his crimes and was not afraid to kill if necessary. She might be willing to risk her safety for a story — but he was not.

EIGHTEEN

Ryan watched Vivian help his mom clear the table, Dr. Murphy's proficiency on the grill evidenced by the stack of rib bones cleaned of their meat. Even Frankie had asked for seconds. *So the guy can cook.* Ryan's gaze switched to the man carrying his mom's cherry cobbler to the table. *And he has a clean record.* Ryan had zero shame for checking into the dentist's records — this was his mom, after all. He'd do the same for Frankie when the time came, which he prayed wouldn't be for a while.

"How's work going? Your mom says you've been busy."

"It's been a hard couple of weeks." Ryan glanced at Vivian again. Since learning the Watcher could be in Walton, he hadn't taken his eyes off of her. Of course, there were other reasons why that was impossible to do, but her safety was the main one.

He hadn't been able to keep her from ask-

x

271

ing questions about the case, despite the lingering cough she still carried from the fire. Ryan had been able to satisfy her inquisition regarding his interview with Lauren by admitting she already knew most of the information: Lauren wasn't aware of the video, didn't know who had taped them, and wouldn't talk about who Olivia's father was.

But Vivian had no intention of giving up on her quest. Her drive to find out how everyone was connected was almost as strong as his was to protect her. Thankfully, she didn't seem to mind his dropping in on her throughout the day with treats or lunch from the Way Station Café. He also had patrols running by her house throughout the night.

"Everyone ready for dessert?" his mom sang out. "Who wants vanilla ice cream with their cobbler?"

"Isn't that the best flavor?" Vivian said, giving Ryan a look.

"Why, yes it is."

Ryan's eyes passed between the two women as they shared a smile. "Nice. You've managed to brainwash my mom."

"She did no such thing." His mom handed him a plate. "I just know a smart girl when I see one."

"I prefer coffee-flavored ice cream." Dr. Murphy whispered loud enough that Ryan's mom pulled back the bowl she had been offering him.

"Excuse me?"

"It's the best of both worlds. Coffee and ice cream. In one bowl." Dr. Murphy looked around the room for support. "Anyone?"

"I can't argue with that," Ryan said.

Vivian eyed him. "Is this boys against girls? Because we both know how that ended the last time."

"I still have the bruises." Ryan rubbed his shoulder. "Frankie, you better get in here before I eat all the cobbler."

"Speaking of coffee —"

"I'll get it, honey." Dr. Murphy stood and pulled out a chair for Ryan's mom. "The meal was delicious." His mom smiled, placing her hand on his before Dr. Murphy lifted it to his lips for a quick a kiss.

Ryan caught Vivian glancing at him. Before arriving for dinner, she'd asked him what he thought about Dr. Murphy, and he didn't have an answer because he didn't know the guy. But in the course of one meal, Ryan had begun to see that Frankie was right. The man did care for their mom, and she was happy. Happier than he'd seen her . . . well, since ever.

Frankie came around the corner and plopped in her chair.

"You don't have to look so depressed, Frankie." Ryan handed her a bowl. "I didn't eat all of the cobbler."

"What?" She looked up like she hadn't realized there was anyone in the room but her. "Oh, yeah. Thanks."

"What's wrong, Frannie?" Ryan's mom asked.

"Bethany's not coming over because she has another *hot* date."

Ryan looked at his mom, who raised her eyebrows with an I-don't-know look. He glanced back at his sister. Frankie had inherited the beauty genes early on. Ryan suffered many a black eye from guys he caught saying inappropriate things about her. There had been no shortage of boys knocking on the door when their mom had finally allowed her to date — and it was only going to get worse. Over the last year, Frankie had grown into more of a knockout.

"I just don't get it," Frankie said around a bite of cobbler. "No boy is worth giving up your whole life for. I don't care how cute he is."

"Sometimes, for the right person" — Vivian's gaze flickered to Ryan for several seconds — "changing your life can be worth it."

Ryan's pulse picked up. He hadn't mentioned anything to Vivian about his discussion with Agent Hannigan. The agent really wanted Ryan in DC where he'd be able to use his skills across several divisions, but just having access to Ryan within the bureau made a position in their Atlanta office an easy concession.

He cleared his throat, drawing everyone's attention. *Here goes nothing.* "Y'all know I've been approached by several agencies about employment that could take me away from Walton." Ryan's mom set down her fork and a flicker of insecurity pierced his nerve, but a quick glance at Vivian's knowing smile encouraged him to keep going. "I've reached out to the FBI and they're considering me for a position in Atlanta."

"Ryan!" His mother pushed out of her seat and rounded the table, bumping into Frankie's arm.

"Heyyy." Frankie frowned at the spoonful of ice cream now sitting in her lap.

"Sorry, hon." Ryan's mom grabbed his face in her hands and kissed it. "I'm so proud of you, Ryan. This is amazing news. Congratulations."

"You're not worried?" His cheeks burned

knowing Vivian was witnessing his mother's unrestrained affection. "I won't be here."

"Honey, you'll be exactly where you need to be. Fighting crime. Saving the world."

"He's not Superman, Mom," Frankie said. Leave it to his sister to keep his ego in check.

"He's more like Captain America, actually," Vivian said.

"Oh, you're right," his mom agreed, pressing another round of kisses across his forehead. "My Captain America."

Frankie faked a gagging noise, rolling her eyes. "Wait." She looked at Vivian and then back to Ryan. "If you guys keep dating, then it really is like Ryan's Superman and you're his Lucy Lane or whatever. You know, because you're a reporter."

"Lois Lane," Ryan and Vivian said at the same time.

"Ew, you guys really are perfect for each other." Frankie scrunched her nose, looking around the table. "I'm, like, the only person at this table who doesn't have a make-out partner."

"Francis!"

Their mother gasped, but there was a lift at the edge of her lips to indicate she wasn't entirely embarrassed by Frankie's suggestion. And Ryan hadn't missed the quick peek Dr. Murphy gave his mom, though at least he had the decency to blush.

"I'm just saying . . ." Frankie finished her cobbler.

"And I'm just saying maybe it's time we call it a night." Ryan lifted his brows at Vivian and she nodded. "I'll clean up."

"No, no." His mom shook her head. "I'll take care of it. Actually, Frannie can do it so the doctor and I can go make out."

"Ew, Mom!" Frankie made a face that matched the one Ryan was sure he was making.

"I'm just saying," his mom mocked before turning her attention to Vivian. "It was so nice meeting you tonight. I hope our family's quirkiness doesn't scare you from coming back."

"I would love to," Vivian said. "It was nice meeting you as well, Dr. Murphy."

"Ryan." Frankie scooted her chair back. "Before you take Vivian home, can I talk to her for a second?"

"Sure?"

Frankie grabbed Vivian's hand and dragged her down the hall toward her bedroom.

"What's that all about?"

"Who knows?" His mom shrugged, collecting Ryan's plate.

"Honey, I'll start the dishes." Dr. Murphy stood and turned toward Ryan. "Congratulations, Ryan. Your mom never stops talking about how proud she is of you."

Dr. Murphy stretched out his hand and Ryan shook it, feeling as though a message was being passed through the gesture, assuring him that he would make sure Frankie and his mom were okay in Ryan's absence.

When Dr. Murphy stepped away and into the kitchen, Ryan's mom smiled at him. "Thank you for coming tonight and getting to know him. And for bringing Vivian. She's a wonderful young lady."

"She is that."

Ryan's mom hugged him and whispered, "She's more than that, and I couldn't be prouder."

"And you've tried talking to Bethany?" Vivian said, after listening to Frannie lament over her friend's sudden absence from her life. "Told her you miss her?"

"Yes, but she shuts down." Frannie hugged a well-loved stuffed bunny to her stomach. "She gets mad at me and tells me to leave her alone."

"Sometimes boys come between best friends, but if your friendship with Bethany is strong enough, she'll come around."

"That's just it. I don't know if she will."

Vivian looked around Frannie's room. The walls were pale pink, and the white bed frame matched the dresser covered in books. Clothes and shoes spilled out of the closet. Her apron from the Way Station Café hung on a chair. Her bedroom wasn't much different from Vivian's own childhood room, except where Frannie had dozens of posters of boy bands tacked to her walls Vivian had exotic images of the Blue Mosque in Turkey, the Giza Pyramids in Egypt, or the smudged faces of brave refugees in Sudan.

Above Frannie's desk was a corkboard filled with photographs of her and Bethany. "You see those pictures?"

Frannie looked over to where Vivian was pointing. "Yeah."

"Those pictures are proof that your friendship with Bethany is way too strong for some boy to come between the two of you. Give Bethany some time to sort out her feelings. New love can be a powerful thing."

Frannie's lips pressed into a thin line.

"What is it?"

Big blue eyes filled with emotion stared up at her. "If it was love . . . with just one guy, maybe I could understand it."

"What do you mean *just one guy*?"

"I don't know." Frannie's eyes flickered to

279

her closed bedroom door. "I don't want to get her in trouble."

"Why don't you explain it to me and we can figure out if Bethany's involved in something that could get her in trouble."

Frannie licked her lips and began playing with her stuffed bunny's ear. "Bethany's parents are super strict. Her dad's the pastor at Community Christian Church and she's not allowed to date." Vivian nodded, remembering those days. "Anyway, Anderson College isn't that far from campus and we go to their games or whatever, no big deal. Except Bethany tells me this guy from Anderson asked her out."

Uh-oh. Vivian's gut clenched. She knew *those* days as well.

"I was kinda excited for her but also kinda nervous. Bethany said it was cool because it wasn't like she was going to be all alone with the guy. He was taking her to a party at Tybee Island and some of our friends from school would be there." Frannie rubbed the rabbit's ear between her fingers, which, based on the worn fur, must've been a habit. "I'd heard about the party and figured it was okay."

"But it wasn't?"

"I expected Bethany to tell me all about it the next day at work, but she called in sick."

"Did she ever tell you about the party?"

Frannie lifted her shoulders. "Some. She said it was fun, but the guy who took her there ended up ditching her. But she met another guy . . . and then she stopped talking to me about it."

"Well, maybe she was embarrassed that the first guy ditched her?"

"Maybe." Frannie chewed on her bottom lip. "But then these guys would stop by work when Bethany actually came in and they would tease her —"

"What kind of teasing?"

"Just say weird stuff about how good she looks and if she was working all the time." Frannie shook her head. "Bethany just ignored them and told me they were some people from the party in Tybee, but some of them looked a little old for college."

The clenching in Vivian's gut was growing tighter and tighter the more Frannie explained. How many times had she read a story or seen a news report about young girls being taken advantage of at parties? Too often the girls allowed their shame to keep them victimized because they somehow felt responsible . . . but maybe she was jumping to conclusions.

"And Bethany hasn't said anything else?"

"Not really." Frannie set her bunny aside.

"I've tried asking her questions like a reporter would — you know, open-ended — hoping she'll tell me something about why she's mad at me or why she doesn't want to hang out anymore."

Vivian lifted the streak of purple hair from Frannie's shoulder and let it slide through her fingers. "Sometimes when we get older we get confused about what we want in life. It's possible Bethany's just trying to figure out her life, and maybe she feels guilty about disobeying her parents and going on a date in the first place. Sometimes people who are guilty of something try to hide themselves because, well, maybe because they're afraid others will see that guilt and make them feel worse."

Frannie tilted her head to the side. "I never thought about that."

"My opinion, if you want it —" Frannie nodded. "My opinion is to keep being there for Bethany so that when she's ready to talk, you'll be the first one she turns to the way best friends always do."

"Thanks, Vivian."

Vivian went to the door, pausing to look at the girl whose concern for her best friend still hung in the sadness at the corners of her eyes. "And promise me you'll put the investigative reporting on hold. I don't think your brother can handle another reporter in his life right now." Vivian winked and Frannie giggled.

"Care to share what that was about?" Ryan said as he climbed into his Jeep.

Vivian fastened her seat belt. Frannie hadn't specifically told her not to tell Ryan, but telling him felt like she was betraying Frannie's trust. "Can I say girl talk and you'll let it go?"

"Definitely." Ryan pulled out of his mom's driveway. "Unless it involves Frannie dating . . . wait, maybe I don't want to know. I'm not sure I can handle any more."

"You have nothing to worry about there."

"Good."

Vivian settled into the drive. "Dinner was really nice tonight. Dr. Murphy seems like a good guy."

"I don't totally hate him."

"You didn't tell me you were considering a job in Atlanta."

Ryan's hand found hers in the darkness. "I wasn't sure how to bring it up with my mom, but it felt right having you there."

"I told you there was nothing to worry about." She squeezed his hand. "I think you could've told them you're moving to Alaska and they would still be proud."

"Alaska?" Ryan glanced at her. "Let's not get crazy, DeMarco."

"I'm just saying, with your family's support, you can do and be anything you want." Vivian wondered if Ryan understood how precious a gift that was. "They'll always be here for you."

"And what about you?"

"I'm behind you 100 percent."

"I appreciate that," Ryan said as he pulled in front of Vivian's house. "What I'm asking is, what do you think about me moving to Atlanta?"

Vivian bit the inside of her lip. "If that's where you want to be —"

"I want to be close to you." His thumb traced the back of her hand. "That's the only reason I'm considering Atlanta at all."

A storm of butterflies let loose in her stomach. "Really? What about DC?"

His blue eyes locked on her. "Are you going to be in DC?"

Vivian let the question linger between them. She wasn't planning to be in DC . . . but could she be? As much as her affection for Walton had grown, the affection she was feeling for Ryan was evolving into something that made her want to be where he was. "I want you to be where you'll be happy."

"I'm happy." Ryan lifted her hand to his

lips and kissed her knuckles. "Just don't ask me to spill any classified secrets. Those pretty little eyes won't get you any headlines from me."

She laughed. "Speaking of headlines, we need to talk about Harold's case. It's been two weeks since the fire and there's not a single new lead? Are you sure you can't force Lauren to tell you anything more?"

Ryan blew out a breath. "You realize you were almost killed in a fire? Maybe it's a good thing our case has stalled. I don't want you pushing yourself too hard."

She eyed him. "Is that why you've been spying on me?"

"I'm not spying on you."

"You stop by my house at least twice a day, and I haven't had to cook dinner for myself since I left the hospital."

"Am I bothering you?"

The hurt in his voice was unmistakable and Vivian ran her hand over his cheek. "Not at all, but I'm fine and ready to get back to work."

"There are other things we can work on, you know?" Ryan said, pulling into her driveway and parking.

"Like what?"

"Hmm, I don't know. Maybe this." He

kissed her fingers, then the inside of her wrist.

Vivian's heart thundered. "Th-this isn't talking."

"Semantics."

Vivian reared back. "Do you even know what that word means?"

"Ever hear of body language?"

"You're too smart for your own good."

"But I'm good." Beneath the glow of the street lamp, Vivian could make out Ryan wiggling his eyebrows.

"Yes, Captain America." She kissed his lips. "You are very good."

NINETEEN

It was disturbing. That was the only way Ryan could describe the way it felt to have the eyes of so many victims staring back at him. Agent Hannigan had emailed him a complete list of the victims' names. Each name was now attached to a photo taped against the whiteboard that he, Charlie, and Sheriff Huggins were now studying, trying to figure out the connection between the Watcher's victims.

"Harold is the only connection I see to Walton," Sheriff Huggins said. He leaned back in his chair, tucking his thumbs into his gun belt. "Are we sure the Watcher lives in this area?"

"We've still been unable to get an exact location" — Agent Hannigan's voice echoed from the speakerphone at the center of the table — "but the links we've been able to track keep leading our techs to an IPN being used within a fifty-mile radius of Walton."

"It doesn't make sense." Charlie went to the whiteboard. "NorthcottPharm is out of Ohio. The Central Kansas State coach is, well, from Kansas. If the Watcher is setting these guys up, how is he doing it? Traveling?"

Ryan folded his arms across his chest. Charlie was right — it didn't make sense. "We need to figure out how the Watcher picks his victims."

"They're all wealthy?" Charlie said. "Powerful?"

"Not all of them," Agent Hannigan said. "We have one victim . . . a, uh . . ." The sound of papers shuffling came through the speaker. "Ah, here it is. Jaxson Middleton, a student at Everson University in Arizona. The Watcher threatened to release a video of him and his underage girlfriend if the kid didn't get caught doping up."

Charlie frowned at Ryan. "The Watcher *wanted* the kid to get caught?"

"Yes. Middleton was the school's star forward and had already been eyed by the NBA as an early draft pick, but the kid wanted to play for the college. When the Watcher sent the email, Middleton went to the police and confessed. The parents of the girl never pressed charges, but social media lit up a firestorm, calling him a rapist and ending any chance he had of playing on the professional level."

"And what about the girlfriend?" Sheriff Huggins asked.

"They're married with a little girl."

Ryan thought about Olivia, Lauren's baby. Besides money, what had the Watcher hoped to gain from Harold and Lauren? "Their reputations."

Charlie and Sheriff Huggins looked over at him.

"Jaxson Middleton didn't have any money to give the Watcher, but he did have something that could be used against him — his reputation. He had something to lose. Northcott could lose their FDA approval. The coach from Kansas could lose his job."

"What about Harold?" Sheriff Huggins's blue eyes studied Ryan. "I've known that man my whole life, and there's not a soul in Walton who'd believe he'd commit any sin with that young lady."

"I agree." Ryan stared at the lineup of victims. "But he had money, and what if Lauren was the one with something to lose? She admitted Harold had been trying to help her, but she still won't admit with what . . ."

"You have an idea?"

Ryan nodded at Charlie. "When I was interviewing Lauren, one topic sent her guard up immediately and Vivian was the one who caught on to it first. Olivia's dad. Maybe the Watcher knows who Olivia's father is and is blackmailing Lauren. Harold had money and could afford to pay off the Watcher."

Sheriff Huggins scratched his chin. "It's a possibility."

"We still don't know how the Watcher is finding his victims." Charlie pulled out a chair and sat. "If we figure that out, maybe we could lure him out of his hole."

Ryan dropped in his chair and slid his computer closer. He typed furiously until the flat screen inside the conference room was filled with the images of the victims. Hundreds of images continued to pop up like a slideshow. One image would appear and then another and another until there were layers of photos with the victims staring back at them.

"Hello?" Agent Hannigan's voice called out.

"Oh, sorry." Ryan sprang forward in his chair, his fingers moving across the keyboard until he finally hit send. "You should be seeing the same thing we are now."

"Why am I looking at Facebook? Or is that Snapchat?" Hannigan asked.

"It's social media. All of it. Every one of these photos is public, which means I didn't need to be friends with any of these people to see them. I just Googled. What if the Watcher is doing the same thing? Look at these photos. You can see where these people live. Where they vacation, eat out, buy clothes. These photos tell you everything."

"Like exactly where to find them so you can set them up," Charlie said, staring at the screen. "An open invitation."

"So how do we find him?" Sheriff Huggins's blue eyes held the glint of a man ready to go to war. Ryan had seen it before when Sydney Donovan was killed. There would be no resting until they caught the Watcher.

"Char— sorry, Deputy Lynch already made the suggestion, and I think it's the right one." Ryan looked from Sheriff Huggins to Charlie. "We lure him."

"How do we do that?" Agent Hannigan said. "Even if one of his victims comes forward, our team still hasn't been able to break through his firewalls completely — unless you've created another program, Frost."

291

Ryan shook his head. "I haven't, sir, but what if we use the same tactic he does? We can find someone who has money, powerful . . . someone with something to lose."

"Most of these people were engaging in something illegal or morally wrong." Charlie looked over the victims' photos. "You know someone who's got a secret they don't mind getting out?"

"No." Ryan rolled his chair toward the back of the room and picked up a copy of the *Gazette.* "But with the right characters, maybe we can create a story worth exploiting."

He held up the newspaper so Sheriff Huggins and Charlie could see the smiling faces of Congressman Daniel Atkins and his wife, Trisha, under the headline: "Congressman Honored, Shelters Saved."

"Now, wait a minute." Sheriff Huggins shifted. "We're not going to start spreading rumors about anyone —"

"Wait." Ryan twisted the paper around, taking in the photo. His pulse spiked. "Sequins." He jumped out of his chair and ran out of the room to his desk where the images of the fire were sitting in a file. He spread them out.

"What in tarnation are you doing, Frost?" Sheriff Huggins said as he stormed over.

"You've got to stop living in that brain of yours and leaving the rest of us behind."

Charlie joined them. "I told Agent Hannigan we'd call him back."

Ryan cringed. He hadn't meant to just run out and would need to apologize to the FBI agent, but right now he needed — "This." He placed the still shot taken from the video outside the alleyway the night of the fire next to the newspaper. "That flash we couldn't figure out." He looked at Charlie. "It's sequins. Look."

Charlie lifted the photo, squinting as his eyes moved between the paper and the photo. "So they're sequins. What does that mean?"

"Not just any sequins. Those are rose gold. Victoria Rose to be exact." Ryan looked down at the paper. There she was — Trisha Atkins standing next to her husband, arm in motion as she waved, wearing the Victoria Rose sweatshirt Vivian had found inside her closet. "Sir, I think we just figured out who the Watcher is."

Vivian pressed the emerald sequin and chiffon gown against her body as she stood in front of the mirror. It was her first major splurge since leaving Washington, DC, and cost almost as much as her car payment, but it would be worth it. She imagined Ryan's face when he saw her.

"He doesn't stand a chance." Pecca popped her head around Vivian's shoulder. "It's beautiful."

"You think so?"

"Girl, you're going to slay him in that dress." Pecca backed away and leaned on the doorframe, tossing a grape in her mouth. "Have you told him about the gala?"

"Not yet," Vivian said, hanging the dress back on the hanger. "I didn't think I was going to be able to bring a guest since it's more of a working event."

"I want a job where I get to wear pretty dresses like that."

"I'd take wearing scrubs over a tight-fitting gown any day of the week. Besides, I think your work is a bit more beneficial to the community." Vivian didn't understand it, but since the night of the fire, she'd been feeling discontentment growing regarding her job. Maybe it was working out of her home while the *Gazette*'s office was getting cleaned. Or maybe it was the fact that every night since, Ryan would come over and they'd cook dinner together, watch an episode of *Arrow,* and then argue over the merits of law enforcement and superhero abilities, which somehow led to kissing.

Ryan was so different from other guys. Vivian could walk into a bar in DC and get hit on by men who thought a single conversation warranted a sleepover where sleep wasn't the main goal. Ryan was . . . a gentleman.

"Hello, Earth to Vivi." Pecca waved her hand in front of Vivian's eyes. "You in there, sweetie pie?"

"Sorry." Vivian blushed, hoping Pecca wouldn't ask what had caused her to daydream. "How's Maceo?"

"Good. He's having a playdate with Noah at Lane's so I can get some cleaning done."

Vivian raised her eyebrows. "This is cleaning?"

"I needed a break." Her hip jutted to the side and she put a hand on it. "Besides, you called me."

Vivian eyed the dress. She couldn't help it. After she bought it, she had to show or tell someone and Pecca was the first person to come to mind. How had Pecca become Vivian's go-to friend? Or friend, for that matter? Vivian had come to Walton with zero pretense of making any connections and yet here she was. Calling Pecca over last minute so they could gush about the dress she'd bought to wow a man she'd had no intention of dating in a town she'd never wanted to return to . . .

"Okay, I'm beginning to think you might need to see a doctor."

"Yikes. Sorry." Vivian moved toward the door. "How about some popcorn and Thor?"

"How about some ice cream and a Hallmark movie?" Pecca said, walking down the hall. "Though I love me a Hemsworth, I'm a little tired of the perfection. I need me a man with a flaw and a woman who can make it better with a kiss."

Vivian laughed. "That is a surprisingly accurate description of those movies."

Pecca plopped down on the couch and grabbed the remote control. "It seems the Walton pool of handsome and eligible bachelors at the sheriff's station has been depleted."

Vivian grabbed some ice cream and two spoons from the kitchen and walked into the living room. "What about the fire department or EMTs? I heard that Troy guy is a real catch."

"Yeah, catch and release," Pecca deadpanned.

Vivian's cell phone rang. "Drat."

"Let it go to voicemail."

"What if it's urgent?"

"You expecting a call from boy genius?"

"Maybe?" Vivian gave her friend a look.

"Answer it. Who am I, in all my single-ness, to stand in the way of true love?"

Vivian moved around the couch and handed Pecca a spoon. Her cell phone went silent. "Ryan's working tonight and told me he would call tomorrow. It's probably a tele-marketer."

Pecca tapped her spoon against Vivian's and winked. Vivian settled into the couch as a panoramic view of a castle filled the screen under the scrolled movie title *Her Royal Ever After.*

Vivian's cell phone rang again.

"Persistent telemarketer," Pecca said, not taking her eyes off the movie.

"They don't usually call back, do they?" Vivian eyed her phone, a thought bringing her to her feet. What if it was Ryan and it was about the case?

"What's wrong?"

"Just checking to see who it is." Vivian picked up her phone and frowned. It was a local number, but one she didn't recognize. "Hello?"

"Vivian." Vivian recognized Frannie's voice, but it was the fear she heard in it that punched the air from Vivian's chest. *Ryan.*

"Frannie, what's wrong?" Her own fear was palpable enough to bring Pecca off the couch, concern radiating in her dark brown eyes.

"It's Bethany. I followed her and I think she's in trouble. There's this guy and I don't know what to do and I didn't want to call Ryan in case she might get in trouble, but Vivian, I'm scared and I don't know what to do."

It took Vivian a long second to make sense of the run-on words filling her ear. "Frannie, I need you to slow down. Where are you?"

"Vivian, you need to get here. I'm scared."

"Okay, honey." Vivian motioned to Pecca to find a pen. "Tell me where you are."

"I don't know. I just followed Bethany —"

"Bethany's with you?"

Pecca returned with a pen and a torn piece of paper. "What's going on?" she whispered.

Vivian shrugged. "Frannie?"

"I'm here," she whispered. "I'm going to send you a pin of my location from my phone so you can find me. When can you get here?"

"Frannie, tell me what's going on."

"It's Bethany. I know you told me not to do anything, but I just couldn't. She came into work today and a short time later got a text message from someone, then said she had to leave because she wasn't feeling well.

But I knew she was lying, because when she first came in, she was like the old Bethany. I asked her why she was lying and she just started crying. Ms. Lane told her she could leave early, and after she left I asked if I could go early too and check on her. Lane said I could since it was slow. I followed her, Vivian. I followed her to a hotel."

"What hotel?"

"I don't know." Frannie's voice was close to a cry and it churned Vivian's gut. "It doesn't really have a name that I can see. Vivian, Bethany's inside a room and there's this guy standing by the door. I'm scared."

"Are you somewhere safe, Frannie?"

"I'm hiding in my car. I don't think they can see me."

They? "I thought you said there was only one guy?"

"He's the only one I can see outside, but there were two more, I think. One's inside the hotel room with Bethany. What do you think's happening?"

Vivian didn't want to think about it or admit what horrid thoughts were running through her mind. "Do not move from your car, do you hear me? I want you to stay right where you are. Keep your phone nearby and on silent in case I need to call you back."

"Vivian, please don't call Ryan. He's going to get so mad at me. And Bethany, I don't want her to get in trouble."

Everything inside Vivian told her not to make a promise she couldn't keep. "I won't." At least she wouldn't until she got there and figured out what was happening. "Hang tight. I'm on my way."

Vivian hung up the phone and quickly explained to Pecca the conversation she just had with Frannie.

"You're going to call Ryan, right?"

"I'm going to see what's going on and then, yes, I'll call Ryan if it's necessary."

"Necessary?" Pecca's brown eyes grew round. "That conversation says it's very, very necessary."

"I'm not disagreeing, but what if Bethany's . . ." Vivian couldn't think of an explanation that would justify not calling Ryan right that second. "I've gotta go."

Vivian grabbed her wallet and keys and then raced out of the house as Pecca offered to pray. *Pray.* In the last several weeks, Vivian had thought more about God than she had in the fifteen years since her dad walked out of her life.

Would God listen tonight? Vivian had no idea what Frannie had gotten herself into. Or Bethany. Her imagination ran through every ugly scenario, leading her to two conclusions. She needed to call Ryan and she hoped this time, when she prayed, God would listen.

TWENTY

There was nothing covert about this approach. Ryan climbed the porch steps up to Congressman Daniel Atkins's home with Sheriff Huggins beside him. While there would be no SWAT team breach of the location, they still had several officers approaching the back of the house just in case.

Back at the office, Ryan had laid out the facts as he saw them: the video of Lauren and Harold, Lauren's refusal to name Olivia's father, the connection between Lauren and Congressman Atkins, and her sudden exit from teaching. A picture was beginning to appear and he hated that the idea came to him after learning about Vivian's father. If Russell Bradley could keep a second family in the shadows, why couldn't Congressman Atkins?

It had taken some work to convince the sheriff to ask Judge Sullivan for a warrant to verify that the rose-gold sequins in the video from the night of the fire matched the ones on the Victoria Rose hoodie he and Vivian found in Trisha Atkins's closet.

Sweat beaded at the back of his neck even though the nighttime temperature had dropped to a balmy eighty-five. Ryan rang the doorbell, recounting the last time he was there with Vivian. It had been playful and, yes, a little sneaky, but he'd had no idea then that he would be back to arrest the Watcher.

His nerves thrummed. The pieces of his case were finally coming together and he was on the cusp of making his first major arrest, putting away the person responsible for not only extorting dozens of people for money but also Harold's death and the fire that could've taken Vivian's life as well.

Ryan's cell phone buzzed in his pocket. He slipped it out just enough to see Vivian's name on the phone's screen. The woman had impeccable timing — like she had some sixth sense he was working the case. A thread of guilt tightened around his chest. Vivian would've wanted to be there for this, but given what the Watcher was capable of, he couldn't risk it. He'd call her after so she could have first access to the story and make her headline, securing her job in Atlanta — where they could be together.

"Hello?"

Letting the phone slip back into his pocket, his hand slid a fraction of an inch toward his weapon when Trisha Atkins answered the door. "Mrs. Atkins, I'm Deputy Frost. This is —"

"I know who Sheriff Huggins is." She smiled, but it didn't match the flicker of fear that passed through her eyes. "How are you, Sheriff?"

"I'm well, ma'am." Sheriff Huggins tipped his wide-brimmed hat. "Is Congressman Atkins here?"

"He is." She backed away. "We're just packing for a last-minute trip. You know, this year has been so crazy and now we're moving. Well, anyway, he's here. Would you like me to call for him?"

"If you don't mind, ma'am, we'd like to speak to both of you," Ryan said, sliding a look to Sheriff Huggins. *A last-minute trip?* "Shouldn't take long."

"Well, I, uh . . ." She smoothed her bright red hair back behind her ear. "I guess that'll be fine." She opened the screen door. "Come on in."

The house looked exactly the way it had on the day of the open house. Again, Ryan's gut twisted with guilt. He hadn't known Vivian for long, but he knew she wasn't going to be happy about being kept out of the loop no matter how good his reasons were. Sometimes her drive for a headline blinded her to the danger she put herself in. He shuddered to imagine what kind of trouble she got into in DC.

Trisha Atkins led them into the large family room with floor-to-ceiling windows overlooking the Ogeechee River. A large deck matched the width of the expansive home, and Ryan could imagine coming home from work to enjoy a meal with Vivian and that view.

"If you'll give me one minute, I'll just run up and get him." She paused at the staircase. "Would y'all like something to drink? Cookies?"

"We're fine, ma'am," Ryan said. He looked to Sheriff Huggins, who also gave a nod and then used his radio to give the other officers their status before taking a seat in a leather wingback chair.

Trisha jogged up the steps and Ryan could hear the muffled murmuring of a conversation. Was she scared? Did she know why they were here?

A moment later, Trisha and her husband, Congressman Daniel Atkins, joined them.

"Sheriff Huggins and Deputy . . ." He looked at Ryan.

"Frost, Ryan Frost, Congressman."

"Aw, call me Daniel, son." He shook Ryan's hand. "We're all family here in Walton, right?"

There was a slickness to the man's tone Ryan didn't care for and it only solidified his suspicion.

"Please, sit." Daniel gestured to the wingback chair next to Sheriff Huggins. He took a seat on the couch and Trisha sat next to him. "I'm sorry I didn't answer the door. Trisha and I were just packing for a quick trip to the beach."

"Which one?" Tybee Island was only forty minutes away but not really where he could imagine the congressman and his wife escaping to. Hilton Head and St. Simons weren't very far and much more fitting to their lifestyle.

"Mexico." Daniel turned to his wife. "Which beach, honey?"

Trisha's eyes darted between the three of them. "Uh, Cabo San Lucas."

"That's right." He placed his hand on Trisha's knee. "We love that place. Almost bought a house there, didn't we, honey?" Trisha gave a tight nod. "So, what can we do for you tonight? I've already talked with my security team about the gala and I think everything is covered."

"We're not here about the gala, Congressman," Ryan said. "We're here to ask you and your wife some questions about Lauren Holt."

The air in the room was sucked out like a vacuum, leaving the congressman and his wife looking desperate for oxygen. A minute passed before Daniel seemed to regain a bit of his breath. His eyes bounced between Ryan and Sheriff Huggins.

"Lauren Holt. I think I remember her. She's a teacher at Anderson. Political science, if I recall."

"*Was* a teacher. Quit two years ago."

"Oh." Daniel frowned. "I didn't realize she left. That's too bad."

Ryan's cell phone vibrated in his pocket. "Did you know she had a little girl?"

Daniel's Adam's apple moved when he swallowed, almost in sync with the lines growing tight at the corners of Trisha's eyes. They knew about Olivia.

"Why would you ask my husband if he knew about —"

"Honey." Daniel's hand found his wife's knee again, silencing her. "It's fine." A message was shared between them that made Trisha slump her shoulders before Daniel's attention returned to Ryan. "It happened one time."

Ryan slid a sideways glance at Sheriff Huggins. "What did?"

"Danny." Trisha's voice held a pleading tone.

"I want you to know I have never done that before. It was a slip. I'd been drinking and working late." Daniel's voice shook. "I confessed to Trisha immediately, and then a month later Lauren shows up at my office and tells me she's pregnant."

Daniel Atkins was Olivia's father. The confession sounded genuine but also made the reason Ryan was there all the more perplexing. Ryan turned to Trisha. "So you knew about the affair —"

"It wasn't an affair. It was a one-time thing," Daniel said. "It never happened again."

Trisha's gaze remained pinned to the ground. Either she didn't believe her husband or she was hiding something.

"Mrs. Atkins, did you attend the Anderson College basketball championship game?"

A few silent seconds ticked off before Daniel Atkins answered. "Yes, we were both there that night, but Trisha didn't feel well and went home a little early."

Even though Trisha's focus was on the thick carpet in front of her, Ryan noticed her wince at her husband's words. When she looked up, the color had drained from her face.

"Mrs. Atkins, is there something you want to tell us?"

And like a dam bulging at the seams, Trisha's green eyes filled to the brim. She blinked and a cascade of tears streamed down her cheeks.

"Trisha, honey, what's going on?" Daniel pivoted to face his wife, his arm protectively on her shoulder. "What's the matter, darling?"

"I-I'm so sorry, Danny." The words were almost inaudible. "I didn't mean to. I was scared and I didn't know what to do. I didn't mean it. I promise." Those last statements came out on desperate breaths. Her green eyes turned on Ryan. "It was an accident, I swear. I didn't mean it."

"Honey, calm down." The congressman looked between Ryan and Sheriff Huggins. "What's going on?"

"Trisha, if you'd like to have your attorney present" — Sheriff Huggins's voice was grim — "you may make that call now. Anything you say can be used against you —"

"I j-just want it to g-go away," Trisha said through a sob. "I'm so sorry, Danny. I was trying to protect you — us."

Ryan's pulse picked up. "What happened, Mrs. Atkins?"

"He was here, the reporter. Asking for Danny. Then I overheard him make a call to Lauren." Trisha wrung her hands, tears streaking down her face. "I panicked."

"Is that when you sent the email to Harold?"

Trisha's teary gaze narrowed on Ryan. "What email?"

"The one of Harold and Lauren. Demanding money." Dread corded through Ryan's gut. "From the Watcher?"

"I-I don't know what you're talking about, Deputy." Trisha wiped the mascara and tearstains beneath her eyes. "I thought you were here because of the peanut oil."

Why wasn't Ryan answering? Vivian steered her car into a dingy parking lot littered with broken glass and trash on the outskirts of Walton. When Frannie said *hotel,* she was being generous — very generous. The motel, if she could even call it that, more closely resembled the hacker motel from an Alfred Hitchcock movie. Half of the windows in the V-shaped, single-story building were boarded up. The pool might've once been an amenity, but now with its muddy water, cracked tile, and overgrown weeds, it looked more like a breeding hole of bacteria and disease. A chill skittered across her skin as she thought about Bethany inside one of the dimly lit rooms.

"Ryan, it's Vivian. Please call me as soon as you get this message. It's an emergency."

Vivian ended the call and dropped her phone on the passenger seat. She searched for Frannie's Honda. A row of dumpsters at the back of the parking lot was overflowing with stained mattresses, shredded chair cushions, and tube television sets that told Vivian this place was old.

Parked in the corner behind the rubbish was a silver Honda. Vivian pulled up next to it, and before she could turn off the engine, Frannie jumped out of her car, yanked open Vivian's passenger's-side door, and slid in.

"Thank you so much for coming." Frannie's voice trembled as she hugged Vivian tightly. "I didn't know who else to call."

"Are you sure Bethany's inside there?"

"Mm-hmm." Frannie nodded. "I went to her house to check on her and saw her walking down the street, so I followed her. At the corner she got into that car."

Frannie pointed out a dark-colored sedan parked in front of one of the rooms with light barely peeking beneath the edges of a curtain. And just as Frannie had said, a silhouette of a person sat near the door, only the orange glow of a cigarette to indicate a face was hidden in the darkness.

"It felt like I was being a reporter. You know, trying to get to the truth. But when we got here" — Frannie's scared gaze landed on the motel — "I freaked out. What are we going to do?"

"We're going to call the police." Vivian picked up her phone, but Frannie grabbed her hand.

"No, please. I don't want Bethany to get into trouble."

"Frannie, if Bethany's in that dump, she's already in trouble." Vivian placed her free hand over Frannie's. "What's your gut tell you?"

"What?"

"When I'm running a lead on a story, I have to listen to my gut. If it tells me to keep pushing for answers, I do. When it tells me to look in this direction or that, I go with it. When it tells me there's trouble, and I'm talking the kind that could hurt someone I care about . . . I have to decide if it's worth it."

Vivian couldn't believe what she was saying. It wasn't that long ago when gut instinct or not, she chased a story. Physical injury wasn't common but threats were, and Vivian knew the difference between a warning given in the heat of the moment and a warning that promised imminent danger if she kept pushing. A year ago she would've crouched outside that hotel room trying to figure out what was happening, but something had changed. With Frannie next to her, Vivian knew whatever was taking place inside that room with Bethany didn't require a reporter.

It required the police.

"Call Ryan."

Frannie released Vivian's hand, and she dialed Ryan's number again, praying he would answer this time. She groaned when it went to voicemail again. What could he possibly be working on that he wouldn't answer any of the ten calls she had placed in the last twenty minutes? An unsettling feeling tugged at her gut. Was Ryan working on the Watcher case? Without her? No. Ryan wasn't like that. He knew how important Harold's story was for her career — for her.

Vivian and Frannie jolted when a scream ripped through the night. The man once hiding in the shadow near the room stood.

"What's happening?" Frannie whimpered.

"I-I don't know." Vivian licked her lips, trying to make sense of the movement happening outside the motel, but they were too far and it was too dark. "I'm going over there."

"Wait, you said we should call the police."

"And you are." Vivian handed Frannie her phone. "Right now. Dial 911 and let them know where we are and that Bethany is in danger."

Frannie's blue eyes became glassy. "What about you?"

"I'll be fine." Vivian put as much courage into her voice as she could. "Stay here and keep talking to the police until they get here."

"I don't want to stay in here by myself."

"Stay in the car, lock the doors, and call the police."

Vivian reached across Frannie and opened up her glove box. She grabbed the small canister of pepper spray she hadn't needed since moving from Washington, DC. Vivian closed her car door as quietly as she could and walked toward the hotel, hugging the tree line and hoping the shadows would keep her hidden from view.

Vivian paused next to an empty and boarded-up room. She could hear two men arguing. She risked a peek around the corner and caught a glimpse of the man still standing near the room Frannie had pointed out. It was too dark to see if he was part of the argument, but another scream followed by the sound of crying shoved Vivian out of hiding.

What am I doing? Vivian didn't need Ryan's warning to know she'd officially found trouble. She peeked at her car, praying Frannie was on the phone with the sheriff's department and deputies were on their way. A shard of glass crunched beneath her shoe, drawing the glare of the man in front of her.

"What are you doing here?"

"I'm here to pick up my friend." Vivian swallowed back the fear that was turning her knees into cooked spaghetti. "There's been an emergency and she's needed at home."

The man stepped into the light of the one working bulb hanging overhead. Unfortunately, it flickered like it was ready to pitch them into darkness, making Vivian feel dizzy. "I doubt your friend is here."

"She is." Vivian stepped forward, trying to see around the man, but his bulk filled the space and made it impossible to see inside the room. "Bethany, it's Vivian. I'm here to take you home."

"What's going on?"

Another man edged past the bigger one and in the shuffle, Vivian caught a glimpse of Bethany huddled on the bed. Her terrified eyes latched on to Vivian's.

"Bethany, come out —"

"She's not going anywhere until I get what I paid for," the second man said. He was much smaller than the first guy. If it were only him, Vivian might stand a chance pushing by him, but with the two of them — she palmed the pepper spray — it would take a miracle.

"I don't know what you paid for, but you're not getting it from her. The police are already on their way. I'm giving you a chance to get out of here before you both end up in jail for a very long time."

A smirk lifted the corners of the small man's lips. The action distracted Vivian for what felt like a second, but in that time, the bigger man's movement was so swift she barely registered the glint of the blade before it was on the side of her neck. Beefy arms crushed her torso, holding her still.

"Honey." The small man breathed on her. "Someone is going to give me what I paid for."

"Vivian!"

Fear ripped through Vivian at the sound of Frannie's voice calling out to her. What was she doing outside the car?

"A three-for-one deal."

The small man snarled. He started for her and Vivian stuck out her foot. He tripped and the big man loosened his grip enough that Vivian lifted her hand and nailed him in the face with a burst of pepper spray.

"Run, Frannie!"

The small man reared back, cursing. He charged Frannie, but Vivian was closer and jumped between them. The momentum sent their bodies crashing into Frannie. The sound of her skull smacking against the concrete silenced her yelp.

TWENTY-ONE

Vivian rubbed the scrape covering her elbow. She had forgotten the sting of the asphalt grinding into her skin the instant she rolled over and saw Frannie wasn't moving. She'd followed the ambulance to the hospital and now was waiting for Charlie or a nurse to come out with an update on Frannie's or Bethany's condition.

"Vivian?" Lane Lynch was walking toward her, holding a blanket and a to-go tray with two covered foam cups. "Charlie called me on his way to the hospital. Said you could use a friend."

Friend. The term still felt fresh and disorienting. Yet it was impossible to ignore the way it pulled at the yearning deep inside of Vivian. When had she allowed isolation to become comforting? Maintaining perfunctory relationships had been her way of protecting herself from letting anyone get close enough to hurt her the way her father had. But, somehow, Vivian had let her guard down over the last several months.

"It always gets cold in here, so I thought a blanket and a warm cup of chamomile tea would help."

"Thank you." Vivian accepted the blanket and tea. "It's late. What about Noah?"

Lane sat in the vinyl chair next to her before removing the lid to her cup and blowing on the tea. "Ms. Byrdie came over after Sheriff Huggins called her. She told me Ryan's on his way."

Vivian breathed in the soothing scent of the tea, trying hard to avoid the emotion building in her chest. "This town is just . . ."

"Small," Lane said with a warm smile before taking a sip.

"No. I mean, yes, but not in a bad way. When I first moved here, I thought every-one was going to hate me for what I . . ." Understanding filtered through Lane's eyes. "But that hasn't been the case. Everyone's been so welcoming — like I belong here."

Lane's lips tilted into a smile. The eleva-tor doors slid open, pulling her attention to Ryan's frantic expression.

"Where is she?"

"They took her back as soon as we got here." Vivian slid off the chair, handing Lane her tea. "Charlie is back there with them."

Ryan wrapped her in his arms and she let herself sink into the embrace. He kissed the top of her head before releasing her, his eyes meeting hers. "You okay?"

She nodded.

A nurse in pink scrubs stood in the doorway. "Deputy Frost?"

"I'll be back," Ryan said before he followed the nurse back toward the patient rooms.

Vivian returned to the chair next to Lane, rubbing her hands together. "I can't believe this happened. He loves Frannie so much."

"His mom and sister are the world to him," Lane said. "Though I'd venture another woman has captured a piece of his heart."

Vivian's cheeks warmed. "It's hard to imagine that."

"Really? Have you seen the way he looks at you?"

"Yes, I mean, I see the way he looks at me and I know how I feel when I'm with him. It's just that I can't figure out what I've done to earn that kind of love."

"The right kind of love isn't earned, Vivian." Lane pressed her hand over Vivian's knee. "I can't tell you how many years I've spent being someone else's idea of perfect, trying to earn their love and affection only

320

to be reminded — painfully — how imperfect I am. That's the beauty of godly love. The kind that is forgiving, unwarranted, undeserved, and unconditional."

Lane sipped her tea, her expression dimming with memories. "I never thought anyone could love me the way Mathias did, and when he died, I wanted to blame God. I did blame God for letting me down. For letting me believe I was unworthy to be loved, but you know what? That wasn't God. That was the enemy wanting me to live in the lies of isolation. And when I finally chose to confront those lies, God reminded me I was never alone — and he gave me Charlie. A man who reminds me daily that I am loved wholly for who I am."

Vivian sat back in her chair. *"Loved wholly for who I am."* Lane's words resonated in the gaping hole Vivian's father had left inside her heart. How many years had she wondered what she could've done to make him love her enough not to leave?

With Ryan, Vivian hadn't felt the need to pretend to be anyone other than who she was because she had no intention of staying in Walton, and now she claimed a piece of his heart? He had chosen *her.* Even over Miss Perfect Holly Newman, who still made Vivian a teensy bit — okay, maybe a lot —

jealous. Ryan had decided Vivian was good enough to be his.

"Vivian?"

Lane nudged Vivian's arm, thankfully missing the tender scrape, sending her attention to Charlie, who was standing in front of her.

"I need to ask you some questions."

Vivian stood. "Yes, of course."

Charlie had taken some information at the scene but said he'd probably have a few more questions. At the time, the main concern had been getting Frannie and Bethany to the hospital. Vivian thanked Lane for coming and waited as Charlie kissed his bride and sent her home. Following Charlie, Vivian searched for Ryan as she walked down the same hallway the nurse had taken him down. Was he with Frannie? Was she okay?

"How are they?"

"Bethany is shaken up and scared, but her parents are on their way." Charlie pushed open a door leading into a room with a sign indicating it was a family waiting room. There was a couch, a small table with two chairs, and a mounted television. Against the wall was a small kitchenette-type area with a microwave, refrigerator, and Keurig coffeemaker. A basket was filled with snacks and supplies to make coffee or tea.

"What about Frannie?" Vivian asked as she sat down.

"Ryan and his mom are talking with the doctor now." Charlie sat across from her, his expression drawn and grim. "How are you? Have you seen a doctor yet?"

Vivian's fingers grazed the tender spot on her elbow. "I'm fine."

"You should probably still see a doctor just in case."

There was concern in Charlie's tone, but he was working his jaw like he had something more to say that had nothing to do with her well-being. "What is it?"

"Do you know why Bethany was at the motel tonight?"

"No." Vivian swallowed, unwilling to offer any guesses as to how Bethany got herself in that position. "But I'll tell you why I was there."

Vivian explained Frannie's call and what happened after she arrived at the motel. Charlie tapped his thumb against the table. "Bethany was there tonight because the Watcher has a video of her."

"Please tell me that's not true." Somehow the whispered words escaped over the nausea closing Vivian's throat.

"He sent her an email about a month ago

and has been using it to get her to do . . ."

Pulsing rage filled in what Charlie couldn't finish saying and Vivian didn't need to hear the words to know what came next. The unspoken truth curled her stomach into a ball of utter disgust.

Footsteps echoed in the hospital hallway and Vivian saw Ryan stalk past. "Ryan."

The steps stopped and then Ryan's frame filled the doorway of the waiting room. His eyes were ablaze and landed on her for less than a second, but she could see the depth of anger and fear radiating in them. She stood and started for him, but he shifted, turning his attention to Charlie. "Did you get Bethany's statement?"

Charlie rose. "Yes."

"Ryan, this is awful." Vivian moved toward him, but he stepped back and she paused. Fear pierced her heart. "Please tell me Frannie's okay."

The furrow between Ryan's eyebrows deepened, his gaze darkening.

Vivian's heart thundered in her chest at Ryan's silence. She searched Ryan's face, desperate for him to answer. Frannie had to be okay. "Ryan?" She touched his arm and his posture stiffened. He pulled away, out of her reach, his hands climbing to the back of his neck as he backed away from her.

What is happening? "Ryan, talk to me. What's going on?"

A flash of emotion flickered over his features before he turned and stormed down the hallway.

"Is Frannie —" She pressed her lips tight, a painful sob cutting into her throat and silencing the question she wasn't sure she wanted to know the answer to.

"The doctor is with her now," Charlie said. "Ryan's just scared."

"Then I need to be with him." She started after him but stopped at the threshold when she saw Ryan hugging Holly Newman.

Coldness seeped into the pit of her stomach. Why was *she* here? But the answer came almost as quickly as the question. Holly was proving to Ryan she'd always be there for him. That *she* was the one he needed. A steady and comforting contradiction to Vivian.

Was that why it had been so easy for her father to walk away? Was his other family everything she couldn't be, making it easy for him to choose them over her? The coldness flowed from her stomach to her limbs. Vivian could never be what Ryan needed. He deserved better and Holly was better. Vivian spun on her heel and rushed toward the double doors, desperate to get out of there.

Moving to Walton had been a huge mistake. Somehow, Harold had managed to chip away at the carefully constructed wall she'd built to protect herself, and with each passing day someone else had chiseled away at it more. Then Ryan had come in like a wrecking ball, demolishing the last of her resistance and bringing with him the hope that maybe she was good enough.

She was a fool. She'd taken her focus off the story and allowed herself to get distracted.

Brick by brick, Vivian would rebuild the wall and never let anyone break her again.

"I know you're hurting, brother." Charlie dropped into the chair next to Ryan. "But was that really necessary?"

Ryan gawked at his friend. "That's not your sister lying in a hospital bed with a gash to her skull and a concussion." He hooked his thumb toward the hospital room behind him. His mom and Dr. Murphy had arrived just after he had and were there when the doctor explained Frankie would most likely be fine, but they would keep her overnight to be sure. "How'd you feel if that was Lane?"

"I'd be upset —"

"Exactly." Ryan roughed a hand through his hair. "I just don't get why Vivian wouldn't tell me."

"You really think she would've done that?" Charlie frowned. "How many times did she try to call you tonight?"

"Yeah, I'm gonna have to live with that the rest of my life." Ryan hated the way Frankie looked in the hospital bed almost as much as he hated the pained expression that had colored Vivian's face when he'd ignored her.

"That's not why I'm bringing it up, man." A call from dispatch crackled over their radios. Ryan turned his radio down while Charlie responded to the operator. Charlie stood and stared into the room where Frankie was resting. "You didn't give Vivian a chance to explain why she was there to-night."

Ryan scoffed. "I know why she was there."

"No, you don't." Charlie's tone shifted from friendly to professional. "Frannie followed Bethany to that motel tonight. She called Vivian to the scene. Vivian told her to stay in the car and call us. She did but then got out of the car when one of the suspects put a knife to Vivian's throat. Vivian stepped in front of the suspects when they went after your sister and that's why Frannie's in that hospital bed tonight. It's not an ideal situation, I get it, but I'd hate to think how much worse it could've been had Vivian not been there and put herself in danger to *protect* Frannie and Bethany."

"How do we know that?" Ryan pinched the bridge of his nose. "She needs this headline to get a job."

"The devastation I saw in Vivian's eyes when she found out about Bethany's video didn't reflect a woman who only cares about a story. Maybe it's time you start to consider that the reason Vivian wants to find the truth has less to do with a headline and more to do with the people she's come to care about."

"Ryan." His mom poked her head through the doorway. "Frannie's awake."

Charlie tipped his head. "Please tell her we're praying for her." Ryan's mom nodded, eyes glistening, before stepping back into the room. Charlie turned to Ryan. "If you need anything, let us know."

Before Ryan entered his sister's room, he took a breath. How could this night have gone so completely wrong? Had he jumped to conclusions? Assumed the worst about Vivian? His throat constricted at the possibility of his error, but he also knew deep down how important the story was to Vivian.

"Why do you look like someone died?" Frankie's voice was raspy. "And where are my flowers? Aren't people in the hospital supposed to get flowers?"

Relief coursed through him. "It's a shame some of your sass wasn't knocked out of you."

"Are you really going to joke about my head injury?" Frankie moved her fingers to the gauzy bandage covering the wound at the back of her head. "I could've died, ya know."

The gravity of the situation returned in a flash and Ryan's mood turned somber. "That's exactly right, Frankie. Do you even realize how badly this night could've turned out?"

Dr. Murphy rose from the chair next to Ryan's mom. "I'll go get some coffee."

Ryan respected the man's intuition to know when to step out of a family affair.

"Honey, I think Frannie understands what she did tonight."

"Yeah, I do." Frankie turned her head side to side. "I'm going to have to wear a hat to cover this ugly bandage."

"It's not a joke, Frankie." His sister flinched at his sharp tone. "I'm sorry, but this is serious. What were you thinking, going to the motel tonight?"

Frankie's lip quivered. "I was thinking that I wanted to make sure my friend was okay. Vivian told me a good journalist observes the details and that's all I wanted to do. Watch and make sure she was okay."

Ryan's chest grew taut at the mention of Vivian's name. "Did Vivian also mention how stupid it is to risk your life for a dumb headline?"

"It wasn't her fault, Ryan." Tears filled Frankie's blue eyes. "I didn't want her to call you because I was afraid Bethany would get in trouble." She sniffled. "Vivian saved my life and Bethany's too."

Charlie's words returned to him. If Vivian didn't know about the video of Bethany, then she wasn't hunting for a jump on a headline when she went out to the motel — she was answering a call for help.

"It was dumb." Frankie's soft voice called his attention back to her. In the hospital bed, she looked small and frail and his anger toward her melted. "I'm sorry I didn't tell you about Bethany in the beginning, but I'm not sorry for following her tonight." Ryan wanted to object, but Frankie kept talking. "Imagine what could've happened if I hadn't followed her or if Vivian hadn't stopped those guys."

Ryan didn't want to imagine the possibilities. Knowing the Watcher had done this to his sister's best friend filled him with such a seething anger, he wouldn't sleep until the monster was caught.

"Don't be mad at Vivian." Frankie's eyelids began to droop. "She makes you cool."

When Frankie had drifted to sleep, Ryan confirmed with his mom that she would stay overnight and keep him updated if anything changed. His footsteps echoed through the quiet hallways of the hospital in a determined cadence.

Cool? That wasn't what Ryan felt Vivian made him. Bold, maybe. Adventurous, definitely. Lucky . . . he'd asked himself at least a hundred times how he'd gotten so lucky that a woman like Vivian could have feelings for him, but it was more than that. Vivian believed in him and made him want to be a better man. So why did he feel like an absolute jerk?

Because you acted like one. Ugh. Ryan's head throbbed at the truth.

"Oh, good, you're still here."

Ryan turned and saw Holly smiling, walking toward him.

She lifted up a paper bag. "They're not as

good as Lane's, but I've heard they're edible."

"It's late." Ryan looked at the cinnamon rolls inside the bag. Edible? They looked hard enough to be hockey pucks. "I hope you didn't stay here for me."

Holly blushed and tucked a strand of blonde hair behind her ear. "My volunteer shift ends at seven. That's when most of the nurses get here and the other volunteers arrive." She looked over his shoulder and back. "Are you leaving?"

"I need to get to work."

"How's your sister?"

"Still has an attitude, but the doctor can't do anything about that."

"Sounds like she'll be just fine." Holly stepped closer, touching his arm. "I'm so glad I was here when she came in. Having someone familiar you can rely on is such a blessing, don't you think?"

There was something veiled in that statement, but Ryan wasn't sure he was coherent enough to make heads or tails of it. And he didn't have time. "I need to go." He handed the bag of cinnamon-flavored hockey pucks back to Holly. "I'm sure the nurses will appreciate these."

Holly took back the bag, a flicker of disappointment passing through her eyes. "Ryan,

I'm really sorry about what happened to your sister and Bethany."

"Thank you."

"Would it be okay if I made a casserole or something and brought it by your house?"

Ryan frowned. "You mean my mom's house?"

"Oh, yeah." She shook her head. "I guess the late hour's getting to me too." Holly toyed with her bottom lip. "I could bring you something too."

"I appreciate that, Holly, but I'm probably going to be pretty busy at the station and don't really know when I'll get home."

Someone wants my attention. Ryan remembered Vivian's words that day outside the Way Station Café and the flicker of sentiment that had crossed her features. Jealousy? It was a feeling that had blossomed in his chest the second he had seen the roses Shep had brought to the hospital. He didn't know much about the guy, but the idea of competing with the wealthy heir of one of the biggest newspaper companies made Ryan feel inadequate. Yet, somehow, Vivian always made it a point to squash those insecurities and make him feel like he was the only one she cared about.

Good grief, he'd made a mess.

"Holly, you've known me since eighth

grade, so you know my limitations when it comes to girls and flirting. But if I've led you to believe my feelings for you are more than friendship . . . I want to apologize."

"Ryan, are you serious?" Holly forced a smile to her lips. "Of course I know that." She fumbled with the bag in her hand to look at her cell phone. "I should probably go check on the other patients and drop these off."

Ryan felt bad, but he wanted to make sure Holly understood there was only one woman whose adoration he sought, and she wasn't going to make him a casserole. No, Vivian was the woman who'd jump into the trenches with a frying pan and can of hairspray to fight off the bad guys. That's who he wanted by his side, but would she stay there? Or give him another chance?

He didn't know, but he wasn't going to sit back and let his own stupidity get in the way. Ryan charged out of the hospital with only two goals.

Admit to Vivian he was a total idiot and beg for her forgiveness.

Find the Watcher.

He wasn't sure which of the two would be harder.

TWENTY-TWO

A night spent on a cot in a jail cell had taken its toll on the woman. Her eyes were puffy and bloodshot, the dark circles beneath deepened by the streaks of mascara she'd cried off throughout the night. Once-manicured nails had been bitten down, and the poise she'd walked in with had diminished to nervous and fearful restlessness.

"I thought Lauren was going to ask for money. Danny already paid her. More than enough to take care of the baby." Trisha Atkins tugged at the sleeves of her sweater. "I just wanted Harold to go away so we could get past the mistake." Her teary gaze landed on Ryan. "I didn't think the oil would kill him. I only wanted to make him sick so he'd leave us alone. It was an accident."

"Deputy Frost, as you've heard, my client made a mistake." Edward Armitage straightened the silk tie that no doubt cost more than Ryan made in a month. The lawyer, in

335

his three-piece suit, had walked into the sheriff's station under no pretense of who he was representing. "Trisha Atkins never intended to kill Mr. Kennedy."

Ryan scowled, not in the mood for the lawyer's attempt to downplay Trisha Atkins's guilt. It was determined fairly quickly that Congressman Atkins wasn't part of his wife's plot. "How did you know about Harold's peanut allergy?"

"When he came by the house, I offered him some cookies. Peanut butter." Trisha sniffled. "He told me he couldn't have any because of his allergy."

Ryan thought he heard her lawyer groan before raising his hand. "Mrs. Atkins never intended to kill anyone."

Was this guy serious? "She used peanut oil to trigger an allergic reaction that *did* kill someone. Not only did her actions kill Harold Kennedy, but then she set fire to the *Gazette,* endangering the life of Vivian DeMarco."

"I didn't know anyone was in there," Trisha whimpered in the chair next to her lawyer. "I thought she'd left."

Ryan ground his molars. When the firefighters pulled Vivian out of the building, he'd never been so scared . . . . until last night. Getting the call about Frankie was beginning to make him think that taking a job with the FBI would be a mistake. And his stupidity at the hospital last night made him doubt he had any future with Vivian in Atlanta.

"Why'd you start the fire?"

"I thought Harold was writing a story about Danny and the baby. When he . . . died, I thought it was over. But then when you and that reporter came to the house, I realized he must've had notes or something. I couldn't let the scandal ruin us."

"It's our hope that my client's candor demonstrates the sincere remorse she feels for what has happened."

"Judge Sullivan will make that determination on Monday morning."

"But that's in two days." Trisha's voice shook. "I can't stay in that . . . that cell for another two days. It's disgusting."

Ryan stood and pushed his chair in, the metal legs scraping against the floor. "That's the intention."

"We want to talk with Sheriff Huggins," the big-city lawyer called out just before Ryan closed the door to the interrogation room. He'd send in Sheriff Huggins, but he didn't think it would matter much. They'd found the Victoria Rose hoodie hanging in her closet and a gallon of peanut oil inside her kitchen pantry.

Forensics was running her prints against some found on the vehicle and outside the old bank building where the *Gazette* office was located. He knew there'd be a match. That coupled with her confession meant Trisha Atkins would need to get used to sleeping on a cot.

Ryan slipped his cell phone from his pocket. After he had left the hospital, he came to work, but Sheriff Huggins ordered him to go home for a few hours of sleep that didn't come. In between the nightmares he had about Frankie, his thoughts were consumed with how royally he'd screwed up with Vivian. It had eaten at him all night, and this morning he would've called her had it been a decent hour . . . or had he known what to say. *Why couldn't I have just let her explain?*

The hurt he'd seen in her face — that was him. He'd caused that, and he didn't know how to even begin to make up for it.

Rounding the corner, Ryan jerked to a stop. Vivian was there. Sitting inside the conference room talking to Sheriff Huggins. Why?

Ryan had to force his feet to close the twenty or thirty feet between them. He tried licking his lips, but his mouth had gone dry.

What could he possibly say to make his behavior last night forgivable? *Start with I'm sorry* —

"Good morning."

Vivian's charcoal-blue eyes landed on him for only a second before returning to the sheets of paper lined up in front of her. "Morning."

Good morning? He wasn't greeting Deputy Wilson or a bank teller. This was Vivian . . . the woman who'd stolen his heart not just with her beauty but with her inner geek. She was unmatchable and the best he could offer was *good morning*?

Sheriff Huggins stood, gathering his coffee mug. "You finished with Trisha?"

"Yes, sir. I think I've got as much information as we're going to get, but her lawyer wants to talk to you."

"I'm sure he does," Sheriff Huggins grumbled. "Deputy Lynch is speaking with Blaise Taylor right now. Let's meet in here in an hour and go over the case."

Ryan shot Vivian a look. She was still working on the case? With him? Sheriff Huggins walked by, catching his attention with a curious lift of the eyebrows that said he knew something was up.

"Sheriff Huggins said Frannie is awake and going to be okay."

His stomach twisted at the waver in Vivian's voice. He pulled out a chair next to her. "She is. My mom called this morning and said they'll probably discharge her this afternoon."

"That's great news."

He thought he saw her shoulders relax, but she still wouldn't look at him. His confidence an apology was going to help was dwindling. "Vivi, I'm sorry —"

"Stop." She looked up, spearing him with stormy eyes brimming with pain. "I'm not here to talk about last night. I'm here to work through these case notes so you guys can catch the Watcher and make him pay for what he did to Bethany and Harold."

"But I want to apologize. Charlie and Frankie told me —"

"Ryan, please stop." Sadness twisted her features for a fraction of a second before she wiped the emotion from her face. "Let's just work on this case and forget everything else."

He didn't want to forget everything else. Not now or ever. Ryan's fingers curled with the urge to draw her close to him so he could wrap her in his arms. If only she'd let him explain. *Like I let her explain last night?*

"Well, that was the most interesting conversation I've had all week." Charlie walked in and dropped a pad of paper in the center of the table, ending Ryan's chance to talk to Vivian alone. But from the look of relief on Vivian's face, it seemed he was the only one bothered by the intrusion.

"Meet Blaise Taylor." Charlie rotated a photo around so he and Vivian could see it. "Another victim of the Watcher."

Vivian picked up the photo. "Another?"

"Wait, wasn't he the one who took Bethany Price to the party where she was drugged and filmed?"

"Yes, but he didn't stay. In fact, he tried to convince her to leave with him, but she wouldn't."

"What does the Watcher have on him?" Vivian asked, setting down the picture.

"The kid might have a killer hook shot, but he struggles in math. Took to breaking into his teacher's desk to steal test answers so he could pass. When college scouts started eyeing him for scholarships, he knew he needed a better-than-passing grade. He basically cheated his whole way through senior year."

"And no one caught him?" Ryan said.

"Nope. He stayed under the radar by making sure his test scores reflected the grades he was getting on his classwork."

"First, how did the Watcher know Blaise

was cheating or going to cheat?" Vivian's nose wrinkled the way it always did when she wasn't buying it. "And second, how did the Watcher get a video of this happening?"

"He didn't." Charlie leaned back in his chair. "He got a video of Blaise cheating at Anderson College."

Ryan tried to wrap his head around the information Charlie was sharing. "So, the Watcher knew about Blaise cheating in high school and then just waited for him to cheat in college?"

Charlie crumpled a piece of paper and tossed it across the room into a trash can. "Do you know how much Blaise will earn this season playing for the Wisconsin Wolverines?"

"Do I care?" Ryan said.

Vivian shook her head.

"You should." Charlie addressed Ryan. "Just under two million. For a poor kid from Taft, Georgia, whose dad is dying from cancer and has no money to cover medical costs . . . it's all the incentive Blaise needed to break into his professor's office at Anderson."

"Okay, but that doesn't explain how the Watcher knew Blaise would do that." Vivian picked up her notes. "All the victims were set up."

"So was Blaise." Charlie raised his eyebrows. "He received an email from his teacher — or so he thought — requesting a meeting. Blaise assumed it was to go over his recent test score, but when he got to the teacher's office, it was empty. Except for the test sitting on his desk."

"Let me guess." Ryan ran a hand through his hair. "It was all captured on video surveillance?"

"Bingo."

"I don't know." Vivian played with the top button of her blouse. "We're still working under the assumption that the Watcher knew Blaise's struggles before and then set him up to be exploited."

Ryan noticed Vivian kept her attention wholly on Charlie. It was a not-so-subtle message. That and her crisp cream-colored blouse, tailored black slacks, and heels said she was here as a professional with a single goal in mind — and it wasn't to forgive Ryan.

"You said Blaise was never caught cheating, yet someone had to have known," Ryan said. "Did Blaise tell anyone?"

"There's only one person who found out about Blaise cheating in high school."

Charlie slid a paper across the table, causing Ryan and Vivian to reach for it at the same time. Their hands brushed for a nanosecond before Vivian pulled hers back.

"Here." Ryan held the paper out to her. "You can look at it first."

"No, it's fine." Vivian scooted her chair over just enough so she could lean across and see the page Ryan was holding. "We can both look."

The vanilla jasmine scent of her perfume tickled his nose and brought back the ache of regret he'd been harboring since he left the hospital. How could he get her to listen to him? To forgive him?

"Who's Jamal Thurgood?"

Charlie looked between Vivian and Ryan. "He might be the Watcher."

Ryan shook his head. "Oh no." He lifted his hands up, palms out. "I already jumped the gun once and was wrong. What makes you think this Jamal guy is him?"

"College scouts went to Taft High School eyeing two players." Charlie held up two fingers. "Blaise and Jamal. Both were good enough to be recruited. Only one made it."

"Blaise." Vivian made a note. "What happened to Jamal?"

"The boys were rivals on and off the court, but Taylor's skills were more refined. It seems Jamal figured his time was running short to win a scholarship, so he upped his game and ended up with an illegal foul that broke Taylor's nose. He was thrown out of the game —"

"Ending his chances to play for college," Ryan added, studying the picture of Jamal again. "Now Blaise is making two million dollars —"

"Two million reasons to extort Blaise," Charlie cut in, folding his arms over his chest.

Vivian rolled her lower lip between her teeth. "It doesn't explain why he'd extort the others though."

Ryan looked at Charlie. "But it gives us enough reason to have him questioned."

"Taft Police Department is already on it."

Jamal Thurgood was not the Watcher. According to an officer with Taft PD, Jamal Thurgood was picked up from his place of business, an auto body repair shop, and adamantly denied being the Watcher.

Ryan made a call to FBI Agent Hannigan to look into Jamal's financial records and to search his computer, but it was an unnecessary call. Jamal Thurgood gave them access to everything and they found nothing. No hefty bank accounts, and the one computer he had at home was more than a decade old — not the kind of machine someone of the Watcher's caliber would use to build a maze of firewalls securing his identity.

"Are you hungry?"

"Hmm?" Vivian looked up from the notes. Ryan was watching her and it was unnerving he had the power to stir the pieces of her broken heart. *Dramatic much?* "Uh, I'm fine."

"You refused the sandwiches Lane brought in for lunch, and I haven't seen you eat anything since you got here. The case will still be here when we get back."

"I think Charlie said there are leftovers."

Vivian turned her attention back to the pages in front of her. She'd been staring at them so long the words had begun to string together in an incoherent blur she couldn't make sense of. It didn't matter though, she would stare at them as long as it took until Ryan left her alone.

Coming into the station this morning, she believed her drive to find the Watcher would outweigh the emotional turmoil still churning within her for Ryan. Vivian had to actively concentrate on the story of the case and not the piercing heartache of their own story ending.

Through a storm of tears last night, Vivian had somehow managed to drive herself home, where she'd given herself permission to wallow in her sorrow. She'd cried until her eyes were raw and there were no more tears left, just body-shaking sobs that echoed in the emptiness of her house.

From the corner of her eye, she watched Ryan's boots finally disappear from the doorway. She inhaled deeply, forcing her shoulders to relax. Vivian had expected he would try to talk to her, and when he started to apologize, it took every ounce of self-control and self-respect to keep from throwing herself into his arms. It had to be this way. She was foolish to ever have believed he could love her wholly.

Once again, she just wasn't enough.

Rubbing her eyes, Vivian rested her head against the back of the chair, wanting just a few minutes to rest her brain. It was hard work keeping her thoughts off Ryan. Thankfully all she had to do was think of him and Holly hugging in the hallway to bring back the grit she needed to stay focused.

Her cell phone rang and she groaned. Opening her eyes, she looked at the screen. *Seriously?* Like the day couldn't be any harder — he had to call. Vivian denied the call, knowing it wouldn't deter Russell Bradley from leaving another message.

Sure enough, a minute passed by and then a message popped up. A glutton for punishment, she played it.

"Vivian, it's Russell. I'm just calling to check in. The Weather Channel says there's a storm headed your way. Um, if you're not too busy, would you mind calling back? I've, uh, well, I just wanted to talk. You have my number. I hope to hear from you soon. Take care."

She stood and went to the only window in the conference room and stared up at the sky. Blue and cloudless. *Guess you were wrong, Russell.* And if he thought she'd ever call him back — he'd be wrong again. What happened with Ryan made her keenly aware of why she'd built a wall around her heart in the first place and what could happen when you let someone in.

"I've got turkey and roast beef." Ryan walked into the conference room carrying a tray. "A cup of pasta salad and half a cookie." He looked at her, his eyes wide with confusion. "Who eats half a cookie?"

Vivian wanted to refuse him. Wanted to reject every attempt he was making at small talk and ignore the way she'd catch him looking at her whenever she dared a peek at him. But her stomach won with an angry growl that made her clutch it in embarrassment.

"Eat, Vivian." Ryan set the food on the

table. "I promise we'll only talk about the case."

She gave in and grabbed the turkey sandwich before choosing the chair at the opposite end of where he sat. Tucking her legs under her, she took a bite of her sandwich, not realizing how hungry she actually was until there was one last bite left. Vivian eyed the cup of pasta salad and the half a cookie.

"Take them both." Ryan stretched across the table, his forearm flexing as he pushed the items toward her. "I ate lunch."

"Thanks." Why'd he have to be so Captain America–like? If he had the arrogance of Tony Stark, it would be a lot easier to hate him.

"What?" Ryan caught her looking at him. "Do I have something in my teeth?"

"No." *Focus on the case, Vivian.* She pushed her attention to the whiteboard, where all the victims' photos were lined up now, including ones of Bethany and Blaise. "It feels like we're so close."

"It's like we're trying to hack into a scrypt."

She rolled her eyes. "I have no idea what that means, Jarvis."

"Nothing artificial about my intelligence," Ryan said, catching her reference to *Iron Man.* "It's a much harder algorithm to crack, like this case."

"We think the Watcher is local or nearby." Vivian set aside the bowl of pasta salad and walked to the whiteboard, putting some distance between her and Ryan. She moved four pictures to the middle of the board. "Harold, Bethany, Lauren, and Blaise. We need to find the connection here."

"Three out of the four didn't have the money to pay the Watcher."

"True," Vivian said. "But, technically, the Watcher wasn't trying to get money from Lauren."

"And if he knew about Congressman Atkins's affair with Lauren, why wouldn't he have taken advantage of that?"

"Because he didn't know." Vivian rubbed her temples. It was right there. That feeling she got in her gut that told her the answer was right in front of her. She just had to . . . look. Vivian pulled Blaise's picture off the board. "Cougar."

"What?"

She turned the picture around. "He's a Cougar."

"No, he's a Wolverine. Plays for Wisconsin now."

"No." Vivian tapped the photo. "He *was* a Cougar."

"Oh, right, for Anderson." Ryan really had

about as much interest as she did in sports. "So?"

"That's the connection." She put Blaise's photo next to Harold's. "Blaise was a student at Anderson and Lauren taught at Anderson. Harold was a guest lecturer at the college."

"What about Bethany?"

Vivian frowned. Dang, Ryan was right. Bethany wasn't connected to Anderson College. The phone in the conference room rang. Ryan walked around the table to answer as Vivian stood back, examining the pictures again.

"Deputy Frost."

Vivian watched him from the corner of her eye, taking advantage of the distraction. The angular structure of his face shifted with the conversation and she edged closer.

"Yes, sir." He nodded. "We'll check into that."

"What?" Vivian said as soon as Ryan hung up the phone.

"That was the officer from Taft." Ryan sat in front of the computer and began typing. "Jamal remembered telling one person about Blaise cheating — a college coach."

"Who?"

Ryan sat back in the chair so she could see the image on the screen. "Meet Anderson College's assistant coach, Pete Robbins."

"I know him," Vivian said, recognizing the man smiling in the photo. "I spoke with him after a few of his players bumped into me."

"That was the day you were asking about Lauren, wasn't it?"

"Yeah. When Otis Jackson grabbed at me." She rubbed her arm, remembering the way Otis's grip dug into her skin. "Why would Jamal tell Coach Robbins about Blaise cheating?"

"From what the officer said, he was trying to prevent Blaise from getting a basketball scholarship."

"Wow." Vivian shook her head. "They really were rivals."

Ryan tapped the edge of the screen. "Check out the class he teaches at school."

Vivian followed Ryan's finger to Coach Robbins's bio. "Computer science." The hair on the back of her neck stood. "Do you think he had something to do with Otis coming after me?"

"I don't know," Ryan said. His gaze grew dark for a second before something flashed in his eyes like he had an idea. "Wait here."

Ryan rushed out of the room, leaving Vivian to stare at the image of Coach Robbins on the screen. It was definitely easy to connect him to the victims at Anderson, but what about the others? She studied the faces of the other victims. Was Ryan right? Did the Watcher troll his victims on social media?

A few minutes later, Ryan appeared in the doorway, his face a mix of emotions. "I just got off the phone with Lauren Holt. I asked her if Harold knew Coach Robbins, and she admitted that he was the reason Harold had helped her. Lauren and Robbins dated. She broke it off with him when she got pregnant with Olivia, but Robbins became obsessed. Started harassing her. She didn't have enough money to move, so she went to Harold for help."

Goose bumps covered Vivian's skin. "It's him, Ryan. He's the Watcher."

"I think so, Nancy Drew."

Vivian didn't know if it was the nickname or the way he was smiling up at her that sent her heart into another one of its betraying flips. *Remember why you're here.* She took a step back. "What happens next?"

"We'll get a search warrant and hopefully find the evidence we need to charge him." His blue eyes searched her face. "Vivian, I'd really like to talk to you about last night."

"There's no need." Vivian moved to the table to gather her belongings. Her willpower was slipping. She needed to get out of there before she did something stupid. *Like take him back.* "I did what I came here to do."

"And now you leave?"

Gah. It was too much. Her hands fumbled with the strap of her bag. "That was always the plan."

Ryan took a bold step forward and grabbed her hand. "I'm so sorry, Vivian."

"I can't." She shook her head, unable to meet the gaze she knew would melt the last of her resistance. "I'm not the one you need, Ryan."

"Says who?"

Vivian pulled her hand free, a shaky sigh slipping from her lips as she blinked back tears. "You deserve someone who can be everything you need and want. She's out there." Vivian's voice caught. "She's the prettiest teacher in Walton."

TWENTY-THREE

"I'm sorry, Frost, but even with everything you've got" — Agent Hannigan's voice echoed from the speakerphone — "it's just not enough."

Not enough? Frustration knotted the muscles along Ryan's shoulders. He looked around the room, seeing his disappointment mirrored in the faces of everyone around him. Ryan had asked Sheriff Huggins and Charlie to come in early to discuss why he and Vivian believed Coach Robbins could be the Watcher.

Unfortunately, besides his connection to knowing about Blaise cheating, they didn't know much about Pete Robbins. Anderson College's website acknowledged his success as the defensive coach for the Cougars, but other than that, the man kept a pretty quiet profile. He wasn't married. Had no children. Lived in a modest home a few blocks away from the school. According to Sheriff Huggins, Coach Robbins was an active member of his church and in the community, volunteering his time whenever needed. From the outside, it appeared Coach Robbins was an all-American citizen, which made it hard to paint him as the Watcher.

Ryan tried to convince Agent Hannigan to look into his financial records, but without a warrant, anything they found would be inadmissible in court. He was not about to let this guy escape on a technicality.

"So, that's it?" Vivian lifted her hands. "We can't even talk to him?"

"Not without tipping him off," Charlie said. "And with this guy's computer skills, I'm worried he already has a contingency plan in place to disappear."

"It's all coincidental, and that's exactly what his lawyer will say." Sheriff Huggins twisted in his chair. "Agent Hannigan is right."

Ryan maneuvered in his chair so he could look at the whiteboard. The faces of each of the Watcher's victims stared back at him like they were waiting on him to do his job. He'd spent all night trying to figure out how to connect the victims to Coach Robbins, but Agent Hannigan was right — he didn't have enough.

He slid a sideways glance at Vivian. She

was studying the whiteboard as well, her brows furrowed in frustration. *"The reason Vivian wants to find the truth has less to do with a headline and more to do with the people she's come to care about."* Charlie's words that night at the hospital came rushing over him. He was right. Sitting here, watching her, Ryan didn't see a persistent reporter, he saw a woman who didn't just watch her boss die, she watched her friend die. And everything in him believed Vivian would do whatever she could — even step in front of a knife — to protect his sister.

Ryan couldn't let this case fall apart. He needed to give Vivian closure. And if she could write a story on that, then great. He'd at least be able to sleep at night knowing she was living her dream.

"We have to go back to our original plan." All eyes turned to him. Ryan stood and tapped the lineup of photos. "The only way we're going to catch the Watcher is to lure him out and catch him in the act."

"Have you forgotten our bait is sitting in jail right now awaiting charges for murder and arson?" Charlie set down his cup of coffee. "The Watcher missed his chance on that one."

"Who else do we know who's powerful and rich?" Ryan asked, scratching his chin.

"Russell Bradley."

Ryan turned on his heel and stared at Vivian. *What is she doing?* "No."

A softness shifted the storm brewing in her eyes before she looked away. "He's rich, famous, and . . . has a secret."

Charlie frowned. "The actor?"

"No," Ryan said. "We use someone else."

"Wait, how do you know Russell Bradley?"

Vivian looked at Charlie, her shoulders pulling taut as though she was steeling herself to answer his question. "He's my father."

"We're not using him," Ryan added. "We'll find someone else."

"Wait now, Frost, this might work," Agent Hannigan spoke up. "Ms. DeMarco, would your father agree to this?"

"No." Ryan's tone grabbed the attention of everyone in the room. "Vivian, we need to talk."

"It's fine."

Ryan turned to Vivian, but her expression was fixed. Determined. "Can we talk?"

Sheriff Huggins stood. "Let's take a little break and get back to this in a few minutes." He walked over to the phone and picked up the receiver, letting Agent Hannigan know they'd call him back. He then headed back to his office, Charlie following behind him.

"What are you doing?" Ryan said, closing the door to the conference room. "You don't have to do this."

"It's fine, Ryan."

But the tremor in her voice told him it was anything but fine. "I want the Watcher caught as much as you do, but not this way."

"There is no other way." Vivian looked up at him. "My father fits the Watcher's profile. And when he finds out Russell Bradley has a daughter he's kept hidden . . . it's perfect."

Ryan sat in the chair next to her, rubbing his knuckles in an attempt to keep himself from grabbing her hands. "I want you to get your story —"

Vivian reared back, her eyes wide. "Is that what you think? You think I'm doing this for the headline?"

"No." Ryan shook his head. "No, I'm saying I want you to finish this story so you can get your job in Atlanta. You've earned it."

She smirked. "I turned down the job at the *Tribune*."

"What?" He tried to read her expression, but she kept her chin tucked as she wrung her shaking hands. "Isn't that what you wanted?"

"I thought I did." She shrugged. "I'm not

sure anymore. I've spent my whole life trying to prove myself . . . trying to get Russell's attention." Her eyes swept up to his. "What better opportunity to confront him than this? At least it'll be for a good cause. Turn his lie into something positive."

"You don't need to do this. You have nothing to prove to your father, Vivian."

Vivian stared ahead. "The day I found out about Russell Bradley, it felt like my entire world shifted. I didn't know what to believe or who to believe anymore. My life was all lies. I went into journalism because I believe truth should be revealed at any cost. No one should have to live in their secret or lie."

A knock interrupted them and Ryan wanted to shout for whoever it was to leave them alone.

Charlie poked his head into the room. "Agent Hannigan is on the phone and wants to speak with you."

Ryan's pulse ticked up. Maybe the FBI agent had found a way to get the warrant they needed to search Coach Robbins's home and computers for evidence he was the Watcher. Maybe they could avoid revealing Vivian's secret. She might think the truth needed to be revealed, but sometimes truth came at a cost. And he wasn't sure she was emotionally prepared to pay.

"I'll be right back."

Vivian nodded but said nothing.

Ryan walked to his desk.

"Is everything okay in there?" Charlie tilted his head in the direction of the conference room. "Seemed intense."

"It's not okay." Ryan lifted his phone. "We need to find someone else."

Charlie nodded, stepping away from the desk. Ryan pressed the button to answer the call waiting.

"Agent Hannigan, we have to figure out another way to flush this guy out."

"I'm not sure there is one." Agent Hannigan's tone was flat. "I'm not sure what's going on over there, but I pulled up the information on Russell Bradley and he's the bait, Frost."

Ryan pinched the bridge of his nose, dropping into his chair. "It's not that easy, sir. There's a history with Vivian DeMarco and Russell Bradley."

"She said he was her father, but I can't find any record of him having a daughter named Vivian."

"There wouldn't be one, sir." Ryan peeked over at Vivian. Charlie was saying something to her that brought a hint of a smile to her lips, but it didn't reach the tension still lingering in her eyes. "Vivian DeMarco *is* Russell Bradley's dark secret. She's the result of an affair the actor had with Vivian's mom for more than a decade."

"No one knows?"

"Not that I'm aware of, sir." He roughed his face. "And I would like to keep it that way."

"We're moving forward," Ryan said as he stepped into the conference room. His grim expression landed on her. "If you're sure you want to do this?"

Sheriff Huggins and Charlie were already seated at the table with her. She swallowed. "Y-yes."

Vivian's suggestion to use her father had slipped from her mouth before she really had time to think on it. The apprehension she saw in Ryan's eyes was making her second-guess her suggestion. Russell's secret was as much hers as it was his. With paparazzi and social media . . . once the truth came out, there was no going back.

"The first thing we need to do is see if Russell Bradley will agree to the plan," Ryan said before looking at her. "You need to call and make sure we can get him here."

"Is it a little too convenient that he just shows up in his daughter's hometown?"

"Which is why Russell Bradley will be the new honoree at the Savannah Yacht Club gala," Ryan answered Charlie. "Good thing they were in desperate need to replace Congressman Atkins."

"I think we should let Vivian call her father before we make any promises." Sheriff Huggins's bright blue eyes turned on her with fatherly compassion. It reminded her of the way Harold would look at her — and the way Russell Bradley never did. "Would you like to use my office?"

"Um, sure." Vivian tucked her hair behind her ear. Even though the sheriff's station was air-conditioned, she was sweating.

Following Sheriff Huggins to his office, Vivian palmed her phone and rubbed her thumb down the side. She could do this. For Bethany and the others. If Russell Bradley wanted to talk to her, she would at least use it to the advantage of protecting others from the Watcher. When she was settled in the leather chair near his desk, the sheriff gave her an encouraging nod before closing the door behind him.

"I can do this." She turned the phone over in her hand and swiped the screen to pull up her contacts. She'd only saved his number to know when he was calling so as to not accidentally answer it. "I can do this."

Her thumb hovered over his number. Closing her eyes, she pressed it.

"Vivian?"

Hearing him say her name stole her breath. She blinked, uncertain of what to say or if she should just hang up.

"Vivian, I can't hear you." His voice sounded a bit rough. "Vivian?"

She swallowed. "Uh, yeah, hi."

"Hi."

This was going to be a lot harder than she thought. Her gaze drifted to the window in the sheriff's office until she found Ryan standing, arms folded over his chest, talking to Charlie. Something changed his mind after he took the phone call with Agent Hannigan. And the stubborn look chiseled into his features told her he still didn't like the idea of using her father.

"Hello, Vivian?"

"Right. I'm here." She ran her hand down the edge of her trousers, taking a deep breath. Hearing his voice took her back to her childhood. How many times had she dropped everything and run to the phone to take his call when he was off on "business" just to hear her daddy's voice? She steeled herself, forcing the emotion back in its place. "I have a favor to ask."

Twenty minutes later, Vivian walked back

into the conference room, numb. Charlie, Sheriff Huggins, and Ryan stood, waiting for her answer. Or rather, her father's answer.

"He's agreed."

There was no enthusiastic eruption of joy but rather a somber understanding that the stakes to catch the Watcher had increased. Vivian wondered how much Ryan had told them.

"Vivian, if you want to change your mind, we support you." Sheriff Huggins towered over her, bringing both hands to her shoulders. "We can find another way."

Genuine concern in both his voice and his eyes came dangerously close to breaching the emotional dam welling up inside of her. Sheriff Huggins had just as much — if not more — invested in catching the Watcher as Ryan did. Walton was his town. The very first time Vivian stepped across the city limits, she recognized the sheriff took his job very seriously. The residents here were more than neighbors and friends — they were family. And it was his job to protect them.

How could she refuse to help him?

"Russell will fly in on the day of the gala." Vivian took her place at the table, turning her focus back on the plan. "He's contacting his publicist to make sure word gets out that he's being recognized at the gala, as long as we're sure the Savannah Yacht Club's committee is on board."

"Half the committee is in Bible study with Byrdie." Sheriff Huggins tucked his thumbs into his gun belt. "When we're done here, I'll give her a call. I don't think we'll have any problems convincing them."

"Good." Vivian returned to her notes. "I'm going to call Shep and make sure announcements run in every edition of his paper and his father's paper. Unless the Watcher is blind . . . there's no way he's going to miss this."

"Except that doesn't answer how he's going to make the connection between Russell and you," Ryan said. "The Watcher has to believe *he* discovered the secret so he can exploit it."

"There are summer clinics happening at Anderson College this week." Vivian pulled out a copy of the *Gazette* and pointed to her article. "Coach Robbins will be there. What if he overhears me talking about Russell Bradley being my father?"

Ryan's face clouded. "It's too dangerous for you to be near him. We don't know what this man is capable of."

"It's the only way," she said. "This will

ensure he believes he uncovered my secret."

"Then I'm going to be there."

Vivian's heart was disloyal. Even after being crushed, it still raced whenever Ryan was near or she caught the spicy scent of his cologne. Or when his desire to protect her was written all over his face like it was right now. Vivian couldn't rely on him or her double-crossing heart. She could rely on only herself.

"You can't be there," Vivian said. "He knows you're a deputy."

"He knows you're a reporter," Ryan countered.

"Which gives me a reason to be there."

The rest of the day passed in a blur of details, and by the time they were settled on what her role would be at Anderson and how she was going to bring up Russell Bradley being her father, Vivian was exhausted.

"Vivian, can we talk?" Ryan waited by the front door of the sheriff's station. "Please?"

"If you're going to try to talk me out of this, you can forget about it." Vivian pulled out her keys. "The plan's in place and it's a good one. Hopefully by this time next week, you'll have the Watcher sitting in the jail cell next to Trisha Atkins."

"I'm not going to talk you out of it."

"What else is left to talk about?"

"I told you this already and I'm going to say it again. I don't want you putting yourself in danger."

"I'm not. Sheriff Huggins said you and Charlie can sit outside the school in case I need you."

"I'm not talking about physical danger this time."

Her heart tripped. "What do you mean?"

"I'm worried about you facing your dad on your own. You told me how much he hurt you, and I" — the muscle in Ryan's jaw ticked — "I won't let him do it to you again."

Ugh — so very Captain America.

"Don't worry, Ryan." Vivian pressed her keys into her palms until she felt pain. "I don't plan on letting myself get hurt like that ever again."

Vivian stepped around him and hurried to her car, feeling the burn of emotion balling in her throat. Why did he have to make it so hard? If he would just leave her alone and stop trying to make her forgive him, then she could move on with her life. *Like I have with Russell?*

"Stop it," she ordered the thought away. "Ryan's nothing like Russell."

Then why can't I forgive him?

The question followed her all the way to

her house, past some still-unpacked card-board boxes in the living room, and into the bedroom, where she collapsed on the bed. If she forgave Ryan and Russell, then she was giving them another opportunity to break her. She couldn't do that. Holding on to that power was all she had left.

Twenty-Four

The Watcher
Walton, Georgia

The house at 1606 White Marsh Lane looked like the one at 1608 and 1610 and 1612. Nothing separated the cookie-cutter veranda-style homes backing up to the Ogeechee Marsh except the flags waving proudly at the entrance of each wraparound porch.

Clemson.

University of Georgia.

And the true rebel — Alabama. *Roll tide.*

His Ford F-250 just fit inside the garage. There were no tools. No pieces of sports equipment. No tubs of ornate decorations like his neighbors filled their yards with each holiday season. The garage was only for his truck.

A blast of cool air welcomed him into his home. He dropped his keys on the table, a zigzagging bolt of lightning drawing his attention to the back window where a Magnolia tree swayed in the storm. Maybe he should've taken his neighbors' advice and had the tree removed.

Large Magnolia trees lined both sides of the home and offered privacy he valued. His gaze moved through the backyard to the private pathway leading down to the marsh behind his home. The murky water was lapping angrily against the dock.

"Ugly water," he muttered before going to his kitchen. After grabbing a beer and the day's paper, he started down the hall as outside another thunderous crash rattled the windows and caused the lights to flicker.

He stepped into a small room set up as an office and flipped on a light. The shades were drawn as they always were because, even though the window of this room was blocked by the dark green foliage of another large Magnolia, one could never be too careful about security.

Settling into the leather desk chair, he turned on his computer, ready to do some work. Letting his computer buzz to life, he pulled a key out from beneath a faux paperweight that looked like an angel and used it to unlock the bottom desk drawer. From there he pulled out a laptop and powered it up.

The electric purr of the computers filled the room and he leaned back in his chair, cracking his knuckles. School had been out for only a couple weeks, but he still had work to do. He rolled his seat closer to the desk and picked up the *Gazette.*

Some people fished with poles and worms, spending hours in the sun waiting for a catch. All he had to do was create profiles on social media. Or read the paper. The apples never fell far from the tree, and self-praise disguised as humble gratitude was always making headlines.

He still wasn't done berating himself for the missed opportunity splashed all over the pages of the paper the last week. *Man, I really missed the payday on that one.* Congressman Atkins's affair was proof politicos were always good for a secret or two. Who knew his pretty little redheaded wife had it in her to murder on his behalf? He fisted the edges of the paper in his hands. So much missed opportunity right at his fingertips.

Lately, his mood had been as dark as the heavy clouds outside. Finding out about the incident with Bethany Price at the motel from the front page of the *Savannah Daily* had kicked it off. According to the story, a deputy ran the plates of the vehicles parked outside the motel in a random safety search when a warrant popped up. Of course one of the vehicles belonged to the man he'd sent to the motel for a night with Bethany. Just his luck. The bust made the headlines, but they kept the girl's name out of it. As far as he knew, she hadn't said anything to lead the police to him. Not that she could. He had taken precautions, but to be sure, he did shut down the website offering female companionship to those who could pay. He'd figure out a way to get his payment out of Bethany Price when she least expected it and the chitchat around town had died down.

And it would die down eventually. Small towns ran on rumors, one circulating long enough for another to take its place. And if another one didn't happen naturally, he knew how to force a new one. He tossed the *Gazette* down. Harold Kennedy's death was the first time he'd truly felt afraid. If he were honest, he wasn't sure he was entirely over it.

When word started to spread through town that the newspaper owner's death looked suspicious, he took drastic measures to make sure nothing came back to him. Harold's laptop had been destroyed, and poor Otis was probably suffering a painful detox in a jail cell somewhere, his brain so fried from the meth he couldn't tell you his own name much less the name of the man who paid him to break into the *Gazette*. All was well.

He reached for the *Savannah Daily*. The season of galas and fundraising was on them, and the pond was fully stocked. His eyes landed on the photo in the lower right-hand corner of the paper.

Russell Bradley, actor, advocate, and honoree at Savannah Yacht Club gala.

Well, that was quick. He imagined the board members scrambling frantically to save face when they discovered their original honoree was an adulterer and his wife a murderer. Just goes to show that everyone has their secrets and not everyone is who they pretend to be. People could try to hide behind their power, money, privilege, or reputation, but eventually the truth emerged — and sometimes it was deadly. It was an important lesson he didn't mind teaching, especially when it came to his father.

He forced his attention away from his past and back to the paper in front of him. The article continued with Bradley's accolades as an actor, including his current role on an award-winning series on prime time and his advocacy for wounded soldiers' rehabilita-

374

tion . . . "making him the perfect honoree, as he'll bring awareness to Walton's very own Home for Heroes."

The photo of Russell Bradley looked like it had been taken from the pages of *People* magazine. From his stylish haircut and relaxed outfit hand-selected by a stylist to the practiced smile of a man who knew how to use it to charm women, he would no doubt bring in plenty of donations at the gala.

Flipping to the sports page, he scanned an article highlighting the advancing career of Anderson College's favorite basketball star, Blaise Taylor. His selection to the Wisconsin Wolverines had made him a millionaire overnight. There was no way the kid was going to get away without showing his appreciation to the coach who got him there.

A flash of lightning lit up the room and then a boom of thunder bellowed around him. He sat forward when his computer screens flickered, but a second later they were fine. He needed to get his work done before the thunderstorm took out the power.

He pulled out a USB flash drive, plugged it into the laptop, and watched the video one more time. The images of the young brunette woman and her friends living it up in Jacksonville caused a smile to play across his lips. He watched as they celebrated her graduation from law school and acceptance to the Long, Langley, and Woodrow law firm. One partygoer pulled out some drugs and he watched the new lawyer inhale, ignorant of how much this one night of festivities would cost her.

His fingers deftly tapped out the passcodes that would gain him the access he needed. With each strike of the enter key, he moved deeper into another secured screen until the last one popped up. It required a 256-bit encrypted password that changed daily and was sent to his cell phone. He pulled out his cell, accessed the code, and entered it. *Bingo.*

The screen opened up to a series of digital links. His eyes found the one highlighted in green, indicating payment had been made. He clicked on it and, sure enough, a deposit of $25,000 had been transferred to an offshore account.

He quickly transferred the money into another account that would split the payment into multiple deposits across several banks, making it as difficult as possible for anyone to track. A few had tried. The ones with the financial means and connections had done their best to hack into his system but they failed — and then they paid.

There were a few who had allowed their egos to convince them they were above reproach . . . that his work wouldn't affect them. But he proved them wrong. A simple click of a button sent video proof of their sin to spouses, parents, bosses, board members, government officials, newspapers, social media . . . maybe it wasn't enough to destroy them, but it certainly hurt them. Or the ones they loved. Enough that it actually became a selling point for his future *clients.* He'd simply attach proof that nonpayment had its own cost. In the end, his clients couldn't deny that it was usually easier and cheaper to pay him.

And they always paid — one way or another.

TWENTY-FIVE

Locker room funk. Reason numero uno why Vivian hated sports. She tried breathing through her mouth, but which was worse — smelling the repulsive blend of body odor, sweat, and multiple scents of Axe or inhaling it, uncertain whether her lungs would recover?

The cacophony of dozens of boys ages seven to fifteen echoed off the tile walls of the locker room at Anderson College. The short tweet of a whistle turned everyone's attention to the center of the room where a man stood in a white polo with a cougar stitched on the pocket.

"You guys played well out there today," Coach Robbins said, meeting the admiring gazes of the boys. "We've got some things to work on, but I want you to get some rest, drink plenty of water, and be here tomorrow morning on time."

Vivian lifted her camera and took a few

more pictures to keep up the ruse. Tomorrow, the *Gazette* would run a feature article in her community column's page highlighting the summer clinic Coach Robbins hosted for underprivileged kids.

"Hands in." The kids jumped up, putting one hand over Coach Robbins's, and in a unified count they lifted them up with more ear-shattering screams.

"Did you get what you needed for your story?"

"I got some really great photos of the kids. A few of them even agreed to talk to me." She smiled as a few boys walked between her and Coach Robbins, giving him a high five on the way by. "I'd love to ask you a few questions about the program though."

"Sure." He flashed her a grin, along with a wink. "Let me make sure the kids get to their rides and I can meet you in my office."

Even if she didn't suspect Pete Robbins of being the Watcher, there was something creepy about him. She'd picked up on it the first time they ran into each other. And the last thing she wanted to do was be caught in his office alone.

"I'm actually thirsty and saw a vending machine by the west entrance of the gym. Can we meet there?" She played with her camera strap. "Maybe I can get a couple of photos of you on the court?"

"Sure." He winked again before grabbing his clipboard from one of the benches and heading toward the same door most of the boys had walked through.

Vivian made her way out of the locker room, sucking in huge breaths of air. She lifted the edge of her blouse and sniffed. *Ew.* She was going to have to burn her clothes. She crossed the gym floor, then pushed through the double doors of the west entrance and pulled two dollar bills from her pocket for a bottle of water. Through the rectangular window on the other set of doors leading to the parking lot, Vivian saw Ryan and Charlie sitting in Ryan's Jeep.

She may not have been ready to forgive him, but she wasn't going to deny that she felt a bit safer knowing he was nearby. Vivian checked her phone to make sure it was on. Pecca would be calling in exactly seven minutes.

The sound of doors slamming notified her of Coach Robbins's presence. She took her water to the bleachers. "I'll take some photos first and then ask you a few questions."

"Sounds good." Coach Robbins's tennis

shoes squeaked across the polished wood of the basketball court. "Should I stand by the hoop?"

"Sounds good. Maybe hold a ball?"

Coach Robbins did as instructed, and two minutes later she had more than enough photos of him. They returned to the bleachers and she took out her notepad.

"First, I want to thank you for taking the time to talk with me. I've heard great things about your summer clinic."

"Well, it's really all about the kids. Some of these boys will never get the chance to play on a real college court or be trained by some of the best coaches in our division." He cleared his throat like emotion had overwhelmed him. "Every kid should get the chance to dream big."

"That's a great quote." Vivian scribbled it down, really wanting to write, "Full of baloney." "I noticed some of your players returned for the summer to help. Is that something you ask of them or do they volunteer on their own?"

"I always want my players to remember where they came from and to give back to the community."

Blah blah blah. She peeked at her phone. Three more minutes.

"I heard the Savannah Yacht Club is

honoring Anderson's coaching team this year at the gala. Are you excited about that?"

"I'm honored that they would want us to be there, but it's never about the recognition. We do what we do for the kids." Vivian wasn't sure if she was still sick from the lingering smell of the locker room or Coach Robbins's false humility. "Besides, I doubt anyone will be paying much attention to me, anyway."

"Why wouldn't they? You made the Cougars champions."

"Maybe." He shrugged. "But with Russell Bradley there, I doubt anyone will pay attention to us little guys."

Vivian smiled, hoping it looked alluring. The weight of this case was on her now. "Don't sell yourself short, Coach. Russell Bradley probably isn't who everyone thinks he is."

Why wasn't Pecca calling?

"Was there anything else?"

Think of something — you're a reporter.

"You've got game on the court, Coach, but does it extend to the dance floor?" *What in the world?*

Coach Robbins gave her a coy look. "I can hold my own on the dance floor, if that's what you're asking."

"I guess we'll see."

Vivian's phone shimmied on the bleacher next to her. She grabbed it and gave Coach Robbins an apologetic smile. "I'm so sorry." She collected her things. "I think I have everything I need."

"Cool." Coach Robbins shook her hand before his grip tightened slightly. "I hope to show you my moves at the gala."

Yep. She was going to be sick. Forcing a smile to her lips, Vivian backed away and walked in the direction of the coaching staff's offices. She wouldn't go in there, but she needed to be close enough for Coach Robbins to "accidentally" overhear her conversation.

"Hey, Mom."

"Girl, I feel like I'm in some action movie." Pecca's hushed whisper filled Vivian's ear. "Like Natasha from *The Avengers.*"

"What are you talking about?" Vivian glanced over to where Coach Robbins was locking a trolley of basketballs into a closet. She raised her voice. "I just found out. Why didn't you tell me?"

"I'm considering cutting my hair? Like pixie or maybe I'll do one of those layered bobs. What's it called? A lob?"

Vivian closed her eyes. Maybe having Pecca pretend to be her mother wasn't such a great idea. She needed to be upset, not helping Pecca pick out a new hairstyle.

"I just don't know why you didn't tell me." From the corner of her eye, she saw Coach Robbins lift his head and look at her. Good. "Did you tell him I was here?"

"I'm also considering joining a dating service." Pecca yelled something in Spanish at someone before she returned to the call. "*Lo siento.* Where were we?"

Vivian sniffled. "Mom, I just don't think I can face him. How did he know I was here?"

"Ooh, you're good, *muchacha.* Give him some more of that."

She would've scolded Pecca, but Coach Robbins had edged closer. Vivian turned so he wouldn't know she knew he was there. "What if he tries to talk to me? I'm not doing it. I won't talk to him. He left us, Mom. We weren't good enough for Russell Bradley and he walked out on us. Walked out on me — his own daughter."

"Oh, girl, you need to be in one of my telenovelas. Seriously."

Vivian peeked over her shoulder in time to see Coach Robbins turn his attention to a spot on the bleachers. "Look, Mom, I'm only going to the gala to do my job. Just because Russell will be there doesn't mean I have to talk to him. I can act like he doesn't exist the same way he's been acting like I don't exist for the last fifteen years."

Pecca sniffled. "Oh, *amiga.* My heart. You poor thing —"

Vivian hung up before Coach Robbins could hear Pecca's cries of pity or amazement, she wasn't sure which, and wiped nonexistent tears. When she was certain she'd adequately played the part, she turned and started for the exit that would take her to her car, which was parked a few over from Ryan's Jeep.

"Hey, um, is everything okay?" Coach Robbins came up to her, putting a hand on her arm. "You seem upset."

Vivian fought the urge to shudder under his touch. "Oh, yeah. Sorry." She sniffled. "Family drama. With my father."

Coach Robbins stiffened, sending a cold fear through her. Did she say too much? Was he onto her ploy? She searched his face, looking for anything to indicate he knew what she was doing, but all she saw was a flicker of . . . empathy.

"I have a painful past with my father too." His hand slid to the small of her back. "Is there anything I can do?"

Yes, rot behind bars for the rest of your life. "I'm good. Thank you." She pivoted away from his roaming touch. "I hope to see you at the gala."

A hungry spark filled his eyes as a smile curved his lips. "Wouldn't miss it."

The second Vivian emerged from the gym, Ryan could breathe again. He'd worked calluses into his palms wringing them over his steering wheel. If it hadn't been for Charlie sitting next to him, he would've burst through those doors to check on her, blowing her cover and their chance at finding out if Coach Pete Robbins was the Watcher.

Ryan reached for his door handle, but Charlie's grip on his shoulder held him back.

"She's fine." His tone was soothing. "Let her get to her car. We'll follow her just like we planned."

Vivian kept her eyes on the ground in front of her, walking swiftly to her car. The minutes felt like hours before she pulled out of the parking lot and onto the road. And more agonizing time passed before Charlie felt like it was safe enough to go after her.

"Take your time, brother," Charlie said, gripping the handle above the passenger's-side door as Ryan took a turn with a little more speed than necessary. "Lane will kill you if I get hurt because of your driving."

Ryan forced himself to slow down and tempered his breathing. Several miles outside Walton, Vivian's BMW was parked on the side of the road. He pulled up behind her and couldn't get his door opened fast enough.

"Be cool, brother," Charlie called out, laughing.

"Be cool, Ryan," he mumbled to himself. As he walked up to the driver's side, Vivian rolled down her window. "Are you okay?"

Vivian nodded like she was trying to convince herself she was. "Yeah, I mean, my heart is racing, but I think it went well."

Her heart was racing? His had been in full gallop from the moment she stepped into that gym. Ryan wasn't sure how he was supposed to let her walk into the gala and face the Watcher on her own. He'd need to convince the sheriff that she'd be safer if he was there with her.

"Did you have any problems? Pecca called you on time?"

"Yeah, he heard everything I said." She squinted up at him. "He already knew about Russell Bradley being at the gala."

Ryan's heart slowed. "Do you think he knows you're his daughter?"

"I basically said as much on the phone with Pecca." Vivian gripped the steering wheel, her knuckles white. "If Coach Robbins is the Watcher and does what we think he will, he'll set Russell and me up at the gala. Catch it on video to use against us."

He hated this. Hated putting Vivian in the middle of this. "I wish there was another way."

Awkward silence ticked off between them before Vivian spoke again. "I better go. Coach Robbins is expecting a story tomorrow morning in the *Gazette.*"

"Right." Ryan tapped the top of her car with his hands, not wanting her to go. It felt like there were a thousand unspoken things hanging between them and he wanted to hash them out. Fight . . . and then make up. Go back to the way it was. But from the way she was limiting their contact, that chance was long over. "I'll, um, see you at the station tomorrow morning to go over the plan before the gala."

"Yes." She started her car and he stepped away, watching her pull back onto the road heading into Walton.

"Did you tell her about the job?" Charlie asked as soon as Ryan got into his Jeep.

"What's the point?"

"Uh, I don't know. Maybe that you love her."

"I don't . . ." Ryan's shoulders slumped

against his seat. There was no denying it. He loved Vivian. Geek boy meets stunning beauty and somehow wins her heart and they fall for each other. Their beginning would've made for a great comic book — at least until he ruined it. "I don't know what to do."

"Have you apologized?"

"Yes." Ryan started his Jeep and merged onto the road. "But it wasn't enough."

"Did you make her believe it?"

Ryan frowned at Charlie. "What do you mean?"

Charlie slid his sunglasses off his nose and slipped them over the bill of his baseball cap. "Think about it, Ryan. How many times do you think Vivian's dad apologized the day she found out he'd been lying to her throughout her whole life? Even if it was a million times, do you think it made a single bit of difference the second he walked out of her life? His actions said she wasn't enough."

Ryan's grip tightened around the wheel. It wasn't hard to imagine Vivian's vulnerability in that moment because he'd witnessed it — experienced it — himself when his own father walked out. *And I did the same thing to her that night in the hospital.* "What am I supposed to do?"

"What would you have wanted your dad to do?"

That was a loaded question. As a kid, Ryan had contemplated a dozen scenarios about what he would do if his dad came home. Would he yell at his father? Hug him and welcome him back? Would he chase him off? Forgive him? So many variables shifted from day to day, until he finally resigned himself to the fact that his father was never coming back and he was on his own. Ryan learned to rely on himself — the way Vivian had.

He flipped on his blinker to take the exit onto Ford Avenue.

Vivian had let him in. Trusted him. And he had let her down. She didn't need him to apologize. She needed him to show her that he would be there for her. No matter what.

"I'm going to fight for her until I make her believe she is enough."

Charlie flashed him a smile. "Yeah, you are, buddy."

After dropping Charlie off at the station, Ryan arrived at his mom's house and was sitting across from her and Frankie, who'd developed a love for brightly colored scarves to cover the wound on her head.

"You look like a hippie."

Frankie's eyes lit. "That's what Ms. Byrdie said too."

"Where's Dr. Murphy?"

His mom sat forward. "He's in Atlanta. The church does a mission trip there every year, and he cleans teeth for people who can't afford it."

"That's cool." It had been impossible to find anything to dislike about the man. He didn't even have a parking ticket. "You're happy?"

"I am." His mom smiled. "Really happy."

"So, Ryan, why'd you call me out here?" Frankie blew a pink bubble with her gum before it popped, covering her lips. "I get enough of their sappy lovefest without you bringing it up."

His mom gave Frankie's leg a playful slap.

"I'm going to take a job with the FBI's Cyber Crimes Division in Washington, DC."

"Washington, DC," Frankie squawked.

"Wow." But the word didn't match the sentiment in his mom's hazel eyes.

"What's wrong?" Ryan shifted in his chair. "You don't think I should go?"

"No, honey, I mean, yes." She reached over and squeezed his hand. "Of course you should go . . . I just thought . . . what about Atlanta?"

Would his mom think him foolish for wanting to go to Atlanta only to be close to Vivian?

"You were moving there to be with Vivian." Frankie's eyes grew round with understanding. "But now you can't because you broke up."

Thanks to all those reality shows, of course Frankie would figure it out.

"You broke up with Vivian?"

Ryan wanted to send his sister a scathing look to tell her thanks a lot, but her apology was all over her face and he just couldn't. *Because she's right.* "It's complicated."

"It doesn't have to be," his mom said. "I've watched you grow into this wonderful man. You're kind, responsible, smart, good-looking —"

"Okay, Mom." Frankie raised her eyebrows. "His ego is already big enough."

Ryan narrowed his eyes at his sister. "Not possible with you around."

"What I'm trying to say is that in the middle of carrying responsibilities that you were never meant to carry, you've allowed yourself to believe you can't have great things."

"Mom —"

"Let me finish." She tightened her hold on his hand. "I didn't realize until you

392

turned down those college scholarships that you were neglecting your dreams —"

"I didn't want to go to the schools."

"Maybe not, but I know you've made choices in your life that put your dreams second to taking care of us, and I don't think you would've ever considered leaving Walton if it hadn't been for Vivian."

Ryan looked down at the floor. Vivian made him want to be a better man, to expect more out of himself. To be worthy of her . . . so she wouldn't leave him.

"Whatever has happened between you and Vivian" — his mom's words brought his gaze back up to hers — "you need to let her know how much she means to you, because going after this dream in DC won't mean as much without her by your side."

"What if she won't forgive me?"

"Then you'll know." She released his hand and wrapped her arm around Frankie's shoulder. "And your sister and I will be here to support you no matter what, right, Frannie?"

"I guess." His sister let out an exasperated sigh. "It'll be pretty cool to tell my friends my brother works for the FBI."

"And it'll be even cooler that I can run background checks on all your friends and hack into their social media accounts."

"You can't do that." Frankie turned to their mom. "He can't do that, can he? There are laws or something, right?"

Ryan smirked. "Sounds like you've got something to hide."

"Come on, you two, let's eat dinner."

Frankie stuck her tongue out at Ryan before getting up and walking into the kitchen. "Real mature for a freshman in college, Frankie."

"It's Frannie," she yelled back.

"I'm never going to call her that," Ryan said to his mom. "The best I can do is Frank."

"Don't you dare." His mom laughed. "Ryan" — she turned to him — "thank you for the way you've taken care of us, son. You've given up a lot. I know God has great plans for the life he wants you to live — and I believe that life includes Vivian. Go after her. You are worthy of her."

Twenty-Six

"Why couldn't I get this part of the under-cover job?"

Vivian stared up at the ceiling of her bathroom, her eyelids fluttering from the second coat of mascara Pecca had applied to her lashes. "Because you have a little boy who needs you."

"True." Pecca's fingers tipped Vivian's chin from side to side. "Still, it would be nice to get dressed up once in a while and pretend I'm the Hispanic Cinderella." She reached for the eyeliner. "Prince Charming would come in on a Harley —"

"A Harley?"

"Who wants to ride in a pumpkin?"

"It's a horse-drawn carriage."

"Exactly." Pecca tilted Vivian's head back and touched up the makeup on her eyes. "Get all dressed up to sit behind horses while they" — she wrinkled her nose — "you know, do their thing."

"But exhaust fumes from a motorcycle are better?"

Pecca huffed. "Way to destroy the dream, amiga."

Vivian laughed. "Sorry."

"How did the meeting go this morning? Or can you not tell me because it's a top-secret mission?"

"Truthfully, I only know my part." She had spent two hours that morning with Ryan and Sheriff Huggins as they went over the plans to catch the Watcher at the gala. Vivian would be arriving as a member of the press, and since Pete Robbins had already RSVP'd, all she could do was wait until he made his move — proving he was the Watcher. What the move would be was anyone's guess, and the uncertainty was creating havoc in her stomach. "Sheriff Huggins said there would be added security tonight."

"As long as Ryan's around, you have nothing to worry about. He won't let anything happen to you."

Vivian shifted on the stool, recalling the way he had watched her this morning as they went over the plan. She'd gotten really good at reading his expressions and knew when he was about to cross the line from professional to personal, but before he had the chance, Vivian would turn the focus back on the mission. It was getting harder and harder to convince herself that she did the right thing by ending her relationship with him. Staying focused was the only way she could protect herself. "He's doing his job."

"*I'm* doing my job." Pecca snorted. "He's preparing to go all Bruce Banner on anyone who hurts you."

"You mean Hulk." Vivian snickered. "Bruce Banner was the nuclear physicist good guy."

"Right." Pecca angled a gaze at Vivian. "Genius boy scout. That's Ryan. Except he'll explode into this massive green monster to protect the one he loves. You're his Natasha."

Vivian pushed Pecca's hand away from applying yet another layer of eye shadow. Trying to keep her mind off of Ryan was already hard enough. She didn't need Pecca planting thoughts of Ryan gallantly coming to her defense — or ripping his shirt off to do so. "First off, impressive knowledge of Marvel characters. Second, I am not his Natasha."

"First off," Pecca said, mimicking, "I'm preparing for the next trivia night. And yes, you are. Natasha brings out the best in

Hulk, right? You do that for Ryan."

Ugh. Why is Pecca making this so difficult? Maybe because it's the truth? "I don't know about that."

"Vivian." Pecca's voice took on that mom tone she'd heard her use with Maceo. "I'm going to be real here and you can hate me or whatever, but what in the world is your issue?"

Vivian frowned. "What do you mean?"

"Ryan was scared. His sister was injured and you both could've been killed. His behavior at the hospital was dumb, I get that, and I told him he was an idiot if he didn't go crawling back to you and apologize. He did, right?"

"Yes."

"Okay, then why are you holding on to it?" Pecca's expression softened. "It's like you're holding on to that single moment as an excuse to push Ryan away."

Vivian stared back into Pecca's probing brown eyes and didn't see an ounce of accusation. She was looking back as a friend trying to understand. *"Amiga."* From the very beginning, Pecca called her friend. Although she hadn't known a single thing about Vivian, it was like she staked a claim on their relationship.

"I'm scared." Vivian's voice wavered.

"Girl, don't you cry." Pecca gave her a stern look. "That's two hours of makeup about to stream off your face."

"That's how you respond to my confession?" Vivian shook her head, unable to keep a smile from her lips. "I pour out my heart —"

"Pour? Amiga, that was like the sprinkling the Pope flicks around." She laughed. "I know you're scared. Knew it the first day I met you. That's why I didn't pressure you to come over or hang out."

Vivian eyed her. "Coming to my house every other day wasn't pressure?"

"No, it was a sprinkling" — she opened her fingers wide — "like the Pope."

"I'd hate to know what a baptism feels like."

Pecca rolled her eyes. "Anyway. I wasn't going to give up on you. And eventually you saw your way to the light, and now look at us. Chatting about boys, doing our makeup — okay, your makeup. We're practically BFFs."

Pecca hadn't given up on her. Neither had Harold. It was because he had believed she was the right one for the job even when she fought it — he never gave up. Emotion bubbled up and Vivian had to work to keep the tears back.

"If I have only one friend in the world," Vivian said as she reached for Pecca's hand, "you're the one I would want."

"Girl." Pecca's thick lashes batted furiously. "Now you're going to make me cry, and I ugly cry."

Vivian's sappy emotion transformed into giggles even as tears slipped down her cheeks. How had she let so much time go by without Pecca's friendship? Or the others? Vivian's life in Walton flashed in her mind, bringing Ms. Byrdie, Lane, and Frannie to her thoughts. Somehow all these people had slipped by her defenses and claimed a piece of her.

"Did I ruin your work?"

"No." Pecca pulled a tissue from the box and started dabbing the skin beneath Vivian's eyes. "I'll just touch it up."

That touch-up took another thirty minutes before Pecca allowed her to start getting dressed. Vivian slipped on the emerald-green gown. She was afraid the beaded bodice would be too heavy, but thanks to the layers of gauzy fabric in the skirt, it wasn't too bad. Vivian stepped out of the bedroom and Pecca's jaw dropped.

"You. Look. Hot."

Vivian grinned, lifting the edge of her dress, and turned. "I know it's not very

Southern."

"Who cares? You're going to put every Southern belle in her place, I do declare."

"Was that supposed to be a Southern accent?"

"Meh." Pecca shrugged. "You ready?"

Vivian toyed with her clutch. "I'm not sure."

Pecca adjusted a strand of Vivian's hair back into place. "What's the matter?"

"I don't know." Vivian placed her palm against her stomach. "Something just doesn't feel right."

"Do you want to call it off? I can call Ryan right now."

"No." Gathering her dress, Vivian moved to the couch and sat on the edge. "I think I'm just nervous. It's been fifteen years since I've seen Russell. What if . . . what if he sees me and it only reaffirms why he left us in the first place?"

"First of all" — Pecca sat next to Vivian — "that's not going to happen. You said he's been reaching out to you, right?" Vivian nodded. "So that must mean he wants to see you —"

"And then what, Pecca?" Vivian ran her fingers over the beading on her dress. "I came to Walton to land a job at the *Tribune*, and when I got it I thought I'd be happy or fulfilled, but instead . . . I feel lost."

"You didn't take the job?"

"No." Vivian shook her head. "My whole life I've set myself goals. Graduate top of my class — check. Get into journalism program at UVA — check. Get job as investigative journalist at top paper — check and double check. It's like it's never enough. Tonight I'm going to face Russell Bradley — my father — a moment I've been waiting for, but now I can't remember why. If he acknowledges me and apologizes, then what? Will he expect me to forgive him? Even if that was possible, where do we go from there?"

"Forgiving someone is not saying what they did to you is okay. Forgiving is saying you will no longer allow what they did to you to control your life." Pecca spoke the words like she knew a thing or two about what she was saying. "Have you considered that maybe you're second-guessing this confrontation because you don't need his approval anymore?"

"What do you mean?"

"Sounds like every goal you've set for yourself stems from this desire to prove yourself to your father."

"I'll never understand why I wasn't good enough for him."

"Your father?" Pecca pivoted on the couch. "Or Ryan?"

The doorbell interrupted the moment, causing Pecca to roll her eyes.

"Figures, right?"

"Right." Vivian stood and gave herself a final glance in the mirror, half grateful for the timely disruption.

Before Vivian answered the door, Pecca caught her by the arm. "You don't have to prove your worth to anyone, including yourself."

The Savannah Yacht Club was lit up like it was the venue for the Oscars. Ryan scanned the long docks decorated in strands of twinkling white lights that matched the ones stretched over the long, wide branches of the live oaks. He was positioned on the south side of the white manor, giving him a view of guests arriving by car and by boat.

"I'm never going to get used to these sand gnats," Charlie said, slapping his palm against his neck. "How are you not getting eaten alive?"

"Native." Ryan shrugged. "They prefer Yankee blood."

"I'm not sure Virginia is considered Yankee territory."

"You wouldn't be getting bit if we were in

there instead of out here."

"Sheriff Huggins tried," Charlie said, swatting at his arm. "The president of the club and the board of directors had already hired a private security firm but agreed that with Russell Bradley's fame, they could use a little extra security outside the gala."

Ryan eyed the area near the front of the club, where a crowd continued to grow. Reporters and photographers not part of the gala's staff were roped off to one section where they could take pictures and ask questions of arriving guests. On the other side was a screen where attendees paused for a photo before entering the gala, though some lingered, and he had to guess it was for the same reason the media had made tonight's event a priority. Russell Bradley's fame.

Two men in black uniforms with big, shiny silver badges pinned to their chests directed traffic. Of the two, Ryan wasn't sure which one he'd wager could actually use the company-issued gun strapped to his waist.

"I guess they're not really worried about security if they're relying on those rent-a-cops."

"Maybe they wanted to save money for the twinkling lights," Charlie said. "They should've used it to spray for bugs."

Ryan looked at his watch. "She's supposed to be here by now. Why isn't she here?"

"Relax, brother. She's right there."

Turning in the direction Charlie was looking, Ryan watched one of the rent-a-cops help Vivian out of a sedan. Her long, dark hair was swept away from her neck, pinned with a sparkling clip that enhanced the way her green dress glimmered beneath the lights. She was radiant. No, stunning. Breathtaking. Vivian was all those things, and a deep urge pulsed within him to rush over and tell her so.

"You okay? Breathing alright?"

"She's . . . I just . . . I'm such an idiot."

"You're not an idiot." Charlie nudged Ryan with his elbow. "Have you figured out what you're going to do to win her back?"

"Not yet." Ryan grumbled as he watched Vivian slip her arm into the crook of George Shepherd Kennedy's arm. "Why did we bring *him* into this again?"

"Because Sheriff Huggins needed someone on the inside who could keep an eye on her."

"What's he going to do, protect her with his nine iron?" Ryan mocked. "The only thing threatening about Shep is his golf swing."

Charlie looked at Ryan with a smirk on his lips. "You just used up all your golf knowledge on that, didn't you?"

Ryan adjusted his vest as beads of sweat trickled down his chest. "Can we just focus?"

"Sure thing, Tiger."

Ignoring Charlie's joke, Ryan turned his attention on a large red pickup that had just pulled up. The valet went around to open the door, but it swung open before he could get there. Coach Pete Robbins hopped out and handed the keys over to the valet.

A couple of reporters called out his name and the coach went over, shook some hands, and posed for photos like *he* was the honoree. But his moment was cut short when a stretch limousine pulled up, drawing everyone's attention. Coach Robbins stepped aside, but his eyes were glued to the passenger inside the car.

Charlie nudged Ryan. "That's Russell."

They watched as Vivian's father stepped out of the car to the roar of his admirers. Russell Bradley made his claim to fame as the doting father and loyal husband on an '80s sitcom, winning the hearts of housewives everywhere and becoming husband goals for younger generations. Since then, his collection of film and movie credits had ranged from action hero to love-torn widower, giving him a long and successful career in an unpredictable industry.

He was also a moron for what he did to Vivian.

Over their radio, Sheriff Huggins confirmed Coach Robbins was inside and Deputy Wilson had eyes on him.

"Now, how does a six-foot-five, refrigerator-sized man like Wilson get invited to this?"

"You forget his skills on the football field led to UGA winning four bowl games," Charlie said. "Georgians don't forget success like that. I've heard they're trying to get him to coach."

Ryan turned to Charlie. "Really?"

"Yep, but according to him the only ball he wants to play is catch with his son."

"He's really like one of those oversized teddy bears from Costco, isn't he?"

"I'll pay you a hundred bucks to say that to his face."

"No deal." Ryan shook his head. "It looks like the last of the guests are arriving. I'm going to head to the van."

Charlie gave him a look. "Remember the plan. We don't interfere unless she's in danger. We have to let the Watcher play this out or we got nothing."

Ryan didn't need Charlie to remind him how high the stakes were. There was a beautiful woman in a heart attack–inducing dress somewhere inside the club to tell him that. Never mind that she also happened to be with Shep.

The back of the club ran parallel to the Ogeechee River, with large floor-to-ceiling windows to give guests a panoramic view worthy of the five-figure dues. A large patio dripping in twinkling lights would beckon guests after their meal for a night of dancing beneath the stars. What Ryan wouldn't give to have the opportunity to lead Vivian out there. He was serious when he told Charlie he didn't want to do life without her. Sure, Holly Newman was the safe bet, and maybe he would've chosen her before, but he was different now. Things had shifted since Vivian came into his life. There was no going back.

Before locking himself inside the surveillance van Agent Hannigan had loaned them, Ryan took in the festivities. The gala was underway as men in tuxedos helped their dates navigate the tight seating arrangements. Waiters walked through, offering glasses of champagne to all. Ryan searched the room, careful to keep to the hedges so as not to interfere with the guests' *experience* — another reason the board gave as to why they wanted the uniformed officers to remain outside — until he found Vivian.

She was seated at a round table close to the front of the room but not directly center. According to Shep, the reporters would be seated together at one table, which meant the empty seat on Vivian's left was where he should be sitting.

Ryan ground his molars. Shep was supposed to be keeping an eye on Vivian, so where was he? His gaze traveled around the room, but Shep was nowhere to be seen. Ryan started to walk to the other side of the building when he spotted Shep at the bar. He was talking with a blonde woman who had her arm draped around his shoulder in a way that suggested maybe she should've been his date. Was he seriously flirting?

"Vivian is by herself while Romeo is at the bar," Ryan spoke into the radio through gritted teeth.

"Frost." Charlie's voice came over the radio. "He probably just went to get her a drink. Did you see Vivian?"

"She's at her table."

"Then she's fine."

Charlie's calming and reasonable voice should've been enough to uncoil the anger tightening in Ryan's chest, but it wasn't helping. Ryan watched Shep buy the blonde a drink, then whisper something in her ear before getting up. Good, he was going back to the table. Only he wasn't. Shep turned in the opposite direction and down a hall.

Ryan moved in the same direction when a door swung open and Shep stepped out, a cigar halfway to his mouth.

"What are you doing?"

Shep jumped, clearly not expecting Ryan to be there. "What? I wanted a smoke."

"You're not here for a smoke." Ryan snatched the cigar and threw it to the ground.

"You realize you just tossed a Montecristo cigar to the ground?"

"I don't care." Ryan seethed. He stepped in close to Shep and appreciated that he was an inch taller so the guy had to look up. "Get in there and keep an eye on Vivian or it'll be more than a cigar that I throw to the ground."

TWENTY-SEVEN

"Coach Robbins, I'd like you to meet Eugene Europa. Star point guard for St. Louis High School and a future Anderson Cougar."

Pete Robbins twisted his attention away from Russell Bradley to the red-faced man wearing a tuxedo bulging at the waistline. Next to him was a young man, smiling sheepishly, his hands tucked behind his back.

Pete held out his hand and the kid gave it an enthusiastic shake. "It's nice to meet you. I've heard good things are happening with the Crusaders."

"Yes, sir." The kid nodded. "We're going to take state next year."

"I'm his math teacher, Brian Garnick. I saw his potential and have helped him achieve it." The teacher tugged at his collar, which was beginning to sink into the folds around his neck. "Eugene here not only has the skills on the court, but he's got the brains to back them up. Scored a twenty-seven on his ACTs."

"That's very nice of you." Pete commended Mr. Garnick while keeping an eye on Russell Bradley. The actor was making his way through the room slowly as people stopped him for autographs and pictures. "Be sure to send me your season's schedule. I'd love to catch a game."

"That'd be awesome, sir." Eugene smiled as his teacher clapped him on the back.

"I'm going to introduce him to Coach Lundy." Mr. Garnick looked around him. "You wouldn't happen to know where he is?"

"Table fifteen."

"Thanks, Coach."

Pete waved off the teacher and student protégé and wondered what a math teacher like Brian Garnick was hoping to get out of Eugene's success on the basketball court. He'd seen it a few times during recruitment season. Players raised not by their own families but by families with access to opportunities they wouldn't have otherwise. These families didn't always have an altruistic motive.

"Ladies and gentlemen." A woman in a black sequin dress stood on the stage with a microphone. "Dinner will be served promptly at eight, giving you exactly one hour to enjoy the delicious hors d'oeuvres our chef has prepared. Please finish up those drinks or grab another" — laughter and cheers went up — "and find your places. I promise you will not want to miss what we have in store for you."

Pete pulled a ten from his wallet and laid it on the bar, then he picked up his drink. It was time to work. He pushed his way through the crowd.

"Great season, Coach." A man grabbed at his hand. "Looking forward to next year."

"Yes, it'll be good."

He continued through the crowd until he made his way into a hallway. It had taken only a simple search of the Central Appraisal District website to pull up the floor plan for the club, which he had studied for less than thirty minutes before arriving to know the layout. The two doors on his right were marked as restrooms. There was a storage closet. And . . . bingo. A sign on the side of the door marked this room as a bridal suite. The yacht club rented out its facilities for weddings and receptions, and Pete guessed this room housed the bride or groom before their nuptials. Tonight it would bring father and daughter together.

Whether it was providence or just plain good luck, when he'd overheard the reporter talking about Russell Bradley being her father . . . it was like winning the lottery. Of course, he checked into Russell Bradley as soon as he got home. No records anywhere indicated that Vivian DeMarco was his daughter. Pete also checked into Vivian's mother and found the only smoking gun he needed — the deed to her house in Virginia was in the names of Genevieve DeMarco and Arthur Russell Bradley. Arthur was Russell's birthname.

Stepping into the suite, Pete took in the room. There was a sitting area with a couch, two chairs, a coffee table, and an end table. On one side of the wall was a long granite counter with stools tucked beneath and a long mirror with lights overhead. Except for a few pieces of art on the wall, some fake greenery, and a wooden bust of James Oglethorpe on a table near the door, there weren't many places for him to hide the cameras.

Normally, he'd outsource this part of the job to keep his hands as clean as possible, but there hadn't been enough time. He reached into his pocket and pulled out three square devices the size of a quarter and two devices that looked like an adapter with a

USB port for the wall. The cameras were small, but with the 155-degree angle, he wouldn't miss a thing.

It took him less than five minutes to set up the cameras and verify through an app on his phone that they were in position. Tucking the phone into his pocket, his fingers grazed the envelope. Part two of the plan. He stepped out of the suite, closing the door behind him, and bumped into someone.

"Oh, I'm sorry, sir, but that room isn't part of the gala event tonight."

Pete looked at the young woman, a server based on her black slacks, vest, and white blouse. He stepped back, painting a confused look on his face. "This isn't the men's room?"

"No, sir." She smiled, pointing to the door behind him. "It's right there."

"Thank you." He winked at her. "One too many sips of the bubbly, I guess."

"No problem. There are also restrooms on the other side of the gala hall, closer to the bar."

"Smart girl." He ran his fingers through his hair and took a step toward her. "Can I ask a favor?"

"Sure, sir."

"There's a girl sitting out there in a green

415

dress with all these sparkly things on it. Table six, I think." He reached into his pocket and pulled out the envelope with Vivian's name on it. "I've been admiring her for a while, but she's sorta out of my league and I don't want to make a fool of myself." Sympathy played in the woman's eyes. "Would you mind giving this to her while I kind of hide out at the bar?"

The server's eyes drifted from him to the envelope and he could see an internal debate happening.

"Yeah, it's probably stupid, huh?" He moved the envelope back toward his pocket. "I'm just not good at talking to women and" — he saw the woman was wearing a wedding band — "I'm old-fashioned. Not into that online dating stuff. It was much safer when we were kids and could pass a note with a box that said, 'Do you like me? Check yes or no.' Am I right?"

"My husband was shy too." She smiled. "I had to make the first move." Her forehead wrinkled. "Come to think of it, I'm still making all the first moves."

"There should be more women in the world like you." He gave her his most charming grin. "You don't have a sister, do you?"

"I do, but she'd chew you up and spit you

out. She's on husband number four."

"Yikes." He started to turn. "Well, I guess I should get back to admiring her from a distance."

"Wait." The woman looked around them. "Give me the note."

"Are you sure?"

"Yes." She took the envelope from him. "I'll be Cupid just this once. You said table six and —"

"Her name is Vivian DeMarco, green dress." He took a step backward. "Your husband is a lucky man."

"I tell him that every day."

Pete turned and hustled back toward the bar. A glance at his watch said he had a little more than half an hour to get Vivian and her father in that suite together. He watched as his Cupid worked her way around the room until she got to Vivian's table and passed her the envelope. Perfect. Now to let Russell in on the plan.

TWENTY-EIGHT

Vivian's fingers trembled over the envelope clutched in her hand. The waitress said she was asked to deliver a message from a secret admirer. Inside the envelope was a note typed with six words.

Please meet me. Bridal suite. Russell.

She knew the note wasn't from Russell. After her initial phone call to her father, she made one more to let him know they could not contact each other until the Watcher had made his move. That way they would know it was him setting them up.

On her way toward the suite, she searched for Deputy Wilson. Ryan and Charlie had told her he would be attending the event as a guest, but she couldn't find him through the crowd and was afraid to waste time in case the Watcher was keeping an eye on her. Vivian had to trust that the plan they had in place was a good one and she would be safe.

Rounding the corner, she lifted her dress

and walked down the hallway until she found the room designated as the bridal suite. She twisted the knob and wondered if Russell was already in there waiting. Vivian wasn't sure if the anxiousness knotting her stomach was from fear or nerves, but it was too late to back out now. Somewhere, the Watcher was . . . watching.

Inhaling, she pushed the door open and was mildly relieved to find the room empty. She closed the door behind her and did a quick sweep, wondering where the cameras were hidden. A closet was at the back of the room and a stab of panic coursed through her — what if the Watcher was hiding in there? Moving slowly to the door, she took another breath and opened it, only to find it too was empty, save for a few hangers.

Vivian exhaled, trying to steel her nerves. Somewhere outside Ryan would watch the whole thing in a van set up to tap into the video feed transmitters — or something technical that only Ryan understood. The only thing she needed to understand was that Ryan was watching her and this footage would give them what they needed for the judge to issue a warrant to search Pete Robbins's computers for evidence he was the Watcher. She just needed to stay calm and wait for Russell to show up.

Why was it taking him so long? Vivian sat on the couch, rolling the envelope in her hand. He was going to show up. He had to. An ugly thought popped into her head. *What if he changed his mind?* What made her think Russell would show up now when he had been absent her whole life? He wouldn't do that, would he? Put their whole plan in jeopardy?

A new fear arrived. What was she going to say when he walked in? "Hi, Dad, it's been fifteen years since you walked out on me. How's it going?"

She thought back to her conversation with Pecca. *"You don't have to prove your worth to anyone, including yourself."* Those words had rolled around in her mind the whole car ride over with Shep. For so long she had believed she was trying to win Russell Bradley's approval. Prove to him he'd made a mistake, only to be ignored. So she'd tried harder. Aimed higher. Anything to grab his attention. Was it coincidental that his phone calls began when she hit her high as a reporter for the *Herald* two years ago?

Suddenly, now, he was interested in contacting her . . . for what?

Vivian's eyes traveled to the long mirror on the wall opposite of where she was sitting. Vivian took in her image. Pecca had managed to make her look like a Hollywood beauty. Would she be enough now?

An ache rippled through her as she contemplated that question. Any minute now, Russell Bradley would walk through that door and they would confront the truth behind his neglect. Only . . . only now she wasn't sure she wanted an answer, because what reason could he possibly give that would satisfy her? Whatever excuse he gave, it wouldn't be good enough. Pecca was right.

Vivian dropped the envelope on the table, pressing a palm to her stomach. The time she had spent writing community event columns for the *Gazette* had made her happier and more content than she'd ever been when she was uncovering stories on corruption, crime, and offensive human behavior. Turning down the job offers at the *Tribune* and *Daily* had been surprisingly easy, given that she didn't know what she was going to do when this was over. It hadn't mattered.

Finding Harold's killer and catching the Watcher had little to do with securing a position as an investigative journalist, or even getting her father's attention, and more to do with restoring hope to the community that had embraced her as family.

Ryan's face penetrated her thoughts,

bringing with it the painful truth Pecca had so aptly pointed out. Vivian had used Ryan's behavior as an excuse to turn him into her father — but Ryan was nothing like him. Even as angry as Vivian had been, Ryan had still pursued her. Still fought for her. When he easily could've picked Holly — the perfect choice by all accounts — he wanted her.

She brushed away the tears on her lashes. She needed to apologize to Ryan for being difficult. She was done using Russell as an excuse to push people away. She wanted a friendship with Pecca and Lane. And she desperately wanted to mend her relationship with Ryan.

What about God?

The thought felt like it came out of the blue, but Vivian knew she'd been pushing that relationship away as well. Where was God in all of this? She inhaled and let the breath come out slowly as though her soul was waking up from a long sleep. How many times had she prayed God would give her back her family? How many times had she felt God had ignored her pleas? It had been too easy for her to assign the sins of her father to God. God hadn't ignored her. He'd answered her prayers in an unexpected way — and it was more than she could've ever hoped for — God gave her a family that had nothing to do with a shared bloodline and everything to do with love.

Vivian sighed. It was time to forgive her father for what he did. She was tired of carrying the bitterness of his abandonment with her and letting it get in the way of loving those who loved her.

"God gave us the gift to bring light out of the darkness. That's been the Gazette*'s mission since my father handed it over to me. As a reporter, I have two choices. I can report on the darkness in the world or I can write the news in a way that restores hope."*

Harold spoke those words to her on her first day at the job, and they had etched their way into her soul, reminding her of why she was there.

It no longer mattered what happened with her father. She didn't have to prove herself to him. Or herself. Vivian only cared about one thing — catching the Watcher.

TWENTY-NINE

Russell Bradley certainly knew how to work his target audience. The actor was still posing for photos and offering congenial conversations with the female guests over forty, their sighs and excited exclamations echoing across the piano music coming from the opposite corner. Pete couldn't blame the guy. Those women had made his most recent romantic drama with Michelle Pfeiffer a blockbuster success. And Pete would cash in on their lusting.

Pete moved around the fabric room dividers so he could get to Russell without having to approach him directly. He paused when he saw a trio of security guards huddled in conversation.

"I heard they're looking for someone."

"Nah, man." One of the men shook his head. "They're just here to control traffic."

"Dude, they don't hire *real* cops to direct traffic." The first one said, shoving into the second guy. "They'd hire us."

"Yeah." The third guy laughed.

Pete looked to his left and out the window in the same direction the guards were looking. He spotted a deputy walking near the patio edge, a radio wire in his ear. Pete's gaze moved farther along the dock until he spotted two more.

A chirping noise erupted from Pete's pocket and the three men looked over at him. He reached into his pocket and pulled out his cell phone. "Thought I turned it off."

The guards didn't look like they cared, then they split up, leaving Pete to answer the alert on his phone. The hair on the back of his neck rose when he saw the flashing red exclamation point flickering over the app he was using to monitor the cameras he'd set up inside the bridal suite. He opened the app and clicked on the cameras filming Vivian. A warning banner popped up on the screen that sent a charge of panic coursing through him. Someone was piggybacking his system, giving them access to his cameras.

Pete looked up, searching around him. It wasn't possible. Even if it was an accidental signal interference, no one would be able to get through the encryption on his app unless they were very good. And even then they'd have to be in close proximity, which meant whoever had breached his program knew what they were doing and wanted to see what he was seeing . . .

His head swiveled toward the hallway leading to the bridal suite. *No.* A sickening reality dropped into his gut like a ball of lead. His eyes moved back to the window. The deputy he'd seen earlier was gone. The other two were farther down the dock, patrolling the boat slips.

"They're looking for someone." The security guard's words slammed into him. It couldn't be. There was no way they were looking for him. He had systems in place. Safeguards. His fingers curled around his cell phone, ready to crush the device when his thoughts went back to the woman waiting in the bridal suite — *her.*

He quickly replayed the video of Vivian walking into the room, watching the way she glanced nervously around and . . . then opened the closet? Pete's jaw clenched as his grip tightened around his phone. How had she figured it out? The email. She must've seen it before Otis broke into the *Gazette* and then somehow linked it to him . . . and then came to his gym and fed him the thickest line. Set him up. And he'd fallen for it. His blood started to simmer.

426

So she'd figured it out? Did Vivian De-Marco really think she was going to take him down?

Pete walked around the curtained partition and through the crowd of women. "Excuse me, Mr. Bradley."

The actor leaned back. "Yes, I'll be with you in just one minute."

"No, sir. I have a message for you from your daughter." Pete moved forward so no one else could hear him. "Vivian." A number of emotions moved through Russell's eyes before concern settled in them. Pete had to admit the actor was good. "It's quite urgent."

Russell looked around the room. "Where is she?"

"I'll take you to her." Russell hesitated for a second, and it was all the confirmation Pete needed. This wasn't part of their plan. A surge of satisfaction tempered his anger. "You should hurry. She seemed pretty upset. I'm not sure how much longer she'll wait for you."

The apprehension lining Russell's forehead softened. "Okay."

Pete led Russell toward the kitchen. "There's a hallway to the left, through that door."

Russell pushed through the door, entering

into another hallway that was dimly lit and empty. Pete knew this hallway would lead to a small kitchen near the boathouse. The club built it so servers could go back and forth between both kitchens while being seen as little as possible by guests.

"Uh, are you a friend of Vivian's?"

"Close enough that she told me you're her father."

Russell's shoulders stiffened as they stepped into the boathouse kitchen. They passed stainless steel prep tables, an oven, and a refrigerator before they paused in front of another door.

"Where is she?"

"Waiting at a table on the other side of this door," Pete said, wrapping his hand around the neck of a wine bottle.

When Russell turned the knob, Pete raised his arm overhead and swung it down against the back of Russell's neck, sending the man pitching into a table and chair, overturning them. Pete froze, listening to see if someone had heard the commotion.

Assured his deed hadn't drawn any attention, Pete used the tip of his shoe to nudge Russell's leg. The man wouldn't be moving anytime soon. He'd give Vivian DeMarco her family reunion — and he'd make sure it was painful.

He waited several minutes before starting back through the kitchen toward the gala, his pulse keeping rhythm with the angry cadence of his steps. Pete paused at the entrance of the dining room. Servers were taking their places near the kitchen to prepare for dinner service. He would need to do this quickly.

Pete slipped down the narrow hall toward the bridal suite where Vivian was waiting. Pausing outside the door, he pulled out his phone and opened the app connected to the cameras currently recording everything happening inside the room — or at least what was supposed to happen. He calmed the tremor in his fingers so he could enter the code. They might've blindsided him, but the tables would turn. He fixed his attention on the door in front of him. *And now she will pay.*

"Can I help you?"

A young man in a black security uniform started for him. He couldn't have been more than twenty years old, a bit on the skinny side with a face still fighting acne like it wasn't sure if puberty had done its part yet.

"Hey, I know you." He smiled. "You coach the Cougars. Coach Robbins, right?"

The tiny name tag pinned beneath a silver

badge that looked as official as one from the toy store said his name was Michael.

"I am, Mike." Pete shook the guard's hand. "You haven't seen a drop-dead beauty about this" — Pete held his hand up near his shoulder — "this tall? Brunette? Green dress?"

"No, sir." Mike shook his head. He tipped his head toward the bridal suite. "That room is closed. Did you check the restroom?"

"Not there." Pete looked over his shoulder in the direction of the dining room. "They're going to start dinner soon and I'm afraid my girlfriend might've spent a little too much time at the bar, if you know what I mean. Would it be okay if I just check this room to be sure?"

Mike looked from Pete to the door and then back, uncertainty clouding his eyes for a second before clearing. "How about I check? Don't want you to get in trouble."

Pete lifted his hands. "Don't want that. These people can be a little uppity."

"That's the truth." Mike opened the door and stepped into the suite, followed by Pete, who silently closed the door behind him.

Vivian stood up, surprise lighting her eyes as they went from Mike to Pete.

"Oh, here you are, honey." Pete walked

past Mike, making his way toward Vivian. "Too much wine?"

"What are you talking about?" Vivian stepped around the coffee table.

Pete stopped her with a tight grip on her arm. "Now, honey, don't embarrass yourself."

"Let go." Vivian tried to pull her arm free, but he held on tight. She turned fearful eyes on Michael. "I'm not his girlfriend. He's a crim— ow." She cringed, grabbing at his fingers with her free hand as his nails dug deep into her skin.

"She's had too much to drink. I'll take her home."

"No!" Vivian pleaded with Michael. "Go get help!"

Mike's expression revealed a mixture of confusion and fear. He backed toward the door, his hand moving toward the gun on his waist. *Why would they give this guy a gun?* Nothing in the kid's posture indicated he was prepared to use it, and Pete was going to take advantage of his inexperience. "Maybe I should go get someone," Mike said.

"That's a good idea." Pete released Vivian's arm and in two short strides closed the distance between him and Mike, putting him close enough to —

The *thwack* of the statue cracking into Michael's skull radiated up Pete's arm as he watched the kid's eyes roll back into his head before he dropped to the floor. Vivian's yelp was muffled by her hands covering her mouth, her expression aghast.

"Sorry, Mike." Pete dropped the statue at Mike's feet. He slipped the guard's gun from the holster, then checked to see that it was loaded before tucking it into his waistband and looking up at Vivian. "You ready?"

Vivian shook her head, backing away from him. "What do you want?"

Pete glared. "To give you the family reunion you so carefully set up." He opened the door an inch and peeked out.

"You really think I'm going to walk out of here with you?"

He pulled the gun from his waistband and pointed it at her. "You don't have a choice. Besides, I'd hate for you to miss your opportunity to confront the man who walked out on you all those years ago."

She swallowed, fear returning to her eyes. "Where's Russell?"

"You're about to find out." He swung the tip of the gun toward the door. "Let's go."

Vivian hesitated and Pete drew back the slide on the gun, engaging a bullet in the chamber. She reluctantly walked close enough to him that he was able to take ahold of her arm and push the muzzle of the gun into her side.

He leaned in close, a curl from her hair touching his lips as he breathed in the sweet scent of her perfume. "Whatever your feelings are for your estranged father, you try anything and his blood will be on you."

She narrowed her eyes on him and tugged her elbow free of his grip. He could see the fire behind her blue-gray eyes. "They're waiting for you out there. You won't even make it past the front door."

The corner of Pete's lips lifted in pleasure. "Watch me."

Pete pulled Vivian close as they stepped out of the suite together. He looked down the hall toward the dining room where he could hear the clinking of silverware against glass. While shoving Vivian forward, his eye caught on the red fire alarm mounted to the wall. He smiled. He wouldn't just make it out the front doors, but he'd do it right under their noses.

Woo-woo-woo.

The bellowing siren screamed through the building, drawing a commotion that echoed from the dining hall. Pete, not happy with the lack of expedience, aimed the gun at the ceiling and fired two shots — the effect immediate.

Screams competed with the fire alarm and a rush of men and women filled the hallway, civility forgotten as they pushed their way to the exits. Pete thrust Vivian into the melee, keeping her close and searching the doors for any signs of the deputies.

There. A deputy was fighting his way through the crowd, panic etched into the corners of his eyes. Pete tucked his chin, but Vivian must've seen the deputy because she raised up on her toes and tried to wriggle free of his grip.

"He'd hit the ground before he even knew what hit him."

Vivian shrank back, her eyes casting one final glance toward the deputy as they walked past him, blending in with the frantic crowd scrambling toward the one thing Pete wanted too.

Freedom.

THIRTY

"Shots fired! Shots fired!" Ryan screamed into his radio as he surged into the crowd of men and women anxious to get out of the building where the gunshots still echoed. His pulse pounded in his ears almost as loudly as the fire alarm's deafening squeal overhead.

"Officer." A man grabbed Ryan's arm, stopping him. "I need your help."

Ryan took in the man. His wispy hair was mussed at the sides and his glasses hung at an angle from his nose. "What do you need?"

"My wife's purse is inside."

"You're kidding?" But the expression on the man's face said he was not. Ryan turned on his heel and left the man confused as to why he wasn't concerned about his wife's belongings.

The radio attached to Ryan's shoulder crackled. The fire department was en route, along with Savannah Metro to help contain the chaos. Ryan should've known something was wrong the second the video feed inside the suite was cut. He should've come in sooner and pulled her out. He never should've allowed her to get involved in the first place.

"Frost."

Ryan looked over his shoulder and saw Charlie cutting through the crowd, but he didn't stop. He needed to get to the suite.

"Hold up."

"She never should've been a part of this." Ryan grabbed at overturned chairs in his way and tossed them to the side. "It's my fault."

Charlie's heavy breathing followed Ryan down the hall toward the suite. *Please let her be in here.* Ryan pushed open the door, his pulse surging when he found it empty of Vivian and a body on the floor.

They dropped to their knees and turned the man over. Charlie felt for a pulse. "He's alive."

"She's gone."

"We're going to find her," Charlie said, radioing in their location for medical assistance.

Ryan ran his fingers through his hair. The man lying on the floor had a purple knot at the base of his skull. Had Vivian done that? He scanned the room. Based on the video feed Ryan had watched on his computer, he could guess the locations of the cameras inside the room.

"It's the Watcher, Charlie." Ryan locked eyes with Charlie. "He has her."

"Wait."

But Ryan was already racing out the door. He paused inside the dining room. Once-decorated tables were shoved haphazardly around the room. Their decorations covered the ground, along with broken glass, shoes, and the remnants of a meal still warm from the oven.

He turned toward the exits. Of all the surveillance videos Ryan had studied while at Quantico, the ones from mass shootings demonstrated crowd control was nearly impossible. People wanted out as quickly as possible, and the Watcher took advantage of that. More than likely, he was the one who triggered the alarm and the gunshots —

Ryan called Charlie over the radio. "Lynch, does the victim have his weapon?"

"It's missing," Charlie responded.

"What's the status on Bradley?"

Another voice crackled over the radio. "MIA."

Vivian was nowhere to be found and now

her father was missing. Ryan stepped over the gala's wreckage, making his way to the back of the club. A familiar face grabbed his attention among the guests huddled in groups along the patio. Shep was talking to a woman with mascara running down her face, her husband's comforting embrace around her shoulder.

It wouldn't have struck him as odd except for the phone Shep held up close like he was . . . like he was interviewing them.

Ryan's temper spiked. He stormed out the doors and grabbed ahold of Shep's collar, spinning the man around.

"Whoa —"

"What do you think you're doing?"

Shep peeled Ryan's grip off his shirt, straightening out his coat sleeves. "My job."

The guy was thick, but Ryan didn't have time to waste on him. "Have you seen Vivian?"

"No. Has something happened to her?" Shep leaned forward in a way that made Ryan question whether concern or journalistic curiosity was behind the look in his eyes.

"I told you to keep an eye on her!"

"Isn't that your job?"

Ryan's fist crunched into Shep's face so fast it felt like an out-of-body experience.

He watched Shep flail backwards into a bush, clutching his bloody nose.

"Are you crazy?" Shep screamed. "I think you broke my nose."

"Come on, Frost." Strong arms pulled Ryan back. "It's not his fault."

Ryan turned to face Charlie. "I know. It's mine."

If Vivian needed any evidence that people were self-focused, walking through a panicked crowd trying desperately to get someone to notice a man shoving a gun into her ribs was it. Her dress caught on her heel and she tripped forward, but Pete's grip tightened on her arm and prevented her from falling as he directed her toward a small clapboard building near the dock.

With all the commotion happening inside of the club, no one was paying attention to Pete Robbins shoving her through a door. The pungent smell of bait filled her nostrils.

"Where's Russell?"

"Soon enough." He pushed her toward another door that led to a snack bar and seating area.

Vivian stopped, Pete's body pressing up against her. She turned and faced him. "I'm not going any farther without proof my father is here."

Pete caressed the side of her cheek with the gun. "Isn't that sweet." He lifted his eyebrows, tilting his head toward a few tables that were pushed to the side. That's when she saw the feet.

"Russell!" Vivian started for him, but Pete yanked her back. She glared at him. "What is wrong with you?"

He smirked. "I told you there'd be a family reunion, but I didn't say it would be a happy one."

Vivian's heart pounded. She'd written enough stories to know the odds of her surviving this weren't in her favor. Her gaze flickered toward the window. Outside, red and blue lights flashed. Was Ryan looking for her? Her gut said he was and that he wouldn't quit until he found her. The thought made an ache well within her. She had to buy some time. Surely, they would search the boathouse.

"Is he dead?"

Pete looked down at the man. "Probably not, but I can take care of that for you." A sick smile played on his lips. "Bet it would feel good to get a little revenge on him."

Disgust agitated in her gut. "Is that what all those —" The videos. Vivian cringed. Their setup had been turned on them, taking with it the evidence they needed to prove Pete Robbins was the Watcher. They could add assault and kidnapping to his growing list of charges, but that was only if they caught him. And from the crazy look in his eyes — the Watcher had no intention of getting caught.

Vivian's free hand skimmed the side of her dress and the rectangular bulge hidden beneath the chiffon folds. Her cell phone. She couldn't risk pulling it out to call Ryan, but if she could just unlock it . . . maybe she could get Pete to confess and record it. *Or record my death.*

Shoving the morbid thought from her mind, she moved toward Russell.

Pete swung the gun toward her head. "What are you doing?"

She swallowed, focusing on Pete's cold glare and not the gun. "The least you can do is let me see him."

Pete snickered. "For what?" He waved the gun around. "No cameras in here to catch your moment."

So, he had figured it out. Pete Robbins knew they were onto him and now was going to do whatever was necessary to keep his secret. "Despite what you think, I've waited fifteen years to see him."

"Have at it." He walked over to a box and smashed the lock off with the butt of the gun. "Not like it'll matter."

Vivian wasn't sure she was supposed to hear that last part, but it sent a chill across her skin. She moved in slow, hesitant steps toward Russell's body, afraid of what she would see. Pete said he wasn't dead, but . . .

Russell's head was turned away from her. Vivian knelt and reached for his wrist — he had a pulse. She peeked over her shoulder and saw Pete picking through rows of keys. Could she risk a run for the door? She might make it, but she'd never outrun a bullet — and she had no intention of getting shot in the back.

Making sure Pete wasn't watching her, she pulled her phone from her pocket, ensuring it was on silent, and then opened up the recording app. When she was sure it was on, she slipped the phone back into her pocket and focused on the man lying in front of her.

This was the first time Vivian had seen him in person since he left her. The tailored tuxedo coat splayed at his waist and his head hung to the side, his eyes closed. She took in the lines at the edge of his neck, near his lips and eyes. Women admired him as dashing, and she couldn't deny the media's comparison with Pierce Brosnan, but tonight — maybe it was the shadows playing on his features coming through the window — he looked tired.

Vivian twisted her lips to the side, trying to keep down the emotion balling in her throat. "Why do you do it?"

"Are you talking to me?"

"Yes." She turned to him. "I want to know what you get out of setting up all your victims. Is it the money? Because I can think of a hundred different ways you could earn a dollar without destroying lives."

"This coming from a woman whose livelihood revolves around unearthing dirty little secrets for the sake of a headline?"

"Maybe at one time that was me but not anymore."

"Yeah right." Pete's attention went back to the keys. He pulled one out and looked at it. "Let's go."

It was too soon. Hadn't anyone noticed they were missing? Maybe not her but certainly legendary actor Russell Bradley. She had to buy some more time and get Pete to confess. "I'm not going with you."

"You are." He pointed the gun at her. "Now, let's go."

"We can't just leave him here."

"You don't have a choice."

Movement near Vivian's leg caused her gaze to flash down at Russell's hand. His fingers moved and Vivian sucked in a breath. *He's waking up.* Careful not to draw Pete's attention to the movement, she shifted, angling herself forward to block Russell's face. His eyelids slid open just enough that their eyes met before he winked. *Winked?* She really hoped he didn't think this was some kind of action flick.

Vivian looked back at Pete. "You still didn't answer my question. Why did you do it? What did Bethany Price or Blaise Taylor ever do to you to make them a target of your sick obsession?"

Pete walked toward her and looked down at Russell. Vivian held her breath, hoping he hadn't noticed Russell move earlier.

"How did you feel when you found out your dad had another family?"

"How did —"

"I can do math," Pete said. "A little deduction and it became clear."

She licked her lips. "It hurt. A lot."

"Right. His secret . . ." Pete squatted and pushed the muzzle of the gun against Russell's forehead, causing her to inhale sharply. "His lie ruined your life. Your father's not that different from the rest of the world. Filled with liars, cheats, and sinners with secrets to hide."

"And it's your job to exploit them? Why?"

"Because they need to pay." Pete grabbed Vivian's arm, yanking her to her feet. "And now it's your turn."

Fear seized her. "What are you talking about?"

"Did you really think I was just going to let you get away with setting me up?"

"I —" She saw movement out of the corner of her eye. Russell was shifting to his side. Vivian couldn't risk him being seen, and maybe if she let Pete believe he had the advantage, Russell could alert the deputies to come after her. "But it didn't work," she said quickly. "We don't have the evidence to prove you're the Watcher."

"I plan on keeping it that way." He shoved her forward toward the side door leading to the boats, but her heel caught on the edge of her dress, sending her crashing to her knees.

She glanced back to see Pete turning around just as Russell was swinging a wooden oar against the side of his head. Pete collapsed to the floor.

"Are you okay?"

Vivian pushed herself up. "Yeah, I think so." She eyed Pete's crumpled body. "Nice hit."

"I had a sparring instructor for a role a couple of years ago." Russell winced and dropped the oar to grab the back of a chair.

She rushed over to him. "We need to get you help."

Russell looked down at her. "Vivian, I'm sorry."

The apology hung in the air between them as his eyes remained fixed on her like he wasn't sure whether she'd heard him. She had, but she just didn't know how to respond.

"I . . ." His eyes closed and he groaned.

"Come on, you don't look good." Vivian went to his side, unable to ignore the burning emotion his words were stirring within her. "Let's get out of here."

Russell nodded, taking a careful step toward her. He put a hand on her shoulder. "Please . . . I" — he took in a breath, waiting until she lifted her eyes to meet his — "I need you to know that I'm sorry. So very sorry."

"It's fine, Russell." She led him to the door. "Let's go."

"Vivian, I need you to hear me." He stopped, his hand moving to the back of his head. "I need you to hear me before it's too late."

She frowned. "What are you talking about?"

"I've got Alzheimer's."

A whoosh of air left her lungs, leaving a sickening void, but it was the bang that had her screaming.

THIRTY-ONE

A gunshot blast has the power to illicit panic or deadly silence. The echo was still ringing in his ears as Ryan surveyed the eerie calm around him. Wide-eyed gala guests sought assurance from him and Charlie, who both had their guns drawn.

"Where did it come from?"

Charlie was an inch taller than Ryan, which gave him an advantage as they searched into the shadows. "I think from over there."

Ryan turned to the boathouse. There was a large window where club members could place orders for food and next to it a door that led inside and to the attached bait and tackle shop. His eyes followed a long, narrow passageway from the café to the main clubhouse most likely used by the kitchen staff — and the perfect way for a person to sneak by undetected.

"Let's go." Ryan charged forward.

Charlie was on his tail, calling in their position to the law enforcement backup. They had begun doing a thorough sweep of the building while trying to organize the guests into groups to be identified.

Ryan paused outside the door of the boathouse, his heart thudding loudly in his chest. What was he going to find inside? If it was Vivian . . . he swallowed. He couldn't let himself think like that. His gaze locked with Charlie's as Ryan reached for the knob. Turning it slowly, Ryan raised his weapon and entered.

"One on the ground." Charlie's whisper directed Ryan's attention across the room with sickening fear.

When he saw a pair of black leather shoes and not the silver ones that had peeked from beneath Vivian's green gown, a small exhale of relief escaped his lips. His comfort was short-lived. Seeing Russell Bradley's body lying on the ground meant the Watcher had just upped his game.

Deputy Hodges and Deputy Wilson entered the boathouse behind them and started taking care of Russell so Ryan and Charlie could clear the rest of the rooms. The search couldn't have been more than a minute, but it felt like an eternity with a horrifying result — Vivian was not there.

"Is he dead?"

"No," Deputy Wilson shouted. "But he's been shot and needs help *now.*"

The urgency in Wilson's voice rattled Ryan as he started toward the back of the boathouse, where another door leading to the docks stood ajar. He needed to find Vivian, fast. "I'm going this way."

"Right behind you," Charlie said.

Both men had their weapons trained in front of them as Ryan went first. He kicked the door all the way open, sending it crashing against the wall behind it.

A scream directed his attention to a boat slip thirty yards away. Pete Robbins aimed his gun and fired off a shot, sending Charlie and Ryan ducking to the ground.

"We can't let him get her on that boat." Ryan edged around the Starcraft deck boat. "We gotta stop him."

"We will." Charlie inched up, his weapon aimed. "It's clear, go."

Ryan did a crouch walk down the dock toward the boat when he heard the rumble of a motor sputtering in the water. He jumped to his feet and ran, but he was too late. With Pete at the wheel, the small speedboat zipped through the water, curving sharply.

Ryan lifted his weapon, but Vivian's terrified look over her shoulder made him lower it. He was unwilling to risk hitting her.

Ryan ran into Charlie on the way back. "We need a boat."

"Savannah PD has one."

Ryan shook his head, eyeing the options tied to the dock. "It's dark out there, Charlie. If we don't go after them now, we could lose her."

"Here." An older man with a scowl that looked like it was permanently etched into his thick face waddled over to them. A wet cigar, chewed at the edge, hung on his lip. "Third one down."

Ryan caught the set of keys he tossed into the air. "Thank you."

At slip 9 they found a slick speedboat Ryan guessed cost double his annual salary, with the name *Dolly* painted on the stern. They both jumped into the boat and he handed the keys to Charlie.

"You expect me to drive this?"

"You're a Marine. Aren't you supposed to know how to drive boats?" The wakes from the boat Pete had sped off in were still lapping against the boat they were in. "Come on, dude. You have your license, right?"

"Barely." Charlie started the boat, the engines purring to life. "Wasn't planning on honing my skills on a twenty-one-footer."

451

Ryan looked in the direction where Vivian disappeared. This part of the Ogeechee River split into more than a dozen waterways that led to multiple creeks and rivers — all unlit and dangerous, depending on the tide.

"Charlie, we're going to lose her."

His friend must've sensed the panic in his voice, because he pushed the throttle, sending the boat lurching forward as they stumbled back, trying to keep their footing.

"Ooh, this baby has power."

"Just take it easy." Ryan held on to the back of the captain's chair. "The river's depth changes with the tide, and I've been on enough boats to know you don't want to ground out."

"No," Charlie said, the boat picking up speed. "Do not want that."

The boat was made for speed, and Charlie was a quick learner. A spray of brackish water whipped against their faces as they zipped along the Ogeechee River. No moon was out tonight. Ryan searched in the darkness, hoping to spot the boat, but the inky water revealed nothing.

"Where is she, man?" Ryan ran a hand over his head, gripped his hair, and sent up a silent prayer. "We've lost her."

"No. There."

Charlie wheeled the boat so that the left side dipped low toward the water, and Ryan saw it. A beam of light bounced off the tall marshland grass. The boat was heading in the direction of Skidaway Narrows.

"Can you get us closer?"

"I'm trying," Charlie yelled over the rumble of the engine as the boat surged forward.

It was too dark for him to see Vivian . . . a sickening thought occurred. Ryan looked around them. What if Pete had thrown Vivian overboard? If they hit her at the speed they were going, they'd kill her.

"Can you see her?" The light from their boat wasn't bright enough. Ryan moved forward, using the windshield to brace himself. "Don't get too close to the sides or you'll —"

"Ground out." Charlie's tone was tense. "I know. I just hope he does."

The boat ahead of them was careening side to side, coming dangerously close to the edges where the water grew shallow.

Ryan had no idea where Pete was headed, but the farther into the narrow inlets they went, the more dangerous it was. And based on Pete's erratic steering, the probability of someone dying tonight was increasing by the second. His grip tightened over the windshield.

I'm coming, Vivi. Hold on.

Vivian dug her fingers into the seat, hanging on as Pete swerved around a curve so fast she was certain the boat was going to flip.

She searched for anything she could use as a weapon, but even if she could find something, she wasn't sure it would be safe enough to let go of the seat for fear of being tossed over the side at the next turn.

There was one thing she was sure of, and that was how much danger she was in.

She couldn't shake the image of her father's face turning a ghastly shade of white before dropping to the floor. Russell should've waited until they were gone and then run for help, but instead, he . . . he tried to save her. And that explained why her heart screamed in horror as Pete dragged her away, leaving Russell facedown in a puddle of blood.

Alzheimer's. The desperation in her father's eyes was unmistakable. *"I need you to hear me before it's too late."* A hot tear streaked down her cheek.

She turned her focus to Pete. "Why are you doing this?"

"You're the reporter." He turned a hard

stare on her. "Shouldn't you have that figured out already?"

"Actually, I don't. You target innocent people —"

"NO! They're never innocent." Pete's dark gaze returned to the river just as they hit choppy water. The boat jumped, hitting hard against the current with a crack. "You of all people should know everyone has a secret."

She shook her head. "No. Not Harold. He was trying to help . . ." Vivian stopped, remembering what Ryan had found out about Pete and Lauren. They had dated. Lauren had been scared of Pete — enough to ask Harold for help.

"You know, your friend might still be alive if he'd minded his own business." Pete used the back of his wrist to wipe at the blood dripping from the wound Russell had left on his temple. "Costly mistake."

"Is that all it is to you?" Vivian clutched at anything her fingers could wrap around to keep herself steady. "Destroy innocent lives for the money."

"You don't get it, do you?" He seethed. "They were all guilty. Even Lauren." He spat out her name like it tasted bad. "I loved her and would've given her the world, but she had to go and sleep around" — the muscles in his jaw clenched — "make me look like a fool." His gaze landed on her. "All she had to do was tell me who he was and I would've taken care of the problem. As a favor. Like I could've done for you."

"A favor?" Vivian reeled. "You shot my father and left him for dead."

"I took care of the problem." He shook his head. "Don't act like that bothers you."

"It does bother me," she screamed, stunned by the implication of his confession. "He didn't do anything."

"Except leave you and your mom." His voice was calm. Too calm. "Now he'll never hurt you again."

Vivian squinted against the salty spray. "Who hurt you? Who turned you into this monster?"

"You'd really like to know?"

"If I'm going to die tonight," she said, her voice trembling, "I at least deserve to know who served you the Kool-Aid."

"I like you." He smirked. "You remind me of my mom." The amused expression shifted back into darkness. "It's what got her into trouble and eventually killed."

Vivian felt sick and hated that she couldn't resist voicing the question radiating in her brain. "What happened to her?"

"My father." Pete's jaw flinched. "He

456

didn't appreciate her sassy disposition — especially after he'd had a few drinks with his buddies. He beat the sass right out of her."

"Did you tell anyone?"

"You don't think I did?" He pursed his lips. "I tried. My father was a stalwart member of the community. A successful banker who plied our neighbors and the police force with his generosity so that even if someone did believe me, they still looked the other way. I had no proof. No power. And no one wants to believe their neighbor, coworker, or friend could be capable of evil."

"But they can be," she offered, hating that while there was no excuse for Pete's crimes, Vivian could empathize. How often as a teenager had she imagined picking up the phone to call the *National Enquirer* and sell out Russell's perfect image as actor, husband, and father? Everyone saw him as ideal. All she saw was the truth he kept hidden behind lies and betrayal.

Pete cursed. Vivian dared a glance backward and caught sight of a boat chasing after them. *Ryan.* Another curse pulled Vivian's attention back to the front of the boat just in time to see the strip of land so dark it was impossible to see until they were almost on it.

"We're going to hit it," Vivian screamed, bracing herself.

Pete gunned the engine, turning the wheel hard to the left. Her shoulder slammed into the fiberglass and she closed her eyes. Was this how she was going to die? The next swerve sent her to her knees and forced her eyes open.

Another sharp turn and the engine made a gurgling noise that sounded like they hit something, causing the boat to slow down. Vivian looked over the side and into the black water, wondering how badly it would hurt if she jumped. Maybe she could swim to the side and wait for Ryan.

Looking over her shoulder, she saw the other boat had gained on them. From the sudden thrust of speed pushing her against the seat, Pete must've seen it too.

"You're going to kill us."

The vibration of the engine shook beneath her with the increase of speed. Vivian's hair whipped across her face, but not before she witnessed the cold stare lighting Pete's eyes. Was that his intention?

Not without a fight. The second Pete's focus went back to the water, Vivian jumped up and aimed her fist right for the bloody welt on the side of Pete's head. He stumbled back, eyes dazed for a second before locking on to her with fury.

Grabbing the throttle, she pulled it back to slow down the boat. Her body and face collided into the control panel at the sudden decrease in speed. A coppery taste filled her mouth.

"You —"

Pete grabbed the back of her hair, ripping it back before he shoved her head into the console so hard it rattled her teeth and stars filled her eyes. Her legs gave out and Pete released her, letting her body drop on the boat's hard fiberglass floor.

As the boat picked up speed, Vivian rolled onto her side, then got onto her knees and tried to stand. She had to get up — had to fight. But how? Her eyes caught on something near Pete's feet. The gun. It must've fallen or he dropped it. If she could get to it —

Pete's growled expletive was the last thing Vivian heard before the jarring impact that hurled her body out of the boat and into the dark night sky.

THIRTY-TWO

"They've grounded out!" Ryan looked on in horror at the boat launched halfway up a sandbar, its occupants missing. "Slow down. She might be in the water."

The hum of the engine softened as Charlie decreased the speed, bringing it almost to an idle. The smell of exhaust, fuel, and burning grass filled Ryan's nostrils. Using his flashlight, he cast a beam around the edge of the boat and into the choppy water, unable to alleviate the fear he was going to find Vivian — dead.

The second the boat had crashed into the sandbar, Ryan's world had slowed down. The grinding noise of the engine running out of water and the speed . . . The momentum had thrown Vivian and Pete out of the boat like a couple of rag dolls, and it made him sick. He searched the landscape, terrified of what he was going to find, but too much dust and smoke in the air made it impossible to see clearly. He clenched his jaw.

"Search and Rescue are en route. A team from Fort McAllister is also on their way with a chopper," Charlie said, setting down the VHF radio mic. He leaned over to check the other side of the boat. "Do you see her?"

"Not yet." Ryan searched the water's edge where the long grass dipped into the water. "Vivian!"

The boat motored forward a few more yards before Charlie cut the engine. "We can't get any closer."

Ryan started to unbuckle his gun belt. "Then I'm going in."

"Wait. What's that?"

Charlie aimed his flashlight over Ryan's shoulder to something in the water. Ryan's heart jumped in his chest. There was something floating. His fingers worked faster over his belt. He tossed it to the floor, then jumped over the side of the boat carefully since he wasn't sure how deep it was. His head went under a couple of feet before he broke through the surface, blowing out a breath against the brackish water.

Ryan swam toward the lump, praying with every stroke it wasn't Vivian. His feet found purchase in the soft sand, forcing him to wade the rest of the way sluggishly until he finally got there. He grabbed his flashlight and lined it up on . . . a hollowed-out log.

Emotion stung at his eyes and choked him as he put away his flashlight. "It's a piece of wood."

The *whop-whop-whop* of a helicopter pulled Ryan's eyes upward and to the south. A bright beam from a spotlight swung back and forth.

Ryan swam back toward Charlie. "Give me my gun. I'm going to the boat on the sandbar."

After Charlie handed it to him, Ryan did a one-arm sidestroke, keeping his weapon above the water with his other arm until his feet could touch. He proceeded around the left side of the boat and lowered his weapon. "Vivian."

His voice echoed against the silent night. Ryan peeked over the edge of the boat to ensure it was empty. Ryan yelled over his shoulder, "Lynch, aim your light over here!"

When the extra light lit up the marshland in front of him, Ryan noticed a depression in the tall grass. His boots sunk into the mud, forcing him to work hard to release the suction-like grip.

"Vivian." Ryan pushed aside some grass and saw him — Pete Robbins, unmoving in a patch of grass. His tuxedo was muddied and torn near his leg, which sat at an odd angle. Blood covered his face. "I've got one! Robbins!"

Ryan made his way to the body and checked for a pulse. Somehow feeling the beat of life still throbbing in this man's body infuriated him. Feet splashed up next to him. Ryan turned to find Charlie trying to make his way through the mud.

"I've got him." He lifted up a pair of cuffs. "Go find her."

Vivian gasped at a searing pain shooting through her side. She turned her face and sucked in a mouthful of briny water. She gagged but couldn't catch her breath. Opening her eyes, all she could see was darkness. She was in the mud . . . no, she was in water. Her head throbbed, forcing her to close her eyes. *Breathe.*

But she couldn't. Her eyes shot open. Trying again, she took a deliberate breath, but there was no air coming in — or at least that's what it felt like. Panicky tears filled her eyes. Ignoring the pain radiating through her body, she tried to turn over, but her legs were tangled in something. Yet . . . she was moving. Or was it the water?

Vivian tried to look over her shoulder, but it was too dark and impossible to know if the slickness running over her body was water or blood. The water covered her from the waist down. She kicked her feet, but her dress was twisted too tightly around her legs. She clawed the slippery, muddy ground.

I'm sliding into the water.

She looked around for the boat. For Pete. But there was no sign of either. How far had she been thrown? Had Ryan seen the accident? Was he looking for her?

"Ry—" she gasped. "Ryan." His name came out like a whisper.

A *thwumping* noise filled her ears and she tried to look up, but her body slipped deeper into the cold water, her lungs catching on a breath it desperately needed. Vivian dug her fingers deeper into sludge, desperate to find something she could cling to as the water lapped against her shoulders.

Then she felt something brush against her side. She froze. *Dear Lord, please don't let it be an alligator.* Holding her breath, she moved her hand through the water slowly, praying she wasn't about to come face-to-face with a cold-blooded reptile. *I just survived a psychopath and a boat accident — a stupid gator isn't going to take me down.*

Her little pep talk was supposed to make her feel better, but it wasn't working. Was she going to die out here? A whimper filled her chest as she stretched her right arm toward some long grass. She twisted her fingers around it, but the mud beneath her shifted, plunging her under the water. Vivian kicked and screamed out in pain before swallowing a mouthful of water. Using just her arms, she fought her way back to the surface, choking and gasping.

"Vivian!"

Ryan. He was calling for her. *Thwump. Thwump. Thwump.* A bright light passed over her. Her arms splashed in the water, trying to stay afloat, trying to get the helicopter's attention. But exhaustion had taken its cue from the pain coursing through her, and she went under a second time. *They're not going to find me.*

Through the murky and watery haze above her, the spotlight passed over her again. *Hurry.* Vivian opened her mouth in a futile attempt. The water showed no mercy and rushed into her mouth and lungs, burning. She closed her eyes and let her arms and head drift in the buoyancy of the water like she was weightless. Weightless and free.

Ryan's muscles burned as he lifted Vivian out of the water. Her head lolled to one side, eyes closed, lips blue.

"She's caught on something."

Charlie ducked under the water, and seconds later it was like Vivian's body had become weightless. He surfaced, snapping his knife closed. "Her dress was caught on a branch."

Ryan pulled her to the side and began CPR. "Don't you die on me, DeMarco." He breathed into her mouth. "You're too stubborn for this." His voice caught, tears burning at the corners of his eyes.

This wasn't happening. He pressed his palms into her chest, starting the next round of compressions. Ryan wasn't going to lose her. Not now. *Please, Vivi, come back to me.*

Vivian sputtered, her lips parting to empty a lungful of river water. She coughed, choking. He rolled her to her side. *Come on, Vivi.* Tears stung his eyes as she coughed up more water. *Please, God.* Charlie rushed over and began an assessment of her injuries. She choked on another mouthful of water before groaning, and it was the sweetest sound to his ears. She opened her eyes and met his gaze, a tease of a smile lifting the corner of her lips.

"Captain America."

He brushed the wet hair from her face with his thumb. "I've never been so scared in my life."

Vivian winced, moving her hand to meet his. She laced her fingers with his and squeezed. "I-I just want —" She wheezed.

"Shh." Her bottom lip was busted and swollen, and there was a mean gash in her leg. Based on her shortness of breath, he guessed she had some internal injuries as well. "Help is on the way."

"Search and Rescue is here," Charlie said, looking over his shoulder at the team approaching in an inflatable rescue boat meant for shallow water.

"I want you to know s-something." Vivian's grip tightened over Ryan's fingers, drawing him toward her. "I w-will never like sweet tea."

Ryan ground his molars and shook his head, trying to fight the emotion welling up inside of him for this woman. He let his lips tickle the edge of her temple. "Why do you have to be so difficult, DeMarco?"

Thirty-Three

The cozy cottage home Harold Kennedy had let Vivian move into months ago looked a little sad with all her personal items packed into a stack of boxes. She wrapped her arms around her waist, wincing when she rubbed against a still-healing tender spot. The doctors considered her punctured lung, the cut on her leg requiring stitches, and some bumps and bruises a lucky break.

Russell hadn't been as fortunate. His gunshot wound had been serious and had required surgery. Vivian sat in the waiting room until the doctor came out with an update that Russell wouldn't be doing his own stunts anytime soon but was expected to make a full recovery. Vivian was unable to ignore the relief that coursed through her at the news, and it was an emotion she didn't really know what to do with.

But for now she was grateful he was healing in the care and comfort of his family in

Los Angeles.

The same could not be said for Coach Pete Robbins, a.k.a. the Watcher. The FBI had taken the part of the case regarding the extortion since the victims were from all over the country. He'd face a separate trial for charges of kidnapping, assault, and attempted murder here in Walton.

The doorbell rang.

Vivian's lips slipped into an easy smile when she saw him standing on the porch. "Captain America."

"Pepper Potts."

She frowned, opening the screen door. "Pepper is Tony Stark's girlfriend."

Ryan stepped inside and drew her to him gently. "Yes, but you see, Pepper isn't just Tony's girlfriend. She's his everything. The one thing he'll give up his alter ego for and the one person — the only person — who drives him to be a better man."

Vivian tucked her chin, blushing, but Ryan tipped it back up with his fingers so that she was looking into those clear blue eyes that had the ability to see into her soul.

"You are the Pepper to my Captain."

Vivian giggled. "I'm sorry." Seeing the hurt in Ryan's face, she covered her mouth to hold back the laughter. "I'm sorry. It's just" — she shook her head — "that sounded more like a Spider-Man line."

Ryan recoiled. "Spider-Man? You're saying my line was juvenile?"

"No. It was cute." She smiled. "Like grade school–crush cute."

"Ugh." Ryan looked at his watch. "You ready?"

She rolled onto her toes and kissed Ryan's neck, wrapping her hands around his waist. "I hate goodbyes."

He pressed a kiss to her forehead. "It won't be for long."

She locked the door, then they walked down the street toward Pecca's house. There was no way she was going to let Vivian get out of Walton without a farewell party. And Vivian had talked her down from a huge event at the Way Station Café to a smaller, quieter, more personal gathering inside her home instead.

"How's Russell?"

"Good." Vivian paused at a neighbor's yard to let the spray of a sprinkler pass. "He's going to start an aggressive treatment to hopefully hold off the effects of Alzheimer's."

Ryan reached for her hand. "What about between you two?"

"I think we made the right decision." She thought back on her conversation with him inside the hospital. "There's nothing to gain by revealing he's my father. His wife and kids know about me and maybe one day I'll meet them, but for now it's enough."

He squeezed her hand. "You're amazing."

"I don't know about that."

"I do." He lifted her fingers to his lips and kissed them.

"What about you?" Their eyes met. "You ready to leave all this behind?"

Ryan had wanted her next to him and his family when he made the call to Agent Hannigan to officially accept the position with the Cyber Crimes Division. It was impossible not to imagine a future with a man who believed the support of those he loved was more important than the dream. Though, technically, he hadn't exactly told her he loved her . . .

"Will I sound like Spider-Man if I say, 'With you by my side, I'm ready for anything'?"

She shook her head. "Sounds very Humphrey Bogart-ish."

Vivian's eyes drifted from Ryan to the cars lined up on the street. She stopped. "Please don't tell me Pecca invited the entire town to her house today."

"Oh-kay." Ryan smiled as he tugged her

up the drive toward Pecca's house. "I won't."

Vivian could already hear the music and voices drifting from around the back. Ryan walked her to the backyard and opened the gate for her.

"Oh, they're here!" Pecca said. "Everyone, they're here."

Vivian and Ryan entered the yard to a round of applause that made her hang on to Ryan's hand even tighter. Everyone was there. Ms. Byrdie, the sheriff, Charlie, Lane, and Noah. Maceo and Sergeant Elizabeth Reynolds. Ducky, Walter, and Clarence.

"Okay, give them some room to breathe." Pecca cleared a path and then hugged Vivian, forgetting about her injuries until Vivian groaned. "*Lo siento.* I forgot."

"It's fine. I thought I said a small party."

"Girl, I didn't think everyone was going to show up." Ryan and Vivian exchanged a look. *No one could tell Pecca no.* "Anyway, Ben Wilson is working the grill. Lane, Ms. Byrdie, and I worked on the sides."

"And we arranged for the desserts."

Vivian twisted around to find Carol Kennedy standing next to Shep, who was eyeing Ryan with contempt — the bruising not entirely absent from his confrontation with Ryan's fist. Vivian had tried to get the story,

472

but neither man was talking.

"We couldn't let you leave without saying goodbye." Carol elbowed Shep. "Right?"

"Yes." Shep groused.

"Don't mind him." She waved off her nephew. "He's just upset you chose a man in uniform over him."

"Aunt Carol." Shep shook his head.

Vivian and Carol laughed as they embraced. "Thank you so much for everything you did to find Harold's killer."

Sadness still threatened to overwhelm Vivian whenever she thought too much on Harold's death. "He changed my life." She leaned back and looked into Carol's watery gaze. "When I felt absolutely alone and rejected, it was Harold who breathed hope back into me and made me a part of this community."

Carol smiled. "He was a good man."

Shep stepped forward and Vivian could feel Ryan's posture tense. "The piece you wrote about Uncle Harold . . ." Shep coughed. "We had to print a second run because we sold out."

Vivian smiled. "I'm glad you liked it."

"I want you to know there'll always be a position for you at the *Daily* or *Tribune.*" Shep cast a glance at Ryan. "If you ever decide to come back south."

"I appreciate that." Vivian looked up at Ryan. "But I think I'm going to enjoy my new job in DC."

"*Blech.* You really are a perfect couple." Frannie walked up with her and Ryan's mom and Dr. Murphy. "When can I visit you?"

"My townhouse has two spare bedrooms," Ryan said after hugging his mom and shaking Dr. Murphy's hand. "One for you and one for Mom."

Vivian gave Ryan's mom a quick hug, noticing her eyes roll, and laughed.

"You think I want to stay in a bachelor pad with you?" Frannie wrinkled her nose. "*She's* the one with access to all of the cute soldiers."

"You know, I hadn't thought about that." Ryan's forehead wrinkled. "Maybe working for Shep's a better idea."

"Then I wouldn't be near you."

"Good point." He snuck a kiss and Frannie appropriately made a gagging noise that made everyone laugh.

Vivian couldn't wait to start her new job at *Veterans' Voice.* The nonprofit magazine worked with military service members to raise money and awareness for issues like homelessness, veteran health care, post-war support, and assistance for those coping with physical and nonphysical injuries. She'd be writing stories about service members or their families, and it felt right. She was following Harold's advice to find light in the darkness.

The sound of clinking glass captured everyone's attention. Pecca was standing on a chair, holding a cup and spoon in her hand. "I want to thank everyone for coming out tonight to wish our dear friend, Vivian, farewell."

Tears stung the corners of Vivian's eyes as Ryan wrapped his arm around her waist.

"She came into Walton like Han Solo." Pecca winked at Vivian. "But is leaving our little galaxy with the entire Force on her side." Everyone groaned. "And she's even taking everyone's favorite Jedi with her." More groaning, but Pecca ignored it all, her smile wide. "Remember, Vivian, you will always have family here in Walton and we're much closer than *far, far away.*"

"Do you think she used up her entire *Star Wars* knowledge on that speech?" Ryan whispered.

Vivian nodded, unable to speak over the emotion clogging her throat. The analogy might've been off, but that only made the sentiment more meaningful. It wasn't just Harold who had breathed hope into her.

The whole town had done so. All this time she had thought *she* was dismantling the wall around her heart, but in truth, each person here was taking it upon themselves to carry one of the bricks marked *abandonment, rejection, alone,* and *unloved* and replace it with *family, friendship, belonging,* and *love.* Her eyes turned to Ryan . . . *chosen.*

"What are you thinking?"

"I'm thinking I need to tell you something before this night is over."

Ryan arched an eyebrow suspiciously. "What's that, DeMarco?"

Vivian tugged on the collar of his polo. "I love you."

A coy smile filled his face.

"What?" She stepped back as a flicker of fear burned her cheeks. Maybe she was wrong to assume — jumped to the conclusion that he loved her too. "You're not going to say anything?"

"I know."

She frowned. "You *know*?"

Ryan drew her to him. "I *know*." He gave her a knowing look like she should *know*. He pointed to himself. "Jedi." He pointed at her. "Leia. I love you. I know." Ryan narrowed his eyes at her playfully. "It's one of the most famous lines."

Vivian pursed her lips and gave Ryan a sideways glance. "Luke was a Jedi. Han Solo was a pilot. *He* said the line to Princess Leia. Luke and Leia were siblings, and that would've been more disturbing than the —"

"Kiss me, DeMarco." Ryan leaned in, covering her mouth with his in a kiss that curled her toes.

When he released her, she looked up and smiled, breathless. "The Force is definitely with you."

"You two are such geeks." Frannie rolled her eyes.

Ryan dipped Vivian in his arms to the roar and pleasure of their family and friends and looked deep into her eyes. "I love you, Vivian DeMarco." And then he kissed her. Full of passion. Full of promise. Full of hope.

ACKNOWLEDGMENTS

I cannot start this section off without first thanking God. Many times during the creation of this story, I felt inadequate, fearful, and anxious. I will never stop being amazed at what God can do in my weakness.

Without the love and support of my family, I could never write my stories. G.I. JOE, you prove every day that you're more than a soldier — you're a great husband and father. To my three bambinos, and now a son-in-love, thank you for all your patience as I work under deadlines that keep my mind preoccupied with fictional characters. I love you guys!

Behind every story is a team of amazing people working tirelessly behind the scenes, and I'm so grateful for my team at Revell. Andrea Doering, Amy Ballor, Karen Steele, Brianne Dekker, and Gayle Raymer, y'all are the best! My agent, Tamela Hancock

Murray, I wouldn't be able to write this page if it weren't for you. Without the encouragement, support, and guidance from this team, my words would never find a page to land on.

Emilie, there's not a single day that goes by that I'm not thankful for you. I won the jackpot with you and am beyond blessed to have you not only as a friend but also as a critique partner who can hear my words, know my heart, and help me deliver a story worthy of being told. Love you, friend!

Jaime Jo, you fill my days with joy, laughter, and the kind of love that will forever make us sisters. Christen, thank you for all the brainstorming on this one. This story is so much better because of your help. Steffani, without you all my characters would be named Jane and John. I'm grateful (and the readers are too) for your skill at naming characters perfectly. Kara, your devotion, love of reading, and support of authors make you invaluable, and I'm blessed to have you in my tribe. Bethany Turner and Joanna Davidson Politano, you both welcomed me into the Revell family with arms wide open and continue to encourage and support me — without you, this job wouldn't be nearly as fun!

To my Newsies, readers, and especially

my amazing Street Team, it's because of YOU that I'm able to do what I love! I never imagined the friendships that could be forged over the love of story, but y'all are proof that readers make the best friends. I'm beyond blessed by your enthusiastic support — thank you *so* much!

ABOUT THE AUTHOR

Natalie Walters is a military wife of twenty-two years and currently resides in Hawaii with her soldier husband and their three kids. She writes full-time and has been published in *Proverbs 31* magazine and has blogged for *Guideposts* online. In addition to balancing life as a military spouse, mom, and writer, she loves connecting on social media, sharing her love of books, cooking, and traveling. Natalie comes from a long line of military and law enforcement veterans and is passionate about supporting them through volunteer work, races, and writing stories that affirm no one is defined by their past.

The employees of Thorndike Press hope you have enjoyed this Large Print book. All our Thorndike, Wheeler, and Kennebec Large Print titles are designed for easy reading, and all our books are made to last. Other Thorndike Press Large Print books are available at your library, through selected bookstores, or directly from us.

For information about titles, please call:
  (800) 223-1244

or visit our website at:
  gale.com/thorndike

To share your comments, please write:
  Publisher
  Thorndike Press
  10 Water St., Suite 310
  Waterville, ME 04901